L
✓ 5

Philip Gwynne Jones was born in South Wales in 1966, and lived and worked throughout Europe before settling in Scotland in the 1990s. He first came to Italy in 1994, when he spent some time working for the European Space Agency in Frascati. Philip now lives permanently in Venice, where he works as a teacher, writer and translator. He is the author of the Nathan Sutherland series, which is set in contemporary Venice and which has been translated into several languages, including Italian and German.

PRAISE FOR PHILIP GWYNNE JONES

'A riveting story of deception and corruption'

– *Daily Mail*

'A playful novel, recounted by a witty and engaging narrator . . . as Venetian as a painting by Bellini (or a glass of Bellini). Oh, and it's also an unputdownable thriller'

– Gregory Dowling, author of *Ascension*, on *The Venetian Game*

'A crime book for people with sophisticated tastes: Venice, opera, renaissance art, good food and wine . . . I enjoyed all that and more'

– *The Crime Warp*

'The Venetian setting is vividly described and Gwynne Jones's good, fluent writing makes for easy reading'

– Jessica Mann,

'A civilized, knowledgeable, charming antidote t(
reaches of the genre, full of entertaining descriptions (
Lovely. Makes you want to book a flight to Venice str

Also by Philip Gwynne Jones

The Venetian Game

Vengeance in Venice

The Venetian Masquerade

Venetian Gothic

To Venice with Love: A Midlife Adventure

The Venetian Legacy

Philip Gwynne Jones

CONSTABLE

CONSTABLE

First published in Great Britain in 2021 by Constable

Copyright © Philip Gwynne Jones, 2021

1 3 5 7 9 10 8 6 4 2

The moral right of the author has been asserted.

A CIP catalogue record for this book is available from the British Library.

ISBN: 978-1-47213-429-5

Typeset in Adobe Garamond by Initial Typesetting Services, Edinburgh
Printed and bound in Great Britain by Clays Ltd, Elcograf S.p.A.

Papers used by Constable are from well-managed forests
and other responsible sources.

MIX
Paper from
responsible sources
FSC® C104740

Constable
An imprint of
Little, Brown Book Group
Carmelite House
50 Victoria Embankment
London EC4Y 0DZ

An Hachette UK Company
www.hachette.co.uk

www.littlebrown.co.uk

In memory of Jan Rudinoff, 31 March 1942 – 4 February 2020.

Thank you for all the good times, my friend. Some of them were even at Venezia matches. I wish you could have read this.

'It is a wise father who knows his own child.'

William Shakespeare, *The Merchant of Venice*

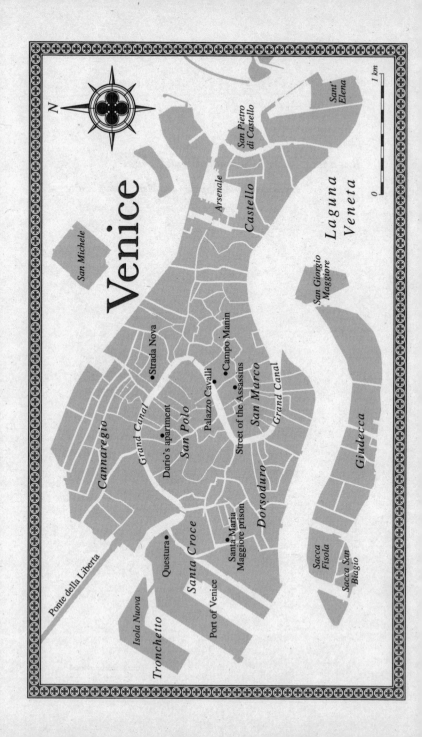

Pellestrina and Lido

Murano

Venice

Santa Maria Elisabetta

Ballarin's office

Lido di Venezia

Malamocco

•Alberoni

Faro Rocchetta

*Santa Maria
del Mare*

N

*Laguna
Veneta*

Pellestrina

Ravagnan's house

*Adriatic
Sea*

Ca'Roman

Chioggia

0 1 2 3 4 5km

Prologue: In the Wolf's Den

'In many ways, crime was the best education I ever had. The first time I went inside I was just a kid. I never even finished high school. You know how they hold you back if you fail a year? Well that was me. The tallest kid in the class. Anyway, the day came when I was too old for them to keep me there any more, so I walked out of the school gates one afternoon and then a month later I walked in through the gates of Santa Maria Maggiore prison. And pretty soon I realised I had to get very smart, very quickly.

'I was a tall kid, but skinny. That's why basketball was always my game, not football, you know? I thought I could handle myself in a fight. I was wrong. Because I wasn't up against school kids any more, but crooks. Hardened criminals. Tough sons of bitches who'd spent half their life inside. And I realised that I was never going to be as tough as them. And even if I was, these guys had friends, you know? I was on my own. I needed to do something to fit in.

'So I figured I had to get smart. The one thing you have in prison is time. So I read. Read a lot. Took my lumps when I had to, and bided my time. And after a while, people used to call me the smart guy or the clever guy. But never the wise guy. Trust me, you don't ever want to be the wise guy.

'If you're smart, you can help people. Maybe the guy in the next cell doesn't speak Italian. You can help him out. You can be his pal. Guy in the next block can't read or write? You write letters for him. You read him the ones he gets in the mail. Now you're his pal as well. And bit by bit walking around prison doesn't feel so bad any more. Because now even the tough guys are leaving you alone. Because maybe one day they're going to want a favour from you.

'That's the thing, you understand? You help people out, and then maybe one day they'll help you out. It's kind of a lesson for life.

So that's what I told my boy. Don't be a sucker. Get educated. Get smart. And don't ever come home from school and show me a bad grade.'

Giuseppe Lupo, in conversation with Gianni Brezzi

Chapter 1

Dario smiled and patted me on the back. 'How are you feeling, Nat?'

'Not sure, to be honest.' I held my hands up in front of my face. 'I think I might be losing all sensation in my extremities. Do you think that's a bad sign?'

'You're nervous, then?'

'I think I am. Shouldn't be, though. It's not as if I haven't done this before.'

'Hmm. You know, I probably wouldn't mention that. Now hold still.'

'Dario, I'm fully capable of doing up my own tie.'

He stepped back. 'Are you sure?'

I stared at my hands. Try as I might, they refused to stop shaking.

'No,' I said.

'Let me.' He fiddled with my tie and tightened it ever so slightly. Then he stood back, frowned and tugged it a little to the right. He patted me on the cheek. 'Okay. You're good to go.'

I took a few deep breaths, and then struggled into my jacket. I looked at the cuffs. There was no getting away from the fact that they'd seen better days. I shook my head. 'I should have got a new one,' I said.

'Too late, *vecio*, way too late for that.'

'No. Wait a moment. There's a place in San Tomà. Near the bakery.' I checked my watch. 'I might just be able to get something there.'

Dario laughed. 'We haven't got time, Nat.'

'We might have. If we hurry.'

'Trust me. There's no time. This is how you're going.'

'I've got to look good, Dario.'

'Nat, man, stop panicking. You look good, okay? You look good.'

'Are you sure?'

'I'm sure.' He paused. 'Well, you look good enough anyway.'

'Gah.' I patted myself down, going through my pockets. 'Okay. I've got everything. At least, I think I've got everything. Have you got everything?'

'I've got everything, Nat.'

'Are you sure?'

'I've got everything. Trust me.'

Gramsci sat on the back of the sofa, staring at us both. He caught my eye, and miaowed a mixture of bemusement and contempt.

I nodded at him. 'Look at him. He's enjoying this. I can tell.'

Dario coughed. 'As I understand, *vecio*, you're supposed to be enjoying this yourself. It's the sort of thing you only do once.'

'Twice, in my case.'

'Yeah. As I said, no need to mention that.' He grabbed my shoulders and shook me as gently as he was capable of. 'Come on, buddy. Let's do this.'

I took a deep breath and nodded. 'Let's do this.'

We made our way downstairs, and past the window of the Magical Brazilians. Eduardo caught my eye, and raised a hand in a clenched-fist salute, mouthing the word *Forza* at me. I smiled as best I could, and waved back at him.

We walked through Calle della Mandola and into Campo Manin. A group of young tourists sat around the statue of the revered hero of the *Risorgimento*, all leaning back into the shadow of the great winged lion at its base, seeking shelter from the midday sun in an attempt to stop their ice creams melting faster than they could be eaten. Daniele Manin looked out from the top of his plinth, right hand thrust inside his greatcoat, imperious and impervious to the heat.

'I'd have got you a gondola, you know? I did think of it,' said Dario.

'You did? Thanks Dario. That was kind.'

'Pal of mine is a gondolier. He'd have done it for free. Well, for a few beers at least. But I figured you wanted to keep everything low-key.'

I nodded. 'That's right. We didn't want a big fuss. Just our best friends, you know. Fede's mum. *Zio* Giacomo. You and Vally and Emily. That's it.'

We walked through to Campo San Luca and made our way to the *Riva del Carbon* where we looked out on to the Grand Canal. Water taxis ferried happy, smiling tourists back and forth, looking fresh and relaxed as they waved to the cramped and sweaty occupants of crammed *vaporetti*.

Delivery men tossed huge multipacks of bottled water to their colleagues on the *riva* without even breaking a sweat, whilst gondoliers did their best to steer their customers safely around the increasingly busy waterway.

Even with sunglasses on, I needed to shield my eyes as I looked over towards the Rialto Bridge, bristling with iPad-wielding tourists jostling each other as they competed for space in trying to capture that perfect shot of what had once been one of the most elegant waterways in the world.

Madness. Utter madness. And yet, there was nowhere in the world I'd rather have been.

I took my sunglasses off, and wiped my forehead.

'Getting hot already, and it's only June,' I said.

Dario nodded, and patted me on the back. I wished he hadn't as I could feel my jacket starting to stick to me. We made our way along the *fondamenta* and into the shade of the Palazzo Cavalli, a handsome sixteenth-century *palazzo* that, nevertheless, felt just a little bit overshadowed by all the splendour that surrounded it.

Federica, of course, was there before me. She tapped at her watch. 'I was beginning to wonder.'

'Sorry. Dario had to help me with my tie.'

She looked at me. 'Oh dear. Have you been getting in a state?'

'A bit of one, yes. Haven't you?'

She looked surprised. 'No. Why would I be?'

'Well, it's just . . . it's just this is kind of a big thing. Isn't it?'

'Well, yes. But it's also supposed to be a happy thing.' She raised an eyebrow. 'So why would one be stressed about it?'

'It's just because . . .' I closed my eyes and took a few deep breaths. 'It's just because I want everything to be perfect, you know?'

She smiled, and touched her forefinger to my lips. 'It's perfect enough.'

I smiled back. 'You look lovely, you know. I mean, you always do, but you look particularly lovely today and I just want to say . . .'

She shushed me. 'And you look very handsome, *tesoro*.' Then she stood back, and put her head to one side. 'It's just—' She reached out and adjusted my tie. 'There. Absolutely perfect now.'

Dario, I noticed, was shuffling his feet and checking his watch. I looked around. Marta, Federica's mother, smiled back at me. Valentina, holding little Emily by the hand, smiled and waved. Even *zio* Giacomo gave a little tip of his hat.

I took a deep breath. 'So, this is it then?'

Fede patted my arm. 'I guess it is. So are you ready?'

I squeezed her hand. 'Oh yes. I think I am.'

I linked my arm in hers, and, followed by our friends, we made our way upstairs to the *piano nobile* of the Palazzo Cavalli.

And that was it.

It took perhaps twenty minutes for Ms Federica Ravagnan to become, well, Mrs Federica Ravagnan. No gondolas, no string quartets, no fuss. Simple, and just the way we wanted it.

Except, of course, that it wasn't quite as simple as all that.

Chapter 2

'So, how do you feel my boy?'

Zio Giacomo clapped me on the shoulder, and then frowned ever so slightly. 'Not quite right.' He adjusted my tie as, I was beginning to understand, everybody would be doing at some point over the course of the day. 'Much better. As I was saying, how do you feel?'

'I don't know. Terribly grown-up I suppose. And it feels different from—' I bit my tongue.

'Yes?'

I decided to be honest. It was my wedding day. I was going to be absolutely honest with everybody, including myself. 'It feels different from last time.'

'My goodness. I'd keep that to yourself.'

'It's true though. I suppose I was very young. Well, still in my twenties. I think that counts as young. Too young, if I'm being honest. And so—'

'And so?'

I laughed and shook my head. 'And so I don't think I really knew what I was doing. I'm not sure either of us did really.'

'But you do now?'

I patted him on the back. 'Yes. Oh yes, I do now. Never been more sure of anything in my life.'

'Well, I'm glad.' He paused. 'I was even younger than you were, I suspect. But I always knew what I was doing.'

We walked on in silence, listening to the chatter from our friends. Giacomo's wife, I knew, had died at a young age. It wasn't something I'd ever felt able to properly speak to him about.

'And yes, I still miss her,' he said, as if following what I was thinking. 'Every day. But I think perhaps that's a good thing.' He blew his nose. 'So, tell me. Where are we going for lunch?'

'The Magical Brazilians. I mean, the Brazilians.'

'Oh. Are we? How disappointing.'

'It won't be so bad, I'm sure. Anyway, we both wanted Eduardo to be there. We've spent a lot of time there over the years.'

'I remember my wedding day. It seemed as if everybody was there. Everyone we knew, all our friends, all our relations.'

'Well, we just wanted a quiet do. Nothing flashy, just ourselves and our closest friends. You and Marta. Just keeping it simple.' We turned into the Street of the Assassins. 'Hang on, what's going on?'

The blinds were down at the Magical Brazilians.

I looked over my shoulder. 'Dario, I thought you'd sorted this out with Ed?'

Dario held his hands up. 'I did. I promise I did.'

'Ed never closes on Tuesdays,' I said. 'He barely closes at all. And he was here earlier. What's going on?'

'Have you tried the door?'

'I can't believe it, Dario. It's our bloody wedding day and

all we were after was a simple round of *tramezzini* and a few drinks with our nearest and dearest, and now it turns out to be the only day of the year when Ed is closed.'

'Try the door, Nat.'

'I don't bloody believe this. Of all the things that could have gone wrong it had to be—'

I tried the door.

It opened.

There was a chorus of '*Surprise!*'

I didn't know everyone. At least not by name. Some of Federica's colleagues I'd only met once or twice before. But there was Sergio and Lorenzo, on one of their rare excursions from the communist bar on Giudecca, Father Michael Rayner from the Anglican Church, Vanni from the *Questura* and even Gheorghe – minus, mercifully, any large dogs.

It was not, therefore, going to be a simple round of *tramezzini* with friends.

I looked back at Dario and grinned.

'You utter bastard!' I said.

Chapter 3

Federica looked over my shoulder, laughed, and then turned to face Dario. She hugged him. 'You utter bastard!'

'Yeah, we've done the "bastards" thing,' I said.

Dario shrugged. 'Hey. It's your wedding day. What was I supposed to do?'

'We said we didn't want a big fuss.'

'I know, but I didn't believe you. Was I wrong?'

There was still quite a lot of cheering going on inside. Ed grinned and waved, and went back to his work lining up Negronis on the bar.

'No,' I said.

Fede hugged him again. 'We'll forgive you. Just the once, mind.'

'Where's Lorenzo?' I said.

Sergio jerked a thumb over his shoulder. 'He's talking with the Tall Priest about Martin Luther.'

'My goodness.'

'Lorenzo likes that sort of thing. He doesn't usually get the chance to talk about it. Never quite been our thing at the club, you know?'

'No. I can understand that.'

'Who's that young guy with them?'

'Him? Oh that's Luciano. He works at the Rialto market. I buy fish from him and his mate every Saturday.' I frowned. 'I wouldn't have thought he'd have strong opinions on Martin Luther.'

'No? Why not?'

'Well, we never talk about that sort of thing.'

'What do you talk about?'

'Fish, mainly.'

'What, so you think because he's a fishmonger he can't know about Martin Luther?'

'No, it's because whenever I see him I'm there to buy fish.' I sipped at my Negroni. 'Anyway, it's great to see you here, Sergio. Thanks for coming.'

He shrugged. 'No worries, *investigatore*.'

'I mean,' I smiled, 'I appreciate you've come a long way.'

He didn't seem to understand the joke. 'It's okay. Haven't been in these parts for a while. It's changed a bit, though. But then the whole city seems to be changing.'

'You ever been married, Sergio?'

He shook his head. 'No. Never found the right person, you know. Or at least, I thought I had but—' He paused. '*Boh!*'

'How about Lorenzo?'

He chuckled. 'Who knows? As far as I know he might actually *be* married.' His expression changed, and he looked serious for a moment. 'I'm happy for you, *compagno*.'

'Thanks, Sergio.' I looked around. Marta was standing on her own by the door. 'Excuse me a moment. I think I need to go and circulate.'

He nodded, and patted me on the back. 'Congratulations again.'

I made my way through the crowd, smiling and nodding all the way. I caught a glimpse of Fede in conversation with two professors from the university and mouthed the words 'I love you' at her. She smiled back with a 'You too'.

Marta was humming something to herself as she stared out of the window. I didn't recognise the tune but there was something mournful about it, a sense of a terrible loneliness that made me pause for a moment.

'Marta?'

She gave me a hug and kissed me on both cheeks. 'Congratulations, Nathan.'

'Thanks.' I noticed that her eyes were red. 'Are you okay?'

'I'm fine. Well, if *Mamma* can't cry at her daughter's wedding, when can she?'

'I suppose so.' I gestured at the crowd. 'This is all rather lovely, isn't it? I mean, I know we said we wanted things kept simple, but, well, we were wrong.'

She nodded. 'Sometimes friends know best. My wedding day was a bit like this. There were more people, though. Both sides of the family.' She looked at me over the top of her glass of prosecco, the question hanging in the air.

'I don't really have any family. Not really. My mother died over ten years ago.'

She touched my arm. 'Oh, I'm sorry. I didn't mean to pry.'

'It's okay. Really. And my dad – well, we haven't spoken in years.'

'I'm sorry,' she repeated. 'That must be difficult.'

I shook my head. 'Not any more. Anyway,' I smiled, 'now I have a new family and a lovely mother-in-law.'

She poked me in the ribs, just as Federica would have done. 'Too much flattery.' Just as Federica would have said. 'But thank you.' She looked around the room. 'Well now, people seem to have left my daughter alone for two minutes, and so I think I should go and speak to her.' She kissed me on the cheek. 'I really am very happy for you both, you know?'

'I do. Thank you, Marta.'

She turned to go, but then both of us were distracted by the sound of tapping on the window. I turned to see a man in middle age, smartly dressed and holding a black leather briefcase, standing in the street. He nodded and smiled at Marta.

'A friend of yours?' I said. 'Ask him in, by all means.'

She shook her head, and her expression was difficult to read. 'No, it's okay. I'll just pop outside for a moment.'

She made her way through the crowded bar, and I watched as she exchanged kisses with the stranger, who smiled, bowed and nodded in equal measure. It was impossible to hear what was being said and neither, of course, was it any of my business. Nevertheless, there was something a little bit disquieting about the expression on Marta's face.

The stranger reached into his jacket, pulled out an envelope and offered it to her. Marta put her hands to her face. He smiled, and spread his arms wide in a gesture that I assumed was meant to be reassuring. She took a step back, nodded as if to calm herself, and then reached out her hand to take it. They exchanged kisses again, and then the stranger turned and made his way along the Street of the Assassins, and into Calle de la Mandola.

Marta ran the tips of her fingers across the front of the envelope before tucking it away in her handbag, her hands shaking. She whispered *thank you* as I held the door open for her, and then looked across the room to Federica.

'Everything okay?' I asked, keeping my voice light.

She could switch a dazzling smile on and off at will. Just like her daughter. 'Yes thank you, Nathan. Now, as I was saying, I really should go and talk with Federica.'

'Okay. We'll talk later, Marta, I'm sure.'

'Yes. Yes, we will. Thank you, Nathan.' Again, her voice had dropped to little more than a whisper. She gave me the gentlest of hugs, and turned away.

I stared after her, and then jumped as Father Michael clapped me across the shoulders.

'Congratulations, Nathan.'

'Thank you, Michael.'

'I've just been talking to that friend of yours.' He nodded at Lorenzo. 'Fascinating man. He knows more about the Council of Reims than I do.'

'Ah well, Lorenzo is something of a Renaissance communist.'

'So, it all went well then? At the Palazzo – what's it called again?'

'Cavalli. Palazzo Cavalli. Yes, all very efficient. In and out in twenty minutes.'

He winced. 'The most noble and holy sacrament of marriage. Efficiently rattled through in twenty minutes.'

'I'm sorry. We really didn't want a church wedding.'

'I understand. It's your day, after all.'

I looked around at the crowd. Many of them were good

friends, some of them I sort of knew and a few were complete strangers. 'It's an odd feeling, you know? All these people are here for us. Now I understand what they say about wanting to be a guest at your own wedding.'

Rayner smiled. 'Maybe you'd better go and circulate some more? Your public will be expecting you. And Nathan—'

'Yes?'

'If you do ever change your mind, I'd be delighted to give you a blessing. Seriously.'

'That's very decent of you, Michael. Thanks.' I was about to add 'but no thanks' and then thought better of it. He would, I knew, have been disappointed that we hadn't got married at St George's, and what he was offering to do was a kind thing. Would it be so bad, after all? 'We'll think about it. Seriously, I promise,' I said.

He patted me on the back. 'Go on, go and circulate.'

I made my way over to Gheorghe, who was in conversation with Vanni and his wife Barbara. Before I could reach them, however, my eye was caught by the sight of Marta and Federica. Marta was smiling and laughing as if all was right with the world. And yet her smile was just a little too dazzling, and her laughter, perhaps, just a little too forced. Then Vanni, Barbara and Gheorghe took it in turns to hug and kiss me, and Marta and Fede were lost from view.

Chapter 4

We sat and watched as Sergio and Lorenzo made their way, a trifle unsteadily, through the door. Lorenzo tipped his hat at us through the window, then Sergio took his arm and they walked off in the direction of San Zaccaria and the next boat to Giudecca. I wondered when they'd last spent an afternoon away from there and, indeed, if they'd ever do so again.

'Just us then,' said Dario. He turned to Vally. 'What do you think? Should we have one before we head off?'

Ed was unable to resist wincing slightly, as he looked around the bar. If it had not exactly been a riotous party (indeed, the phrase 'riotous party' had different connotations in Italian, as opposed to English where it might genuinely suggest an actual riot) there was, nevertheless, a certain amount of clearing up needing to be done before opening for business tomorrow.

Vally caught his expression, and shook her head. 'I don't think so.' Emily lay asleep with her head in her lap, and Vally stroked her hair. 'Time to get this one home. She's been very good but let's not push it.'

Fede smiled. 'She's been great. She was the real star in some ways. Who wants to talk to the newly married couple when there's a cute little girl to make a fuss of?'

I thought for a moment of the man outside the window, who'd taken quite an interest in talking with the mother of one half of the newly married couple but that, I thought, could wait for later.

Dario sighed. 'I suppose you're right.' He got to his feet, yawned and stretched. 'Perhaps we need an early night?'

Vally smiled. 'I think perhaps at least one of us does.'

'Okay then.' I turned to Eduardo. 'Thanks, Ed. You've been a star. Sorry you've got so much clearing up.'

He grinned. 'It's no problem, Nat. It's nice to see you looking happy, man.'

'Thanks.'

'I mean,' he continued, 'sometimes it's hard to remember the sad middle-aged man who used to drink alone in here all those years ago.'

'I don't know who you could possibly mean.' I reached into my jacket. 'We should settle up.'

He shook his head. 'No you shouldn't.'

'No, really.'

He shook his head again. 'Really. It's sorted. Call it a wedding present.'

'Wow.' I reached across the bar and gave him an awkward hug, whilst taking care not to send a tray of empty glasses crashing to the floor. 'Thanks, Ed.' A thought struck me. 'I suppose in that case, we might as well stay for one—'

Fede interrupted me. 'Or, perhaps, we might as well not.'

'Oh.'

'Really. Let poor Ed go back to work while there's still a chance of him getting home before midnight.'

'Yeah. You're right. I'll see you tomorrow though, Ed.'

'Or the day after,' said Federica.

'Or the day after.'

'Or perhaps the end of the week. Come on.' She leaned across the bar to give him a peck on the cheek, and then linked her arm in mine. 'Let's go.'

We made our way outside, and took part in one of those very Italian farewell rituals where neither party wants to be the one that actually turns their back and leaves. Eventually, though, we were done and we waved goodbye to Dario, Vally and Emily.

'So. That's that then,' I said.

'It seems so.'

'A job well done, *signora* Ravagnan.'

'Indeed so, *signor* Sutherland.'

'So. Shall we go to bed then?'

'I think we should.'

We went upstairs to my apartment – or *our* apartment, I reminded myself. The keys rattled in the lock as I pushed the door open, and I waited in expectation of the usual grumpy greeting from Gramsci. Fede gently pulled me back as I was about to step inside.

I turned around. 'What's going on?'

'You've forgotten something.'

'I have?'

She sighed. 'Aren't you going to carry me over the threshold?'

'What? Seriously?'

'Absolutely.'

'I didn't think you held with that sort of thing.'

'*Caro mio,* until recently I didn't hold with lots of things.

Marriage being one of them. And yet here I am. So if we're going to do this, we're going to do this properly. Come on.' She slipped an arm around my shoulders.

'Hmm. Right. Okay.' I put my arm around her, and then reached down to scoop her up as best I could. 'I've got this. I've absolutely got this.'

I carried her through the door, into the bedroom and attempted to set her down gently. Then a yowling sound came from between my feet, where Gramsci had tangled himself up, and the two of us toppled on to the bed together.

I kissed her. 'I love you, you know?'

'I do. I love you too.' She wriggled out from under me, and brushed her hair out of her eyes. She looked over at me and patted my chest. 'Oh, this is annoying. What were we thinking of, getting married on a work night?'

'Hmm. We didn't really think that through, did we?' I stroked her hair. 'Normal people would have booked time off. Honeymoons. Things like that.'

'I know. But given that we're probably only going to be able to afford to go away once it makes more sense to wait until August. We could go up to the mountains. Escape from the heat.'

'Or I suppose we could just have got married in August?'

'Only mad people get married in summer, *caro*.'

'Ah well. So, are you back at the Querini tomorrow?'

'Afraid so.'

'Early start?'

She smiled, and leaned closer to me. Then she kissed me, properly.

'Not too early,' she said.

In the Wolf's Den

The Old Wolf is unhappy. I can tell that from his body language. He touches his face, covers his mouth more than he did at the start of our interview. He seems less willing to make eye contact. He smiles, at times, but I can feel him forcing the expression on to his face. Work as a journalist long enough and you start to recognise things like this. For the first time in our conversation I feel as if I am the one in control.

'Would you like to tell me about your family?' I repeat.

He breathes deeply and then nods. He takes a cigarette from the packet in front of him and taps it on the table.

'I was born in Mestre at the start of the war. This you know. I never knew my father. I imagine that this, too, you know. He never came back from the war, so mamma *brought me up alone.*'

There is something about the way he says 'mamma'. *As if the word should be in capital letters.*

'She never spoke about him. Never. Sometimes I would ask questions. When I was little, she would hug me and say that not all boys and girls have a papà. *And that would be enough for me. But when I was older, if I asked the same question, well, then she would get angry. Tell me that I wasn't too old for her to spank my arse. So after a while, I just stopped asking.*'

'She never spoke about him at all?'

'No. Now, you need to imagine me as a young boy exploring our house. It wasn't big of course, but it seemed so through the eyes of a child. One day, when she was out at the market, I went down to our cellar. It was full of all kinds of junk, old chests and suitcases. I rummaged through everything. There were photos, of course – so many of them of nonno and nonna. I found Grandfather's service revolver from the First World War.' He chuckles. His eyes twinkle and, for a moment, the Old Wolf looks like everyone's favourite grandfather. 'I took that and hid it under a loose board in my bedroom. I kept it for years.'

His expression becomes serious and he shakes his head. 'But there was nothing belonging to my father. And when I say nothing, I mean there was nothing at all.'

'Why do you think that was?'

He shrugs. 'Tell me about your father, Brezzi. What did he do in the war?'

I am unable to stop my chest puffing out, just a little. 'He was a partisan. With the 8th Garibaldi Brigade.'

He sees my reaction and smiles. 'You must have been very proud of him.'

'I was. I am.'

I worry, suddenly, that I might have revealed too much. The Old Wolf closes his eyes. Then he sings, under his breath, the words of the old partisan anthem . . . 'O partigiano portami via . . . o bella ciao, bella ciao, bella ciao ciao ciao'.

'We're a sentimental people, Brezzi. We all like to imagine that our fathers, our grandfathers were partisans. And that, somewhere in our basement, is a chest full of good memories. But, of course, they can't all have been partisans. And those memories

might not necessarily be good ones. And so, you see, I envy you.'
He pauses, as if thinking to himself. 'Perhaps all this explains
why I've always felt closer to women than to men.'

I smile. 'Is that something you've just thought of?'

'I think it is,' he replies, and for the first time there is a feeling
of some genuine warmth between us. But the next question, I
know, is going to be difficult.

'Tell me about your mother,' I say.

He shakes his head. 'You know about her already.'

'I know. But I'd like you to tell me.'

'Why?'

'Because this is why I'm here. Everybody knows the facts
already. There's no story in that. The story is in what you say.'

'"There's no story in that",' he repeats. He taps the cigarette,
once again, and this time he lights it up. I suppose I should say that
his hands shake, but that would be untrue. He sits across the desk
from me and smokes, quietly and calmly, as if wondering what to
say. Suspects under interrogation do this to buy time, but this, I
think, is not the same. He is genuinely thinking about his words.

He smokes until the cigarette is burned down to the filter.
Then he taps it out into the ashtray and folds his hands together.

'There have been two remarkable women in my life. My
mother and my wife. Both of them left me when I needed them.
When I was vulnerable. My mother died when I was in my late
teens. I do not think I ever really, properly grieved. For me it was
a sudden freedom. Freedom to do everything I wanted. And of
course, everything I wanted to do was stupid, childish. Within
a year I was in prison.' He looks at me. 'You aren't that much
younger than me. Is your mother still alive?'

'No,' I say. 'She died when I was not quite fifty.'

'I'm sorry.' He pauses for a moment. 'Did you have time to say goodbye?'

'I did. She was in hospital. Breast cancer.'

'Again, I'm sorry.' He pauses, once more. 'Would you tell me what you said to her? The last time?'

I realise that he has turned the interview on its head, and he is now asking questions of me. Nevertheless, there seems to be no good reason to refuse, and so I continue. 'I told her how much I loved her, of course. And how much I owed to her. That the sort of man I had become was because of her.'

'Good. That's a beautiful thing. And . . .'

'And?'

'Nothing else?'

I pause for a moment. Again, I think, these are questions that I should be asking of him. 'I told her I wished . . .' My voice tails off.

'You wished?'

'That I could have been a better son.'

'Ahhhh,' he whispers, and reaches over to pat my hand. 'Of course. Of course. But you were lucky. I never had that chance. I came back from school one day to find Mamma was dead, and an empty packet of drugs by the side of her bed.'

Now it's my turn. 'I'm sorry.'

'And so I went, you might say, off the rails. Drink, drugs, violence, prison. Step by step by step. Strangely enough it was the Church that saved me. I remember our old priest telling me that I had to let all that anger go. That there were always things we wished we could say to the departed. But we had to realise that the moment had gone. There were things, sadly, that would always remain unsaid.'

*'You said there had been two remarkable women in your life.
Would you like to tell me about your wife?'*

*He shakes his head, and his shoulders drop. For a moment he
looks older than his years, gaunt and fragile.*

'No. Not yet. Ask me something else.'

*I take a deep breath. Immediate family, then, is not some-
thing the Old Wolf wishes to talk about. At least, not yet. I decide
to move the interview on.*

'Tell me about the Mestrini,' I say.

Chapter 5

I slept in the next morning until Gramsci's mewling became unbearable. Then I pottered around, and half-heartedly tinkered with a PhD thesis I was translating on the themes of identity and ambiguity in the works of Luigi Pirandello, but my heart wasn't really in it. I supposed I could go up to the Rialto to buy fish instead. We might not be going on honeymoon, but I could still afford to cook us a good dinner. Expensive fish, perhaps? I checked my wallet. Well, moderately expensive at least.

The doorphone buzzed. The post? Maybe a belated congratulations card or even a present?

'*Chi è?*'

'*Ciao,* Nathan. It's Marta.'

'Marta?' I tried to keep the surprise out of my voice. 'Come up, please.'

I opened the door for her and took her jacket. 'I thought you were going back to Chioggia today?' I said. 'Anyway, it's lovely to see you. Federica's out at work, but I can give her a ring. Perhaps we could meet her for lunch or—'

She smiled, but looked tired. 'No thank you, Nathan. Actually it's you that I wanted to see.'

'Oh right. Lovely. Well, do sit down. Can I get you a coffee?'

'That would be nice, thank you.'

'Machine or Moka?'

'Moka, please. I worry what these capsule machines are doing to the environment.'

'Well, me too, to be honest. But they are useful when I'm holding a surgery. Most people who call are emotional at best, and in a right old state at worst. Sometimes the ability to make a coffee in seconds is the only thing that wards off tears.'

She smiled. 'Yours or theirs?'

'Frequently both.'

Gramsci hopped up on to the sofa, and padded towards Marta, who shrank back. I reached out and pushed him to the floor. He leapt up again.

'You don't like cats, do you? I mean, you really don't like them?'

She shook her head.

'Okay, come with me. You can watch me make coffee, and I'll keep him at a safe distance.'

'Thank you.' We went through to the kitchen. I filled the Moka and put it on the hob, all the while prodding Gramsci away with my foot. 'So, what can I do for you, Marta?' I checked my watch. 'It's a little early, but I could make us both lunch if you like?'

She shook her head. 'That's kind, but it's not necessary. I just wanted to talk. About yesterday.'

'It was lovely. I hope you enjoyed it too?'

She nodded.

'I'm glad you're here, by the way. There was something I wanted to ask you yesterday. I never quite found the time.'

'Oh?'

'That tune you were humming. It's so pretty, and it's kind of been going round in my head since I heard it but I can't place it for my life.'

'Oh that. *Candida Rosa*. You don't know it?'

I shook my head.

'It's from a woman to her daughter before her marriage. She tells her how much she loves her, but then realises she is going to be alone now. I think it's Hungarian originally. Which makes me think Hungarian weddings must be terribly serious.

'I remember my mother singing it to me before my own and her being very brave as she tried not to cry. I didn't understand why she was so sad. I think I do now.' She patted my arm. 'Don't be offended, Nathan. It's just that it's a big thing for me as well, you understand? For years after Elio left there was just Federica and myself. Just helping each other along. More like two old friends than mother and daughter. And now things will be different between us. Between the three of us.'

'I'm sorry,' I said. 'I don't want you to be upset.'

She smiled. 'It's not your fault, silly. I'm just being *Mamma*, that's all.'

'I'll be a good son-in-law. I promise.'

'I know you will.' She looked around the kitchen, and shrank back when she saw Gramsci sitting on a cupboard directly behind her.

'He's staring at me,' she said.

'That's just because he likes you.'

She narrowed her eyes. Gramsci did likewise. 'That's not actually true, is it?'

I sighed. 'No. Not really. Sorry. Take the coffee through to the living room. I've got an idea.'

I shook Gramsci's box of kitty biscuits at him, just as he was about to follow her. He immediately turned his attention to me, mewling and waving his paws in the air. I put the box down, just out of his reach, and then turned and slipped out of the kitchen, shutting the door behind me. An outraged series of *miaows* came from the other side. I would, I knew, pay dearly for this later.

'Tell me, Nathan. Does Federica ever talk about her father?'

Elio Ravagnan, I knew, had died almost ten years ago, long before Fede and I had even met. 'Not really. Hardly at all, to be honest. It's funny, you know, neither of us talk about our families. Apart from you, of course.' I realised what that sounded like. 'I mean, we don't talk about you like *that*, if you know what I mean.'

'I know what you mean. Go on.'

'There's not much more to say. I know you broke up some years ago now. I know that—' I took a deep breath. 'Well, I know he had an affair. We don't talk about much more than that.'

Marta sighed. 'No. Neither do we. Or at least, we haven't for some time.'

I nodded. 'I understand. So tell me then, Marta. What sort of man was he?'

'A new man, I suppose you'd call him. He cooked, he cleaned, he helped around the house. He put Federica to bed, sang her to sleep every night and read her stories. *Pinocchio.* It always had to be *Pinocchio.* Yes, I think you could have called him a new man.' She paused. 'And then he went and screwed his secretary on the side.'

I almost choked on my coffee. I knew it had to have been something like that, but hadn't expected Marta to be quite so blunt.

'God, Marta, I'm so sorry.'

The words felt inadequate, but she smiled, and patted my arm. 'Yes. I was too, Nathan.'

We sat there in awkward silence.

'You saw me talking to that man, of course?'

I nodded. 'Nothing serious, I hope?'

'I don't know.' She sighed. 'His name is Michele Ballarin. He was Elio's business partner. As was his father before him.'

'A lawyer, then?'

'Yes. I believe the practice is still called Ballarin–Ravagnan.' She took an envelope from her handbag, and passed it to me. 'He gave me this.'

I turned it over in my hands. 'No stamp, no postmark?' I said.

'Michele tells me it's sat in the safe in his office for over ten years.'

There was just one word on the envelope. *Federica*. 'Beautiful handwriting,' I said.

Marta nodded. 'Elio's. He used to say that's why he became a lawyer and not a doctor. It's strange. Seeing his writing after all these years.'

'I can imagine. You don't have any other letters from him?'

'We had quite a number at one time. Those he'd written to both Federica and me. Saying how terribly sorry he was. That sort of thing.' She smiled. 'We burned them all late one night, after a girls' night in.'

I smiled back, as best I could. Marta Colombo, I remembered, was someone I never, ever wanted to get on the wrong side of. And neither, for that matter, was her daughter.

'So, what is it?'

'Something for Federica. For her wedding day. Something he left for her, years ago. Before he died.'

'I don't quite understand.'

'Michele Ballarin didn't come out from the Lido just to deliver this. He wants Federica to get in touch with him.' She paused. 'It seems Elio might have left her a little something.'

'What, you mean a legacy?'

She sighed. 'I can't imagine it would be anything very substantial. I don't think he had very much left when he died. There was his house in Malamocco, but we sold that and split the money.' She sipped at her coffee. 'All of this might be difficult for Federica, you understand?'

'I think so.' I smiled. 'You really do love your daughter, don't you?'

'She's my best friend, Nathan.'

'So what do we do now?'

'You show her the letter when she comes back. Tell her about Ballarin. And then . . .'

'Then?'

'Then, whatever it is, we'll all deal with it. Together.'

Federica put the phone down, and I could see that her hands were shaking, ever so slightly. 'I think I need that spritz now,' she said.

I went through to the kitchen and fixed us a brace.

'So. Did Ballarin tell you anything about it?'

'He said he probably shouldn't do that over the telephone. So I made an appointment for us to go and see him tomorrow.'

'Both of us?'

'Of course. What's mine is yours, *tesoro*.'

'Gosh, thanks. And likewise, you know.'

'I know.' She paused. 'What is that exactly?'

'My record collection. My film library. Gramsci.'

'Oh.' She kissed me on the cheek. 'Well it's the thought that counts.'

We clinked glasses. 'So,' I said, 'what do you think it is?'

'I honestly don't know. I thought everything had been sorted out when he died. I don't think there can be much left. Perhaps some jewellery of *nonna*'s. That would be nice.' She leaned back, closed her eyes, and took a deep breath.

'There's also the letter,' I said.

She opened one eye, and nodded.

'Are you going to open it?'

'Do I have to?'

'You don't have to. But it'll still be there tomorrow.'

She shook her head and swore under her breath. Then she smiled. 'God, I can tell you've been talking to my mother.'

'Is it that obvious?'

'It is. I don't think you understand how this mother-in-law thing works. We're supposed to gang up on you. Not the other way around.'

'Sorry. I'm sure I'll get the hang of it eventually.'

She gave me a gentle smack on the back of the head, and reached for the envelope. She ran her fingers over the single word on the front, and then tore it open as carefully as she could. Whatever was inside must have been a tight fit, as she had to worry at it with her fingers before being able to draw it out.

It was simply a postcard. The Madonna enthroned, surrounded by a swirl of tiny angelic figures and a group of rather stern-looking holy men.

'Andrea and Bartolomeo di Paolo. *The Virgin in the company of twelve saints.*' Fede rubbed her eyes. 'From our old church in Malamocco. It was the first restoration project I ever worked on.' She turned the card over, then sighed and placed it face up on the table.

I nodded towards the bookshelves, lined with cards from friends. 'Do you want me to put it with the others?'

She nodded. 'Yes. I think that would be nice.'

'Are you okay?'

She rubbed her eyes again. 'Not sure.' Then she nodded to herself. 'But I will be.' She got to her feet. 'Come on. It might be a long day tomorrow. Time for bed.'

I placed the card next to the one from Dario, Vally and Emily. I turned it over to look at the message on the back.

There were just six words. *For Fede. With my love. Papà.*

Chapter 6

'Okay, Gramsci,' I said. 'You've got food and water sufficient for six hours. Multiple sleeping places are available. When we come back, can we be reasonably certain that nothing will have been destroyed?'

He looked up at the sound of my voice with a lack of interest that was almost palpable. Then he curled up once more, throwing a paw over his eyes in order to block out the world at this unholy hour of ten o'clock.

I pulled on my jacket.

'You won't need that,' said Federica. 'It's going to be hot.'

'We're going to see a lawyer. I won't feel properly dressed without one.'

She shrugged. 'As you like.'

I felt the blast of hot air across my face as soon as we stepped outside and realised immediately that she was right. I decided it was too late to admit that now. The jacket would have to stay.

'So,' I said, as we settled into our seats on the *vaporetto*, 'tell me about this guy.'

'His name's Michele Ballarin. He was a partner of my father's.'

'Did you know him well?'

She flushed, ever so slightly. 'A bit.'

'A bit?'

'Yes. A bit.'

'You're blushing.'

'I am not blushing!'

'Yes you are.'

'Okay, yes I am. We had a bit of a thing.'

'A thing?'

'Yes. I was fifteen. He was seventeen. Just a bit of a thing.'

'Oh.' I nodded. 'How long did that go on for?'

'About three months.'

'Three months. Does that count as a thing?'

'It does when you're fifteen.' She paused, and then smiled. 'Hang on a moment, are you – jealous?'

'Jealous? Hah! That's a laugh!'

'You are! You're being jealous of a seventeen-year-old.'

'I am not!'

'In fact it's worse than that. You're being jealous of a seventeen-year-old boy a quarter of a century ago.'

'I am not being jealous and I am not— Look, anyway, can we just move on from this? So, yes, you knew him and there was a thing. I understand.'

She shook her head.

'Am I being a disappointing husband?'

'You are. So, moving on. We used to see quite a lot of his father. Antonio, his name was. A lovely man. A lovely, gentle man. He'd been in partnership with *papà* for years. He used to come to us for dinner quite frequently.' She frowned. 'Before everything went wrong.'

'I see.'

'We never really saw much of him after *papà* left. Sometimes we'd see him in the street, and he'd wave but never stop to chat. I think he felt embarrassed. I went to his funeral when he died. Just sat at the back, and slipped out before the end. And later I heard that Michele had taken his place in the firm.'

We were past the *bacino* of San Marco by now, with the green dome of the votive temple on the Lido still distant. I shifted uncomfortably in my seat, and tugged at the cuffs of my jacket.

'You can take that off, if you like,' said Fede.

'Is it that obvious?'

'Just a bit.'

I stood up and struggled out of it, its sleeves already clinging to me in the heat. I folded it up as best I could, and laid it in my lap.

'I'm going to have to carry this around all day now, I suppose?' I grumbled.

'I did warn you, *caro*.'

'It's just that summer always seems to arrive in a rush. One day, it's spring and you're walking around enjoying the warmth and the sunshine and the next day you wake up and realise you're not going to be able to stand in direct sunlight for the next three months.'

'It could be worse. And the weather was just right for the wedding, wasn't it? I'm sure you look ever so smart in the photos.'

The *vaporetto* pulled in to the *Giardini* stop, where dozens of black-clad and lanyard-wearing young people got off and made their way to the pavilions of the Architecture Biennale.

'So,' I said. 'What do you think this is all about? Your *legacy*, I mean?'

She shook her head. 'I don't know.' She looked relaxed enough, but there was a tightness to her voice.

'Are you sure?' I looked more closely at her. 'Are you all right?'

She smiled. 'Yes, of course. Why wouldn't I be? It's just going to be strange, that's all. Being back in my father's office again. I was so young last time. Barely out of my teens.'

'Okay,' I said, and decided to change the subject. 'So what are we going to do for lunch?'

'No idea. Is there nothing in the fridge?'

'Hardly anything. We could go to the Brazilians, but Eduardo's probably sick of the sight of us by now. We should have an event lunch.'

'An *event* lunch?'

'Exactly. We had a budget wedding, so we should go somewhere nice.' I checked my watch. '*Ai Mercanti* won't be open yet. I'll give them a call later.'

'Lovely,' she said, but she seemed distracted again.

Ballarin's office was in one of the main residential areas of the Lido, between Via Sandro Gallo and the Venice Tennis Club. Fede nodded at it as we walked past. '*Papà* always said how lucky he was to have an office here. I remember how he used to love playing tennis when he was younger.'

'You were never interested?'

'No. He took me along a few times but he could tell I was just doing it to please him. I think that made him a bit sad. Still, it could have been worse.' She pointed to the far end of the road. 'If his office had been just a hundred metres in that direction he'd have been next to the rugby club.'

'A lucky escape.'

'I think so.' We stopped outside what appeared to be a regular apartment block. 'This is it.' She traced the fingers of her right hand over the brass nameplate that read *'Ballarin–Ravagnan. Studio Legale.'*

'Nice that they kept your dad's name.'

She nodded, but said nothing. She let her finger rest on the doorbell for an instant, and closed her eyes. Then she nodded once more, and rang the bell.

'Chi è?'

'Michele. It's Federica.'

'Federica. Please come up.' The door clicked open. 'Second floor.'

Everything about Ballarin's office suggested probity and reassurance. With its polished parquet floor, and shelves lined from floor to ceiling with thick leather-bound books, it had the look of an old-fashioned bank manager's office; the sort where you might be offered a glass of sherry and a cigarette before settling down to business.

Ballarin was a dapper figure with a neatly trimmed beard and shiny black hair that, I thought, betrayed the use of expensive products. He wore a smart, light-blue suit, and an open-necked shirt was his only concession to informality.

We exchanged hugs and kisses. Good aftershave, I thought. Expensive aftershave. He smiled at us, and I smiled back, trying not to dislike him. It had been a quarter of a century, I told myself. I was not going to be jealous of a 'thing' a quarter of a century ago.

'A good journey, I hope?'

Fede smiled back, but said nothing.

'It's getting a little hot,' I said. 'On the boat, that is.'

'Of course. I imagine it must be.' He picked up the remote control on his desk and turned the air conditioning down by a couple of degrees. 'That should help. Can I offer you a coffee?'

Fede shook her head. 'Just water for me, please.'

I nodded. 'That'd be lovely. Black with sugar.'

'Of course.' He went over to a table by the window where a Nespresso machine sat, its shiny modernity incongruous in its surroundings. He clunked in a capsule.

'George Clooney,' I said.

'I'm sorry?'

'That machine. It's the one George Clooney advertises. I've got one myself.'

'How marvellous,' he smiled. 'Now I'm afraid I don't actually have any sugar. Trying to watch this.' He patted his stomach. 'But I can offer you one of these.' He took out a packet of *Baci* chocolates and put one on the saucer next to my coffee. 'They're nearly as good as sugar.'

'Thank you.'

'My pleasure. Please do take a seat, and we'll get down to business.'

We sat down, and I suddenly noticed that the Nespresso machine was not the most incongruous thing in the room. There, on Ballarin's leather-topped desk, was a small plastic statuette. A little man composed of red, white and green blocks with a tiny football for a head. '*Ciao*'. The official mascot of the 1990 Italian World Cup.

Ballarin saw the expression on my face and smiled. 'Italia '90. Do you remember, Federica, we watched the semi-final against Argentina in that bar they'd set up on the beach? Music playing, everybody dancing. *Notti Magiche,* they called it.'

I looked at Fede, who put her hand to her face and pushed a lock of hair away. She might have blushed, ever so slightly. 'I remember,' she said.

I forced a smile on to my face that both Fede and Marta would have been proud of. 'Lovely,' I said. 'Lovely.'

Ballarin smiled back at us. Just a little bit too long, I thought.

Fede gave a little cough. 'So, this is about my father?'

'As I mentioned to your mother.'

He took a folder from his desk, withdrew a sheaf of papers and riffled through them. 'Everything you need to know should be in here. But the crux of it is,' he folded his hands together and smiled at Federica, 'your father had always wanted to leave you something. After your wedding day. He'd arranged it with my father. Years ago now. And so this is it.' He licked his forefinger, and spun round the top sheet so that it was facing us.

Federica, I knew, had expected nothing more than perhaps a few pieces of her grandmother's jewellery. I'd hoped that perhaps we'd see a couple of lines of figures, together with a deduction for tax and a net amount at the bottom that might buy us a modest honeymoon.

There were neither of those. There was just a picture of a house.

Federica was silent.

'I don't understand,' I said:

Ballarin looked at Fede. 'I'm sure you recognise it. Your father's property on Pellestrina. He wanted you to have it.'

'Pellestrina,' I said. 'You've got to be kidding.'

Fede reached over and grabbed my arm tightly. Painfully so. 'He's not kidding,' she said, and her voice shook.

'Your dad had a place on Pellestrina? You never mentioned it.'

'It's – well, it's not somewhere I've thought about in a very long time.'

Ballarin pushed the folder towards her. 'There are some things for you to sign, of course. But otherwise everything is here. Title deeds, keys, everything you should need. No utilities connected, of course. That's something you'll need to sort out. Or I can sort them out for you, if you'd prefer.'

Fede put her hands to her face. They were, I could see, shaking.

I put a hand on her shoulder. 'Fede. Are you okay?'

She nodded. Then she took a deep breath and looked at Ballarin.

'This is impossible.'

Ballarin put his head to one side. 'I don't understand, Federica?'

'It's impossible. My father left us everything when he died. I thought there was nothing left.'

Ballarin stroked his beard. 'I know it must be a shock. And it's certainly unusual, but not quite unheard of. Your father wanted to keep something special for you for your wedding day. As a surprise.'

'Oh, it's certainly that.' Her grip on my arm was almost painful now. 'Do I need to sign anything at this moment?'

He shrugged. 'You don't have to. That's very much up to you.'

'Okay. Good.' She pulled the folder towards her. 'Can I take these away? Just for a couple of days? Just to have a look through everything?'

'Of course, Federica.' He paused. 'I can still call you Federica, can't I?' It was, I thought, slightly late for that but I judged that it probably wasn't the moment to say anything. 'Take them away and have a good look through everything. If you have any questions, just give me a call. And then, when you're happy, just make an appointment and we can arrange to have everything signed.'

She nodded. 'Okay. Thank you, Michele.' Then she turned to me. 'I think I'd like to go now.'

Chapter 7

Pellestrina. The impossibly thin strip of land that lay south-west of the Lido and stretched towards Chioggia, the embankments on its seaward side serving as a barrier between the Adriatic and the lagoon. Accessible only by boat, and remote from the city that now acted as its parent – a city that was depopulating year after year – it seemed incredible that anybody should still live there. And yet, nearly four thousand people did, surviving on fishing, boat-building and tourism in a climate that – like the rest of Venice – felt brutally hot in the summer and yet fragile and painfully exposed to the elements in winter.

A place on the very edge of things, not quite Venice and yet not quite Chioggia. A place, it seemed, where we now had a property.

We sat outside again on the *vaporetto* on the return journey to Venice, making the most of the cool breeze that blew across the lagoon. Another month, perhaps even another few weeks, and the sun would be enough to drive us inside, leaving the rear seats to tourists eating rapidly melting ice creams. But, for the moment, it was enough just to sit there and watch the Lido receding in the bright sunlight.

'So,' I said, 'would you like to tell me about it?'

She shook her head. 'Maybe later. There's a lot of things I need to get my head around.'

'You've inherited a house. I mean, that's pretty cool. Think what we could do with it. Rent it out, use it for holidays . . .'

'Stop it, Nathan. Please, just stop it.' Her voice was tired.

'I'm sorry. I thought you'd be pleased.'

'I don't know what I'm feeling just now.' She reached over and squeezed my hand. 'I'm sorry.'

'It's okay.'

'I need to talk to *mamma* about this.' She paused. 'As soon as possible. Is that okay?'

'Sure. She's in town for a few more days, isn't she? Shall we just go round to her hotel?'

'Nathan—' She paused again. 'I think I need to do this on my own.'

'Oh.'

'I'm sorry. We'll talk about it later, though. Promise. Do you mind?'

'No, of course not.' A thought struck me. 'What about lunch?'

'I'm not really in the mood right now.' She forced a smile on to her face. 'I'm sorry. I suppose technically we're on honeymoon. I'm sure this isn't what you expected.'

'Well, it's a bit weird, isn't it? I mean, two days ago I thought you were a woman of slender means. Today you're an heiress.'

She smiled, properly this time, and punched my arm. 'Stop it!'

'It's very confusing. I mean, I thought I'd married you for love and now – all this.'

She said nothing, but dabbed at her eyes and blew her nose. And then she laid her head on my shoulder for the remainder of the journey back to Venice.

I fussed and fretted around the apartment all afternoon, finding it difficult to settle or concentrate. I really did need to get started on translating the PhD thesis, but my eyes kept sliding off the text. Eventually I put *Dark Side of the Moon* on the stereo, lay down on the sofa and closed my eyes.

The bells chiming at the beginning of *Time* woke me from my half-doze, and then Gramsci chose to leap on to my chest, his claws sinking in through my second-least-horrible T-shirt.

I scratched him, briefly, behind the ears.

'Okay, Grams, it's like this. Lovely secondary care-giver has recently been promoted to the position of joint primary care-giver. Now, this may not mean much to you, on account of you being a cat. But what you need to understand is that Federica now needs to be treated with the same love and respect that you show to me. Are we good with that?'

He said nothing – again, on account of being a cat – but I felt pretty sure my words were sinking in.

'So when she comes home this evening – given that she's had a bit of a trying day – we're going to have to do our best to make things as good as they can be for her. Aren't we? Which means no violent or potentially destructive behaviour from you. And from me,' I reached for the remote control and turned the volume down, 'it means perhaps choosing some music that is not actively distressing. Can we do that?'

He sank his claws in, just a little more, drawing an 'Ow!' out of me.

'I'll take that as a yes. Okay?'

I wasn't sure what remained in the fridge. I'd got back too late to go and buy fish, and the nearest butcher's shop would, I knew, be closed. I could pick up some stuffed pasta from *Prix* or we could just go out for pizza, but we were still in our first days of married life and not bothering to cook wouldn't seem like the best of omens. There'd be something in the kitchen that I could do something with, I was sure. Gramsci, meanwhile, showed no signs of moving, so I closed my eyes, trying not to wince as he occasionally flexed his claws in appreciation, I assumed, of the music.

I was woken up by the sound of keys rattling in the lock, and Gramsci yowled as I leapt to my feet.

'*Ciao, cara.*'

'*Ciao, caro.* Sorry, did I wake you?'

'Oh, I've not been asleep.'

She smiled. 'You really are a terrible liar.'

We stood in silence for a moment.

'So,' I said, 'is everything okay?'

She nodded. 'I'm not sure. I think so.'

'Would a hug be good?'

'A hug would be very good.'

I held her, and stroked her hair, and we just stood there until she broke the silence.

'I suppose we need to talk,' she said.

'Only if you want to.'

'I think we do. Is it time to start drinking?'

I checked my watch. It was past six o'clock. 'Oh, definitely.' I went through to the kitchen and came back with two glasses of prosecco.

She raised an eyebrow. 'No spritz?'

I shook my head. 'No.'

'Don't tell me my husband has embraced healthy living. I'm not sure I'm ready for that.'

'Nothing so drastic.' I paused. 'But you're upset. And I've never seen you upset before. Not properly. And so I thought prosecco would be more sensible than a spritz.'

She slumped down on to the sofa, leaned her head back and closed her eyes. 'You're right, *caro*. You know, you really might have the right stuff for this "husband" job after all.'

I sat down next to her. Gramsci leapt up on to the arm of the sofa, and made to jab her with a paw but I mouthed the words 'What were we just talking about?' at him and he slunk away.

'Come on then,' I said. 'Tell me all about it.'

'Where would you like me to start?'

'Wherever you like. I never knew about Pellestrina.'

'I'm sorry. I suppose I should have mentioned it. It's just that it's so long ago now that I've half forgotten it myself.'

'Bad memories?'

She opened her eyes, and looked at me in surprise. 'No. Good ones.'

Chapter 8

'*Papà* wasn't from Pellestrina, of course. Neither was his father. Ravagnan isn't *pellestrinese*. But someone, somewhere back in our history must have been. Because as long as I remember, there'd been the house. Every summer, when the schools broke up, we'd travel down from the Lido to the house by the sea. The house that smelled of old wood and pipe smoke. Me, *Mamma*, *Papà*. And *nonno* and *nonna* – my father's parents.

'We all lived in Malamocco in those days. Not quite the Lido, not quite anywhere else. That's somewhere else we should go again. I think I'd like to spend some time there. It's been so long.

'So, as I said, every summer we'd go down to Pellestrina. The summers last for ever when you're young, don't they? And you might think it would be boring for a little girl, but it wasn't. I made friends there. We'd play on the beach. *Nonno* would cook us fish for dinner every night. *Nonna* was the better cook actually, but Grandfather thought that fish was something a man ought to be able to cook. So that's what he did. And then, in the evenings, he'd light his pipe and sit in his usual chair and tell us all stories that we'd heard a hundred times before.'

'Including *Pinocchio*?' I said.

'No.' She shook her head. 'That was always something that *papà* had to do.' She smiled. 'I wouldn't let anybody else read that.'

'It sounds lovely,' I said. 'Idyllic, even.'

'It was. I think even at the time I realised how lucky we were. And then, one day *papà* came and spoke to *mamma* and myself. I wasn't a little girl any more, you realise, but he was still finding it difficult to treat me as an almost grown-up. *Nonna* was very ill, he said. We needed to be very brave, and we needed to make sure that we looked after *nonno*.

'I don't remember the last time I saw her. But I remember thinking that everything would be different from then on. That summers would never be the same.

'We went back to Pellestrina the following year, of course. But it was different. *Papà* took over the cooking. *Nonno* would just sit in his chair. Sometimes he'd smoke his pipe. I asked him, once, if he'd tell us one of his stories. And he smiled, and he ruffled my hair like he always did, and he started. And then stopped. He was crying, ever so quietly. Tears just running down his face, silently. I hugged him, and told him it was all right. He said that I shouldn't be worried, that he was just a silly old man.

'I remember that I wanted to cry as well but I knew it would break his heart to think he'd upset his granddaughter. So, I told him that he'd never, ever be silly to me. But, for the first time, he seemed like an old man.' She paused. 'And there were no more stories after that.'

'He sounds like a lovely man,' I said.

'He was. Oh, he was.' Fede's eyes were red now. 'You should

have met him. Oh, he'd have liked you. The arguments you'd have had about cooking fish! You think *Zio* Giacomo's bad?'

She wiped her eyes. 'He didn't live much longer. You know how we talk about "losing the will to live"? I'd always thought that was nonsense. But it seemed as if he just didn't see much point in going on any more.

'There was one more summer on Pellestrina. After *nonno* died. But it wasn't the same. The house was that little bit too big for just three voices.

'That was when it started to go wrong, you know? I don't think I realised just how much father relied on *nonno*. He no longer seemed like the same man. He started coming home later and later, saying he'd had to stay on at the office. And then sometimes he wouldn't come home at all. He was working too hard and fallen asleep at work, he'd say. I was at university by then. Maybe I didn't pay attention to it as much as I should have done. But I think mother always knew.

'Then one day he came home and told us he was leaving. He'd look after us, he said. He'd always look after us. But he'd met someone else. Someone who made him feel young again. Like it was when *nonno* was still alive.' She took a deep breath. 'Some crap like that, anyway.' She rubbed her eyes once more.

'Are you okay?' I said.

She forced a smile on to her face. 'I'm sort of okay. I'd be more okay with a strong drink and a cigarette. Except—'

'Except that we don't do that any more,' I said.

'Exactly.' She smiled, properly this time. 'God, look at me, I went to bed with Nathan Sutherland last night and woke up with Mr Sensible Husband this morning.'

'I'm sure it won't last,' I said.

'It better not.' She kissed me. 'But thank you. So, as I was saying, *papà* moved out of our house in Malamocco. And then three months later he telephoned. He'd made a terrible, terrible mistake, he said.'

She paused to drink the last of her prosecco.

'I think it was the hardest thing mother ever did, you know? Not taking him back. I'd see him around the town, of course. But I never spoke to him.'

'Never?'

'No.' She seemed surprised. 'Why would I? I found out he'd been at the house on Pellestrina with *her*.'

'Her?'

'Sofia. Their secretary.' She shook her head. 'It was like he'd spat on my childhood.'

'I understand.'

She shook her head. 'I don't think you do.'

'Try me. I'll tell you about my family sometime.'

She took a deep breath. 'I'm sorry. Well, there isn't much more to say. His partner Antonio died. He'd been a friend to us, when I was growing up. I went to his funeral. I saw *papà* there, briefly. He tried to make his way through the crowd to speak to me, but I slipped away.

'I think that was the final straw, in many ways. Antonio was older than he was. Somewhere between a big brother and a father figure. When he was gone, I think *papà* must have felt terribly alone.

'And then, late one evening, he drove back to Malamocco just a little too fast. There's a section in the road there that the locals call the *curva della morte*. "The Curve of Death".

If he'd been just a little slower, taken one less drink, he might have made it.' She shook her head. 'Nearly ten years ago now.'

We sat in silence for a while.

'I think it's time for that spritz,' I said.

She nodded. 'I think it's well past time.'

I gave her a hug and got to my feet. 'So,' I said, 'any thoughts about what we should do?'

'I think so. We didn't have any plans did we, about going on honeymoon? There was nowhere either of us particularly wanted to go.'

'Well, I did wonder if we might have a short visit to Aberystwyth. So you could see my old stomping ground. But I'm not sure I'd class that as a honeymoon.'

'Would it make a difference as to what time of year we went?'

'None at all. Bound to be raining, whenever.'

'Okay. Let's take a couple of weeks and just see what it feels like being back on Pellestrina.'

'Are you sure?'

'Absolutely. I don't know how I'm going to feel about it. But I think it's something I need to do. Is that all right?'

I smiled. 'More than that. It's a great idea.'

She took my hand. 'Thank you, *caro*. I can take a few weeks away from work. What about you?'

'I've still got some – by which I mean a lot of – work to do on translating that thesis. But that's fine, I can do that anywhere.'

'What about the consulate?'

'The consul in Mestre deals with problems on *terraferma*.

I'll give him a call. He can cover for me, and I'll return the favour next time he needs to get away.'

'So we could have a second honeymoon in Mestre next year?'

'We certainly could.'

'Well, aren't I the lucky girl?' she smiled. 'Aren't people going to be a bit cross if they have to go to Mestre to get their problems sorted out?'

I shrugged. 'Possibly. But then anyone who needs the services of the consul is going to be cross by default. I'll give Marcus a call tomorrow just to give him a heads-up.'

'Have you got anything important in your diary?'

'There is no diary. There's just a guy in prison I need to visit.'

'Really? How exciting.'

'It's not really. He gets out in a couple of months and so I need to go and explain to him what happens when he's released.'

'So what does happen?'

'The Italian state kicks his sorry arse all the way back to Britain.'

'Oh. Is that what you're going to say to him?'

'Well, I'll find a way of taking the edge off it. But more or less.' I got to my feet and went into the kitchen. 'And now it really is time for a drink.'

I fixed us a brace of spritz Nathans and took them back into the living room. Gramsci yawned and stretched on the back of the sofa, and a thought struck me.

'I was just thinking about what you were saying. About the house being too big for three voices.'

'Yes?'

'Well there's only two of us. Except, of course, there's also,' I inclined my head towards the cat.

Gramsci yawned again, and curled his paws over his eyes.

Fede looked from me to Gramsci and then back again. 'You're kidding?' she said.

'I haven't said what I was thinking yet.'

'You want to bring your cat on honeymoon with us?'

'Strictly speaking he's our cat now. And, well, yes.'

'Can't you get someone to look after him?' I looked at her, and raised my eyebrows. 'Okay, stupid idea. Can't you take him to a cattery?'

'Kitty prison. Tried that once. I paid dearly for it when I got him home again.'

She sighed. 'Okay. I understand. But you'll have to get him there.'

'Trust me,' I smiled. 'He'll be no trouble.'

In the Wolf's Den

'Tell me about the early years', I say. 'The 1970s. The gangs.'

He shrugs. 'What else is there to say? You know all this stuff already.'

'I do. But I want to hear it from you.'

He smiles. 'Okay. If you think it's interesting.' He closes his eyes, and folds his hands together. 'There were so many of us in those days. Italy seemed like a country where you could do anything you wanted. There was chaos, of course. Political chaos. Aldo Moro. The Red Brigades. What we called the Years of Lead.' He shakes his head. 'Never had any time for any of that nonsense.'

His voice is warm, smoky. The Old Wolf is telling me a bedtime story.

'Who did we have? The San Donà clan. The Mestrini. Clan Giostrai.' He chuckles. 'I did a few jobs for them. Always ended in chaos. Stupid of me. Never work with amateurs. Never work for anyone where there isn't a proper boss. Otherwise you just end up fighting. And if you end up fighting you end up dead, or in prison.

'I ended up running with the Mestrini. I was married by then. Albino was just an infant. We were living in some flophouse

in Mestre, and getting by on what I could steal and what I could deal. And then one day some guy – he's not a friend, he's not even a friend of a friend, he's just some guy – says he knows people who've seen me selling on the streets. Now normally they'd be pissed off because this is their territory, but they think maybe we can work together. All I have to do is deliver a few packages.

   'And so, for the next few months, that's what I do. I drive to Trieste – for the first time in my life, I've got a car, imagine how that feels – I pick up a package, and I drive it back to a safe house in Mestre.'

   'Drugs?' I say.

   He looks surprised. 'Of course.'

   'You were okay with that?'

   Again, he looks surprised. 'Do you smoke?'

   I nod.

   'So you know the risks. Do you want me to go on?'

   I'm about to speak, but bite my tongue.

   'I run this route for maybe six months. And then one day, it's not my usual contact in Mestre, but a roomful of cops.

   'My lawyer tells me to come clean, make a plea bargain.' He shakes his head. 'Never been that kind of man. I say I met some guy on the street, he asked me to deliver a package. No, I don't know what the hell is in it. No, I don't know anyone at the address in Mestre, it's just an address I was given, you know? No, I didn't know they were drugs, I'm a poor Mestrino down on his luck and I just needed some money.

   'I got two years. And I was just going to keep my mouth shut, and do my time. Except one day, I meet this guy. We're on exercise, and he comes up to me and pats me on the shoulder. He's heard good things about me, he says. I'm a good guy. A smart* guy. I've just made one mistake. Throwing my hat in with the Mestrini.

'I tell him I've got nothing to say to him.

'He smiles at me. Says that things are changing. All these old gangs – the Mestrini, the Giostrai boys. Amateurs. They won't be here for much longer.

'He's got an accent. Sicilian. I'm still not sure I want to be his pal, but I have the idea that maybe he has something interesting to say. I ask him how he ended up in the Veneto.

'He laughs, and tells me that the government has sent him on holiday. I don't understand, of course, so he goes on to tell me that he and his kind – by which I mean convicted mafiosi of course – are being moved out of the South. To keep them away from their associates. Stop them communicating. In this way, the thinking goes, they can break it all up. But now, of course, everybody in the North – anybody with a bit of ambition – wants to learn from the Sicilian masters. And I could be part of that. If I want to.

'I shake my head. Drugs are a mug's game, I say. I've been burned by that already.

'He shakes his head. They're not interested in that, he tells me. There are plenty of people – cheap crooks, stupid kids – that they can use on the streets. But those who've been inside the Mestrini or Clan Giostrai – these are the guys they'd like to meet.

'I tell him I just want to do my time and get out.

'Of course, he says. But he gives me a number for me to call when I get out. Just in case I ever feel like talking. He pats me on the shoulder again. Lupo, he says. That's a good Sicilian name.

'So, I kept my nose clean. Trust me, I was going to be a good guy when I got out. Look after my family, be a proper father. And

*so one day, I walk out of the gates of Santa Maria Maggiore yet
again with the clothes I'm standing up in, a packet of cigarettes
and a few coins in my pocket.'*

'*And so you made that call?' I say.*

*The Old Wolf laughs, a great smoky chuckle. 'No. I went for
a beer instead.'*

Chapter 9

Federica will tell you about the journey to Pellestrina. How the sun shone on the waters of the lagoon on the way to the Lido; how the bus made its way along the tree-lined avenues that led to Malamocco and on past the sand dunes of Alberoni; of the ferry that took us across the lagoon to the tip of Pellestrina, and of the journey down through the island itself, following the line of the *murazzi*, the great seawalls made of Istrian stone that served to protect the island, and, by extension, Venice itself from the high waters of the Adriatic. She will tell you of the short walk to our final destination, warmed by the early summer sun, and cooled by the lightest of breezes.

I remember none of that.

Gramsci had howled for the entire journey. This had initially meant having to sit outside on the *vaporetto*, which was no great sacrifice on a summer's morning. Then our fellow passengers on the back seats decided that perhaps they would leave the three of us to our own company and retreated inside.

By the time we reached the Lido and got on the bus to Pellestrina, Federica had also decided that the two of us might prefer to be alone, and retreated to the opposite end.

The journey from Piazzale Santa Maria Elisabetta to the *traghetto* at Alberoni is not a short one. Having discovered that Gramsci did not like travelling by water, it then transpired that he was equally unenthusiastic about travelling by road. The ferry service that carried the bus across the short stretch of water to Pellestrina, therefore, combined the worst of all possible worlds. The final stretch along the straight, unchanging main road down through the island was, mercifully, a bit of a blur. A few small children expressed an interest in peering through the bars of Gramsci's travelling box, in the hope of getting a look at the cute kitty inside. Some of them, in spite of my best efforts, even poked their fingers through the bars, before snatching them back quickly. The adults on the bus glared at me as one with the darkest of looks. I smiled and muttered apologies as best I could, but my accent did not seem to improve matters. *Stranieri*, it seemed, were descending on Pellestrina with their unfriendly cats.

I caught sight of Federica preparing to get off the bus for our stop at Madonna dell'Apparizione and forced my way through the crowd to join her. The two of us stood there at the side of the road, breathing in petrol as we watched the bus retreat into the distance.

I held Gramsci's box up so that I could look directly at him. 'There we go, old son. That wasn't so bad was it?'

He sat there and looked at me in silence for a moment, before starting to howl again.

Federica said nothing but shook her head.

'I suppose that could have gone better,' I said.

She nodded.

'You might have sat with me.'

'Yes, but I was afraid that people might think we were together.'

'Well we're here now. Tell me it's not far, eh? Please tell me it's not far.'

'Just five minutes.'

'Oh good.'

'You know, this isn't really how I imagined my return to Pellestrina.'

'Sorry. I was thinking that we'd just have to move here. I'm not sure I can face the return journey.'

'I thought perhaps that was something you two might like to do by yourselves. Come on.'

She led us across the road, and along a narrow street that led down to where the blue lagoon spread out before our eyes. Boats were moored along the front with scarcely any space between them. Not the monstrous maxi-yachts that one saw in Venice, but fishing boats with great metal cages fixed to the front. Ramshackle fishing huts stood on stilts further out in the water. The street itself was lined by small houses in shades of pink, terracotta, blue and yellow, and the smell of fried fish came from a nearby restaurant making my stomach rumble as I wondered how far off lunch could be. My jacket was clinging to me uncomfortably in the midday heat, and Gramsci was still howling away and attracting unwanted attention from passers-by, yet, in spite of myself, I smiled.

Federica patted me on the arm. 'First time?'

'It is. It seems terrible, but I've been here ten years now and never made it out here before. And it seems—'

'—like another world?'

'Almost.'

'It's busier than I remember, mind you. But still, it's nothing like Venice.'

I nodded at the restaurant. '*da Celeste*. Do you know that place?'

She smiled. 'I do. It was here when we used to visit. It was a special treat to go there. We had to be very careful though. If we went there too often *nonno* would get all grumpy and say that we didn't like his cooking. And then we'd have to make a big fuss of him and say that of course his food was better but we didn't want him to work so hard.' She patted my stomach. 'Are you thinking of food already?'

'Not just food. I'm thinking a drink would be very good indeed.'

'Me too.' She looked down at the cat box. 'But we need to get your little friend settled first.'

'You mean our little friend.'

'No, I think I was right the first time.' She reached inside her handbag and took out a bunch of keys. 'It's just over here.' She led me past the restaurant and to a small terracotta-coloured house, its tiny garden overgrown and the grasses browning in the sun. The gate juddered open, and she smiled. 'It was always like that. Nobody ever got around to fixing it.'

'The garden needs a bit of work.'

'That's a project for you, *caro*.'

I held up the cat box. 'How about that, eh, Grams? A whole garden for you to run around in. Well, to lie around in.' He remained unimpressed, and the howling continued.

Federica walked up to the front door, and ran her fingers over the horseshoe-shaped nameplate, pitted with age, but with the name 'Ravagnan' still just about legible.

She turned the keys in the lock, and we went inside. I was expecting it to smell of damp and must, but it appeared to have been recently cleaned.

'Michele must have got someone in,' she said.

'Shame they couldn't have done the garden as well.'

'That's a little treat they were leaving for you.' She took a deep breath. 'Here we are then.'

We were in a large wood-panelled living room. A couple of ancient sofas sat on the bare stone floor. To our right was a small kitchen. To our left, a wooden staircase led up to the first floor.

A bookcase stood against the rear wall, almost empty except for a shelf of hardbacks and some boardgames stacked up on the bottom. Federica walked over to it. 'Monopoly. Trivial Pursuit. My goodness.' She sighed. 'I wonder—?' She ran her fingers along the spines of the books, and then gave a sharp intake of breath and took one of them down. The cover was torn, and yellowed with age, yet she lifted it to her face, and rested her forehead against it, her eyes closed. She opened it up, and breathed in, deeply. Then she smiled. 'It still smells the same. Come and look.'

I stood next to her, and put an arm around her shoulders. 'Look.'

The colours had faded, but there was no mistaking the image. A small boy, in red shirt and green shorts, with a conical hat upon his head and a comically long, thin nose. Carlo Collodi's *Le avventure di Pinocchio*.

She turned to the frontispiece. 'Happy Birthday, darling Fede. With all my love. *Papà*.'

'I can't believe it's still here. After all this time.'

I became aware that Gramsci was still howling away. 'I suppose we ought to let him out?'

'Oh?' She looked at him as if she'd forgotten he was there. 'Oh yes, I suppose so.'

I put his carrying case down, unclicked the grille, and then snatched my hands back as I expected him to shoot forth like a rocket from a bottle. Immediately, the howling ceased. He sauntered forth, sniffed around the sofas and gave one of them an experimental scratch before hauling himself on to the back, curling up and falling asleep.

The silence was almost tangible. Fede made to speak, but I shushed her. 'No. No. Let's just enjoy the moment.' I stood there, eyes closed, breathing in the unfamiliar smells and listening to the noises from the street outside.

Fede gave me a hug. 'Better now?'

'Much better.'

'Do you want to see the rest of the house? Or is it time for lunch?'

Gramsci purred in his sleep, as I tip-toed towards the door and pulled it open as gently as I could. 'I think, Mrs Ravagnan, that it is very much time for lunch.'

Chapter 10

I pushed my plate back, patted my stomach and sighed.

'Better?'

'Much better. All's well with the world.' Then I noticed the level in our glasses. 'Well, almost. Do you think we need another round?'

'*Caro*, we're here to decide what to do with my – our – new property. It's not just a chance for a month of incessant eating and drinking.'

'It isn't? Oh dear.'

'And we're not going to be able to eat here for every meal. We're going to need to get you back in the kitchen.'

'Oh I know. I'm looking forward to it. But it's our first day, I've had a long ride in a hot bus with an angry cat and–'

She put her index finger over my lips to shush me. 'Oh, very well.' She turned to the waiter and smiled. 'Two more glasses of prosecco, please.'

I looked out over the lagoon, shimmering cornflower blue in the midday sun. A gull perched on a nearby mooring post, scanning the water for fish that might stray too near the surface, and then flew off, disturbed by the sounds of a motorboat packed with young people.

'Do you get many tourists out here?' I asked.

'Some. They usually only come for the day though. But those are probably locals.'

'Must be a strange place to grow up.'

She nodded. 'And difficult, I think. There are no high schools on the Lido. Not any more.'

'So, what, if you're going to school you—?'

'Take the bus. Then the ferry. Then another bus, and then the *vaporetto*. And then walk. Every day.'

'Bloody hell,' I whistled. 'It was a twenty-minute walk for me. And I used to complain about that.' I looked around at the fishing boats that were moored, all of them with great, ungainly metal cages fastened to the front. 'I've always wondered – what's with these?'

'*The vongolare?* The scoop at the front dredges molluscs out of the floor of the lagoon. Very efficient. Too efficient. Every so often the *Guardia* have a clampdown on illegal fishing. Then things quiet down for a few months. And then, well, they stop being so quiet and things go back to normal. *Nonno* had all sorts of stories about his father and his pals fleeing from the police after they'd been caught overfishing. Some of them might even have been true. He used to show us a scar on his leg which he said happened when he was shot running away as a young man. But then *nonna* said it happened when he fell off a ladder while painting the house.' She looked serious for a moment. 'And if anybody worries about overfishing today, well, they try to put it out of their minds.'

I looked down at the empty pile of mussel shells on my plate and, similarly, tried to put it out of my mind.

Fede pointed at the building a few doors down from her

grandfather's. 'He lived practically next door to the *carabinieri*. I don't think he ever did anything really bad. Even they might have noticed. But he liked to make out that his father was a bit more of a rogue than he ever was. I grew up telling my friends that Great-grandfather had been a smuggler.'

I laughed, and Fede waved for the bill. She patted my hand. 'Come on then. There's a pizzeria nearby. I think that'll do us for dinner. In the meantime there's somewhere I'd like to go.' She took out a few banknotes from her purse, and smiled at the waiter.

'Oh right. Fine. Well, I need to do some shopping as well.'

'You do?'

'Yes. For Gramsci.'

She opened her mouth, and then shook her head. 'Forget it, I probably don't want to know. Do you need an actual pet shop or would a supermarket do?'

'A decent-sized supermarket would probably do.'

'Oh God. Okay, we'll do the best we can. But we need to do my thing first.'

'Where are we going?'

'The Adriatic.'

'Won't that take rather a long time?'

'It's a two-minute walk. Trust me, you'll be in the supermarket buying whatever essential supplies your – *our* – horrible cat needs before you know it.'

I grinned. 'I don't believe it. *Our* – you said *our*!'

She looked at me for a moment, muttered something that sounded like *pffft*, and half dragged me to my feet, leading me back in the direction of the bus stop.

***

We climbed up a series of stone steps that had been cut into the side of the embankment, leading to the top of the *murazzi*.

'You get a better idea of them from up here,' said Fede. 'From the road, they just look like a big, grassy dyke. But from here . . .' Her voice trailed off, as she spread her arms wide, to indicate the great piled-up slabs of white Istrian stone that curved away in both directions, protecting the fragile lagoon from the Adriatic.

'Bernardino Zendrini,' she continued. 'One of the greatest engineers of the Republic. He really believed he could hold back the ocean itself.'

'It looks to me like he did a pretty good job,' I said.

'He did. Until 1966. Still, that was a run of about two hundred years. That's probably better than the MOSE project will ever do. And cheaper as well.'

'I hadn't thought,' I said, 'were your family here in 1966? During the great flood, I mean?'

'*Papà* had left home by then. But *nonno* would talk about it for hours if we let him. No electricity. No way to know if help was coming. No sound except the roar of the waters, and people screaming.' She raised her hand to shield her eyes, and looked out towards the sea. 'Seems difficult to imagine on a day like today, doesn't it?'

I nodded.

'*Nonno* was very philosophical about it. He said it was just the order of things. Sooner or later, the sea would win and everything would be swept away.' She looked at me and smiled. 'But not today, though. Come on!'

She took my hand and led me across the *murazzi* to the beach beyond.

'There,' she said. 'What do you think?'

I took a good look around. The sand, it had to be said, was never likely to be described as 'golden' even on the sunniest of days, and was broken up by patches of scrubby vegetation and studded with flotsam and jetsam. Directly in front of us, a breakwater in pink and white stone jutted out into the sea, a tumbledown shack-like structure at its far end.

'Well,' I said, 'it's not the Lido.'

She punched my arm. 'I know it's not much, but it's what they've got. No beach clubs here. No one to run around after you, carrying umbrellas and loungers. No bars, no restaurants. No showers. Just this.'

As I looked around, I could see more of the ramshackle huts dotted along the beach. Some were little more than a few poles with rope stretched between them. Others had flimsy roofs that provided a modicum of shade. A few had folded up deckchairs, umbrellas and children's beach inflatables inside.

'I'm not sure I quite understand,' I said.

'Think about it. If you live on Pellestrina, you're never more than a couple of hundred metres from the beach. Therefore no need for a bar, or a shower, or somewhere to eat. You can just go home. Or just barbecue fish on the rocks. So, every year, everyone kind of constructs their own little space. Just somewhere to leave things and give you a bit of shade.'

'I still don't understand. What's to stop other people taking your space. Or just nicking your stuff?'

Federica shrugged. 'It's Pellestrina. People just don't.'

'So, did you have one of your own?'

'Of course. We'd put it up when we arrived, and take it down again when we left. Not much – just a couple of poles with some rope between them. And then we hung towels over them for shade.' She paused, and looked at me. 'There should still be some umbrellas and deckchairs in the attic.'

'Right,' I said, starting to wonder where this was going.

She continued to look at me.

'Oh no,' I said. 'You don't mean that?'

'What?' she said, with *faux* innocence.

'You want me to go up to the attic, and root through God knows what rubbish in the hope of finding some old beach gear from over twenty years ago. And, if it hasn't rotted away, you want me to build some sort of beach shack thing?'

'I'll help. Well, not with the attic, I don't think there'll be room for two of us up there.'

'You have got to be kidding. I've had a hard day transporting the worst cat in the world all the way from Venice, and now you want me to do this?'

'All you've had to do this afternoon is have lunch and a stroll on the beach. And all you have to do tonight is get the things down from the attic and eat pizza. Come on. It'll be fun.'

'It won't be fun. It very much will not be fun.' I folded my arms. 'And I'm not going to do it.'

Chapter 11

'Success?'

I wiped a cobweb from my hair, and then realised that my hands were thick with dust and that it might not have been the smartest thing to do.

'I think so. I found a few deckchairs and a couple of umbrellas.'

'Do you think they might clean up?'

'Do you mean, do you think I might be able to clean them up?'

'Yes.'

I sighed. 'Probably.' I looked down at myself. 'You know, maybe a white T-shirt wasn't the best thing to wear.'

'Maybe not.' She smiled, tried and failed to find a non-dusty part of me to kiss, and settled for blowing me one instead. 'Well done, *caro*. What's it like up there?'

'Dark. Dusty. Watertight though. Oh, and I think there might be a rat. There's definitely something scurrying away under the floorboards. And there's loads of boxes of stuff. Newspapers and the like.'

'That'll be because of *nonno*. He was a terrible hoarder. Used to drive *nonna* mad.'

'Oh, and something else. There's a box of photos. Your family I guess?'

'My family? Couldn't you tell?'

'I had a look but it was dark and, besides, you were probably about ten at the time. So no, I couldn't.'

'Exciting, though. Well done. We can have a look after dinner.'

'Dinner sounds good. Slumping into a chair with a spritz sounds even better.'

She looked me up and down. 'I'm not sure slumping into anything would be a good idea until you get cleaned up. Go on, you have a shower and I'll go and bring us back some pizza.'

She made to hug me, but then decided against it. So this time I blew her a kiss, and trudged upstairs to the bathroom.

'How was yours?'

'Pretty good. Probably better than anywhere in Venice.'

'I think this place has a wood-fired oven. You don't find that in the *centro storico*.'

That was true. The use of open pizza ovens reaching a terrifying heat was, for the best of reasons, not allowed in Venice itself.

'I should have cooked, though.'

'No, you shouldn't. It's not an evening for you spending hours in the kitchen. It's an evening for eating pizza straight from the box and drinking cold beer from the bottle.'

I reached over to give her a hug. 'Ah, I can't think why I wanted to marry you.' I got to my feet and took the empty boxes through to the kitchen. 'There. All cleared away.'

'You can cook tomorrow. If you're missing it.' Then she saw the expression on my face and frowned. 'What's wrong?'

'Mmm, I've had a look in the kitchen. I kind of miss all my pots and pans. And knives. I don't think these are quite up to it.'

'This is just dinner at home, you realise?'

'I know, I know. But we're on honeymoon. I want everything to be perfect.'

'And it is. So stop fretting. If you really think you can't manage without your precious pans and knives you can always go back to Venice to pick them up.'

'I guess I could. It seems a long way, though.' I sighed, and flung my arms wide. 'Oh, I *suppose* I could try and improvise with what I have.'

'Well done. I appreciate the sacrifices you're having to make. Now why not come and sit down? Come on, I want to have a look at what's in this box.'

I sat down next to her on the uncomfortably sproingy sofa. To be fair, it had probably never been resprung, nor, in all likelihood, would it ever be.

We sat and looked at the box together.

'Go on then,' I said.

'Me?'

'Of course. They're your family.'

'Your family as well, now.'

'I hadn't really thought of that. Is it possible to have a father-in-law you've never met?'

'I don't know.'

'Anyway, you open it. Your dad, your box.'

Fede reached over, picked it up and put it on her lap.

She ran her fingers over the lid, then nodded to herself and removed it. The box contained a pile of newspaper clippings and photographs. She leafed through them.

'Wow.'

'Family stuff?'

'Most of it.' She showed me a framed photograph. 'That's all of us. *Nonno* and *nonna* were still alive. I was so young then.'

'You look like your mother, you know. Actually, more than that, you look like your grandmother.'

'Thanks.' She gave me a kiss on the cheek. 'I hope so.'

'Weird though, isn't it? When was this taken? Maybe thirty years ago?'

'That sounds about right. But it looks like it's from another world. It could almost have been in sepia.'

She stood it on the table, and took out another one. 'This is me. I think it must have been the year I graduated. And this is *nonno* and *nonna* again.' She passed me the photograph. Both of them were smiling, but the old lady's face was noticeably lined and thinner this time. Federica sighed. 'I think this was the last photograph of the two of them together. We came to Pellestrina, as usual, for the summer. I think *mamma* and *papà* must have known it would be the last time. In the end, we only stayed two weeks before *nonna* had to go into hospital.'

'These were probably on your dad's desk at work, weren't they?'

Fede nodded. 'Strange to think about. Years after he'd left, there we all were, looking on as he worked.' She rubbed her eyes. 'God, this is a bit difficult.'

I rubbed her shoulder. 'Are you all right?'

'I think so. But it's strange. Looking at that photo and thinking that there's only *mamma* and me left now.' She lined up the three photographs on the table. 'You don't have any of this stuff, do you?'

I shrugged. 'Not really. A few photos here and there. But all this—' I indicated the photos and the contents of the box. 'I think I envy you this.'

'I understand.'

'Even if he wasn't the man you thought he was, or the man you wanted him to be, it must still be nice.'

'Yes. I think so. Oh dear, are we getting all morose?'

'I think we're allowed to.' I nodded at the clippings. 'What are those?'

'All sorts of things. They go back years. There's a clipping from the *Gazzettino* with a list of newborns. Including me. One recording their wedding. Others recording the deaths of *nonna* and *nonno*. My graduation. So much stuff.' She rummaged through the few remaining papers at the bottom of the box. 'I think the rest of it might actually just be rubbish.' She took out a brightly coloured leaflet and laughed. 'Pizza delivery company. Now what else have we got here?'

Gramsci surveyed the near empty box, and his muscles tensed as he readied himself to pounce. There was a large brown envelope at the bottom which I snatched away just in time. He gave a little yowl of delight and squeezed himself in as best he could manage. The sides bulged alarmingly.

I opened the envelope. More photographs. I spread them out on the table. Six men, all shot at medium distance. One of them was using a public phone box, another was getting out of a car. Others were simply photographed in the street.

'Who are these guys?' I said.

Fede shook her head. 'I don't know. Not family though.'

'Could they be, I don't know, unknown cousins or something?'

She sighed. 'Nathan, I'm Italian. The concept of "unknown family" does not exist here.'

'Strange.' I took another look inside the envelope. 'Wonder if there's anything else in here?' I noticed a small white piece of plastic, perhaps half the size of a matchbox, and tipped it out.

'What's that?' I said.

Fede picked it up. 'Oh. It's a USB stick.'

'I know what it is. I'm just wondering *what* it is. If you see what I mean.'

'More photographs, perhaps?'

'Could be.' I got to my feet. 'Back in a minute.'

I brought my laptop down from the bedroom.

'You took your computer with you on honeymoon? Well, that's flattering.'

'I thought I ought to. The phone is fine for emails, but I thought I'd need the laptop in case I get the time to crack on with that translation job.' I laid it flat on the table, and waited for it to start up. I slotted in the USB stick.

A warning message popped up. 'Data might be corrupted. Do you wish to continue.' I clicked on the box. 'Yes I do. Now it's running an anti-virus scan, so that might take a while.' The file manager window popped up. 'And on the other hand, it might not.'

'What do we have?'

I took a closer look. 'Nothing very exciting, I'm afraid. No photos. Nothing very much at all. Just a single file.'

'Zipped-up photos then?'

I shook my head. 'I don't think so. It's a PST file. What's a PST file?'

'No idea.'

'Am I going to open it?'

'I don't know. Are you?'

'I suppose so. If it's anything nasty the antivirus software should pick it up.' I double-clicked on the file. 'Ah, it's password protected. That's a shame.'

'Odd. I wonder why. What's it called, anyway?' She peered over my shoulder. '*Ghost Dog*. What does that mean?'

'No idea. Does it mean anything to you?'

'Not a thing.'

I ejected the drive and stuck it in my pocket. 'I'll have a play with it some other time. See if there's any other way of opening it. And if not I can always reformat it. A spare USB stick is always useful.'

'You can't do that. There might be something important on there. Maybe I've inherited something even more fabulous.'

'You're right. Do you know anyone who's good with this sort of thing?'

She shook her head. 'I'm an art restorer, remember?'

'You use computers, though.'

'Yes, for things like tonal and textural analysis. We don't do cryptography. If somebody forgets their password we're as lost as anyone else. Do you know anyone?'

'No one I can think of. I can ask around.'

Fede yawned. 'No hurry though. It'll wait until we get back to Venice. Is it time for bed?'

'I think so.' I tapped the side of the box. 'Are you spending the night down here, Fat Cat?' Gramsci made a sound somewhere between a purr and a snore, and woozily raised himself from the box before making his way upstairs. 'Time for bed then, I see.' Then I frowned and looked at Fede. 'You're right though. It's a strange name. *Ghost Dog*. I wonder why?'

Chapter 12

I passed an uneasy night. Gramsci had detected the presence of something under the floorboards – a rat or a lizard – and had spent hours scratching away at the wood in an attempt to reach it. At some point past midnight I'd got up, deposited him outside the bedroom and closed the door. Then I decided the piteous mewling from outside was more annoying than the scratching and I let him back in again.

Federica, as ever, slept through it all. I nodded off shortly before daybreak and was awoken shortly afterwards by Gramsci jumping on to the bed and demanding breakfast.

Sleep, obviously, was going to be impossible. I pulled on a T-shirt and trousers, and padded downstairs. I measured out Gramsci's kitty biscuits, and then stood there in the kitchen yawning and stretching. I was, I supposed, on holiday. Nothing to do and all day to do it.

I should start by making breakfast. Except, of course, that in my haste to ensure Gramsci was properly provided for I'd forgotten to buy anything that resembled breakfast goods for ourselves. Coffee? How had I forgotten to buy coffee? Not even any tea for Federica.

Okay, then. I'd go out and forage. There was, I remembered,

a bar just a couple of doors down from the *carabinieri*. I'd pick up two coffees – my hopes of finding a bar that sold Earl Grey tea were not high – and a couple of *brioche* and bring them back for us. What could be more romantic?

I slipped on my shoes and a jacket and went outside. Two kids on a Vespa puttered by, blithely ignoring the laws on wearing helmets, and I smiled as I saw a *carabiniero* shaking a finger at them. He followed me into the bar, presumably heading for breakfast as well.

The *barista* smiled at him. '*Ciao*, Marco.'

'*Ciao*, Renzo. Coffee and croissant, please.'

'As always?'

'As always.'

Marco the cop took a paper napkin from the dispenser, and a pastry from the cabinet. 'I've just seen the two Zennaro kids on their bike. No helmets again. One day I should speak to their parents.' He shook his head.

The *barista* fixed his coffee, and then turned to me. '*Buongiorno*.'

'*Salve*. Could I have two croissants please. And—'

Renzo raised an eyebrow, and I realised what I was going to have to say.

'—and,' I muttered as *sotto voce* as possible, 'two coffees to take away.'

Marco stopped in the act of eating his pastry and turned to look at me. 'I'm sorry,' said Renzo, 'could you say that again?'

'Two coffees. To take away. *Da portare via*. Please.'

A strangulated sound came from Marco which might have been a cough turning into a laugh, or a laugh being concealed as a cough. 'I'll see you later, Renzo, okay?' He grinned at his friend and muttered something under his breath in what, I assumed, was a *Pellestrinese* version of *Veneziano* that might, possibly, have meant something like 'good luck with this one'. He picked up his cap from the counter, and gave the brim a quick polish with the sleeve of his jacket. He smiled at me. 'Good morning, sir!' he said with a little nod of his head, before turning and leaving.

I took two croissants from the cabinet. Renzo was still looking at me.

'You're going to tell me you don't have any paper cups, aren't you?' I said.

He shrugged. 'Sorry. We've never really done that. It's not like being over there.' He pointed in the general direction of Venice.

'I suppose not.'

'Anyway, why take your coffee away? You could just stand here, read the paper, talk if you want. Life is never so busy that you need to drink a coffee in the street, surely? Take a bit of time. Enjoy your holiday.'

'Oh, I'm not on holiday,' I protested. Then I thought about it. 'No, hang on, I actually am. I suppose I'm a tourist.' That felt a bit strange.

'Well, you're very welcome. I'm sorry, but I still don't have any paper cups. Who's the other one for?'

'My partner. I'm sorry, I mean my wife. We're on honeymoon.'

He smiled and reached across the bar to shake my hand. 'Ah, congratulations.' He looked around as if expecting to see her.

'She's sleeping in. I thought it would be a nice thing to do,' I explained.

He smiled again. Perhaps, I thought, just a little too much. 'Look, I can probably find two plastic cups.' He rummaged around in a cardboard box at the back of the bar, and took out two transparent plastic glasses. 'These are usually for people who want a glass of wine outside on the street. Will they do?'

'Er yes. They'll be perfect. Thanks.'

'No problem.' The Gaggia hissed as he poured a shot into the first and then the second cup, the plastic buckling with the heat. He put his head to one side. 'Hmm. Are these okay?'

'They'll be fine.'

'Sure?'

'Absolutely.'

'Okay. These are on the house. Congratulations again. Come in any time, next time I'll give you a prosecco. Where are you staying, by the way?'

'Just a couple of doors down. Past the police station, before the restaurant.'

He looked confused for a moment, and then his face cleared. 'Oh. You mean Giulio Ravagnan's house.'

'That's the one. Did you know him?'

He laughed. 'Mister, how old do you think I am? He died when I was a young boy.'

'Sorry. I should have realised. Anyway, it's my wife's house now. I suppose you'd say she's inherited it.'

'Your wife's from Pellestrina?'

'From the Lido. Giulio Ravagnan was her grandfather.'

'I see. Well, I'm sure it's a lovely place. It'll be cold in the winter, mind, but so's everywhere round here.' He slid the glasses over the counter. 'Sorry, I haven't got covers or anything like that for them.'

'Don't worry. It's not as if I have far to go.'

He gave me a paper bag for the *brioche*, which I tucked into my jacket pocket as best I could. Then I wrapped each cup in a napkin, in order to stop my fingers burning.

Renzo gave me a wave. 'See you later, yeah?'

'Depend on it. Thanks again.'

I made my way back along the street, breathing in the smells of petrol and fish. Tables were being wiped down at the restaurant. The *vongolare* in the lagoon were setting out for their morning's work. Pellestrina was waking up.

I prodded the gate open with my foot, and walked up the garden path. Then I turned to look out at the lagoon again. I wondered what it would be like in the very height of summer? Busy, of course, but surely nothing like the choking hordes that crowded through Venice? And in winter?

Surely it couldn't, wouldn't, be possible to stay here all the time? Even something as simple as having a beer with Dario would become an epic journey. I could translate here as well as anywhere, but it would be impossible to keep the consulate going. And yet, there was something so lovely about the idea.

I shook my head. Our coffees would be cold by the time I'd finished daydreaming. I place the plastic glasses on the front step, and searched in my pockets for the keys.

It didn't take me long to remember that they were at the side of the bed.

This put me in something of a quandary. I could, of course, just ring the bell and get Fede to let me in, but waking her up – if I could manage it at all – would probably take the edge off my big romantic gesture. The alternative, however, was to wait for her to wake up, get showered and dressed, wonder where I was and come to find me holding two cold cups of coffee on the doorstep.

I was about to ring the doorbell when I heard a voice from behind me.

'Excuse me?'

The speaker was a pale, dark-haired woman in middle age. In her right hand she held a bunch of keys.

'Good morning,' I said. 'Can I help you?'

She smiled, a little awkwardly, and shook the keys. 'I'm sorry, sir. I thought perhaps I might be able to help you.'

'You have keys?' I said, stating the obvious.

'Of course, sir.' *Sir*, again.

'I'm sorry, I'm sure I'm being very stupid. My name is Nathan Sutherland and I've locked myself out. The house belongs to my wife.'

She nodded. '*Dottoressa* Ravagnan. *Si*.'

'You know her?' I said, feeling more stupid by the minute and wondering if perhaps it might be useful to start the conversation all over again.

'Of course. My name is Giulia. I'm the housekeeper.'

'The housekeeper?' I shook my head. 'I'm sorry, we seem to be stuck in one of those conversations where I just repeat the last thing you said. I didn't know we had a housekeeper.'

'*Signor* Ballarin thought it might be useful. Just until you get settled. I'm sorry, I didn't realise you'd be moving in so soon.' She nodded at the overgrown garden. 'That's too much for me I'm afraid, but I'll see if my husband can do anything with it.'

'That's very kind.'

She shook the keys, once again. 'May I . . . ?'

'Yes, of course. Thank you.'

She unlocked the door, and I bent to pick my rapidly cooling cups of coffee from the step. I took them in and sat them down on the table, along with the slightly crushed paper bag of *brioche*. I would, I knew, be removing flecks of pastry from my jacket for days to come.

Gramsci, curled up on the sofa, raised his head and narrowed his eyes.

'He'll be fine,' I said. 'Just dust around him, or whatever you have to do. He'll be tired, anyway. He was up all night hunting rats.'

'Rats?'

'Or lizards. Something in the floorboards or the walls anyway.' I looked at the coffees. 'I really should take these up to Federica. Sorry, I hope we're not getting in your way.' She shook her head. 'I'll be down shortly.'

'No need, *caro*.' Federica's voice came from the top of the stairs.

'You're awake?'

'And you're remarkably observant this morning. I heard you going out.' She came down the stairs. 'Coffee?' she said.

'I'm sorry. I thought asking for an Earl Grey in a plastic cup to take away would be too complicated. Anyway, this is *signora* Giulia,' I said. '*Signor* Ballarin was good enough to arrange a housekeeper for us. Just until things are straightened out.'

Ballarin, I remembered, had mentioned reconnecting utilities. Had he mentioned cleaning? Probably.

'He did? Oh good. It all looks lovely, thank you. Is there much left to do, Giulia?'

'Very little, *signora*. But I can clean every day and cook for as long as you're here.'

'Thank you. But to be honest, I think all we need to sort out is the garden. Everything else seems to be fine. I don't think it's fair to expect you to clean up after us every day.'

Giulia smiled. 'It's no trouble, *signora,*' she said. 'No trouble at all.'

Chapter 13

It was, I have to say, my best honeymoon ever. Admittedly, I only had one other point of reference, but I was pretty sure this was as good as it got.

We went swimming every day. I cooked us fish every evening. We went to bed early and got up late. And, sometimes, in the morning we would just lie there, saying nothing. Not because we had nothing to say, but simply because we had no need to say it.

But then, of course, there was Gramsci.

He had deposited what looked like the same lizard on our doormat for the third time in as many days. At least, I assumed it was the same lizard. They all tended to look very similar.

I sighed, and reached for a dustpan and brush. I was getting to be a dab hand at this by now. Attempting to grab it, I knew, risked hurting it. But a quick flick of the wrist with the brush would sweep it into the pan, where the gentlest of pressure would hold it immobile until I was able to deposit it, unhurt but presumably both shaken and stirred, in the garden. Where it would remain until Gramsci decided to repeat the game. It was, I thought, either the luckiest or the unluckiest lizard on all Pellestrina.

'Why do you think he does that?' said Federica, after we'd gone to bed and the familiar scratching sounds had begun again.

'I think it's the hunter-gatherer instinct kicking in. You'd have to say it's quite impressive, given the speed those lizards can move. He's obviously in better shape than we thought.'

'Yes, but he doesn't do anything with them. He just brings them in, drops them at your feet and waits for you to deal with them.'

'I think he's just trying to be nice. In his own peculiar little way.'

'Very peculiar.' The scratching stopped. 'Thank God for that. Do you think he's finished for the night?'

The scratching started again. Fede pulled a pillow over her head. 'It's no good,' she said, her voice muffled. 'You're going to have to deal with it.'

'Can't you just sleep through it? You can normally sleep through anything.'

'Not through that. Go on.'

I grumbled away but got out of bed anyway. 'I can't even see him.'

'Mfffff.'

'I'm sorry, what was that?'

She whipped the pillow away. 'I said "I think he's under the bed."'

'Oh right. Good. What better way to spend the night than trying to extract an angry cat from under the bed?'

'He's your cat.'

'He's *our* cat, remember?'

'You had him first. You deal with him. Anyway, he respects you.'

'I don't think he does.'

'Okay. I made that bit up. But just deal with him, put him outside, lock him in a room on the other side of the house. Anything.'

'All right. All right. But I'm blaming you if I get a splinter.'

I knelt by the side of the bed, and craned my head underneath. Gramsci was crouching there, his claws scrabbling away at the floor.

'There's nothing there, daft cat.'

I pushed him away. He yowled, snatched at my hand and then went back to his original position, scratching and picking away at the floor.

'There's nothing there. No lizards. No mice. Nothing to play with. See?' I pushed him away once more, and ran my fingers over the floor in the hope that would convince him.

And then it moved.

A floorboard little more than two feet long and perhaps six inches wide, moved ever so slightly under the pressure of my fingers.

Gramsci miaowed in delight, and leapt forward again, sinking his claws into both the floorboard and my hand. The shock made me jerk upright, banging my head on the bed frame.

'Aargh!'

'What's the matter?'

'Bloody cat.' I swept him up in my arms, holding him so that his claws, scrabbling through the air, could do no damage, then walked to the bedroom door, deposited him outside, and slammed the door behind him. Immediately he started to howl.

Fede looked at me. 'I'm not sure that's really an improvement.'

'Bloody cat,' I repeated. 'Just give me five minutes. There's a loose board down here. Whatever he wants is under it. So I'll just take a look, get rid of whatever's there, and then, who knows, we may even get something that approximates to a proper night's sleep.'

She sat up and swung her legs over the side of the bed. 'Where is it?'

I knelt down again. 'Just over here.' I picked at it with my fingernails. 'See, it's come loose. Something's got under there.' There was a reasonable degree of play in the board, and it was easy enough to pull it up with my fingernails until I could get the rest of my hand under it. I moved it aside. There was a faint smell of damp from within, but nothing worse. Whatever was there was at least still alive.

I made to reach inside, but Fede grabbed my hand. 'What are you doing?'

'I'm just going to see if I can feel anything.'

'A lizard would be one thing. A hungry rat would be another. Take a look first.' She picked up her mobile phone from the bedside table and switched the torch on. 'Here. Use this.'

I shone the beam through the gap. 'Still a bit difficult to see. But there doesn't seem to be anything moving. Neither can I hear anything. Whoah!'

I yanked my hand back as a small lizard scurried out of the hole, looked left and then right, and then hurried away, squeezing itself under the skirting board.

I was about to replace the loose plank but then something

caught my eye. 'Hang on. I can see something now. It's a plastic bag or something like that.' I tugged at it. 'Surprisingly heavy.'

I pulled it out, laid it on the floor next to the bed, and brushed the dust from it. Not a plastic bag, but a small leather briefcase. Builder's tools, accidentally left behind from the last time the house had needed repairs? Yet it looked quite expensive.

I clicked the hinges open, and shone the light from Fede's phone inside.

I jerked upright with a start.

'Oh, bloody hell.'

'What is it, *caro*?'

I held the case up for her to take a look. At the dark-blue plush-velvet interior, which held a small black and grey handgun.

'Oh, bloody hell,' said Federica.

Chapter 14

There are times in life, when dealing with Italian bureaucracy – with any bureaucracy for that matter – when you want the person on the other side of the desk to think well of you. Attempting to hand over a firearm to the *carabinieri* was one of those occasions.

I was unsure how best to go about it. I was, however, pretty certain that taking a gun out of my pocket would not be the best way to start.

I approached the officer on the front desk, and held up the briefcase.

'*Buongiorno.*'

He did not look up, but merely nodded as if to acknowledge my existence, and carried on making notes in the folder in front of him. In the past, I would have repeated my greeting or perhaps coughed in order to try and attract his attention, but by now I had learned that this was just part of the protocol to be observed when dealing with those in authority.

He stopped writing and nodded to himself. He replaced the cap on top of his pen, and laid it down. He closed the folder, and filed it away. Then he frowned, and made a minute adjustment to the position of his pen. He took off his glasses, gave them a quick polish with the cuff of his uniform, and then smiled at me.

'*Buongiorno.*'

'I wonder if you can help me. It's just that I've found – something – and I think you're probably the best people to deal with it.'

He nodded. 'One moment please.' He reached above his head to a shelf lined with folders and ran his fingers along the spines until he found the one he wanted.

'Here you are. Just fill out one of these please.' He switched to imperfect English and pointed at the salient fields on the form. 'Name, address, birthday. Your passport number. And sign here. And here. And here.'

I took out my ID card. 'Can I use this? I don't carry my passport around.' He nodded, and I scribbled away.

'You live in Italy?'

I nodded. 'Venice.'

'Holiday?'

'Honeymoon.'

'Congratulations.' The corners of his lips turned up, just a fraction.

'Thank you.' I checked the form once more, then turned it around to face him and slid it under the glass screen. I held up the briefcase once more. 'Don't you want to know what it is?'

'Separate form. You can leave that with us.' He pointed to his left. 'Just slide it under the hatch over there.'

'Why did I need to fill that form out then?'

He shrugged. 'Everything needs to be documented in this job. Anyway, maybe somebody will come along for their property and think, ah, a public-spirited citizen, perhaps he deserves a thank you or a reward.'

'Trust me, I don't think that's going to happen here.'

'No?'

'No.' I held up the briefcase, higher this time. 'Because I've got a gun in here. You understand? I've got a bloody gun in here.'

He removed his glasses again, and stared at me.

'Ah,' he said.

I wasn't sure if I was allowed a telephone call or not, but made one anyway. Lunch, I told Federica, might be delayed a bit. I was still relatively confident about dinner.

I had not, to the best of my knowledge, actually done anything wrong. But it also seemed that my first attempt at behaving like a public-spirited citizen was not working out as it should.

The tiny waiting room was starting to feel uncomfortably hot. I looked up at the wall-mounted air-conditioning unit but there seemed to be no way of switching it on. For the third time, I read the posters on the walls. Warnings against drug-dealing. Warnings against smuggling. Identifying those at risk of human trafficking. A few images of long-missing people, the posters now curling up at the edges.

A vending machine stood in the corner. Perhaps a cup of coffee would make something happen. 60c for a cup. Not too bad, I supposed. I checked my pockets. I had a 20 euro note and a 50c coin.

I sighed and sat down again.

'Mr Sutherland? Mr Nathan Sutherland?'

The speaker was a tall, distinguished-looking man with a shock of grey hair and glasses which, in contrast to his military uniform, combined to give him a somewhat professorial appearance. I tried to work out his rank from his shoulder insignia, but he spared me the trouble. 'I'm *maresciallo* Busetto. I'm told you've brought something very interesting for us to see.'

'Well, I'm glad it's of interest.' I looked at my watch. 'It's just that I was hoping to deposit it here and be off. I'm on holiday, you see, and, well, lunch over the road seemed like a nice idea and instead . . .' I trailed off.

He smiled. 'I'm sorry to have kept you waiting. Would you like a coffee? A proper one?'

'That'd be nice.'

'Good. Come with me please.' He looked me up and down. 'It is rather hot in here isn't it? We're not supposed to turn the air conditioning on until the end of June. Saving the planet, they tell us. Saving money, of course.'

I followed Busetto through to his blissfully air-conditioned office. Two coffees were waiting on a tray, along with two Ferrero Rocher chocolates. The briefcase lay open on the desk, displaying the gun.

'Sit down please.' He sipped at his coffee, and then looked concerned. 'I'm sorry, would you prefer sugar? My wife tells me it's bad for me. So having a small chocolate with coffee is my little vice. I find it takes the edge off it.' He unwrapped it, and bit it in half. This, evidently, was becoming A Thing.

'Erm, thank you. A chocolate will be fine.'

He indicated the weapon lying on the desk, next to the

coffee cups and the wrapping paper from the chocolates. 'Do you know much about guns, Mr Sutherland?'

I shook my head. 'I've had a couple pointed at me.'

He raised an eyebrow. 'Really? You're not a private investigator are you?'

'No. I'm a translator.'

He gave a dry, rattly little laugh. 'I'll assume you're teasing me. You don't know what this is then?'

'No idea, I'm afraid. Beyond being a gun.'

'Mm-hmm. Could you tell me how you came across it?'

'My cat found it.'

'Really?' He raised an eyebrow again.

'He was searching for lizards. Or mice. Or anything small that presents a modest challenge. And, well anyway, there's a loose board in my bedroom and underneath it,' I gestured at the table, 'I found a gun in a briefcase.'

He smiled. 'It seems you have a very talented cat, Mr Sutherland. A veritable Macavity.'

'You like TS Eliot?' I said, trying to keep the surprise out of my voice.

'I've only read the ones about the cats, I'm afraid. I found the others a bit difficult. What's his name?'

'Gramsci.'

He raised an eyebrow, and gave a slight 'hmmph'. He drummed his fingers on the table. 'Well, it's probably nothing that need concern you, Mr Sutherland.'

'I'm not sure I like the sound of that "probably". That's too much like "it's probably nothing to worry about".'

'Well it is – probably – nothing to worry about. Have you told the owner of the property about the weapon?'

'Well, yes. She's my wife. We're on honeymoon.'

He smiled. 'Oh, many congratulations. She owns the property, you say?'

I tugged at the collar of my shirt. I was starting to feel uncomfortable, despite the air conditioning.

'It's been hers for less than a few weeks. It belonged to her father, who died nearly ten years ago. But he never lived here either. It was his father's property really. He was a fisherman here for years.'

'I see. But she has been here before?'

'On holiday. When she was young.' I corrected myself, and smiled. 'Younger, I should say.'

He waved his finger in mock admonishment. 'Ah, you're learning already, Mr Sutherland. And what about during the period since her father died?'

'As far as I know she hasn't been here since. It wasn't her house to visit. Look—' I tried to force some jollity into my voice. 'My wife's an art restorer. She's not a gangster.'

He laughed. 'Oh, my dear Mr Sutherland, I'm sure she isn't. But go on: who was responsible for the house during the period since her father died?'

'Her late father's business partner. He's a lawyer.'

'Lawyers.' He gave a little chuckle. 'Mm-hmm. Do you have a name, contact details?'

'His name's Michele Ballarin. I don't remember his address. Somewhere halfway down the Lido. If you look for the Ravagnan–Ballarin practice you'll find it easily enough. Or the Ballarin–Ravagnan practice, I can't quite remember.'

He raised his hand. 'Okay. Okay. *Tranquillo.*' He scribbled away on the pad in front of him, and then paused. He raised his head and stared directly into my eyes. 'Ballarin–Ravagnan, you said?'

I nodded. 'Yes. Does that mean anything?'

'*Boh.*' He smiled, gave a little shrug and went back to scribbling on his pad. I tried to read his writing upside down, but couldn't decipher it. I wondered if he was actually writing anything intelligible at all or if it was just for effect.

'So. How long do you think it's been down there for?' I said.

I wasn't expecting an answer but, to my surprise, he took the question seriously. 'Difficult to say. There are people here who could give us an estimate, either based on the gun or on the case.'

'I'm wondering what a retired fisherman would be doing with something like this.'

He smiled, again. 'Indeed. You're sure you're not an investigator, Mr Sutherland?'

'I try not to be.'

'Well I wouldn't worry about it. Just leave it with us. It's probably nothing.' That word *probably* again.

'So am I free to go?'

'Well of course.' He sounded genuinely surprised. Or, at least, he gave a very good impression of it.

'It's just that I am, technically, on honeymoon and,' I checked my watch, 'my wife is going to be wondering just how long I'm going to be and we're in danger of missing lunch.'

'And that would never do! Thank you for coming in, Mr Sutherland. Very public-spirited of you.'

I turned and made my way to the door. Any second now, I thought, any second now. I rested my hand on the doorknob.

'Oh, Mr Sutherland. Just one more thing.'

Bingo.

'Are you staying on Pellestrina for a while? Just in case we need to contact you.'

'At least a couple more weeks.'

'Wonderful. Thank you, Mr Sutherland. Enjoy your lunch!'

I smiled as best I could, and made my way outside, texting the words 'Lunch. Now!!!' as I walked.

Chapter 15

'Better?' said Federica.

'Much better.' I took another soft-shelled crab from the plate. 'These are just the best things in the world, aren't they?' I held one up. A small red-golden crab, perhaps the size of my palm, perfectly preserved and fresh out of the frier. I bit into it. There was nothing that tasted so intensely of the sea, so intensely, well, *crabby*, as *moeche*. 'I think that, if my doctor told me I was only allowed to eat one thing for the rest of my life, these would be it.'

'Is that something you think about a lot?'

'Oh yes. More than you might think.'

'*Nonno* used to tell me how they were once the food of the poor. Just like oysters. Something that everyone could afford. And then they were overfished. Even in those days.' I was holding the last one up in front of my face, admiring its crabby perfection, when she reached out and took it from me, bit it in half and passed it back to me.

'Oi!'

She smiled as she munched away.

'I was saving that!'

She dabbed at her lips, and drank a little prosecco. 'There'll always be other crabs, *tesoro*. But you've never done these at home?'

I shook my head. 'I did, once. Never again. I've never liked deep frying. I always worry about the house going up in flames. But more importantly, there was the combination of Gramsci and a sink full of small, live crustaceans. It was an unequal struggle.'

She laughed, and we looked out over the bay together. A small group of *vongolare* were coasting up to the shore.

'This is a bit magic, you know?' I said.

Fede said nothing, but nodded.

'I can't imagine what it must have been like. Being a kid here, during the summer. You and your family, cooking fish on the beach. Grandfather telling stories. All of that. I'm jealous, you know?'

'Don't be.' Her eyes, I could see, had reddened. 'It's just nostalgia. And I'm not sure that's ever healthy.' She rubbed her eyes with the back of her hand.

'Ah, I'm sorry. I've upset you. I didn't mean that.'

She reached out and took my hands. 'I know you didn't. It's just all this,' she pointed towards the lagoon with one hand and the house with the other, 'is a bit much to take in all at once. All those good memories, yes. All those good, lovely, warm memories. And then my father did what he did, and that makes me wonder how much of it was real, and how much of it was just people putting on masks and playing little games to hide what was really going on.' She shook her head, shaking the memories out. 'Let's talk about something else.'

'Well, Dario's coming over tomorrow. That'll be nice.'

'Yes. I did wonder. First you wanted your cat to come on

honeymoon with us, and now you want your best friend here as well.'

'It's not like that. They're only here for the day.'

'I'm surprised you didn't ask them to stay for a few nights.'

'Well, I did think about it but then I thought – well, the business with the gun and everything. I don't like the idea of little Emily wandering around, and possible Bad Things being hidden under floorboards. That sort of thing.'

'What, you think there's a concealed weapon in every room just waiting for small girls to chance across them?'

I shrugged. 'Why take chances?'

'So anyway, tell me properly what happened at the *carabinieri*. You were a long time. I thought you'd just go along, say "I've found a gun" and be back within five minutes.'

'Wasn't quite like that. I think everything's okay though.'

She paused, with her glass halfway to her lips. 'You *think*?'

'Yes. Pretty sure.'

She sighed, and rubbed her eyes again. 'Go on then. Tell me the worst.'

I did my best to explain.

'So,' she said, 'you've been asked not to leave town.'

'Well, he didn't put it quite like that. He just sort of said it'd be nice if we kept in touch.'

'Oh. Okay. That's fine then. Anything else?'

'I might have used the expression "My wife is not a gangster."'

Fede held up the empty jug of wine and waved it at the waiter. 'I think we're going to need another,' she said.

***

By the time we made our way home, we had – just about – convinced ourselves that we had simply been behaving as public-spirited citizens and were not helping police with their enquiries.

'So, what are we doing about dinner tonight?' I said.

'We've only just finished lunch.'

'I know, but I always like to plan at least one meal in advance. I get nervous otherwise.'

'Up to you. Do you want to cook fish again?'

'I could do. All we need is some fish.'

She checked her watch. 'Too late now. I suppose I could cook. Actually, no, I suppose I couldn't. Pizza then?'

'Nah, not again. We've had a good lunch. I'll just do something simple. Just spaghetti with oil, garlic and chilli.'

'That's good too. Do you need any parts?'

'Er, spaghetti, garlic and chilli.'

'Right.'

'Oh, and oil.'

She sighed. 'Okay, one of us needs to go and pick up essentials.' She looked at me, expectantly.

'Well, I could do it. But one of us needs to go and entertain Gramsci. He's been on his own for a while. Just in case he's brought any little friends home.'

'Hmm. Okay then.' She gave me a peck on the cheek. 'I'll just be fifteen minutes or so.'

The house, as ever, smelled of old furniture and old books, warming in the early summer heat. It would be difficult to endure come August without air conditioning. I wondered how Federica had found it when she was growing up. But maybe Italians felt things differently. Or, perhaps, it had just been a blessed couple of degrees cooler in those days.

Gramsci was nowhere to be seen, but I could hear him scrabbling around upstairs and miaowing in agitation. He must have heard me coming in.

I sighed. A little lie-down would have been nice. 'Come on then, puss,' I shouted up. 'Let's throw a few balls around, eh?'

The scratching and scrabbling stopped, but he gave no sign of making an appearance. I made my way upstairs. The main bedroom door was closed and, for a moment, I feared the consequences of having locked him in by accident.

'You're not under the bed again, are you? It's only a lizard for God's sake. Have pity on it, can't you?' I dropped to my knees to take a look.

Something was not right. I had, I was certain, replaced the loose board the night before. I was sure it had been in place before I'd gone to the police station. And yet, there it was, ever so slightly out of place.

I supposed it was possible that there was something else down there and that Gramsci had been looking for it. And yet, the door had definitely been shut and his powers, to the best of my knowledge, did not – yet – extend to the operation of door handles.

I moved the board further aside, reached down into the gap and groped around. There was nothing except bare wood and dust and my hand came away dirty and cobwebbed.

For a moment, just for a moment, I thought I heard the sound of footsteps on the stairs, and then the door opening and closing.

'Fede?' I said.

There was no answer.

'Fede?' I called, once more.

I replaced the floorboard and stood up, testing it with my foot. Whatever I had or had not done that morning, it was securely in place now. I went through to the landing, and then to the bathroom in order to wash the grime off my hands. The curtains, I noticed, were blowing in the afternoon breeze. Perhaps, then, I had left the bedroom door open and it had later slammed shut in the wind. But was it possible that Gramsci had managed to claw the board up all by himself?

I dried my hands, and made my way downstairs. 'Fede?' I called again.

She was nowhere to be seen. Gramsci, however, wandered out of the spare room, leaving behind him some suspiciously ragged-looking curtains. I tossed some balls for him until she arrived, ten minutes later, with a bag of shopping. 'Everything you asked for. Some tins of tomatoes just in case. Campari in case we run out.' She caught the expression on my face and frowned. 'What's wrong?'

'I don't know. Listen, this sounds daft, but did you just come back and go out again?'

She looked puzzled. 'No. Why would I do that?'

'Don't know. I assumed you'd just forgotten something.'

'No. What's going on?'

'I don't know. When you went out this morning, that floorboard was back in place wasn't it?' She nodded. 'Except that when I went up there just now, it wasn't quite right. And I don't think it was Gramsci.'

'And so? What are you thinking?'

'I'm thinking that only one other person has a key to this place. At least as far as we know.'

'Giulia?'

'Exactly.'

She wrinkled her nose. 'It doesn't seem very likely. She seems honest. I mean, nothing's gone missing, has it?'

'No. But we know nothing about her.'

'She doesn't seem the "murdering people whilst they sleep" type.'

'I hadn't thought about that. But now I'm thinking about that.'

She laughed. 'She's a middle-aged cleaning woman. I don't think there's much to worry about.'

'I suppose not.'

'But if it'll make you feel better, I'll call Ballarin and ask about her.' She looked at her watch. 'He probably won't be there now. I'll call in the morning.'

'If we're still alive,' I muttered in the most sepulchral tone I could muster.

Fede laughed. 'We can put the chain on the door if you like, *caro*.' But then she looked serious, just for a moment. 'I will call him, though.'

Chapter 16

Federica hung up. 'He's not there,' she said.

I looked at the time. 'It's still reasonably early. Maybe he's a late riser.'

'Maybe so. His office, I suppose. If he doesn't want to go in early, that's up to him.'

'You could call him at home?'

She shook her head. 'No point. I left a message on his answerphone. Anyway, don't things seem a bit different in the cold light of day?'

'Not at all. We've still found a gun under our bed, and I'm certain someone was in here and moved that floorboard yesterday afternoon.' I took out my wallet, counted out a number of banknotes, and then wedged them underneath a candlestick on top of the fireplace.

'What are you doing?'

'There's sixty euros there. I just want to see what happens to them.'

'What, this is some sort of test to see if Giulia's honest or not?'

'If you like. There are six ten-euro notes there. Easy to take one, even two, and assume that the rightful owner will just think he's miscounted.'

I heard the rattle of keys in the door, and I fixed a broad smile on to my face as I turned around.

'*Ciao*, Giulia.'

'*Ciao, signor* Sutherland.'

'Call me Nathan, please.'

She looked a little uncertain, but nodded.

'Giulia,' said Fede. 'Have you noticed the loose board in our bedroom?'

Her eyes darted between Fede and myself, as if wanting to know what I was thinking. 'I have, *signora*.'

'Okay. I think we need to do something about it.' She pointed at me. 'Nathan noticed last night that it had come loose again.'

'Has it, *signora*? I hadn't noticed.'

'Do you know anyone who might be able to put it right? I'm sure it's not the most difficult job in the world, but I suspect it might be beyond Nathan.'

'Oh, thanks,' I muttered.

Giulia paused, unsure as to where this was going. 'I'm not sure, *signora*. Maybe.'

Fede brought out one of her most dazzling smiles. 'Good. I'll call *signor* Ballarin now, and he can arrange things with you.' She took out her phone.

Giulia shifted her weight from one foot to another. 'There's no need, *signora*. I can do it later after I finish work.'

'Oh no. Let's do it now. Anyway, you've done such a lovely job for us that I'd like to tell Michele personally.' The smile never left her face. She tapped away at her phone, and held it up to her ear. There was a fine bead of sweat on Giulia's forehead. It didn't go unnoticed by Federica, who made a little fanning motion with her other hand. 'It's getting hotter, isn't it?' She held the phone out in front of her so that Giulia could hear the dialling tone. Then she shook her head, and looked disappointed. 'It seems he's not there.' She put the smile back again. 'Perhaps you could call him later, as you suggested?'

Giulia's shoulders seemed to un-tense. Just a little. She responded to Fede's smile as best she could. 'Yes, of course. Of course, *signora*.'

'Good. Wonderful. Thank you so much for your help, *cara*. If we don't see you later, have a good day.' She patted her on the shoulder as she passed, and Giulia couldn't resist flinching slightly.

Fede turned to me. 'Come on, *caro*. You've got fish to buy if you're going to dazzle us all with your barbecuing skills.' I smiled and nodded to Giulia as we left, trying to avoid making eye contact with Gramsci and his accusing little face.

'What happened to all this "in the cold light of day, it's probably all nonsense" stuff?' I said.

Federica shrugged. 'Oh, it probably is. But I just thought it might be interesting to see her reaction if I suggested we all have a little chat with Ballarin.'

'And was it?'

'Oh, I think so.'

'And what if Ballarin had actually answered?'

'Then that, I think, would have been even more interesting. Now then, *caro,* Dario and family will be here soon and there is fish to be bought.'

In the Wolf's Den

'Small decisions can take your life in different directions, can't they? I could have made a phone call with that money in my pocket. But I wanted to stand at a bar and have a beer, just like a regular guy.'

The Old Wolf smiles, and, for a moment he looks genuinely happy. 'And that's how I met him. Sandro Vicari was a good guy. A bravo. You know, Brezzi, I've never had many friends in my life. Just business partners, and that's not the same. But Vicari was a pal.

'I went into the nearest bar I could find and had my first beer in two years. It was a hot day, I remember, and it tasted like the best thing in the world. And this young guy walks past me, he's waving at a girl or somebody on the other side of the street, not looking where he's going, and he bumps into me and my glass falls off the bar. There's broken glass and beer everywhere, and the barman is swearing at me and my out-of-prison suit is soaked and I'm going to smell like a tramp for the rest of the day.

'So I ball my fist, and I think I'm going to hit this cheeky sonofabitch in the face. And then he just grins at me. He's got this silly, cheeky smile on his face and the thing that strikes me is that he doesn't seem afraid. He just says sorry, can I buy you a beer?

'And so I tell him he'd better and is he going to buy me a new suit as well? You know what the cheeky bastard does? He looks me up and down and says "That's a terrible suit anyway." For a moment I think I'm going to hit him again, but then I just start laughing. And so does he. "Come on," he says, "I'll buy you a beer. But only if we sit outside, because you stink of booze."

'So we sit outside all afternoon, and drink and smoke. I ask him what he does, and he says he's a student. A fine arts student. I've got no idea what the hell that means. Anyway, the time comes when he says he needs to get back home. He lives in Malamocco, so he's got a long journey. He asks me where I live. I say I'm not sure, but I think I've still got a wife and boy waiting for me in Mestre.

'Vicari pauses for a few seconds and then he nods. I'm sorry, he says. That must be tough. And it is tough. Because I haven't heard from Maddalena in over a month, and I hope she's going to give me yet one more chance but part of me is afraid that when I go back to our apartment my keys are no longer going to fit the lock.

'It's been good to talk, I say. I tell him I'll see him around.

'He grins at me. "Not if I see you first," he says.

'I make my way over to Mestre. I've got no money left for the train by now, but nobody ever checks. And Maddalena is there, with Albino, and she can smell the booze on me and starts crying. The boy doesn't even recognise me, and he starts howling as well.

'Eventually, she dries her eyes and she lays it on the line. No more last chances. No more prison. Because her parents have told her she can move back in with them, they'll move to the other side of the country, and I'll never see them again.

'And I try. I swear to you, Brezzi, I really try. But it doesn't

*take long to discover that not many people want an ex-con, and
nobody wants a multiple ex-con. We have rent money due, we
have bills to be paid, and I need to get some money fast. So I take
the last few lire in my pocket and go out on to Corso del Popolo
to find a phone box. I take out the piece of paper with a number
scrawled on it that I've carried around for nearly two years. And
I make the call.*

*'Someone picks up the phone, and I start stammering out why
I'm calling and what my name is, and he cuts me off before I can
say too much.*

*'"We've been expecting you," he says. And they give me an
address in Mestre to go along to. One hour later I'm sitting in a
room with actual, genuine* mafiosi.*'*

'How did that feel?' I ask.

*'In all honesty? I was scared. Because this was serious now.
This was at a different level to the Venetian gangs.'*

'Were any of the big figures there? I'm thinking of people like
Felice Maniero, Francesco Tonicello?'

The Old Wolf shakes his head. *'No. It wasn't as easy as that.
It was years until I even met Maniero. I had to work my way
up and prove I could be trusted. But they knew I was smart
and I had knowledge that they could use. About the Mestrini
gang. About Clan Giostrai. Names, faces, places that people met.
The Mala del Brenta were learning from the Sicilians, and they
wanted to be the only game in town.'*

'There's something I don't understand,' I say. 'You were seen
as a man of omertà. Somebody who'd keep his mouth shut no
matter what the circumstances. And so I don't understand why
you effectively betrayed both gangs to the Mala del Brenta.'

'Honour among thieves, you mean?'

'I think that's what I'm trying to say.'

He shakes his head. 'I've always been good at knowing which direction the wind is blowing. I could see these guys moving in, and I knew there was only ever going to be one winner if it came to a war between gangs. I wanted to be on the winning side. Simple as that. Nothing personal.'

'People were killed, of course.'

He nods, slowly.

'People were killed, because you'd identified them. Because you supplied information on their whereabouts and their daily routines.'

Again, he nods.

'How do you feel about that?'

'Nobody needed to get killed. If they'd just gone along with things, become part of the new order, everything would have been all right.'

The answer sounds practised, lazy and dishonest. The Old Wolf, I imagine, has said this to himself many times. I decide not to press him any further.

'Tell me about Felice Maniero? Were you friends?'

'Angel Face,' he smiles. 'I'm not sure anyone ever called him a friend. But he was someone I trusted.' He laughs, hollowly. 'That turned out to be a mistake, didn't it? Felice Maniero is alive and well and living in freedom and me – well – here I am.'

'What about Francesco Tonicello?'

'It took me a few years to meet Tonicello. I knew who he was, of course. I was kind of in awe of the guy. Remember, I'm just out of prison, and I'm doing any crappy job that comes along in order to make my way in the organisation. Tonicello is the smart guy, moving money around, forging passports, fencing artworks, dealing in jewellery and gold. It seemed more glamorous than drugs and guns. It also seemed a hell of a lot safer. But his world was a long way away from mine.

'Anyway, a couple of months later, I'm back in Venice for a few hours, I take a drink in the same bar and the same young guy comes in again. He's just finished studying for the day and he's got his portfolio under his arm. He looks at me and laughs and says "That's still a terrible suit, brother." I cuff him on the back of the head and say, you can buy me a beer for that, you cheeky bastard.

'And again, we spend the day just talking and smoking and drinking. He shows me some of his work, and I tell you, this guy is just amazing. Just a master, you know? And not just at drawing, he shows me photos of some of his sculptures. He tells me he makes jewellery as well. I think this kid's like Leonardo. I ask him what does he want to be once he leaves university. He says he has no idea, probably a struggling artist.

'I told him I had a better idea.'

Chapter 17

'You think these will do?' asked Dario. 'I picked them up at the Co-op.'

He held up two disposable foil barbecues.

'Probably. I've got to be honest, I don't really know what I'm doing here. How about you?'

He shook his head. 'Nat, I've only just started cooking at home. Cooking on the beach seems like a step too far for me.'

'You never did this when you were growing up?'

'Sure. But I never really paid much attention. Everyone had a different job. The women would be looking after the kids. Just like now.' He pointed to the shore, where Fede was walking with Vally at the edge of the sea, each of them holding one of Emily's hands.

'Then there'd be the old guys. Their job was to stand around staring at the barbecue and nodding. That seemed to make things happen.'

'And what was your job, Dario?'

He grinned. 'Hanging around with the girls and being cool.'

'Okay. Well today, it seems, we're in the role of the old guys. Do you think we're up to it?'

'I reckon so.'

'Good man.' I showed him the contents of the cool box. 'So, I've got some squid. The trick here is to cook it either for a very short time or a very long time. Anywhere in the middle and it'll resemble a car tyre. We have more prawns than we should know what to do with. I don't think there's much to go wrong with them. Then we've got some sea bass fillets – no bones to mess with, but the difficulty here is going to be stopping them from sticking.'

'How do we do that?'

'I think the trick is to stand around and stare at them. Nod occasionally, if you like.'

'Right.'

'Oh, and there's this.' I took out a sad-looking bag of pre-packed salad leaves. 'In case anyone's interested.'

Dario tried, and failed, to look enthused.

'What about Emily? Do I need to go and pick up something for her?'

'Nah, she'll just have what we're having.'

'Marvellous child.'

He grinned again, the corners of his eyes crinkling. He looked out towards the sea. 'This is her first time, you know? At the beach.'

'Wow. Really?'

'Yep. We only moved here in November, remember? The weather's not been right until now.'

'That's kind of a big thing. I'm flattered you chose to share it with us. So, how do we get this thing started?'

Dario removed the plastic wrapping and put the two barbecues down on a flat area of rock. 'That's pretty much the extent of my knowledge, *vecio*. All we do now is light them and then I think we wait.'

'Okay. We can do that.'

We stood in silence for a moment, and then Dario looked at me.

'So. Go on then.'

'What?'

'Light it up.'

'You've not brought anything?'

'No.'

'Neither have I. I don't smoke any more, remember. I don't carry lighters or matches around these days.'

'Ah.'

'Great. First ever barbecue and it's fallen at the first hurdle. The stage of actually lighting the bloody thing. A stage which, although I haven't read many books on barbecue cookery, is generally considered to be an essential one.'

He shrugged. 'Okay. Okay. I think I see a way round this. There's a *tabaccheria* just back the way. Can't be more than five minutes.'

'I suppose not. Bah!' I threw my hands in the air. 'It's going wrong already.'

Dario shook his head. 'You worry too much, *vecio*. It's just a barbecue. Not *Masterchef*.'

'Yeah, but I'm on honeymoon, and you've come all the way over here and I just want it to be perfect, you know?'

'Barbecues aren't meant to be perfect. It's just about hanging out together. Having a beer, chatting, watching the kids play.'

'I guess you're right.'

'Still, getting the thing lit would make it a bit more perfect. Come on, I'll keep you company.' He waved at the girls, who were now swinging Emily by the arms just above the surface of the sea, accompanied by her excited little shrieks. 'We'll be back in ten minutes, okay?' he called.

Vally shouted something in return, but I couldn't make it out.

'Did you catch that?'

'No. They probably think we're off to buy beer.'

'You didn't bring any beer?'

'I did. But we could probably do with more.'

We walked off towards the main road. 'You know, Dario, there's something you might be able to help me with . . .'

We stood around the barbecue, feeling its heat starting to spread and nodded at each other. Dario took another look at the image on my phone and rubbed his chin.

'You recognise it?' I said.

'It's a Beretta pocket gun. Maybe a Tomcat, but I can't be absolutely sure.'

'Okay. What does that mean?'

'Easily carried, lightweight, easy to conceal. Used to be called a *lady's gun* but I don't think we're allowed to say things like that any more. You found one of these under your bed?'

'Under the floorboards to be precise, but yes.'

'Who do you think put it there?'

'I don't know. I was hoping Fede's grandad brought it back from the war and kept it as a souvenir.'

He shook his head. 'No chance. Army don't use guns like that.'

'No.'

'No. Not much stopping power. Anyway, this is a new model. 1990s, maybe later. Long after Grandad's time. You said it was in a case, as well?'

I nodded, and brought up the photo for Dario to look at.

'That's a Negrini case. Expensive.' He paused. 'Professional.'

'Okay. So who uses a gun like this?'

'People who need a weapon they can conceal easily. Cops – undercover cops, anyway – like them. Magistrates, judges – people who might need protection.' He lowered his voice. 'You know. Down south. People who might have pissed off the mafia. Private investigators as well. My pal Franco has something like this.'

'Is it legal?'

'Legal, yes. Difficult to get, though. He got one for a private security contract he was working on. But it's not easy. It takes time. Cops don't like the idea of people walking around with an easily concealed gun.'

'I thought you said they didn't have much stopping power?'

'They have *enough* stopping power. That's the only reason to have a gun like this. It's a weapon of last resort.'

'Bloody hell.' I shivered despite the ever-increasing heat from the barbecue. 'So what the hell is one doing in our house?'

'I don't know, Nat. If I was you, I'd be looking at whoever's been staying in that house since Federica's dad died.'

'And what would you do?'

'Hell, I'd ignore it. The cops have it now, let them deal with it.'

'I thought you'd say that. And that's just what I'm going to do.' I looked down at the barbecue. 'I think we're just about done here?'

Federica waved at me from the shore. 'Any chance of eating today, *caro*?'

'Any minute now,' I called back. 'Well. Almost any minute now. You can't rush this sort of thing.'

'You could at least put the food on.'

'We're nearly there. I don't want to jeopardise the delicate process though.'

'It's a barbecue on the beach. Not *Masterchef.*'

'That's the second time I've been told that. Come on then. Prawns. Shouldn't take long.'

Fede waved at Vally and Emily. 'Just in time I think. Emily's seen the sea now. I think she might be getting bored with it . . .'

I lay on the beach, my hand across my forehead, and wished that there was just a bit more shade. We weren't quite in the height of summer but tomorrow, I feared, I would be just a little more pink and a little more uncomfortable than I'd have liked.

Dario snored away to my right. Fede to my left. Nearer the shore, Vally, with seemingly inexhaustible reserves of energy, was building sandcastles with Emily. Small children, I was coming to realise, required an even greater degree of entertainment and attention than Gramsci.

I raised myself on to one elbow and looked around. The beach was almost deserted. Still a little too early in the season for Italian families to be descending *en masse*. A group of young people were kicking a football around in the distance.

Nearer to us, an older couple snoozed in two deckchairs. He was ruddy of face and silver of hair, the chunky watch on his wrist and thick gold chain around his neck marking him out as a man of some wealth, if not necessarily one of taste. This was not going to save him from a nasty case of sunburn upon awakening.

Dario and Fede snoozed and snored away the effects of what I considered to be a modestly excellent lunch. How nice it would be to join them, I thought, but I was starting to find the direct sunlight increasingly distressing. I needed to find a bit more shade. Perhaps I'd walk back towards town and pick up ice cream for everyone.

I supposed I should find out what everybody wanted. But that would involve waking people up which didn't seem very fair. Besides, ice cream was ice cream. One might have one's preferences but I couldn't imagine one being refused.

I waved at Vally and Emily. Vally gave me a wave in return. Emily ignored me. To be fair, construction of the castle did seem to be at a critical phase.

I made my way back over the *murazzi* and towards the lagoon, from where the *vongolare* were returning with their catch. There was something about their appearance that made me smile. Perhaps it was the contrast of these hulking asymmetrical beasts with the elegance of those boats that had historically plied their trade in the lagoon. And yet, the Venetians were nothing if not practical when it came to boats. *Vongolare* looked the way they did because that's how they could work best and, in their own unique way, they were just as much a part of the city as the *gondola* and the *sandolo*.

I stopped to watch them depositing their catch, taking my phone out to capture the moment. A young woman, walking in the opposite direction, broke her stride in order to avoid walking through my shot. I smiled and mouthed *grazie* at her. I thought about how often I'd done this myself in Venice. My usual routine was to stop and mentally count to three. That, I thought, seemed like a reasonable amount of time to allow someone to take a photograph. And then I realised what I was doing, and smiled to myself. I was being a tourist. As the crow flies I was perhaps ten kilometres from the Street of the Assassins and the Magical Brazilians, and yet I was being a tourist. I was on holiday for the first time since I could remember.

I snapped off another few photos. Tens of kilos, perhaps hundreds of kilos of molluscs were being poured on to the shore, together with those fish that had also had the misfortune of being swept up in the great metal cage. Some of them thrashed and flapped helplessly on the quayside. Two guys in waterproofs sorted through them, occasionally throwing those ones that didn't make the cut back into the sea. Most of them, I knew, would not survive.

'Stop it. Stop it. Stop it now.'

One of the workers was shouting, striving to make himself heard over the roar of the machinery. His companion looked at him and then at the contents of the grille at the front of the boat, and then joined in with the shouting, waving frantically at the crew on board.

The crew member operating the crane mechanism nodded and shut it off, shrugging as if to ask what the problem was. He walked out on deck.

'What's going on, guys? What's the problem?'

'I don't know. Something's trapped in there. Can't see what it is.'

The two men on shore moved closer, making their way through the field of flapping fish and inert crustaceans. Suddenly, one of them grabbed the other's shoulder.

'*Dio mio!*'

The other moved closer and then stopped, crossing himself.

Something was dangling from the metal grille. No, not something, but *someone*. At first I thought of the figure of Gregory Peck's Ahab, lashed to the side of the great white whale at the end of *Moby-Dick*. Then I saw that there was something even more grotesque about it.

He – for it had been a he – was hanging upside down, in the manner of an inverted crucifixion. His feet appeared to be secured together, and had caught on the cage. His jacket, sopping with water, hung down behind his head. His arms dangled and swung in the air, whilst his tie, still knotted neatly around his neck, partially obscured his face.

No. Not Ahab, but Mussolini, dangling from a lamppost outside the Villa Belmonte.

One of the dockhands made his way over to the boat and reached up.

'Mauro, don't touch him,' his friend called out.

'We can't just leave him like this.'

'He's dead. He must be dead. Leave it to the police.'

Mauro shook his head, but then seemed to think better of it and stepped back. He crossed himself once more.

The body twisted rhythmically in the breeze, slowly turning 180 degrees clockwise, and then back again. As it turned to face me, I got a clearer look at the face, and started.

For a moment the grotesque sight in front of me, and the stink of dead and dying fish, made me want to vomit. I shook my head to clear it, and then slowly picked my way across the quayside in order to stand next to Mauro.

His friend shouted at me. '*Signore*! Stay back please. Sir, please get back!'

I reached up to grab the jacket of the dead man and stop the body from turning. Mauro grabbed my arm. 'Sir, Alvise is right. We should leave this to the police.'

I nodded. 'Yes. Yes we should.' I turned to Mauro. 'But I think I know this man.'

'*Dio*,' he breathed.

I looked up at the face hanging above me. Bloated and blue from the effect of the seawater, the eyes staring sightlessly – fish-like – into my own. Almost unrecognisable. But not quite. It was a face I had seen just twice before, and yet I had absolutely no doubt.

'I do know him,' I said, and my voice, too, was little more than a whisper. 'His name was Michele Ballarin.'

Chapter 18

Busetto stared down at his desk, and scribbled more of his unintelligible notes. Then he raised his eyes to us and smiled. 'Mr Sutherland. *Dottoressa* Ravagnan. Thank you for coming in.'

'A pleasure,' I said.

He raised his eyebrows. Fede dug me in the ribs.

'Sorry. Wrong thing to say. Just trying to be polite.'

'So, just to run through the events of yesterday afternoon. You and your friends spent the day on the beach, at some point you decided to go and buy them ice cream,' he might have smiled here, but I couldn't be sure, 'walked back towards the lagoon,' he paused, 'at which point the – *unfortunate business* – was discovered.'

Describing a brutal death as unfortunate business was about the most incongruously English thing I could imagine at that moment. I was tempted to smile but Fede, I knew, would elbow me in the ribs again.

'That's about the shape of it,' I said.

He tapped his pencil on his pad. 'I'm just wondering why you felt it necessary to approach the body. After all, the usual reaction of the man in the street to an event like this would have been to turn away.'

'I'm impressed by your faith in the man in the street.'

'Perhaps I exaggerate. But still—?'

'I've seen dead bodies before.' He opened his mouth to speak, but I shook my head. 'No no. I'll tell you about it another time. But you might need to put a couple of hours aside. Anyway, as I saw the body turning I caught a clearer glimpse of his face. Yes, I know it was upside down and bloated from the sea. And I realise I'm talking about a man I had literally seen twice in my life before. But I recognised him. Or at least I thought I did.'

Busetto nodded and scribbled away. 'So, did you notice anything else?'

I shook my head. 'Nothing I can think of. I didn't care to look for too long.'

He took out an envelope. 'I have some photographs. Or would you prefer I describe them?'

'Describing them will be enough. More than enough,' said Fede. I nodded in agreement.

'Of course.' He smiled. 'The cause of death was easy to establish. Drowning, of course. There are other injuries, however. Severe bruising to the face and to the upper body.'

'Could that have happened when the body was dragged up?'

'Post-mortem bruising? It happens, yes. I suspect not in this case.'

He fell silent, waiting for us to respond. 'Go on,' I said.

'His feet were bound together. With a plastic cable tie.'

Fede nodded. 'So he was murdered. That's what you're saying.'

'I'm afraid so, *signora*.' He corrected himself. 'I'm sorry, *dottoressa.'* He pushed a box of tissues across the table. 'I'm sorry,' he repeated, 'did you know him well?'

She gave him a withering look, and pushed them back. 'I suppose I did once. But many years ago. It wouldn't be true to say I really knew him.'

'I understand.' He took a deep breath. 'There are some things we will need to check out . . .'

'I don't understand?'

'*Dottoressa,*' he chuckled, 'a few weeks ago you inherited a property on Pellestrina that was once the possession of your father. The estate was administered by *avvocato* Ballarin, a partner in your late father's practice. And now, just a few days after you visit Pellestrina, the unfortunate *avvocato* Ballarin is found dead – murdered – also on Pellestrina.'

I raised my hand. 'Isn't it possible that he was killed somewhere else in the lagoon, and the tides washed him over here?'

Busetto shook his head. 'You have more faith in coincidence than I do, Mr Sutherland. As I said, his ankles were lashed together. With a plastic cable tie. Not his hands. He would have been able to float for some time, of course. How long, though, I wonder? He would have known it was impossible to break the bonds around his feet. How long would he have been able to stay afloat for?'

'You're saying whoever did this did it to torture him?'

'To be cruel. Deliberately cruel. Now why, I wonder?'

He looked at Fede, who shook her head. 'I have no idea,' she said. 'This is a man I've had no contact with for years. Then he appeared out of the blue on my wedding day, to tell my mother that my father had left me what he described as "a modest legacy".'

Busetto whistled. '*Avvocato* Ballarin and I might disagree on the definition of "modest".'

'Likewise. But as I said, I've only seen him once in the last decade. A couple of weeks ago.'

Busetto smiled. Then he removed his glasses, gave them a polish, and smiled some more. He leant towards Federica, just ever so slightly. 'You also telephoned him in the last twenty-four hours, of course.'

Fede started. 'How could you know that?' Busetto tried to wave it away, but she continued. 'No, wait a moment. I didn't personally speak to anyone in his office. So the only way you could possibly know that is if you had an *intercettazione* on his line.' She smiled. 'Isn't it?'

Busetto looked apologetic, embarrassed even. 'Correct, *dottoressa*. You understand this is something I'm not allowed to discuss with you?'

'Oh, that's clear. Very clear.'

'But could I ask you why you called him?'

'I wanted to ask him about our housekeeper. Specifically, where he found her.'

'You have a housekeeper?' He raised his eyebrows, and scribbled away. 'You don't trust her?'

'I don't know if we do or not. But after we found the gun it struck us that we know nothing about her at all.'

'Has there been anything to make you suspicious? Money going missing?'

Fede shook her head.

'Telephones or tablets? Watches? Jewellery?'

Fede gave a hollow laugh and muttered the words 'if only', before giving me what I thought was an unnecessarily hard stare.

'Next birthday, okay? I promise.' I turned to Busetto. 'Nothing's gone missing. It's just that I was alone in the house one day and I had the feeling – just the feeling – that someone else was in there with me. And the floorboard – the loose one, under which we found the gun – that had moved. I'm sure of it.'

Busetto nodded. 'Okay. This is interesting. Do you have the name of this *signora*?' He poised his pencil over his notebook.

'Giulia,' I said.

He wrote it down, then looked up at me expectantly. 'Giulia . . . ?' he said, as if to prompt me.

'Giulia. That's all we know.'

'No address, phone number?'

'No.'

'Photographs?'

'She's my cleaner. Why would I photograph my cleaner?'

'Not even a surname?'

'Not even that. I'm sorry, we never exchanged life stories. I do understand that this is of limited use.'

He looked down at the name scrawled on his pad, and then struck it out with three very precise strokes of his pencil.

'Yes,' he said.

We sat in silence for a while. 'Can we go now?' I said.

Busetto nodded. 'Of course. My thanks for coming in, as I said.' He got to his feet and held the door open for us. 'I'll be in touch.'

I slumped on to the sofa, pushed Gramsci away with one hand, and closed my eyes.

'I suppose we need a drink,' said Fede.

I nodded.

'Are you going to get us one then?'

I opened my eyes. 'Why have you got to phrase that as a question? What you really mean is "Go and fix us a drink, Nathan."'

'I don't know. I think perhaps I picked it up from you.' She smiled. 'Gosh, perhaps that means I'm becoming more British?'

I got to my feet and stretched. 'Well, saying "gosh" is certainly a sign of something. Okay, I'll do it. Prosecco?'

'Perfect.'

Gramsci followed me through to the kitchen, and I reached down to scratch him behind the ears. 'The annoying thing is, he'd have seen exactly what went on the other afternoon when I thought someone else was here. Except he can't tell us about it.'

'Because of being a cat?'

'That, and his bad attitude.'

I returned with the drinks and we clinked glasses.

'You know what?' I said. 'I wish Vanni was dealing with this.'

'Why so?'

'Well, I know where I stand with him. I can't work Busetto out at all. He seems to be playing good cop and bad cop simultaneously.'

Fede gave a hollow laugh. 'Trust me, Nathan, Busetto is not being a bad cop. You'd know if he was.'

'I just don't get it. Why's he so interested in us?'

'I don't think it's us. It's the house. Or, more precisely,

the house and Ballarin. You don't get permission to monitor someone's telephone line without good reason. Ballarin – and this is just a guess – was involved in something not strictly legal which was of interest to both the police and whoever it was who killed him.'

'You're discounting suicide?'

'I think we can.'

'And his body turning up not quite but almost on our doorstep?'

She sighed. 'I don't know. But I do know what I'm going to do about it.'

I sat there in silence for a moment. 'Okay. I give up. Tell me.'

'Forget about it. That's what I'm going to do. That's what *we're* going to do. This is our bloody honeymoon. This is the house where I spent every summer of my childhood and I am not ready to give up and go back to Venice any time soon. So tonight we're going to go to the restaurant across the road, drink just enough prosecco, eat just enough seafood and then come home and make mad crazy love.'

'Gosh.' I leaned over towards her. 'I don't mind skipping dinner, you know?'

She pushed me away. 'No, I really am quite hungry.'

My phone plinged. I checked the message and quickly texted back.

'Anything important?'

'Dario. Just hoping everything's okay. I told him it was. He won't believe that, of course, but that's just Dario.'

She caught the expression on my face. 'You look sad.'

'Just a bit.'

'Want to tell me about it?'

'Well, it was supposed to be a happy day out for everyone . . . and then all this.'

'There'll be other days. Come on. Happy honeymoon, *caro.*'

'Happy honeymoon, *cara*. I'm sorry, it's not really turning out to be the sort of one we expected, is it?'

She shook her head. 'No.' Then she leaned over and kissed me. 'But there's nowhere else I'd rather be.'

I tried to look cool and immediately failed. 'Me neither.'

Chapter 19

I was woken by the sound of the doorbell and rolled over to check my watch, fumbling with my glasses as I strained to see the face. Ten o'clock. We'd overslept. Still, we were on honeymoon, we could bloody well sleep in if we wanted to. I had vague memories of getting up a few hours previously in order to feed a cantankerous Gramsci, but couldn't be absolutely sure. That might not have been today.

I threw on a T-shirt and pair of jeans, and went downstairs. The bell rang again, and yet again by the time I reached the door. I threw it open, prepared to be grumpy.

It was Busetto.

He smiled at me. 'Good morning, Mr Sutherland,' he said.

I nodded. 'It certainly is.'

'May I come in?'

I scratched my head and rubbed my eyes. 'I'm sorry, I've only just got up. The place is a bit of a mess. Could you come back later?'

He shook his head. 'It would be much easier if we could speak now.' He looked over his shoulder. 'And it would be better if we could speak indoors.'

Sleep was still fogging my thoughts, but I waved him inside.

'Coffee?' I said.

'Let me. You sit down.'

'What?'

'Seriously.' He looked over towards the kitchen. 'I can see a Moka on the hob, and I assume the jar that says "coffee" on the side has coffee in it.' He unscrewed the pot and grimaced at the dregs inside. 'Is there a bin here?'

'Under the sink. Look, *maresciallo*, can I ask what you're doing here? My girlfriend – I mean, my wife – will be downstairs soon, she's going to wonder why I've taken to asking policemen round for breakfast, and frankly I'd appreciate having time to prepare the explanation I'm going to have to give.'

He knocked the dregs into the bin, refilled the pot and put it on the stove. Then he turned to face me, leaned back against the sink and folded his arms. He was about to speak when Gramsci padded through. His face lit up.

'Ah, so this is your famous Macavity!' He was about to bend down to stroke him, when Gramsci hissed at him. He straightened up again.

'Sorry. He's not really a people cat.'

The coffee started to bubble, and Busetto smiled at me. 'How many cups should I fill?'

'My wife's a tea person. Coffee is good for me. And have one yourself, of course.'

'Sugar?' I nodded.

He sat down opposite me, and slid my coffee over. It caught, for a moment, on the irregular surface of the table, slopping into the saucer.

'I'm so sorry.'

I shook my head. 'Doesn't matter. So, what can I help you with, *maresciallo*?'

'I was on my way to work and I was thinking about something you said yesterday. That you'd only seen *signor* Ballarin twice in your life?'

'That's correct. Through the window of a bar on my wedding day. And a couple of days later at his office.'

'Mmm. And your wife, she also said that she'd only seen him once in recent years?'

'Yes. In Ballarin's office. The same time as me.'

Busetto stirred his coffee, and tinked his teaspoon on the side of the cup.

'I thought you didn't take sugar?'

'I don't. But coffee taken outside the office doesn't count.' He smiled at me. 'Please don't tell my wife.' He turned the smile off. 'As I was saying – both of you have only seen *signor* Ballarin on one or two occasions in the past few weeks.'

'Years. Or in my case, my life. But that's basically it.'

He sipped at his coffee, closing his eyes and smiling. Then the eyes snapped open. 'You're quite sure about that?'

'Absolutely sure. Look, can I ask what this is about?'

'It's just that we've found Ballarin's car.'

'You have?'

'Yes.' He paused. 'It's outside your house.'

'You what?'

He moved towards the door. 'Take a look.'

'No, it's okay. I believe you.'

He turned the smile back on. 'Take a look.' He paused. 'Please.'

I shrugged. 'Okay.' I opened the door and looked outside.

There was a black BMW parked directly in front of us.

'You didn't mention this when we had our little talk yesterday.'

'I don't notice these things. I'm from Venice. Cars don't make much of an impression on me. Anyway, I had no idea what sort of car he had.'

'He didn't call on you?'

'No.'

'Are you sure?'

'I'd have remembered. Yes, I'm sure.'

'I'm just wondering what might have brought him down here from the Lido?' He got to his feet, and stretched. 'Well, I'm sorry to have disturbed you. Thank you for the coffee anyway.'

'Not at all. Thank you for making it.'

'A pleasure. Well, I'll be in touch. If I need to be.'

He was about to turn towards the door, when he suddenly stopped and stared down at the table. I followed his gaze. He was looking at the photographs of the six unknown men we'd found in Elio's box of memorabilia.

He looked at me. 'May I?' I nodded. He slid the top photo from the pile, and then repeated the action with the others, spreading them out into a grid.

'Can I ask where you found these, Mr Sutherland?'

'They were in a box in the attic. Under a pile of family photos.'

He nodded, and smiled once more. 'Okay. Well, thank you.' He turned and made his way to the door. 'As I said, I'll be in touch.'

***

Federica, barefoot in jeans and T-shirt, padded downstairs, and shooed Gramsci off the adjacent seat to mine. She looked at the two empty coffee cups. 'Have we been entertaining this morning?'

'We're always entertaining,' I smiled.

'Who was it?'

'Busetto.'

'Oh. Was he a being a good cop or a bad cop?'

'He made me coffee. That counts as a good cop. Then he seemed to be interested in those photos we found. That made him slightly less good.'

My phone rang. I looked at the screen. Number unknown. 'That's probably him now. He's going to do his "just one more thing" again, I know it.' I clicked Receive. '*Pronto?*'

'Good morning.' A woman's voice. 'Is that Mr Nathan Sutherland?' Nathan, pronounced in the Italian way, with a short 'a'.

'It is.'

'British Consul Nathan Sutherland?'

'Honorary Consul. Can I help you?'

'I wonder if I could speak to your wife, Mr Sutherland?'

'I should think so. Can I ask what this is about? Don't you have her number?'

'You're easier to find. My name is Sara Scarpa. I'm from *Il Gazzettino*.'

Fede had been close enough to overhear. She looked at me and nodded. I passed her the phone, and she tapped at the keypad, putting it on to speaker. She placed it on the table, between us.

'*Signora* Scarpa?'

'*Dottoressa* Ravagnan.' Her voice was light, breezy. 'I was wondering if we could have a quick chat about the events of two days ago. The body that was dragged up from the lagoon.'

'Uh-huh. Carry on.'

'I understand he was known to you?'

'Slightly. It's not unusual in a city this size. Most people are vaguely known by most other people.'

'But this man – Michele Ballarin – had been a business partner of your father.' Fede fell silent, and Scarpa continued. 'Elio Ravagnan. They were lawyers, weren't they?'

'That's correct. I think that was well known.'

Scarpa continued, her voice as bright and sunny as ever. 'I wonder if we could just have a little chat. About your father and Michele Ballarin.' She paused. 'And about his relationship with Giuseppe Lupo. Anything – everything – that you can possibly remember. No matter how small.'

Fede's chair scraped against the floor, as she started. 'Giuseppe Lupo? Are you being quite serious here?'

'Absolutely, *dottoressa*. As I was saying, anything you know about him. Did he ever come to visit your family? Did you ever go on holiday together? Did he ever come to your house on Pellestrina?'

Fede was laughing now. '*Signora*, I think I should stop you there before this conversation descends further into insanity. Why on earth would my father have had anything to do with Giuseppe Lupo?'

Scarpa ignored the question. 'What was your father's connection to him? On a professional basis, on a personal level.'

'I don't know where you've got this from, but he had no connection to him. None at all. This is ridiculous.'

'So your father never spoke to you about him?'

'I hardly spoke to my father at all in the decade before he died.'

'So there could have been something – just that you didn't know about it?'

'As I said, we rarely spoke. And certainly my mother never mentioned his name.'

'Your mother. Of course.'

'We know nothing about this. Nothing at all.' Fede's voice was breaking now. I reached for her hand, and she squeezed it tightly, her wedding ring digging into my fingers and drawing an 'Ow' from me.

'*Dottoressa* Ravagnan, we've got off on the wrong foot. I'm sorry. I'm trying to help you here.'

'That's very kind of you. Very kind of you indeed. But why, I wonder, would you want to do that?'

'It's my job to manage news. The story about Ballarin's murder is in every paper in Northern Italy. Tomorrow, maybe, in all of Italy. I can help you manage it. I can let you give your side of the story.'

'There is no story. And there is nothing to say. So you can drag every journalist in the Veneto to our front door and the answer is going to be the same. I have no idea what you're talking about. And there is nothing more to be said.'

Scarpa sighed. 'Very well, *Signora* Ravagnan. I do hope you'll remember that I tried to help.'

Fede hung up, and we sat there in silence, staring at the phone.

I checked my watch. 'Ten thirty. Okay, well I guess the day can only get better from here.'

Fede didn't reply.

'Are you okay?'

She said nothing.

'Would a cup of tea help?'

She nodded.

I brewed her up a cup as she sat in silence, and set it down in front of her. She sipped at it, wincing slightly at the heat.

'You know what would be better?' she said. 'The uncomfy sofa, and a hug.'

'Both of those sound good,' I said. I flopped down on to the couch. 'Come on then.'

She came and sat next to me, and put her head on my shoulder. And we just sat there, without speaking, waiting for her tea to cool down.

I waited until I thought sufficient time had passed. 'So,' I said, 'do you want to talk about it?'

'Not really.'

'I know. Probably be good though.'

'You're right.' She sighed. 'Come on then. Where would you like me to start?'

'Giuseppe Lupo.'

'I thought it might be.'

'I've got one question about Giuseppe Lupo.'

'Which is?'

'Who's Giuseppe Lupo?'

She closed her eyes for a moment, and then took a sip of her tea. Then she reached for the heaviest cushion she could find and smacked me around the back of the head with it.

'Feeling better?' I said.

'Much.' She was smiling now.

'So go on then. Who's this legendary figure and what's his connection with your father.'

'Giuseppe Lupo is – was – a senior boss in the Mala del Brenta.' She could see the realisation dawning in my eyes, but spoke anyway. 'The Venetian Mafia.'

Chapter 20

'Seriously?'

'Seriously, was he a boss in the Mala del Brenta? Yes. Seriously, did he know my father? No, of course not.'

'So where on earth has that woman got the idea from?'

'I don't know. It's nearly ten years since my father died. Ten years in which Michele Bastard Ballarin might have been doing some sort of dirty deal with the Mala del Brenta.' She took a deep breath. 'My father was a bad husband. But he wasn't a crook.'

I looked over towards the kitchen. I liked the idea of coffee but neither of us, I felt, needed more caffeine. Moreover, it was starting to get warm now and the air felt uncomfortably close. The air felt thick with the atmosphere of an awkward conversation and the threat of a potential row. Fresh air might be good.

'Shall we go for a walk?' I said.

Fede looked surprised, and then suspicious. 'That's not like you. When did you last suggest we just "go for a walk"?'

'Probably never. But I think it might be a good idea.'

She took a deep breath and then nodded. 'I think you're right.' She yawned and stretched. 'But first you need to get showered and shaved. Oh, and iron a T-shirt.'

'Is that the most important thing right now?'

'It certainly is.' She gave a hollow laugh. 'You need to look good. A mafia daughter, after all, can't be seen with just anyone.'

Blue *bricole* studded a blue lagoon, shimmering under a clear blue sky. A veritable preponderance of blue. The smell of cooking came from *da Celeste* and I could see a few early-birders were already taking their seats for lunch.

Fede guessed what I was thinking, and smiled. '*Caro mio.* Always thinking at least one meal ahead.'

'Well, as I've said, these things are important.'

'I know. But would you be okay with just a sandwich?'

I squeezed her arm. 'I'd be more than okay with that.'

'In a bit then. Come on, it's not even midday. Let's just walk for the moment.' She led me back to the main road and the *murazzi*. We climbed up the steps that led to the top of the wall, and sat down and looked out over the Adriatic, enjoying the feel of the gentle breeze that came in off the sea.

I pointed towards the horizon. 'So,' I said, 'what happens if you keep going in that direction?'

'You hit Croatia. After about a hundred kilometres. Not that far really. Lots of Venetians go there on holiday. The beaches are better. My friend Cristina even goes to the dentist there.'

'The *dentist*?'

'Sure. It's a lot cheaper than here, even with the cost of getting there.'

'Have you ever been?'

'To the dentist?'

'To Croatia.'

She nodded. 'A few times. After Father left. Mother wanted things to be different. I suppose Father would have let us use the house if we'd asked but,' she shook her head, 'too many memories. No, it had to be somewhere else.'

'Did you like it?'

'Very much. And it was nice, you know? Just Mother and myself. I was grown up by then, so it was more like two girls going on holiday together than mother and daughter.'

'We should do it. All three of us.'

'That's a nice idea. We should. One day.'

We sat there, and looked out over the sea, listening to the sound of it crashing on the shore and the occasional roar of traffic from behind us. I laid my head on Fede's shoulder and could, I thought, have quite happily gone to sleep. Then she touched my arm.

'You never asked me, did you?'

'What about?'

'If I knew anything about this. About Lupo and my father.'

I shrugged. 'There was no need.'

She smiled, and hugged me. 'Thank you.' She got to her feet. 'I think it's time for that sandwich.'

We made our way back to Renzo's bar and ordered some *tramezzini*. I chose two with grilled vegetables just to feel virtuous. Then I decided that was quite virtuous enough for one day and that I'd earned a small octopus on a stick as well.

A buzzing sound came from Federica's handbag.

'I think that's your phone.'

She nodded, gulping the remains of her sandwich in a hurry.

'*Ciao, mamma.*'

I could hear Marta's voice on the other end of the line, but couldn't make out the words.

Fede's face drained of colour. She held the phone away from her ear, and pressed the mute button, looking around the bar as she did so. 'I need to take this outside.' She lowered her voice, 'I'm sorry. There are too many people here.'

She walked outside, speaking into the phone. '*Mamma*, just tell me about it, calmly. *Mamma*, please don't cry . . .'

There was an awkward silence in the bar as everybody pretended not to have heard. An old guy, seated in the corner and rolling a cigarette, caught my eye and gave a little shrug. *Mothers, eh?*

I could see Fede walking up and down outside the bar, her hand gestures becoming ever more animated, and began to realise that this was not going to be a lunch to linger over. I paid for our sandwiches, and wrapped up Federica's remaining one in a napkin.

I nodded at Renzo. 'I think I'd better go.'

'No worries. Have a good afternoon, yeah?'

I wasn't sure at all that that was going to be the case. Because I had never, ever heard Marta Colombo crying before.

Fede was leaning her head against the wall, her eyes closed and breathing deeply. I could see her lips moving. She was counting to ten.

I let her finish. She opened her eyes again, and then looked at her phone. Her knuckles were white. She dropped it into her handbag, and took another deep breath.

'I brought your sandwich,' I said, holding it out to her.

'Thank you. You know, I'm not hungry right now. Maybe later. Better still, you have it.'

'Okay. So. What now?'

'I think we should go home. Because I think I might be about to start screaming, and I don't want to create a scene in the street.'

'We can do that. Is there anything I can do?'

'You can let me have a good old scream and swear.'

'Okay. I'll answer the door to the police as well. Just in case they think there's a murder going on.' She didn't smile. 'Are you going to tell me about it?'

'Later.'

I offered her my arm, but she shook it away and walked – stalked – off in the direction of the house, leaving me struggling to keep up with her. Her hand shook as she tried to find the right key, and she dropped the bunch to the ground. I bent to pick them up and she snatched them from me, still shaking.

'Let me.' I reached out my hand. 'Come on, let me.'

She slapped it away.

'That's not fair. I don't know what's happened but I'm pretty sure it's not my fault. Come on, tell me about it.'

She finally managed to get the key to turn, and went inside. I followed, and closed the door as gently as I could. Fede stood in the living room, resting her hands on the table, her head bent and hair hanging down over her face.

I gave it as long as I dared.

'Do you want to talk?'

Her head snapped up. 'Shut up,' she hissed. 'Shut up, shut up, shut up.'

'Okay. I under—'

'I said just bloody shut up. Just for a bloody moment. Just stop being Mr Understanding, just for a few minutes. Are you capable of doing that?' Then she lowered her head again. I stood there, in silence, wondering what the hell I was going to say or do. Then she wrenched out a scream, sweeping newspapers, ornaments and coffee cups from the table to smash on the floor. Gramsci howled and fled up the stairs.

I stood there, looking at her, as the echoes faded and the terrible thought came into my mind that, for the first time in our relationship, I did not know what to do.

She raised her head, and stared into my eyes. 'We should never have come here, should we?' The question sounded like a challenge, as if she was daring me to disagree.

'No. I'm sorry. I never thought it would make you so unhappy.'

'I've never heard my mother cry before. You understand? Never. Not when my father left. Not when he died.' She walked over to the bookcase, screamed once more and swept the books from the top shelf. One of them dropped at her feet. *Pinocchio*. She picked it up, took a deep breath and screamed yet again as she hurled it across the room.

'Fede. Please. Don't do this. At least tell me about it.'

'That journalist. That pig of a journalist telephoned her and asked her the same questions as she asked us this morning. Only worse. *What can you tell us about Giuseppe Lupo? Was your late husband in collusion with the Mala del Brenta? What was it like being a mafia wife?*' She choked out a laugh. 'A mafia wife. For Christ's sake. She said if she could have a full, exclusive interview with her then she might be able to take the edge off the story. If not – *pfft* – who knows how long it might be until someone leaks the story to the newspapers?'

'Bitch.'

'I don't know what we're going to do, Nathan. I just don't know what we're going to do.' Her voice cracked and I realised that I had never seen her cry either. I pulled her to me, and she rested her head on my shoulder in order to hide her face; her body shuddering with misery and anger. We stood there, amongst the scattered newspapers and broken crockery, holding each other.

I stroked her hair. 'I know what we're going to do, my love. I don't know exactly how. But we're going to sort this out.'

She raised her head, and I could see that her eyes were red. 'How?'

'I've got no idea. But we're going to sort this out. The two of us, together.'

She nodded, and forced a smile on to her face. 'Yes. We are, aren't we?'

In the Wolf's Den

The Old Wolf draws on his cigarette, then leans his head back, eyes closed. He smiles.

'Those were the good years, you know? The best of years. Everyone loved us – Vicari and me. Right from the very start. You see, anyone can sell drugs on the street. Anyone can knock over a jewellery store. But then what do you do with the stuff once you've got it?

'Vicari had a talent for making paste jewellery look like the real thing. And he could make the real thing look like worthless crap. And if you know someone who can do that, then moving the stuff around becomes so much easier. If we stole stuff in the Veneto, Vicari would work his magic and conceal it, and then we'd launder it on the other side of the country.

'Not just jewellery either. If you had a painting that you needed to be certified as real – or if you had one that needed to be certified as fake – he could find you someone who could do it. There was a guy in Venice who used to help us out with this. Domenico Moro. You might remember, he died not too long ago.

'If you stayed with the Mala long enough, you'd get yourself a nickname. Kind of like being a Brazilian footballer, a mark *of respect. I was the Wolf of course, because of my name. Vicari was the Deacon.'*

Lupo closes his eyes and laughs again.

'We all went to Mass, you see? And it made sense — we'd give him dirty goods, and he'd make them shiny and new and spotless for us. So that's what we were. The Wolf and the Deacon. And we made a lot of money. A lot of money, very very quickly. Yes, good years.'

'And also for your family?' I say.

He opens his eyes. 'Of course.'

'Will you tell me about them?'

'Is it important?'

'I think it is. Without your family, you're just the face of a crook on the front page of a newspaper. With your family, you become a person.'

He chuckles. 'Just the face of a crook. You're a brave man, Brezzi.' Then he nods his head, and his face grows serious. I can see him age in front of me again.

'Well now.' He lights another cigarette and smokes in silence for a while. 'It was the late 1960s. I'd just come out of prison for — I think — the second time. Long before the Mala del Brenta. I was just running with the local gangs.' He looks at me. 'You remember the sixties?'

'Just about.'

'Good time to be alive. Everybody has a little bit more money. And every cheap crook in the Veneto thinks they can strike out on their own in the big cities, Milan, Rome, wherever. But not me.'

'Why not?'

'Always seemed like a dumb idea. You may be a big figure in Mestre, but you go to Milan — you're just going to be a punk.

Like I said, prison was an education. Those guys, those wise guys, who thought they were going to be a big noise in the big city,' he shakes his head, *'dumbasses. They never made the most of a good prison education. You'd see them driving around in flash cars, before heading off to Milan. And then maybe one day, somebody says to you "Hey, remember Gino? They found his body dangling from a bridge the other day." Dumb kids. I never had a flash car. Even when I could afford it. But I remember my first scooter. Vespa 125.'*

He smiles and drags on his cigarette again. 'Lovely thing. Girls loved it too of course. And I was a young guy, good-looking enough, with clothes that were smart enough. I remember there was a club I used to go to on Saturday nights. They were just starting to play pop music — American music, British music, you know? And so that's where I met Maddalena. Lovely name. Lovely girl. Religious family, never liked me. But I kept going to Mass with her on Sunday and one day they just accepted that it didn't matter whether they liked me or not.'

'But they knew what you did?'

'I think they pretended they didn't, even to themselves. "My son-in-law is a businessman", that sort of thing. Which, in many ways, I was.'

I wonder if the Old Wolf is pretending to himself as well. When he speaks to me about his family, I notice that his voice changes. He no longer sounds like a gangster, but rather as the man I know him to have become. There are questions I want to ask, but he's in the mood to talk and so I feel it best not to interrupt . . .

Chapter 21

'Are you going to be all right on your own?'

'I should think so. It'll be a bit strange. But Gramsci will be around. It'll be like old times. Not that those old times were good times,' I added, hurriedly. 'Now, have you got everything?' I looked at the small case that Fede was carrying.

'I don't need much. It's only for a couple of days. You do understand, don't you?'

'Sure. She's upset. You need to be with her.'

'The trouble is that now she's going to feel guilty as well. Taking me away from my husband on our honeymoon.' She checked her watch. 'Okay, my bus is in ten minutes. I could come back this evening, you know? Chioggia isn't far.'

'I know. But you need to be with your mum. I understand that. And give her my love.'

'Thank you. It should only be for one night.' She touched my cheek. 'And what are you going to do?'

'What we discussed. I'm going to read up on Giuseppe Lupo and the Mala del Brenta and see if I can find anything – anything at all – that might link him with Michele Ballarin.'

'Nothing else?'

'Nothing else.'

'Nothing stupid?'

'This is the bloody mafia! Of course I'm not going to do anything stupid.'

'Promise?'

'I promise. Just some research. Nothing else. Oh, and I suppose I might be allowed the occasional cheeky Negroni?'

'Of course, *caro*. There's nothing at all desperate about drinking Negronis alone.'

'I'll have you know I did that for many years.'

'Many lonely, unhappy years?'

'Well, yes. But that's beside the point.'

She was smiling again now. 'I made out a list of things for you to do. I've left it on the kitchen table.'

I set her on her way with a hug and a kiss. Then the door closed, and I found myself alone in a strange house, with only the company of an unfriendly cat.

I considered going out for breakfast, but I'd promised Fede I would knuckle down to work straightaway. So I put some biscuits down for Gramsci, and made myself a coffee instead. I picked up her list of instructions.

1) Buy prosecco.

2) Book restaurant for tomorrow evening.

3) Solve mystery.

4) Do not do anything stupid.

5) If tempted to do anything stupid, please refer to point 4.

I smiled to myself.

'Okay, puss,' I said, 'I can't believe I'm saying this, but today we're going to try and learn all about the Venetian mafia. Are we good with that?'

Gramsci gave a great, *basso profondo* purr.

I scratched the back of his neck. 'I know, I know. It's probably a stupid idea. And investigating too far will most likely get me killed. Which will mean someone else will have to feed you.'

He continued to purr.

'But yes, you're right. Someone else would probably step in and take over that arduous job. So let's see what there is to find, eh?'

I flipped up the lid of my laptop and set to work. I was not, I told myself, going to do anything stupid. I was, nevertheless, just a little bit relieved that Federica was going to be away from Pellestrina for a few days.

You in the North, you make me smile you know? Always it's the South that's holding you back. Always the South, with their superstitions and their mafia and their omertà. *Murder someone on Saturday, say your prayers on Sunday. This third world country in the middle of your own. If only you could be free of us, you say. How lucky you would be. You could be like the Austrians, the Germans, God help us even the British. And we in the South would revert to barbarism, to our own dark little ways.*

But don't forget how much we taught you. What were you before we arrived? Bums, petty crooks working fairground rackets. Shady taxi drivers, frigging the meter to cheat tourists. Unlicensed shops selling Chinese glass to Americans. That's where you'd still be without us.

'A' – former member of the Mala del Brenta

Clan Giostrai? Sure I know about Clan Giostrai. You could call them organised crime. Me, I called them disorganised crime. A bunch of cheap crooks who worked the fairgrounds on the look-out for drugs, sex and the chance to fleece their customers. And then all of a sudden, it wasn't selling a little blow or shagging a schoolgirl behind the rollercoaster. It was bank robbery. Jewellery heists. Kidnapping. Extortion.

So what happened? Well, we happened. I know, I know, we're supposed to blame the South for everything but this shit-storm really was our fault.

We invited them in. You understand that, we invited them in?

In the sixties, in the seventies, we decided that we could beat the mafia by splitting them up. We sent them into what you might call 'internal exile'. People like <name redacted>, <name redacted>, <name redacted> – all these bad sons-of-bitches – what did we do? We stopped them returning to Sicily, and we moved them to the Veneto. We might as well have given them a palazzo and hung a sign over the door with 'School of Crime' on it. And all of a sudden, every crook in the region is beating a path to their door, wanting a slice of the cake. Wanting to learn from them. And so one day even these bums in Clan Giostrai decide that maybe there are better ways of earning money than selling bags of weed at the carnival.

'Paolo', former *carabiniero*, dismissed for corruption in 1994

The Mestrini – those guys weren't part of the Mala del Brenta. Not at first. Each side knew who the other was, but they kind of left each other alone. No one stepped out of line, you know what I mean? Everyone had a boundary. The Mestrini, they were tough guys, bad guys, you didn't want to screw with them. They had *their own turf on Mestre for drugs. In Venice they ran the taxi and hotel rackets. But the Mala del Brenta were professionals — real professionals from the South — and bit by bit they took over all the others.*

Then there were the Veneziani, the old guys. They were here long before anyone else and they held out the longest. The Rizzi brothers, they thought they were friends — personal friends — of Felice Maniero from the Mala. Until one day they weren't any more. Maniero had them gunned down during peace talks.

'Giulio', retired police officer

Gianni Brezzi, The Mala del Brenta: A plague from the South

I took my glasses off and rubbed my eyes. There were pages and pages of this stuff, some in English, some in Italian and even a few less official-looking sites in Veneziano. I looked down at the notes and diagrams I'd scribbled in a failed attempt to make sense of the various organisations and personalities involved. Personalities that frequently had the word 'jail' scribbled next to them or had simply been crossed out in the event of them being permanently removed from the scene.

I had, I suppose, always assumed that there was some kind of Venetian mafia, if only because of the hand-painted sign that hung from a *palazzo* near the Rialto Bridge bearing the words *'No mafia — Venezia è Sacra'*. If there was one, I assumed it was relatively low-key, extremely unlikely to be interested in me and possibly even a little bit cuddly; nothing more serious than crooks running dodgy taxis and selling fake Murano glass.

I had been wrong. It seemed to comprise a multiplicity of organisations and appeared to be anything but cuddly. Bank robbery, drug trafficking, kidnapping, extortion. One organisation had links to war criminals in ex-Yugoslavia, and had trafficked guns to Croatia in the 1990s. Another had gunned down heads of rival clans during a supposed peace meeting at a restaurant.

Gianni Brezzi, it seemed, was a Venetian journalist who'd written a number of books on the subject, as well as contributing to a number of national newspapers. I scribbled his name down as well. It might be good to get in touch with him at some point. I wondered if he knew who Sara Scarpa was.

Brezzi had a lot to say about the career of Giuseppe Lupo, who had been a senior member in the Mala del Brenta. After suspected involvement in a series of armed robberies throughout the Veneto, he'd been arrested in Chioggia in 2011 whilst trying to fence two stolen diamonds. X-ray analysis had linked them to a set stolen from a jeweller's in Padua in 2003. A robbery in which the shop owner had been shot dead.

Lupo had been an old man even at the time of his arrest. If he'd been just a few years older he might not have gone to prison at all. But, instead of turning *pentito*, he'd said nothing to implicate his former associates or reveal the location of the stolen goods, and seemed content to accept his punishment in stoical silence.

He had died in jail just one month ago; six months before he was due to be released. That did, perhaps, explain the sudden interest in him from the press.

Okay. I now had a vague idea of who Giuseppe Lupo was and more information than I was strictly comfortable with

regarding the Venetian mafia. But had there been any connection between Lupo and Federica's dad? If there had been,
it surely would have found its way into the newspapers. And
surely Fede and Marta would have known?

I didn't feel at all comfortable about searching for this,
but it had to be done. I checked the *La Nuova* website. Then
Il Gazzettino. Then *Repubblica, La Corriere, La Stampa* and,
when I could think of no more Italian newspapers, I checked
the British ones as well.

There was nothing. I leaned back in my chair and sighed.
Everything Sara Scarpa had said appeared to be a load of
nonsense. There was nothing to be found in the press regarding any possible link between Giuseppe Lupo and Michele
Ballarin, and neither was there anything regarding Elio
Ravagnan. I picked up the phone. I'd call Fede and tell her
not to worry. She could put her mother's mind at rest and,
who knows, maybe she'd be back tonight?

And yet, and yet . . . just one more search. Something
broader. 'Lupo Ravagnan' brought back any number of hits
– Ravagnan was not an uncommon surname in the Veneto –
but the first few pages of results returned nothing of interest
and I was prepared to let it go at that.

Then I searched on 'Lupo Ballarin'. Again, I scrolled
through pages and pages of results with nothing to show for
it. It was done. I rubbed my face, and then looked at my
watch. Time for lunch. I'd be on my own, which wasn't ideal,
but, by God, I'd earned a good one. I might even treat myself
to a Negroni beforehand.

And then I saw it. Not in a newspaper, not on a social
media site, but on the home page of the church of the

Madonna della Marina in Malamocco. It could scarcely be defined as an article, and the layout of the webpage, with its overuse of Comic Sans, made my eyes ache. But the caption left no room for doubt. '15 August, 2004. Michele Ballarin, Giuseppe Lupo and Sandro Vicari on this joyous occasion for God's holy church.'

There were three people in the photograph. Despite the shaky quality of the image, I could just about recognise Ballarin. Strangely, however, he looked older – was his hair a little thinner? Perhaps he'd had work done in the meantime? His arm was around a thin, bespectacled man with silver hair. The third member of the party was perhaps between them in age, shaven-headed but compensating with a neatly trimmed grey goatee.

'Joyous occasion'. What did that mean? There was nothing to indicate a baptism or a wedding, and funerals, I was pretty sure, wouldn't meet the definition at all. I scratched my head, trying to remember the significance of 15 August, then gave up and googled it. *Ferragosto*. The feast of the Assumption of the Virgin. An appropriately joyous occasion, then, for a church dedicated to the Madonna.

Seven years after this photograph had been taken, Lupo had been arrested in Chioggia attempting to fence stolen diamonds. A cheap little crime, I thought, and somewhat out of keeping with the image I had of a mafia boss.

So who was Sandro Vicari? It didn't take long to find out. Another suspected member of the Mala del Brenta, he'd been linked with a series of jewel robberies, forgeries and art crimes over a period of twenty years, before being shot dead in Padua in 2010.

Christ. Two of them. And there was now evidence – actual genuine photographic evidence – of a link between Michele Ballarin and the mob.

This did not, of course, mean that there was any connection with Fede's dad. But it was a link, no matter how tenuous. And it was something I needed to check out before she returned. It was midday now. Plenty of time to travel up to Malamocco and back. But the prospect of a lunchtime Negroni had receded.

I looked again at the names I had scribbled down. Or, at least those without the words 'jail' alongside them. None of them, I thought, were people that I had a particular interest in meeting. I was also very keen on them not developing a particular interest in me.

Chapter 22

I'd only ever been to Malamocco once before. Fede had taken me there, not long after we'd got together, in those slightly awkward early days of a relationship where you realise 'Yeah, we're together now' but before it actually seems like something real you might both settle down to.

Fede got to her feet. 'Next stop,' she said.

'Are you sure? I thought we still had a way to go yet.' I unfolded the map, not caring about looking like a tourist. 'Look, it's definitely the one after.'

'I know that. I just want to go the last stretch on foot.'

'What, like a pilgrimage?'

'You can call it what you like. But we should. I'll tell you all about it when we get there.'

We were the only passengers to get off the bus. I could see the outskirts of Malamocco in the distance, and it looked further than I'd care to walk on a hot day. Yet there was something about Federica's manner that made me feel it might be as well not to complain too much.

There was no pavement on the lagoon side of the busy road, and no pedestrians were to be seen. Cars and motor scooters whizzed past us, both faster and closer than strictly comfortable, whilst a sign warned of a sharp left turn up ahead.

Federica walked to the sharpest point of the curve, and jumped over the crash barrier on to a patch of rough ground that, within ten metres, dropped away into the sea.

'This is where it happened,' she said. 'Where Father died. You know what they call this place? The *Curva della Morte*. The Curve of Death. Venetians, eh?' She laughed, but there was no humour in it. 'We do have this love of melodrama.' She ran her hand across the top of the crash barrier. 'This wasn't there at the time. They put it in the year after. There were two other deaths the same year as father. That's how it got its name.

'You don't realise how sharp the bend is at night. People drive along here just a little faster than they should. Maybe it's late. Maybe you've had a drink. And all of a sudden the bend is on top of you, and time – your time – has run out.'

She paused. 'There's a terrible Italian word. Carbonizzato. Carbonised.' She shuddered. 'We'll never know what happened that night. People said Father had been working too hard. Others said that he'd started to drink a little too much. Probably it was a bit of both. All we know is that one night he drove along here just a little too fast – with not quite enough care – and that was enough. Mother and I heard the following morning.'

'I'm sorry,' I said. 'Should we have brought flowers? I could pick some up in Malamocco and bring them back?'

She shook her head. 'That's kind of you, but there's no need. Besides, there's something a little mawkish about roadside shrines, don't you think?'

A car whizzed by, throwing up dust and pebbles and choking us with petrol fumes. 'Come on,' she said. 'It's not exactly a *place to linger. Let's walk into town and I'll show you our old house.'*

'You never talk much about your dad,' I said.

'You never talk much about yours.'

'Fair enough. We've had no relationship for years, though.'

'We didn't either. Not in the years before he died.' She stopped walking, and paused. 'But—'

'But?'

'I was thinking of something our old priest said, at Madonna della Marina. People die, and, if we're not careful, we can spend our lives beating ourselves up about what we did or did not say to them whilst they were alive. Perhaps we argued on our last meeting? Perhaps we hadn't spoken in years? If only we could put things right, speak to them one last time. But of course, we can't. And we have to put those "if onlys" out of our head right away. Because there's nothing to be done. And the "if onlys" will kill you if you let them.

'Would I change anything? No. Probably not. My father was, in the end, a disappointing man. But when I was growing up, at least, he was a pretty good father. I think you can love someone without actually liking them, can't you?'

I was trying to think of a suitable response, but then realised it was a rhetorical question. She shook her head, and then smiled at me. 'Come on, then. Let's go. I'll show you our old house. And I'll take you round the church as well.'

'Great. Any chance of a drink and a sandwich afterwards?'

'Only if you're good.' Then she reached up and pecked me on the cheek. 'Thank you.'

'What for?'

'Nothing in particular. But thank you.'

I linked my arm in hers, and we made our way – carefully – around the Curve of Death, keeping as close to the side as possible, and down into Malamocco.

As soon as I reached Malamocco I regretted not having spent more time there in the past. The loveliest of little towns, a miniature Venice in itself, it had also been the first settlement on the Lido. I'd imagined us going there for long weekends in the summer but Federica had shown no particular interest in that idea. Too many memories, she said. Visiting once was fine for nostalgia, but that was enough.

I walked past her old house. I'd feared it might have been boarded up or, worse, become a bar or restaurant, but two small, brightly painted bicycles parked outside showed that normal life was still going on and I smiled.

It was tempting to pull up a chair outside one of the little cafés alongside the canal, to drink a coffee and just watch the world go by, but I had work to do. I'd left what should have been sufficient food for Gramsci, but come early evening he'd start getting grouchy and I'd need to be around. I turned my feet, not without some reluctance, in the direction of the church instead.

The Church of the Madonna della Marina had stood in Malamocco, in various shapes and forms, since the fourteenth century. Its plain white façade was unassuming and it was inevitably overlooked by tourists in favour of the nearby Santa Maria Assunta with its huge campanile – modelled on that of San Marco – which towered over the small town. I hadn't had any particular desire to visit – there was, as far as I was aware, no great art to be found there – but Federica had insisted we should.

Fede, I knew, rarely went inside a church except for work, yet I was struck by the fact that she crossed herself as soon as we entered. She must have caught the expression on my face, and she smiled and squeezed my hand. 'Old habits.'

She led me up the aisle until we were five pews from the front. 'Let's sit down.' We sat there and I looked around at art that, as I had expected, was not quite of the first rank; breathing in the familiar odour of stale incense and old furniture.

'This is where we used to sit on Sunday mornings.' Then she frowned and looked around. 'Or perhaps it was the row in front. Or maybe even the one behind. Anyway, it was definitely somewhere around here. And one day – I think I must have been in my early teens, and being dragged out of bed early on Sunday morning to go to Mass was starting to lose its appeal – I remember staring up at that painting.' She pointed to the chapel to the left of the altar. 'The Virgin with Saint Cosma and Saint Damiano. Tintoretto. Or at least some people say it is. Possibly people from the Malamocco tourist board. Anyway, I remember I used to look at that painting every week, when old Don Luca was preaching away and telling us how terrible we were. I used to think how sad it looked, how dusty and dirty and unloved. And one Sunday, it came into my mind that that's what I was going to do. I was going to restore things. I was going to make old things look beautiful again.' She beamed at me. 'I still remember that. Perhaps it was divine inspiration?'

'Perhaps so,' I said.

'Anyway, I thought one day, after I'd been away to university, I'd come back and I'd work on that painting – actually, no, it *wasn't the painting, it was the frame – I was going to come back and make it shine like gold.'*

I turned to look at her. 'And did you?'

She shook her head. 'No. There was a project but we never got the money. Poor old Tintoretto or not-Tintoretto is as dusty as he ever was.' She nodded to herself. 'It would have been nice, though. But I did work on one in the sacristy. Well, sort of. I was a very small part of quite a big team. Come on, I'll show you.'

She led me to a door set into the wall on the opposite side of the Tintoretto chapel and rattled the handle. 'Locked,' she said, with a look of disappointment on her face. 'I remember when they didn't have to lock churches at all.'

'We could come back after lunch,' I said.

She smiled at me. 'You've been very patient,' she said. 'Lunch it is, then.'

We never did come back.

Chapter 23

A Ferrari was parked outside the church, bright red against the plain white exterior, in defiance of the No Parking sign.

Why the hell would anyone have a car like that on the Lido, a strip of land where the speed limit never went above sixty kph? But I supposed that anyone with sufficient money to afford a car like that would be as worried by speed limits as they were by parking restrictions.

I went in and sat in what I hoped was the same pew as five years previously. I wondered what on earth I was going to say to the priest, if he ever appeared. *Excuse me*, padre, *but is it true that a member of your flock was a gangster?*

The church was a blessed relief from the heat of the day. I sat there, and looked at the altarpiece in the chapel on the left. It looked convincing enough to be a Tintoretto to me, but I was no expert. It was, evidently, in need of some work and I felt sad that Federica and her colleagues had never had the chance to work on it. Perhaps its attribution hadn't been convincing enough to attract attention from the great international organisations that poured money into restoring the city's artworks.

I heard the door creaking open behind me, and a flash of

sunlight spread out along the nave, lighting the way to the sanctuary. Then the door closed again, and I heard footsteps behind me. I didn't care to turn and look, feeling it would be disrespectful, and so waited for him – or her – to pass in front of me.

He was a man in early middle age, in a well-cut suit and dark glasses, carrying a briefcase. He walked to the steps leading up to the sanctuary and set his case down. He removed his glasses, and folded them away inside his pocket. Then he ran his hand through his hair – as if to make sure he looked quite correct before approaching the altar of the Lord – and genuflected and crossed himself, before moving to the front pew. Then he replaced his glasses, thinking, perhaps, that he needed to cut a *bella figura* even in the eyes of the Almighty. He sat there, bent over, his hands clenched together and lips murmuring in silence.

Someone to whom it was important to come and pray for a few minutes in the middle of the day in the middle of the week. Once, that would have seemed strange to me. But after a decade in Italy I was coming to understand that it made perfect sense.

The door to the sacristy opened, and a young man came in. He kneeled and crossed himself in front of the main altar before taking down the candles and refilling them from a bottle. Evidently, they were not real. Then he kneeled and crossed himself once more.

I got to my feet and walked down the aisle, my feet echoing on the stone floor. The man in dark glasses was still kneeling, a rosary clasped in his hands and his lips moving silently in prayer.

'Excuse me?'

The young acolyte turned to face me. 'Yes, sir?'

'Is the *padre* here?'

He looked over his shoulder towards the sacristy. 'I believe so, sir. I'll just go and see.'

I stood there in the near-silence, listening to the fervent, whispered prayers of the man in dark glasses, and wondered again just what I was going to say.

'Good afternoon.'

The young acolyte – the sacristan? – had returned in the company of a little man who stared at me from behind thick, bottle-bottom glasses. He was dressed casually, a small crucifix on his lapel the only concession to his office.

'*Padre*. I hope you're not too busy?'

'Not at all. Not at all.' He switched into English. 'I'm Don Francesco. How can I help you?'

'My name's Nathan Sutherland. Erm, I don't want to put you to too much trouble, but I'd like to talk about Michele Ballarin. If that's okay with you of course.' Maximum Britishness, I had decided, was the way to go.

Dark Glasses stopped praying for a moment and looked up, and the little priest craned his head to whisper in my ear. 'I think we're disturbing that gentleman. Come with me please, it will be easier to talk in the sacristy.'

'I'm sorry,' I whispered back. I nodded at Dark Glasses as if to apologise, but his lips were already moving again in prayer.

Don Francesco took me through into the sacristy, which was larger than I might have imagined from the dimensions of the building. My eye was immediately caught by the large polyptych on the wall. *The Madonna and the infant Christ in the company of twelve saints*. Federica's first restoration project.

'That's quite lovely,' I said.

Don Francesco smiled for the first time. 'Isn't it? I think we're very lucky to have it. I suppose it should really be in the body of the church but,' he sighed, 'it's not my job to move poor old Tintoretto or whoever he may be after so many years.'

'My wife worked on it, you know?'

'Really? How interesting. But before my time I'm afraid.'

The room was dimly lit but I could still make out, on the opposite wall, an area of plaster of identical dimensions to the painting, somewhat lighter than the surrounding area.

Don Francesco saw the quizzical expression on my face. 'We had to move it,' he said. 'The natural light in here isn't good, and there's nothing we can do about the positioning of the windows. Not without expensive remodelling and permission from the *Comune*, which they won't give us. Every so often someone proposes a scheme to have some proper lighting installed but it never comes to anything. So many other projects, so little time and,' he gave a dry little laugh, 'so little money. Many visitors think we can just send a begging letter to Rome, and the money will arrive by return of post, but no. There's no money in the Church these days.'

I took another look around the room. A small writing desk was placed near the door, with, incongruously, a large pine IKEA wardrobe next to it. The door was ajar revealing a rack of vestments, in all shades of the liturgical year.

Don Francesco chuckled. 'The last one fell to pieces. Centuries of woodworm. It would have cost proper money to have one made by hand and so a flat-pack it had to be. We must move with the times Mr— I'm sorry, remind me again?'

'Sutherland. Nathan Sutherland.'

'From England, I assume?'

'More or less,' I smiled.

'And were you a good friend of *signor* Ballarin?'

'I'd met him once. Twice if you count seeing him through the window of my local bar.'

'I see. Well then, Mr Sutherland, I'm afraid I'm a little confused.'

'It's just that *signor* Ballarin was the business partner of my late father-in-law.'

Don Francesco looked confused for a moment but then his expression cleared.

'Oh, Elio. Elio Ravagnan.'

'You knew him?'

'In his later years. He started coming to Mass again a couple of years before he died. His marriage had broken up, but I imagine you know that. He seemed lonely. I think returning to the Church was of some comfort to him.'

'And Michele Ballarin?'

'I have to say I never really knew him.'

'This wasn't his church?'

'When he was a boy. Before my time. He moved away, somewhere near Santa Maria Elisabetta. But his memorial service and funeral will be held here. He'd left instructions that he wished to be buried with his mother and father.' He sighed. 'And I don't think he had any other church to call his own.'

'I see.' I thought back to the photograph on the website. 'Malamocco must be a lovely place to live and work.'

'Oh, it is. It can be hard in the winter, though. I can't remember how many times we've been flooded out. It's lovely, yes, but it can be difficult at times.'

'I can imagine.' I tried to keep my voice as light as possible. 'How long have you been here, *padre?*'

'Fifteen years now. I've been very lucky. So often the Church moves you on just as you seem to be settling down, but not in my case. This, I think, will be my last position and that pleases me.'

'Fifteen years. Uh-huh.' I paused. 'Do you remember a man called Giuseppe Lupo?'

He removed his glasses, and worried at them with the sleeve of his shirt. 'Lupo?' He bent over a little, the better to observe his polishing and avoid my gaze. 'I don't think I know the name.'

'Or Sandro Vicari?'

'No. No. I'm not sure that means anything to me.' The little priest, I was convinced, would soon have the cleanest glasses in Christendom.

'It's just that there's a photo of the two of them on your church website. Back in 2004. Laughing and joking together with Michele Ballarin on what's described as a "joyous occasion".'

'Mr Sutherland, I'm afraid I don't administer the church website.' He forced out a little laugh. 'Given my computer skills, I think it's best for all concerned that I don't. And 2004 is quite a long time ago.'

I decided to be blunt. '*Padre*, Lupo and Vicari were members of the Mala del Brenta. They were *mafiosi*. And your church website has a photograph of them in the company of Michele Ballarin, my father-in-law's business partner, who was killed three days ago.'

I must have raised my voice because he shushed me and looked towards the door with some alarm.

I raised an eyebrow. 'Afraid someone might hear?'

'I don't think it would be pleasant for visitors or those who come for prayer to have to listen to shouting, do you?'

'I'm not shouting.' I lowered my voice. 'But I'm sorry.'

'Mr Sutherland, I'm still not quite sure exactly what you want from me?'

'I want my wife and mother-in-law to stop being hassled. And to do that I need to find out what connection – if any – Michele Ballarin's law practice had with organised crime. And to do that I need you to help me. Please, *padre*. What was the connection between Ballarin, Lupo and Vicari?'

The air was stuffy now, and Don Francesco had begun to perspire. 'I'm sorry, Mr Sutherland, but I'm really not able to do that. 2004 was a long, long time ago.'

I took a deep breath. 'Okay. I understand. Thanks for your time, *padre*.' I looked around the sacristy. 'It's been lovely to see inside here though. That polyptych is a lovely thing.'

He smiled and nodded, feeling on safer ground now. I cast my eye over the other works on display. Panel paintings, nibbled away by woodworm and brown with age. Faded vestments from long-dead and long-forgotten priests hung in glass cabinets, their original owners identified by semi-legible scrawls on yellowing pieces of card. Pyxes, ciboriums and incense burners, once bright and shining, sat dulled and dusty behind dirty glass panes. I looked back up at the polyptych. It was not, perhaps, as great a work as all that but it was at least a point of light and colour in a room that seemed suffocatingly brown. I felt the need to be out in the fresh air and sunlight again.

Something caught my eye amidst the dullness. I took a closer look and wondered how I had missed it before. In a glass case, surrounded by dusty candlesticks and chalices, stood a monstrance. A gold stand supported a shining sunburst around a small crystal window; the entire piece surmounted with a golden cross.

I whistled.

Don Francesco came over to stand next to me. 'Lovely, isn't it?'

The excesses of the monstrance stood out in sharp relief to the objects that surrounded it. I thought that there was perhaps too much gold to be strictly tasteful, but thought it best not to say so. 'Beautiful,' I said.

The little priest reached into his pocket and took out a key, rusted with age. He fiddled it around in the keyhole for a moment, and opened the cabinet. He took out the monstrance and held it before his eyes, a spark of genuine joy in his eyes.

'Do you know what this holds, Mr Sutherland?'

I shook my head.

'Look closer. In that central crystal chamber.'

I took out my glasses and peered more closely. A thin brown sliver of wood, sharp and pointed.

'Is this what I think it is?' I said.

He smiled. 'From the Crown of Thorns.'

'Wow.' The word seemed inadequate so I quickly added a 'My goodness' as well, which still seemed to lack something. I held out my hands. 'May I?'

He looked unsure for a moment but then his gaze softened. 'Of course. But please be careful.'

I took it from him, and held it up, turning it so as to allow the sunshine to stream through the crystal, my face just centimetres from a thorn that had pierced the flesh of Christ.

'Brought from the Holy Land by pilgrims in the eighth century. St John took it from the foot of the cross, before the Saviour's interment. It is the most precious thing we have.'

I looked at the tiny fragment encased in crystal, and realised that I did not believe a single word of what Don Francesco was saying. And that thought made me just a little bit sad.

I passed it back to him. 'You're very lucky.' He locked it away again and I thought that, surely, it deserved a more secure place to be stored. Then I noticed that the gold had flaked away from the lower part of one of the rays of the sunburst, revealing the base metal beneath. Beyond its contents, then, it perhaps wasn't as valuable as I'd first thought.

I bent closer to look at it, and noticed a faded typewritten label fixed to the shelf. *Restored 2004. With gratitude to Giuseppe Lupo and Alessandro Vicari.*

A 'joyous occasion' indeed. I decided not to say anything. Not yet.

Don Francesco made a show of glancing at his watch.

'I'm sorry, *padre*, I've kept you too long. I do appreciate your help.'

'Well, I'm not sure I was of much use. But I hope things work out for you and your family.'

'Thank you. And thanks for the opportunity to look around here.' I made my way to the door, rested my hand on the handle, and then turned to face him one last time.

'And I do understand, you know. If you can't help.' I stressed the word *can't*, just ever so slightly. I turned again and made my way outside, blinking at the sunlight, and struck by the sudden warmth. The red Ferrari was still there. I was disappointed to see that it didn't have a ticket.

Chapter 24

I had definitely earned a spritz. I chose a bar on the opposite side of the square, and sat there watching life in Malamocco pass by as two old guys on the adjacent table smoked furiously and argued politics over a game of cards. Everywhere, it seemed, had its own local version of Sergio and Lorenzo.

I had chosen the bar deliberately because of its view of the church and sat there nursing my spritz until the ice melted, leaving the Campari tasting warm and sticky. The barista offered me another, but I shook my head. Keeping it clear, I thought, would be a good idea.

Then, across the square, I noticed the man in the dark glasses leaving the church in the company of Don Francesco. The two of them were deep in conversation until the businessman – as I thought of him – gave a stiff little bow of his head, and extended his hand for Don Francesco to shake. Then, as if the ice had been broken, the taller man clapped him on the back with a degree of force that sent the little priest stumbling forward a step. His companion beamed down at him, all the while continuing to vigorously rub his back in a manner I felt would have seemed a little bit familiar between priest and parishioner. Don Francesco was evidently popular amongst his flock.

Dark Glasses turned and walked away. Then he jumped into the Ferrari, and the engine rumbled into life. He gave a wave of his hand and roared away in a squeal of burning rubber. I supposed if one could afford a Ferrari, the cost of tyres – and, indeed, of parking tickets – would seem relatively unimportant.

Don Francesco stood alone, staring at the rapidly disappearing vehicle. Again, he removed his glasses and gave them a furious polish, before making his way with a stiff, deliberate little walk across the square. I raised my glass to him as he passed but he appeared, or pretended, not to notice.

He had told me that he could not remember meeting Giuseppe Lupo, a known mobster and a man whose photograph was to be found on his own church's website. I supposed I should be charitable and take his word for it. But whatever the truth was, he evidently had some very interesting parishioners.

I supposed I should go back to Pellestrina and think about what I'd found, but there was something I needed to do first. I called out to the *barista*. 'Excuse me, but can you tell me if there's a florist around here?'

Federica was right, I thought. There was something just a little mawkish about leaving flowers at accident sites. But Elio Ravagnan, whatever sort of man he might have been, was the father-in-law I'd never meet. He deserved at least a few minutes of my time and a bunch of flowers.

There had been changes since I'd last been at the Curve of Death with Fede. Further accidents had led to a public campaign to erect even heavier-duty crash barriers in addition to the rather grim sign that recorded the number of incidents in the previous twelve months.

I hopped over the barrier, and made my way to the edge. The lagoon, glassy still and calm except for the passing of a few small boats, lay spread out in front of me, whilst the abandoned island of Poveglia lay to my right, overgrown but the remains of its crumbling mental hospital still clearly visible.

I examined the drop. It really wasn't that far. If you were lucky and took the curve that little bit too fast, you might just be left with a recovery job, an expensive insurance claim and a story that you might dine out on for years to come. If you weren't lucky . . . I looked around the grassy area, and saw several hefty trees, one of which had a wilted bunch of flowers laid at the base. I placed mine next to them, and stood there for a few minutes in silence.

I walked on for perhaps a kilometre, thinking about Elio's last journey. The road stretched out before me; a long, straight strip of tarmac. You could, if you were so inclined, hoon around like a lunatic if you were possessed of a big enough engine and small enough genitals.

I turned and looked back towards the lagoon, and the Curve of Death.

It would be quite easy to get it wrong, I thought, as I started my walk back into Malamocco. Late at night on a nice straight road. Turning up the heating against the chilly night outside. One drink too many before setting out. One for the road. It's a short journey, home in ten minutes, what harm can it do? Perhaps you're driving just a little faster than you should, but the police never check along this stretch at this time of night. And then the curve is upon you. You wrench at the wheel, the tyres screech but there's not enough purchase. You run out of road. And then you run out of time.

I was almost back at the curve, lost in my own thoughts. A few cars passed by me, and one of them parped his horn, the driver jabbing his finger in the direction of the pavement on the other side of the road. Quite right too, I thought. It was a silly risk to be taking. I should cross over.

I heard the scream of the oncoming car before I could even turn my head to check for traffic. The red Ferrari had returned, its engine howling as it barrelled towards the curve.

Towards me.

Jesus!

I froze but only for a fraction of a second before I hurled myself over the barrier, rolling over and over in an attempt to put as much space between myself and the car as possible. I heard another screech of tyres over the blood pounding in my ears, and then I felt myself thud into a solid object. Something soft crumpled under my chest, and I winced as I felt something penetrate my skin.

I lay there, my eyes closed, panting, as the sound of the car engine receded. I breathed deeply, and then opened my eyes. I was at the base of a large tree.

I looked down to see Elio's bunch of flowers crushed against my chest, and my T-shirt torn and bloody from where the thorns had scratched me through the fabric.

Shaking, I got to my feet, and dropped the flowers to the earth. Then I immediately felt guilty and bent to arrange them as best I could against the base of the tree. Then I slumped back down in order to keep them company as I waited for my legs to stop shaking before I set out on the walk back into Malamocco.

Chapter 25

I stopped back at the bar opposite the church for a second, but completely necessary, spritz and went into the bathroom to try and clean myself up as best I could. A few leaves were tangled in my hair, my jacket and trousers were covered in dried mud and my T-shirt was torn and bloodied. I'd left the bar just thirty minutes ago looking as dapper as I ever would. Now I looked as if I'd been in a fight.

The barista gave me a curious look, as well he might. My hands trembled as I drank my spritz and he gave a sad little shake of his head.

'I can explain this, you know,' I said.

His face assumed the tired expression of someone who was well practised in dealing with people who began sentences with 'I can explain this, you know.' He nodded as if to indicate that he was going to at least pretend to be interested whilst all the while doing something else, and turned to attend to some glasses which had suddenly become in urgent need of polishing.

'No, really, I can explain this. I was walking out of town – just by that bend in the road, the one you call the Curve of Death. And I was, I suppose, on the wrong side of the road.'

He turned round to look at me, shaking his head and wagging his finger. 'Ah, *signore*, that's very dangerous. You need to be careful there. Cars come round there very fast, you don't see them until it's too late.'

'You're not kidding. I almost got run over.'

He smiled, thinly. '*Signore*, I think I can see that. You've been very lucky.'

I wondered whether I should push it any further, and decided I should. 'It was a red Ferrari. I suppose it would have been a glamorous way to go.'

He stopped polishing glasses, and swore under his breath.

'Do you know who has a car like that?' I said.

He nodded. 'I know.'

'Would you like to tell me who?'

'It depends. Would you like to tell me what you're going to do?'

There were times, in Italy, when being as English as possible paid dividends. This, I decided, was one of those. 'I'm going to jolly well give him a piece of my mind,' I said.

He burst out laughing.

'What's so funny?'

'Mister, that car belongs to Albino Lupo. You don't give him a piece of your mind. Unless you want a piece of yours to be splattered against a wall.'

'Lupo.' I frowned, as if trying to recall the name, and tinked the edge of my glass with a fingernail. 'I think I know him. But I thought he'd died recently?'

'That's his father you're thinking of. Albino is his boy.'

'I see. I saw him in church earlier. Praying quite fervently. And then he left and started driving equally fervently. Not the most practical car to have on the Lido, I'd have thought?'

'He doesn't live here. He just brought the car over with him. Nobody knows what he's doing here. People say it's just "a business trip".'

'And he needs the muscle car for that?'

'He doesn't need it at all. He only has it to show that he has it. And if he wants to drive like a maniac up and down the *litorale* every day, then no one seems to care.'

'I'd have thought the police might?'

'Mister, nobody wants to get involved. Albino Lupo wants to bring his big expensive car over here? Fine. He wants to eat in the finest restaurants, drink the finest wines? Fine. He wants to drive back to his hotel a bit faster than he should?'

'Fine?' I said.

'Fine. As long as he doesn't hurt anyone. And if he kills himself one day on the *Curva della Morte* . . .' His voice trailed off.

'Also fine?' I suggested.

'*Beh*, you didn't hear that from me. Better to say, the sooner he sorts his business out the sooner he can piss off back to the mainland.'

'I understand.' I sipped at my spritz. The ice cubes had almost melted now, a sign that summer, proper summer, was on its way; when a crisp and bitter Campari spritz needed to be chilled within an inch of its life to save it from becoming sticky and sickly.

The barista seemed happy to have finished the conversation, and turned away from me in search of an imaginary job to do.

I wasn't quite finished yet. 'I mean, I understand why you

want him to be gone. But I don't understand why you tolerate this.'

'I'm sorry?' He looked genuinely confused.

'Why do you put up with this shit? The guy's father was a *mafioso*. He turns up here driving his flash car for inadequately endowed men up and down every day. Why do you put up with it? The guy's probably a crook and he's rubbing your faces in it every day. Why are the cops tolerating it?'

'Mister,' he shook his head, 'you're not from around here are you?'

'I'm from Venice. That's thirty minutes away.'

'That's not what I meant. And this is Venice as well. How long have you been here? In Italy?'

'Maybe ten years.'

'Ten years. Okay. So you should know by now. Firstly, the police don't arrest him because nobody wants to. You want to be the guy who arrests a suspected *mafioso*? Really? You got a lovely wife and children at home? Maybe you want them to live under police protection for the rest of their lives? For what? Because the guy broke a few speeding laws?' He shook his head. 'Second thing is this. I remember back in the nineties. I lived out on *terraferma* then. We knew something was wrong when every Billy Big Balls started driving around in Ferraris, Lamborghinis, Porsches. That sort of thing. Where did they get that sort of money from? Working in *papà's gelateria*? There was the *Mala del Brenta* and also *Clan Giostrai*, you know, the Carnival boys? And the Mestrini gang. And who knows how many others. Then in the 1990s the cops — there were brave ones you know, smart ones – they brought it all down.

'It never quite went away. But we could pretend it had. Not so much violence at any rate, and that was enough. And now this prick is here, driving up and down in his big car. But one day he'll go away and we can pretend everything is back to normal again, because he'll be someone else's problem. Somewhere where they're used to dealing with proper crooks. Do you understand that, Englishman?'

I nodded, and drained the last of my spritz. 'I do.'

'I'm sorry about,' he ran his hands through his hair in order to indicate my general state of dishevelment, 'what happened to you.'

'Thank you. And don't worry, I'm not going to do anything stupid.'

'Good.' He wagged his finger at me. 'You be sure you don't.'

I took out my wallet and laid five euros on the table. '*Arriverderci*,' I said, and turned to go.

He called after me. 'Mister, a spritz is two fifty.'

'Let's call it a tip,' I said.

'Thanks. It's a hell of tip for one drink.'

'Yes, but you might just have helped to save my life as well. I reckon that's worth two fifty.'

Chapter 26

It was mid-afternoon by now. I could have gone back to Venice. It would have been nice to have had a beer and a chat with Dario. I wondered if Vanni might be able to help me – a chat with a friendly cop seemed like a good idea. But I felt dirty and sweaty and the thought of a long *vaporetto* journey in a hot cabin didn't appeal. I wanted to be back on Pellestrina, to have a shower and a lie-down, and then I could throw foam balls for a grumpy cat, call Fede, and think about what to have for dinner.

Most buses were air conditioned these days but it was always a bit of a lottery as to whether it would be switched on or not. Today, inevitably, my numbers had not come up and the crowded bus felt sweaty and sticky. I would have taken my jacket off but was aware that I might look in even more of a state if I did. So I stood there and swayed and sweated as I hung on to my strap, until the bus reached the terminus at Faro Rochetta for the ferry to Pellestrina.

This time, at least, there was no angry cat in a box to carry. I got off the bus and stood there with the other passengers on the ferry as we made our way across the lagoon.

I kept half an eye on the bus. Most of the passengers had

disembarked, in search of a blessed breath of fresh air. If I timed it right, I could grab a seat for the remainder of the journey. Or would that be dishonourable?

'*Signore!*'

Someone was shouting on the other side of the ferry. I closed my eyes and leaned my head back against the bus. The metal was uncomfortably hot so I straightened up again and opened my eyes.

'*Signore*. Hey, Mister!'

A man on the opposite side of the ferry, leaning against the edge with a cigarette in his hand, was calling out to me.

'Hey, Mister. Are you okay?'

I really, really did not want to get into a conversation. All I wanted to do was to get into a hot shower and a cold Negroni. I nodded and smiled and said, 'Fine, thank you.'

He grinned and chucked his cigarette over the side. Then he walked over to me.

Oh crap.

He leaned back against the side of the bus, and patted me on the shoulder. 'Good. Good. It's just I saw you with your shirt all,' he made a wiggly gesture with his fingers in order to demonstrate just what a state he thought my T-shirt was in, 'and I thought, hey, maybe that guy's not doing so well? Maybe he needs a hand?'

He took out a packet of cigarettes and offered me one. I recognised the packet. JPS reds. Cheapo fags. Desperation fags. I waved it away.

'Thanks. I've given up.'

'You've given up. That's fantastic. I wish I could.' He lit up and turned his head away from me in order not to blow the smoke into my face, but the light breeze wafted it back in my direction.

I was hot, and feeling just a little battered and bruised. The reek of the cigarette smoke combined with the smell of petrol, added to the possibly inadvisable but necessary two lunchtime spritzes, made my head spin. I wanted nothing so much as to throw up and crawl into bed. But bed was still a long way away.

'My wife says to me all the time, Rico, these things are going to kill you. Won't you give them up for me? And I say, sweetheart, of course I will. But not just yet, you know?'

We were, perhaps, just five minutes from the landing on Pellestrina. Then just another ten minutes down the road. I could do this. I could smile and nod and say 'yes' to my new companion for as long as it took.

The engine of the bus rumbled into life, sending hot exhaust fumes blowing around us and making my stomach lurch once again. I got back on board. Let there be a single seat. Please, let there be a single seat. That way I can sit by myself and my new pal Rico will not be able to sit next to me.

No seats. No seats at all. Still, the bus was crowded. I could push my way to the opposite end of the bus.

'Mister. Hey, mister!'

Almost against my will, I felt myself turning around. Rico had bagged a double seat and was patting the one next to him. 'Over here, mister.'

I didn't think I could refuse, and made my way to the back. I sat down next to him and gave as thin a smile as I could whilst still being polite.

'Thank you.'

'No problem my friend, no problem. You see the old *signora* down the front there?'

I looked. An elderly lady was hanging on to the overhead strap and swaying alarmingly whenever the bus made a slight turn.

I nodded.

'She got on at the middle door by mistake. Couldn't get here in time. I just beat her to it.' He laughed and laughed, which then turned into a coughing fit.

There was perhaps one way out of this. 'Oh, she's older than me,' I said. 'I should give her the seat.'

I made to stand up, but he pulled me back into my seat again. 'Are you kidding? You look like shit, my friend – no offence. You need this seat more.'

'That's kind, but—'

'Kind, nothing. Besides,' he coughed up a laugh again, 'she's not that much older than you.' He clapped me on the back. 'Joking, again.'

I didn't dare to look at my watch. Surely, by now, it had to be less than ten minutes. Perhaps I should just get off and walk the rest of the way. But what if that turned out to be his stop?

Don't do anything stupid, Fede had said. And now I appeared to have met the most irritating man in Italy, and he wanted to be my friend.

'You're English, aren't you?' he said, suddenly switching languages.

'I am, yes.'

'I thought so. Your accent, you know? That's okay, we can speak English. My teacher always told me it was important. Learn English and travel the world, she said.'

I smiled. 'Well, she must have done a good job.'

'Good job, shit. All my English I learned later. After I left school.' He jabbed me in the arm. 'Were you good at school?'

'Erm, I guess I was okay.'

'University?'

'Yes.'

'I thought so. I thought you seemed like a scholar. Where are you going, mister?'

'Madonna dell'Apparizione.' I was too tired to bluff it out.

'Ahhhh!' He raised his eyebrows and his hands in perfect synchronisation. 'That's where I've seen you.'

Oh. Crap.

He shook me by the shoulder. 'Yes, I remember. You're the Englishman staying in the old Ravagnan house.'

There seemed little point in denying it. 'Yes. That's me.'

He looked puzzled for a moment. 'But you're with an Italian woman?'

'My wife. Yes. We're on honeymoon.' I bit my tongue but it was too late. Why in God's name had I mentioned that?

'Ahhhh! Congratulations, sir!' For a terrible moment I thought he was going to lean over and kiss me. 'So where is your wife today? Don't tell me,' he elbowed me in the ribs and grinned, 'she's still sleeping, yes?'

'Actually, she's visiting her mother.'

'Her mother?' He threw back his head and laughed, slapping me on the thigh. 'She's gone back to her mother's already? My friend, you must be the unluckiest man in the world.'

'Well, right now I kind of feel like it,' I said, through gritted teeth.

He laughed some more, and shook his head. Then he jabbed the shoulder of the man in front of us and muttered something in *Veneziano* to him. The man smiled politely, but turned away with a look of vague disgust.

I tried to size up my companion as best I could without looking directly at him. Inexpensively but relatively smartly dressed with neatly cut hair. Short but powerfully built. Smoked a cheap and nasty brand of cigarettes. No smell of alcohol on him – unlike me, I had to admit. But there was nothing that marked him out as someone who'd hassle a complete stranger on the bus for a merciless quarter-hour.

I could get off at the next stop, I thought. It was only a few kilometres. A few kilometres in the afternoon sun, feeling hot and bruised and beaten up, but manageable nevertheless.

Tempting. But there was the possibility, no matter how remote, that my new best friend might choose to follow me and I'd be stuck with his company for longer. I risked a glance at my watch. Maybe five minutes. That seemed manageable in a way that a long walk in the heat did not.

Finally, blessedly, the bus pulled up at Madonna dell'Apparizione. I nodded and smiled at my new pal and shuffled my way through the crowd to the doors. I stepped off, breathed in the fresh air mixed with the scent of petrol, closed my eyes and sighed.

'That's better, eh?'

My eyes snapped open.

'This is my stop,' he smiled.

I thought about it. He knew I was staying in Elio Ravagnan's house. So it was entirely possible he lived nearby.

There was, indeed, a dreadful possibility that we were going to have to be best friends until we left Pellestrina.

'You live here then?' I said.

He looked confused for a moment, and then shook his head. 'Me. No. I'm just visiting like you.'

I nodded at him. 'Have a good evening,' I said, in the hope that that would be enough. I made to turn into the narrow street that led down to the lagoon, but a car cut right in front of me making me jump.

He put his hand on my arm. 'Careful now.' He leaned over and stared directly into my face, close enough for me to smell the cheap cigarettes on his breath once more. 'Are you sure you're okay? You look shook up.'

I stepped back, but he did not remove his hand. 'I'm fine. Just a bit tired that's all.'

He grinned. 'Your honeymoon. I understand.' He punched my arm again. 'I'm joking, my friend.' He looked right and then left. 'Okay, no cars coming.'

We walked past the small supermarket on the corner. There were a few things I needed to get but I had the horrible feeling that he'd follow me in. So we made our way down to the lagoon front and I tried to think of a polite way to shake him off, all the while cursing myself for being so British.

I could see our house in the near distance, and imagined he'd seen it as well. I was not going to invite him in for a cup of tea, but I could imagine a long, long chat on the doorstep as I prayed for him to leave. Or, worse, having to go for a drink with him.

I put my hand to my jacket pocket and felt my mobile

phone there. I supposed I could suddenly invent an emergency phone call, summoning me back to Venice, or Chioggia or the Lido or, well, anywhere that seemed a reassuringly long way away.

Was I really going to do something so childish? Was I really going to do something so pathetic?

Yes. Yes, I was.

I was reaching into my pocket when my companion spoke up again.

'So. Elio Ravagnan's house, then?'

I took my hand away from my pocket, and stopped walking. 'Yes,' I said, guardedly.

'Is it a nice place? It looks like a nice place.'

'It is. It needs a bit of work, I suppose.'

'Ah. I could find you someone there. A good carpenter, a good plumber. Whatever you need. You've gotta be careful you know. Get the wrong person, they hear you with an English accent and then,' he spat on the ground, 'they double the price. These guys won't. These guys are honest.'

I paused, weighing my words carefully. 'I thought you didn't live on Pellestrina,' I said, keeping my voice as light as possible.

'Me, no. I told you, I'm just visiting.'

'Ah, okay. It's just that you seem to know people. Tradesmen and the like.'

'No no. These guys live on the Lido. Not *Pellestrinotti.*'

'Sure. I understand. Well, thank you. I'll bear it in mind.'

I was slowing my footsteps now, to put off the evil moment of arriving at the house.

'So. Did you ever know Elio Ravagnan?'

I shook my head. 'He died about the time I arrived in Venice.'

'Your wife ever tell you the stories about him?'

I stopped walking and turned to face him.

'There are no stories about him,' I said.

He laughed. 'Apart from the ones about where he got his money from. He and his business partner.'

'What do you mean?' I said, my voice rising.

'That he let that house out. As a safe house. To *mafiosi*.'

I snapped, and grabbed the lapels of his jacket, trying to pull him closer to me. 'Listen here. I don't know what crap you've heard but you keep it to yourself. You understand?'

He slapped my hands away, and stepped back. I moved towards him and tried to grab him again, but he evaded my grasp and slapped them away once more. A group of kids were starting to stare at us in the hope that a particularly crap fight might develop into something more interesting.

He was laughing now. 'Mister, mister. Stop. Please.'

I stepped back, and lowered my hands, breathing deeply.

He held up his hands. 'I don't want any trouble. Really. I can help you.'

'You can? Oh good. Beyond getting me a really good plumber what can you do?'

'Listen,' he lowered his voice. 'The stories about Elio. You know they're a load of shit. I know they're a load of shit. The trouble is the press know all the stories. And after his partner was found dead – well, they'll swarm all over you.' He paused. 'I'm surprised they haven't been knocking on your door already.' I said nothing, but my face must have betrayed me. 'Ah. They've been round then?'

I sighed. 'One telephoned yesterday, yes.'

'And what did you tell her?'

'We told her to leave us the hell alone.'

'Okay. That was the right thing to do. I can help you with this.'

'As I said, you can? Tell me how.'

'I know people, you know. Journalists. People in the press. I can stop them harassing you.'

I looked him up and down. 'And just how are you going to do that? And what's in it for you? Do you want money?'

He looked affronted. 'No no. No money. I just need you to be honest with me. Tell me about Ravagnan. About Ballarin. Be honest with me. Everything you know about them, about the house.' He paused. 'And about Giuseppe Lupo.'

I shook my head. 'Oh Christ. You're another journalist, aren't you? This is pathetic.'

'Mister, I'm not a journalist. I'm your friend. I'm trying to help.'

We'd reached the garden gate by now. 'You're not my friend. And the best way you can help me is – and I say this with absolutely no respect at all – is to get the hell out of here.'

He held up his hands again. 'Okay. Okay. I'm going. But have a think about what I said.'

'I've thought about it. It's a shit idea. Now go.' I heard scrabbling from the other side of the front door. 'I'm on my way, Gramsci,' I called out.

Rico looked confused for a moment. 'Okay. But if you change your mind, just let me know.' He paused. 'See you around, my friend.' I watched him make his way down the street until he was safely out of sight, and then went inside.

I closed the door, leaned my back against it, and sighed. Gramsci sat at the top of the stairs looking down at me.

'You know, Grams?' I said. 'This morning the worst thing that was going to happen to me all day was my dead father-in-law being linked with the Venetian mafia. Oh, and my wife going back to her mother's. That wasn't great either. But no, that wasn't actually as low as it could go. The worst thing, it seems, is that the most irritating man in the Veneto wants to be my friend.'

Gramsci miaowed, whether in sympathy or from need of food I couldn't tell.

'Although, now I think of it, there might be something just a little bit worse than that. And that could be that he's not simply the most aggravating man on the planet. But maybe something more and just a little bit scarier.'

Gramsci padded downstairs and allowed me to scratch him behind the ears for a second, before jumping on top of the sofa, and, from there, leaping on to the top of the book-shelf in order to glare down at me.

'So what do you think, eh?'

I went over to the shelves and ran my fingers across the spines of the books.

Something wasn't right.

Federica had taken *Pinocchio* from the shelves yesterday, prior to throwing it at me. I'd laid it down on the table, and then replaced it on the right of the shelf. It was now in the middle. Indeed, as I looked closer, I could see that all the books that had previously been on the right of the shelf were now on the left, and vice versa. As if somebody had taken them down in two stacks, and put them back in the wrong order.

Why?

Were they looking for something? Had they put the books back in the wrong order by accident? Or – and this worried me even more – had they done it on purpose, hoping I'd notice, just to screw with my head?

I replaced *Pinocchio* where it had been and went back to the front door. I ran my hands over the wood. Nothing splintered, nothing forced. I put on my glasses and looked at the metal around the lock. Nothing scratched – at least not recently. Then I went to the back door and did the same.

Nothing.

Whoever had done this had not needed to break in. Which meant they had a key. Which meant that they could come back at any time.

There was something else my new acquaintance had said. *What did you tell her?* Why had he assumed the journalist was a woman?

I looked at the books on the shelves, and then back at Gramsci. I went to the kitchen, poured myself a glass of pro-secco and slumped into a chair.

'He's not just a profoundly irritating little man, is he, Grams?' I took a drink, and then pressed the cool glass against my forehead. 'This, I'm afraid, is something worse.'

Gramsci miaowed.

Chapter 27

I woke up next morning and decided I needed a cop. And that meant Vanni.

There were plenty of other things I needed. A bottle of milk in the fridge, Gramsci to start being nice, a beer with Dario. Federica being home would have been good as well, but she'd telephoned to say that she was spending another day with Marta. I'd been sparing in what I'd told her. I hadn't mentioned my new friend, and a near-death experience involving a fast car driven by a possible *mafioso* had also slipped my mind.

That was the problem. The big five-letter word.

Mafia.

Before I ever moved to Venice, friends asked me – only sometimes in jest – if I was worried about the mafia. My reply was that I was going to work as a translator, and not as an anti-corruption judge and so I didn't think they'd pay very much attention to me.

Well, here I was, still working as a translator and now very much concerned that if I wasn't careful they might start paying an uncomfortable amount of attention to me. This wasn't something I dared mess around with. I needed professional help, and I wasn't sure if Busetto was the ideal person. I telephoned Vanni, and arranged to meet him for a late breakfast. Then I called Dario and arranged to meet him for a late lunch.

The long journey back to Venice at least gave me the chance to read the newspapers thoroughly. Michele Ballarin's death was still big news. His memorial service had been scheduled for the following day at the Madonna della Marina. That was something to pencil in. It might be interesting to see the sort of people who'd turn up. Hopefully Fede would be back by then. It would be a nice thing to do together on our honeymoon.

'Just coffee?' said Vanni.

'Thanks.'

He narrowed his eyes. 'Not *corretto*?'

I shook my head. 'Too early in the day, even for me. I need to keep a clear head.'

We stood outside Bar Filovia, watching the crowds in Piazzale Roma come and go. Tourists piled on to crowded vaporetti, whilst locals fought their way in the opposite direction, prior to cramming on to buses that would take them to Mestre and beyond. Japanese visitors with suitcases that could have blocked out the sun battled for space with old ladies and their shopping trolleys. A queue was forming at the ticket office whilst tourists stood in line at the ticket machines, baffled by the range of transport options on offer and the fact that the selection seemed to vary according to language.

'I thought we might have gone somewhere more private, Vanni. This is kind of a delicate matter.'

He nibbled away at his brioche, trying and failing to stop flakes of pastry falling on his shirt. 'I thought this was the best place.'

'Are you kidding? All the world and his brother seems to be here.'

'Yes, but nobody's paying any attention to anything except where to go and where to get a ticket.' He laughed. 'Did you want us to meet in a church, like in the movies?'

'I thought somewhere quiet would be good.'

'This is quiet. As long as we don't listen to other people. Trust me, this is one of the most anonymous places we could be. Hiding in plain sight, you might say.'

'I see. If you say so.'

'Also I was hungry and wanted to get out of the office. Breakfast is better here.'

'Oh.'

'So. You want to talk about Giuseppe Lupo.'

I looked around us to check if somebody had picked up on the name, as if even mentioning it was capable of summoning his shade from beyond the grave. Vanni noticed and chuckled. 'He's not capable of doing you any harm now, Nathan.'

'I'm not so sure.'

'Cold in the ground one month now.' He reached for his phone. 'Take a look at this.'

It was face of the man I'd seen on the website of the Madonna della Marina. He looked somewhat older, and his hair had thinned, yet he was smiling at the camera and there was the ghost of a twinkle in his eye.

'Looks like your favourite grandfather, doesn't he?' I nodded. 'The difference is, Grandad here was quite capable of having you killed.' He showed me another photo. I didn't recognise the face at first glance, hidden as it was behind a long white beard. His hair was dishevelled, and he peered out at the camera from behind glasses. The expression on his face, however, was the same, and the twinkle in the eyes was still there. He looked as if he'd just played an elaborate practical joke on someone and was pleased at his cleverness.

'This was taken in early 2011. Looks a bit different, doesn't he?'

'Like Gandalf. No, not that. Not quite twinkly enough. More like that Bosnian war criminal. Karadzic. Just after they tracked him down.'

'Heh. That's what I thought. Although I don't believe anyone ever accused Mr Karadzic of twinkliness. And, just like him, Lupo was so convinced of his own cleverness that he thought the beard was enough of a disguise. This was taken just after he was arrested in Chioggia.'

'It was definitely Chioggia then? Not Pellestrina?'

'No. Why do you ask?'

'Vanni, people have been asking us questions about the house that belonged to Federica's dad. Or perhaps it's better to say that they've been *telling* us things – that it had been used as a safe house for *mafiosi,* including Giuseppe Lupo. I don't know if they're trying to blackmail us, or if there's something important that we're supposed to know about it – but whatever it is, it's not going away.'

Vanni said nothing.

'Vanni, this is nonsense. Isn't it?'

'Hmm. Well, it's probably nonsense. Except—'

'Oh God.' I drained my coffee and set the cup down. 'Except?'

'There were stories circulating at the time. That Lupo had been seen on Pellestrina. The *carabinieri* denied it of course.'

'Why would they do that, if there was any truth in it?'

'Nathan, Ravagnan's house is a two-minute walk from the *carabinieri* station. Remember what I said about hiding in plain sight? They wouldn't be in a rush to admit that a senior member of the *Mala del Brenta* had been living practically next door for months without them noticing. And remember – until he tried to fence those two diamonds, he hadn't actually done anything wrong in the eyes of the law.'

'I suppose not. But why wasn't this in the papers?'

'Ballarin and Ravagnan were lawyers. Very good ones. And so they might have also have been very good at keeping stories out of the papers. The problem is,' he sighed, 'both Ballarin and Ravagnan are now dead. If there is any truth in this – and I'm not saying there is – there's nothing to prevent it all coming out now. You'll need to speak to Federica about it.'

'There's no easy way of doing something like that, Vanni.'

'Welcome to married life, Nathan. You'll find a way.' He paused. 'You've come a long way to speak to me.'

'I didn't know who else I could speak to.'

'Nobody on Pellestrina?'

'There's the *carabinieri*. The main guy is a *maresciallo* Busetto. But—' I searched for the right words. 'I keep thinking he's waiting for us to trip up somehow, or say the wrong thing. He just seems to be suspicious of us for some reason.'

'Busetto.' He shook his head. 'I don't know him. Perhaps

he hasn't been there that long. But then I don't know all that many *carabinieri*.'

'You don't speak to them?'

He sighed. 'Not as much as you might expect. Not as much as we ought. Historical reasons and all that nonsense, you know?'

I nodded. 'I'm not sure I'll ever understand the difference between all your police forces, no matter how long I live here.'

Vanni chuckled. 'I'm not sure if I ever will, to be honest.'

'Anyway, this whole business about Fede's father and the Venetian mafia. It's nonsense of course, but he seems to be worrying away at it like a dog with a bone.'

'Well of course he is. He's a cop on Pellestrina. Pellestrina! How much crime do they get there? Petty theft, or illegal fishing. And now he's got a case which might involve actual *mafiosi*. This would be the highlight of his whole career. Stories in the newspapers, perhaps a nice transfer upstairs. Maybe even a book deal? I can imagine the film rights.'

'Oh, marvellous. Marvellous.'

He patted me on the back. 'Look, Nathan. If he wants to speak to you, then speak to him.' He wagged a finger at me. 'I'll be honest with you. I can't go treading on his toes.' He paused. 'However—'

'However?'

'You can always give me a call, you know? I'll do what I can, even if that might not be much.'

'Thanks, Vanni. You're a pal.'

'No problem.' He checked his watch. 'And now I need to get back.' He reached for his wallet. 'I'll get these.'

'That doesn't seem fair.'

'I insist. Call it another wedding present. Talking of which, where is the lovely Federica?'

'She's gone back to her mother's.'

Vanni laughed and then saw the expression on my face. 'You're serious?'

I sighed. 'It's a long story . . .'

Chapter 28

I had time to kill before meeting Dario, and so took the long walk down through Cannaregio. I stopped to take money out of a cashpoint, straining my eyes to make out the instructions on screen that were barely visible in the bright sunlight, and singeing my fingers on the burning-hot keypad. Summer had definitely arrived.

I folded the notes away inside my wallet and turned to make my way down Strada Nova, nearly tripping over two tourists who'd sat themselves down next to the ATM without me noticing. I apologised, it being the British thing to do, and they nodded at me as if to say apology accepted. They were eating spaghetti in tomato sauce from a cardboard container. Pasta to go. That was the latest thing. Time had become so precious to us that we now needed to eat spaghetti in the street.

I shook my head, and continued on my way, swept along by the hordes of visitors. Down through Cannaregio, past Rialto, into Campo San Salvador and along the *calle* into Campo San Luca and then Campo Manin. The crowd, thankfully, had thinned out a little and I sat for a moment at the base of Manin's statue, sweeping my damp hair out of my eyes. I looked up at him and shook my head. 'Ah, Daniele, this is becoming hard work, isn't it?'

Manin said nothing, that being the way of statues. He'd ended his days teaching Italian in a girls' school in Paris. That must have seemed even harder than organising a rebellion against the Austrians. I closed my eyes, and wished I was back on Pellestrina, sitting on the *murazzi* and looking out at the sea, with only Federica for company and just the sound of the gulls and the sea in our ears.

I shook my head and got to my feet. Manin, I was sure, would have had none of this nonsense. Time to get to work, Nathan.

Dario and I were the only people sitting inside the Brazilians, every other visitor making use of the tables outside. But sitting in the heat was not a novelty if you had to face a Venetian summer every year and, since I'd given up smoking, there was no longer a need for us to be in the open air.

We clinked glasses. 'It was nice to see you all the other day, you know?'

'Yeah. It was for us too. Just how I'd imagined it when we moved back to Venice. All of us on the beach together, you grilling fish, Emily taking her first walk on the sand.'

'Dead man being dredged up from the bottom of the lagoon?'

'Mmm. Yeah, that wasn't so great.'

'Sorry about that.'

He shrugged. 'Wasn't your fault.'

I sighed. 'I think it might be. Listen . . . it's a bit of a long story.'

***

Dario drained his glass, and then held it up to the light as if to confirm that it was, indeed, empty, and nodded. He turned to Eduardo.

'I think we need another round of drinks.'

Ed nodded. 'I think you do.'

Neither of them were smiling.

'Are you serious about this, Nat?' said Dario. 'Really, properly serious?'

'Sure I am. We're going to prove that Federica's dad had nothing to do with the mafia, and life will get back to normal. Maybe we'll have another barbecue, you can all come over again, and this time nobody will have to be dredged up from the bottom of the sea.' I turned to Ed. 'You should come as well, Ed.'

He smiled. 'Really? Thanks, Nat.'

Dario was still not smiling.

'You don't agree?' I said.

He shook his head.

'Ed won't get in the way. I promise.'

Dario exhaled, slowly.

'Okay. I'm joking. But, seriously, what would you do?'

Dario looked me straight in the eye. 'I'd leave it,' he said.

'You're serious?'

'Absolutely.'

'Dario, you don't really believe that any of this is true? That Fede's dad was linked with the mob.'

'No. I don't believe it. But obviously some people do. That *carabiniero* on Pellestrina. That journalist you told me about.'

'If she was a journalist. I'm not convinced.'

'Doesn't matter. If she is a journalist so much the better. Alternative is worse. Much worse. And then there's that weird guy who you met on the bus.'

'Uh-huh.'

'All of these people believe it. And, trust me, that's gonna cause you problems. Just let it drop and hopefully they'll all go away.'

'You mean I should just let them sniff around as much as they like, digging up as much dirt as they like – whether it's true or not doesn't matter – on Elio. Harassing my wife and my mother-in-law. That's what you're saying?'

Dario set his glass down on the table. 'Yes. That's exactly what I'm saying.'

'Okay. That's not the answer I was expecting. Are you going to tell me why?'

'Because you're my friend. You both are. And I don't want to see you get hurt.'

'Dario, I think I can handle it.'

'With respect, *vecio*, I don't think you can. This isn't some old crooked guy with a collection of fake art. This isn't a soprano with a sugar-daddy conductor. This is the mob. So don't get involved. Step away. And hopefully it will blow over.'

We sat there together in silence, and I thought about what he'd said. He was right, of course. There was only one sensible course of action.

'But I can't do that,' I sighed.

Dario dropped his gaze and patted me on the shoulder. 'I know you can't, Nat,' he said.

'What would you do, Dario? You'd try and sort things out, wouldn't you?'

'You know I would.' He took a deep breath. 'So. What can I do?'

'At the moment nothing. But that's fine. Anything apart from telling me I'm a crazy bastard who's going to get himself killed is fine.'

'Nat, you are a crazy bastard and – if you don't take care – you are going to get yourself killed.' I grinned and his eyes crinkled as he smiled back. Just a little. 'But you're sure there's nothing I can do?'

'Nothing. At least for the moment.'

'Okay. You'll tell me, though?'

I nodded. 'Dario, this is going to seem like a strange question. And I don't know if I feel comfortable asking it. But have you ever come across anything like this? Mafia, you know?'

He gave a half-laugh. 'What is this, "you're Italian, you must have met the mafia?" That kind of thing?'

'You know I don't mean that. But seriously – have you ever had anything to do with them?' His face darkened. 'Whoah, sorry, badly expressed. I mean have you ever come across anyone who you knew was in the mob?'

'Hmm. Once maybe. It's not all that dramatic though. Vally and I were on holiday. Sicily. There were these fish – little, tiny baby fish – *neonati*. I'd only ever tried them once, and thought they were just about the best things in the world. Anyway, we were at this restaurant. It was our anniversary so it was somewhere smart, you know? And I remember asking the waiter if they had any *neonati*. And the guy looks shocked, kind of offended. "No sir," he says, "of course not. It's against the law to catch them at this time of year." So I do a lot of apologising, say I'm from up North and things are different there. Choose something else from the menu. And then – then – two guys come in. They're smartly dressed, but nothing flash. Could just have been two businessmen. They sit down, one of them flicks through the menu. He sighs, closes it. He looks bored. But the thing is he wants everyone to notice just how bored he is.

'He calls the waiter over. He asks him – and he's speaking just about loud enough for people to hear, because he wants to be heard – if there are any *neonati*. And the waiter nods. He doesn't say "Of course, sir" or anything. The expression on his face doesn't change. He just nods. And he goes away, fetches these guys a plate of little fish. And the two of them just sit there and eat, they don't even look like they're having that great a time. Maybe they're not. Because they've ordered these damn fish not because they want them, but just because they can. And because they can be seen to be doing it.' He shook his head. 'You understand what I mean?'

I nodded. 'I do.' I checked my watch and then finished my beer. 'Okay, I need to be going. I've got a bag of kitty biscuits for Gramsci to pick up from the flat. Come on up for a moment.'

'Sure.'

I waved at Ed. 'Okay, Ed, I'm not sure when I'll next see you.'

He furrowed his brow. 'You mean you're going to prison or you're going to be killed?'

'No, I mean I'm on my honeymoon having a lovely time with my lovely wife. And so I don't know when I'll be home again.'

'Oh that. Right. You both have a good time, yeah?'

'We will. Cheers, Ed.'

We made our way outside, and weaved our way through the tables that were encroaching into the narrow *calle*.

'How's he enjoying it? Gramsci, that is. Does he like Pellestrina?'

'Oh, he loves it. Perhaps a little too much. There seems to be an endless supply of small lizards and little birds for him to play with. It's going to be difficult to get him home. And it wasn't easy to get him out there.'

I pushed my key into the lock, but the door swung open at my touch.

'Oh shit.'

I stepped into the downstairs hall. The *calle* never got much sunlight, even on summer afternoons, so I flicked the light on. The bare lightbulb illuminated the dusty hall.

I took a closer look at the door. The lock had splintered away from where it had been forced.

'For Christ's sake.'

'It could just have been kids, Nat. Drunks maybe.'

'You don't believe that, do you?'

He shook his head. 'I don't get it, though. Wouldn't your neighbours have heard?'

'I don't have any neighbours. Not any more. They moved out to Mestre a year ago like everyone in this bloody city seems to be doing.'

'Ed, then? Or the other guys at the Brazilians?'

'Ed closes at eleven. Sometimes earlier if it's quiet. There's the guy in the antique bookshop over the way, but he's not around at night. No. Turn up late enough and nobody will be here to hear you. If you do it quickly.' I sighed. 'Okay. Let's check upstairs.'

We made our way up to the first floor. The *porta blindata* was scuffed around the base, and a few dusty footprints indicated that my unwelcome visitors had taken out their frustration on it. Nevertheless, they hadn't managed to make much of an impact and, although some of the plaster had crumbled away around the outside, there seemed to be no real damage done.

Dario patted the door. 'It takes proper work to break in through one of these. Kick it, shoulder charge it, all you're going to hurt is yourself.'

I turned the key in the lock and heard the reassuring sound of the five metal bars in the lock sliding back. 'Okay,' I sighed, 'let's just get these bloody kitty biscuits and go.'

'Sorry, Nat. Listen, I can get a locksmith around to look at the front door if you like?'

'Are you sure?'

'Of course I am. You've got enough to worry about. Least I can do.'

'Thanks, man. That's kind. It'd be nice if it was done by the time we get back.' I gave a hollow laugh. 'If we ever get back.' I sat down heavily on the arm of the sofa. 'Oh bloody hell, Dario. This isn't good, is it?'

He gave a half-smile, caught the expression in my eyes and decided to be honest with me. 'No. It's not good.'

'Whoever's doing this thinks we have something. They've been looking on Pellestrina and they've been looking here. But for what?'

'Drugs?'

'I'm the Honorary bloody Consul!'

'Money?'

'I'm an honest Honorary bloody Consul.'

'Weapons?'

'What do they think I've got, an AK47 in the safe?'

'Art?'

I was about to snap out another glib reply when I paused. 'You know, that's not such a stupid suggestion.'

'Oh thanks. Just trying to help.'

'No no. Let's just think on this for a moment. Stolen art, as we know, is an easy way to move collateral around. Something small, perhaps. Something Elio might have given Federica. She mentioned her grandmother's jewellery. It's a possibility.'

'Yes, but would that really be enough for the mob to take an interest?'

'Perhaps not. Still, let's keep it in mind, eh?' I drummed my fingers on the arm of the sofa. 'Yes, it's a thought. Find out what they – whoever they are – think we've got and maybe that will start to unlock things.'

He frowned again, the wrinkles around his eyes deepening. 'You're not going to do anything stupid? Not without me being there anyway?'

'Nothing more stupid than I've already done, Dario. And tomorrow I have nothing more serious than a memorial service to attend.' I remembered the USB stick. 'Are you still in touch with your mate Franco? The private eye.'

He nodded. 'We don't see each other that often. Even less so since I moved back to Venice. But we keep in touch.'

'Okay. I wonder if he could do me a favour.'

'He might do. Do you want to hire him?'

'Not exactly. There's just something he might be able to

help me with.' I took out the USB stick. 'There's something on here that's password protected. It's a PST file – whatever that is – called *Ghost Dog*.'

'What's that?'

'No idea. But it was in a box of Fede's dad's possessions. Do you think he'd be able to unlock it?'

'Well, if he can't he'll know people who can.'

'Fantastic. Listen, could you do me a big favour and pass this on to him? I'll pay for his time, of course.'

Dario shrugged. 'Okay. I don't know how long it'll take him, but he'll probably offer me a mate's rate. I'm in Mestre tomorrow, I'll give it to him then.'

'Thanks. There's more.' I took out the envelope of photographs and spread them on the table. 'Do you recognise any of these guys?' He shook his head. 'Okay, can you ask Franco? Just in case.'

'Sure.' Dario paused. 'Why don't you ask Vanni?'

'Because if it's anything serious he'll be obliged to investigate. And I don't want that. Not at the moment anyway.' I put the photographs back in the envelope and passed them to Dario.

He dropped the USB stick inside and nodded. 'Okay, *vecio*. I'll see what I can do.' Then he looked up at the row of cards on our bookcase and smiled. 'I see you've got ours there.'

'Pride of place, Dario, pride of place.' Then a thought struck me. 'Tell you what, I'll take these back to Pellestrina. It'll be a surprise for Federica when she gets home.'

Dario patted me on the back. 'Ah Nat, you're learning about this *husband* thing quickly.'

Chapter 29

I winced a little as the bus taking me back to the ferry terminal at Faro Rocchetta took the Curve of Death just a little quicker than felt absolutely safe. I looked back towards the church as we passed through Malamocco, but the red Ferrari was nowhere to be seen.

The sun was shining directly on my face through the window, making it uncomfortable to read my newspaper, so I folded it away, shaded my eyes, and did my best to enjoy the view. As one travelled further and further away from Santa Maria Elisabetta, and passed through Malamocco and on to Alberoni there was a feeling – despite the presence of traffic – of remoteness. Turn your head in the right direction and Venice could feel a long, long way away.

I got off the bus in order to stretch my legs during the ferry crossing. There was no sign of my new friend, and I felt the muscles in my shoulders and back starting to unclench.

My mind kept drifting away from the main problem in hand and on to dinner. I'd thought about taking the opportunity to stop by the Rialto market in order to buy some fish, but ultimately decided that carrying a bag full of squid or mussels for a long distance on a hot bus would be antisocial.

By now the fishmongers on Pellestrina would have closed. I didn't really know what to do. I could probably pick up something unexciting at the supermarket, but my heart was never really in cooking something unexciting. The pizzeria, of course, would be open, but Federica had been there only a couple of nights ago and the odds were we'd be there in the near future.

That left *da Celeste*. Sitting out on a warm night under a cloudless sky. The only sound being the lapping of waves, and the occasional buzz of a passing Vespa. Friends and family sitting together, laughing together. A jug of cold prosecco and a plate of soft-shelled crabs. Perhaps a roasted sea bream as well? I patted my stomach. I felt I was hungry enough.

But then Federica wouldn't be there. Would it be right to go without her? Going to 'our' restaurant on our honeymoon by myself. I wondered if that was just a little bit like cheating. And, besides, it wouldn't be as much fun on my own.

On the other hand, the alternative would be a takeaway pizza with Gramsci, and that was an evening that did not have the word 'fun' written all over it.

I was still wondering what to do when I turned my key in the lock of the door.

'*Ciao, tesoro.*'

I gave a strangulated 'N'yargh' and dropped the keys to the floor.

'Sorry. Did I startle you?' Fede was stretched out on the sofa, Gramsci standing guard over her.

'You did rather. I wasn't expecting you.'

'It was supposed to be a surprise.'

'It certainly was.'

She got to her feet, and stretched and yawned.

'Have you been asleep?'

'A couple of hours. I had a late night last night. *Mamma* wanted to have all her friends round to meet me. So lots of talk about weddings, lots of photos. Quite a few tears. You know what we're like.'

I smiled. 'I'm glad you're back.'

She threw her arms around me and tried to lift me off the ground. She failed, but not through want of trying. 'Me too. I've missed you.'

'Prosecco?'

'That would be good.'

I poured out two glasses, and stood the bottle on the table. 'So,' I said, 'how's your mum?'

'Mmm. Not quite sure. She was fine as long as I was there. Or as long as other people were there. When we weren't – even if I just went out to the shops – she had time to think. And when she had time to think, well,' she shook her head, 'not so good.'

'I'm sorry.'

'What worries me is that she's not answering the phone. Not if she doesn't recognise the number. She's got it into her head that an unknown number could be a journalist. Somebody rang, three times, when I was there. She just let it ring out. Didn't even want to pick up and hang up. She was scared that would show that the number was valid.'

'Hell. So how is she now?'

'She's okay.' Fede sipped at her prosecco. 'Oh, we had a nice time really. You should have been there. All her friends want to meet my glamorous British husband.'

'My goodness.'

'Well, I think *mamma* might have built you up a little too much. Don't worry, I did my best to put them right. Otherwise expectations might have been a little too high.'

'Oh. Thanks.'

Fede smiled, and rested her head on my shoulder. 'So she's okay. At least for now.'

'That's good.' I kissed the top of her head. 'I've got a surprise for you!'

'Oh, how lovely. Is it flowers?'

'Ah, no. I did buy some flowers yesterday, but, well, there was a bit of an incident. I'll tell you about that later. No, I brought all our wedding cards back from Venice. I thought it'd be nice to put them up.'

'Thank you.' She kissed me. 'That really is quite thoughtful.'

I took them out and lined them up on the bookcase. Then Fede followed after me, putting them into what I could only assume was the correct order.

'Lovely,' she said.

'Not bad at all.' I thought back to our earlier conversation. 'You know, Fede, there's one thing I don't understand.'

'Go on.'

'This is your mother. Marta Colombo. I used to be quite scared of her. Sometimes I still am. And, well, I know being hassled by journalists is upsetting but she's a strong woman. I don't quite understand why this is cutting her up so badly.'

Fede raised her head, and took another drink. 'You have to understand, *caro*. This is where *nonno* was brought up. This is where *papà* came when he was a boy. And this is where we came on holiday, as a family. All of us. Grandpa telling stories. Grandma and *mamma* in the kitchen. *Papà* holding me up when I was sleepy, so everyone could give me a kiss goodnight. It wasn't just about being on holiday. It was about being wrapped up in love.

'And then *papà* turned out to be someone other than the person we thought he was. And so all those long hot summers . . . well now they seem like something different. And if it turns out that,' her voice broke, just ever so slightly, 'if it turns out that he was working for the mob, then everything is broken. Everything that was warm and lovely about growing up. About being a family. All of that is gone.'

I nodded. 'I understand.'

'Yes. I think you do.' She paused. 'It's Michele's memorial service tomorrow.'

'I know. I was assuming we would go.'

'Are you sure?'

'Oh yes. There might be people we need to speak to.'

'Speak to?' She narrowed her eyes. 'You haven't done anything stupid, have you?'

I looked over towards Gramsci, who avoided my gaze and jumped down behind the sofa. 'I've met a weird bloke who wants to be my friend and who knows more about the journalist who telephoned us than seems feasible. Oh, and I nearly got run over by someone who might just be a member of the Mala del Brenta. But really, I think, it depends on your definition of "stupid".'

Fede was about to speak but I gave her my most disarming smile. 'But, on the plus side, if we leave now *da Celeste* should be able to fit us in for dinner.'

Chapter 30

'Is this going to do?' said Federica.

'Black T-shirt. Black jacket. Black jeans. Yes, I think you have the "black" thing nailed down.' I ran my hands through my hair. 'How about me?'

Fede grimaced. 'It's okay. I mean, it will do. That jacket's seen better days.'

'I'm sorry. I pulled it out of a bush two days ago.'

'And haven't you got any black shirts? Nothing like that?'

'I'm on my honeymoon. Mourning wear wasn't the first thing on my mind.'

'Don't worry about it. It'll be fine. Well, fine enough.' She patted my chest. 'You're sure this is worth doing?'

'I think so. Think about it. The *padre* at Madonna della Marina seems to be fairly relaxed about the sort of people that make up his congregation. I'm interested in who's going to turn up. It might be interesting.'

'To be fair, *caro*, your friend Father Michael might say the purpose of the church is not to care about who turns up in their congregation.'

'Up to a point. Pope Francis recently excommunicated *mafiosi*. I'm wondering how far the message has filtered down.'

***

We waited outside the church for the mourners to arrive, and Fede exchanged smiles and nods with people she recognised.

'How do you feel,' I said, 'being back here?'

Fede shrugged. 'It's okay. At least I think so. It's strange, it's only a few kilometres away and yet it's been years since I've been back. Once *mamma* had moved away there was no real need to come here.'

'Do you want to take a walk past your old house later?'

She shook her head. 'I don't need to.'

'It's still being lived in, it seems.'

'That's nice.' She checked her watch and looked around. 'Okay, I don't know how many more are going to turn up now. Shall we just slip in at the back?'

I nodded, and she took my arm. She paused on the threshold in order to cross herself. Then she saw the expression on my face and squeezed my arm. 'Old habits,' she whispered.

We took our seats at the back of the crowded church. I nodded at Federica. 'Good turn-out,' I said.

She gave me a dark look.

'Sorry, that probably wasn't the best choice of words. I'm just surprised to see so many people, that's all.'

'He'd lived on the Lido all his life. He'd have known a lot of people. Worked with many of them, helped many of them.'

'It's nearly four o'clock. Why are we starting so late?'

'Not sure. Might be because of his sister, Margherita. She lives in Rome.'

A chord sounded gently from the organ, and I looked up to the gallery where four people – two men and two women – had got to their feet. The organist played the chord again, as an arpeggio this time, and nodded at each of them as they hummed each note back to him in turn. Soprano, alto, tenor, bass. He nodded, raised his right hand, and they began to sing.

Mozart. *Ave Verum Corpus.*

A woman in an immaculately tailored dark suit walked down the aisle and laid a wreath of flowers at the entrance to the sanctuary, then genuflected and crossed herself before making her way to the front row.

The overwhelming smell of lilies mixed with the mustiness of the church, as I closed my eyes and listened to the choir. Absurdly, I felt my eyes prickling. Tears for a man I'd seen twice in my life. *Esto nobis praegustatum, in mortis examine.* Clever man, Wolfgang Amadeus.

We sat and listened until the final notes echoed away into silence.

'Is that her, at the front?' I said. 'The sister, I mean.'

Fede nodded. 'That's her.'

'Were they close?'

'I don't think so. But still . . . hush, we're about to begin.'

The little priest, Don Francesco, began to read.

'In life Michele Ballarin cherished the Gospel of Christ. May Christ now greet him with these words of eternal life . . .'

'Let us go forth with the love of our brother Michele in our hearts, and may the peace of God which passes all understanding be with us this day, this week and always.'

The small choir began to sing. Mozart once again, this time the *Lacrimosa* from the *Requiem.* Too much for four singers and an organ, but still beautiful. Row by row, the congregation stood and made their way out into the *campo*, where they would line up to pay their respects to Ballarin's sister.

I got to my feet and was about to follow, when Federica grabbed my arm and steered me in the opposite direction.

'What are you doing?' I hissed in her ear.

'I want to take a look in the sacristy. I want to see exactly what they've done to my painting.'

'Oh. Right. Well, promise not to get cross.'

'I promise.' She stopped dead in her tracks. 'No, scratch that. I don't promise.'

She walked into the sacristy and looked up at the enthroned Madonna and the grim-faced apostles.

'I don't believe it.'

'I'm sorry, I did tell you. Is it so bad?'

'Yes it is.' She threw her hands up towards the painting. 'It was deliberately hung on the opposite wall so that it at least got whatever natural light there was. Here, it's in perpetual shadow.'

'Maybe they didn't want the sunlight to damage it?'

'It's oil on canvas. There's no problem with sunlight.'

'We could have a word with the priest?'

'I'm going to have more than a damn word with him. I can't believe they would simply move this without asking anyone who'd been involved in the restoration. I don't know what's worse, the arrogance or the ignorance.' She sighed, and shook her head. 'Look. I know it's not the best painting in Venice. It's not even the best painting in Malamocco. But it was the first proper job I worked on, and it meant a lot to me. Trying to make it look beautiful again. Trying to make it shine again. And now it's as dull and colourless as everything else in here.'

'Well, not quite everything else,' I said.

'What else is there? Some not very good art on the wall that's probably not from the period they think it is. Vestments. Lots of them. God knows why the clothing of dead priests is thought to be worth preserving, but nevertheless it is. And—' She broke off as she noticed the monstrance.

I smiled. 'Note the label. Restored by Lupo and Vicari.'

She bent down to take a closer look at it, her lips moving as she read the caption. Then she straightened up and shook her head. 'Over-restored. But there might be something quite interesting somewhere underneath all that fake gold.'

'Fake?'

'Of course. Don't tell me you thought it was real?'

'I did, rather. I'd assumed they would have had the money for the real thing.'

'But the real thing wouldn't have had quite as much bling as this.'

'I'm sorry. You've lost me. I still don't understand why?'

She shook her head. 'Don't you?' She tapped her hand against the glass. 'Giuseppe Lupo. Gangster boss. A man who's probably had people killed. And, like so many of these people, he still considers himself to be a good religious man. So, what can he do? He's getting older. Starting to worry about the state of his immortal soul.'

'Because of all the murders and everything?' I said.

'Exactly. And then, perhaps, one day the parish priest suggests that maybe, just maybe, you might like to make a contribution to restoring the church's most sacred relic.'

'A fragment of the Crown of Thorns. Embedded in a vessel designed to display the very body of Christ.'

'Exactly. Think of it. How many sins might you scrub off by paying for its restoration? But then, of course, with these people the temptation is always to go too far. Make it look shinier, brighter, sexier than it ever would have looked in the past. "Pimp my Monstrance", we could call it.' She shook her head. 'You know what, I wouldn't mind betting that they insisted on having the painting moved. Just so there was no danger of their precious work being overlooked. It's disgusting. Disgusting.' She sighed. 'Come on. We should go before Margherita leaves. I should at least say hello to her.'

We were not quite the last people to pay our respects to Margherita Ballarin. Parked in its usual, illegal, space was the bright red Ferrari of Albino Lupo. And there, next to Margherita, stood the man himself, primped and preening in a suit that could have made even me look good. His beard was neatly trimmed, lending him a slightly – and presumably desired – Satanic appearance; whilst he smiled down at Margherita from behind a pair of Gucci sunglasses. I was unsure if the effect he was going after was that of a gangster, or simply a man with too much money. Quite possibly both.

He inclined his head and bent to kiss Margherita's hand. An expression of disgust crossed her face, and she attempted – too late – to yank her hand back.

He never stopped smiling, but bent closer to her in order to whisper into her ear. Then he straightened up, and reached into his pocket. He took out his wallet, extracted a card and passed it to her.

Margherita looked at it, and turned it over in her hand before slowly and deliberately crushing it and dropping it at his feet. Then she stepped back and slapped him across the face, the crack ringing out like a shot and making me start.

Albino rubbed his cheek, with a rueful smile on his face. He raised his voice so that the rest of us could hear. 'Well, I suppose I deserved that. *Arrivederci, signora.*'

He laid his hand upon the door of the Ferrari, and was about to open it when he paused and turned to look at the two of us. His smile widened. He made his way over to Federica and gave a little bow.

'*Signora* Ravagnan?'

'*Dottoressa,*' I said.

He didn't even look at me, but smiled at Fede. She took a step back.

'Oh, don't worry. I'm not going to kiss your hand. I don't want to risk being slapped twice in one day.'

'I'm sorry,' I said. 'I'm not sure we've been introduced.'

Again, he ignored me. 'Albino Lupo. My father was a great friend of poor *signor* Ballarin.' He paused, and his smile grew ever wider. 'And, of course, of your father.'

Fede shook her head. 'I think you must be mistaken.'

'No. No, I don't think so. They were very close.'

'That's not possible. He wouldn't—' Her voice broke.

'Wouldn't – *what, signora?*'

Fede shook her head, and gathered herself. 'They didn't know each other. I'm sorry, but you really are mistaken.'

'Great friends,' he repeated. 'Great friends they were. But we can talk about this some other time, *signora.*' Then, for the first time, he turned to me. 'I'm sorry, I mean *dottoressa* of course.' He looked me up and down, and reached out to tug a loose thread from my jacket. He rolled it between his fingers, before letting it drop to the ground with an expression that mixed distaste with pity. 'I think we might have met, Mr—?'

'Sutherland. Nathan Sutherland. Yes, we have. Or rather, we almost bumped into each other a couple of days ago.'

'Yes. Yes, that must be it.' He turned back to Federica. 'Don't forget what I said, *signora*.' Then he jumped back into the Ferrari and was gone in a screech of burning rubber.

'Wanker,' I muttered.

Fede patted my back. 'Red Ferrari, eh? I wonder how long it'll be before he decides he needs to gild a monstrance?'

'Are you okay?'

She took a deep breath, and nodded, slowly. 'I think so. How about you?'

'Yeah. I think so too.'

'I could do with a spritz, though.'

'Me too. There's a place round here I was at the other day. The barman seemed like a good chap. We should go there. It'll be nice for him to see me looking as if I haven't been in a fight and—' Fede was staring over my shoulder. 'You're not listening to me, are you?'

She shook her head in irritation, and shushed me. 'God,' she whispered.

'What's the matter?'

'That woman. Over there.'

I followed her gaze. There, outside the church, stood a blonde woman dressed in black.

'Oh God. It's her.'

Chapter 31

'Fede, I don't know her. Who is she?'

The woman was staring back at us now. She put her hand to her mouth, and looked to her left and then her right as if searching for a way to escape. Then she shook her head and walked, haltingly, over to us.

'Oh God,' whispered Federica again.

'Federica?' I could see the woman more clearly now. She was, perhaps, just a few years older than Fede. Her eyes were red from crying.

Fede nodded. 'Sofia.'

I smiled and gave a little wave of my hand. 'Nathan,' I said. 'Federica's husband.'

'Pleased to meet you.' Her voice wavered.

Fede, I knew, hated many things. Seafood on pizza, wobbly scaffolding and most Italian governments being among them. I had seen her look angry before. But I had never seen her look at anyone the way she looked at the blonde woman. It wasn't just hatred. It was utter, withering contempt.

I shook Sofia's hand and let it drop. She half extended it to Federica, and then let it drop to her side. Silence hung in the air, thick and awkward.

'Okay, I'm at a disadvantage here. You know each other?' I offered.

'We do know each other,' said Fede. 'She knew my father better.'

Oh. God.

The blonde woman took a handkerchief from her bag and dabbed at her eyes. 'Federica, darling, please don't be angry with me.'

'I'm not your darling. And don't presume to think you have such an effect on me.'

'I know you hate me but—'

'If I thought about you at all I probably would. Again, don't presume too much.'

I reached for Fede's arm, but she shook it off and flashed me a glance that told me my most welcome contribution would be a silent one.

'Why are you here, Sofia?'

She dabbed at her eyes again. 'He was my employer, Federica. I had to come. I have to talk to you.'

'You don't have to. You don't have to do anything. You didn't have to jump into bed with my father. But, okay, tell me why.' Fede folded her arms.

'I know it's difficult for you. But I just have to—'

Fede grabbed my arm and spun on her heel. 'That's the third time you've said "have to". You're boring me now. Goodbye.' She half marched, half dragged me down the street. I could hear the other woman's feet tic-tacking along the tarmac, and her breath labouring as she half sobbed, 'Don't go. Please. It's about Michele and Elio and—'

Fede stopped. She didn't turn around, but her grip

tightened on my arm. 'And—?'

'You know what I'm going to say. But I'm not going to say it here. Please. We need to talk.'

Fede's grip tightened even further, becoming painful. I tried to prise her fingers from my arm, and then she looked into my eyes as if realising what she was doing for the first time. She patted my hand, and looked away, almost absent-mindedly.

She turned around. 'Okay. So let's talk.'

'Not here. Back at my apartment. Please.' Fede stared at her and Sofia was unable to hold her gaze. 'Please,' she repeated, this time in a whisper.

'Are you still in the same lovely flat, Sofia? The one that was so close to our house?'

'I moved, years ago. After – well, I moved years ago. I live near Santa Maria Elisabetta now.'

'How lovely. We were almost neighbours for a while, then. What a shame we never ran into each other.'

'Will you come? I'll drive you. Please.'

Fede continued to stare at her. Then she closed her eyes, and nodded. 'Okay,' she said.

'Coffee?' said Sofia.

Fede shook her head. I nodded. 'That would be nice, thank you.'

'I'll fetch you one now.' Her voice trembled, just a little. 'Are you sure I can't fetch you anything, Federica?'

'Quite sure.'

'Sit down, please.' She fumbled with the dials of an old Bakelite radio and classical music blared out. She gave a little jump and yanked the dial to the left, reducing the music to a more bearable level. Mozart. *Così fan tutte*. Was it going to be Mozart all day?

She turned, and was about to go to the kitchen when Federica called out to her.

'It's still a little loud.'

'I'm sorry. I'm sorry.' She scurried back to the radio and turned it down further, her hands shaking.

'Did you think you'd need it to drown out the screams?' Fede smiled.

'I'm sorry.'

'So you keep saying. Make Nathan his coffee, why don't you?'

We sat down on a slightly musty green cord sofa. I looked around the room. The carpet just a little bit too worn, the arms of the sofas raggy. I leaned over to Federica and whispered in her ear.

'Why are you being so horrible?'

She looked at me in blank incomprehension. 'How would you expect me to be?'

'I don't know. But she's trying to be nice.'

'Being nice to my father was the problem.'

'I understand, but can't you just be civil?'

She shook her head. 'Oh, stop being so bloody British.'

Sofia re-entered and we sprang apart, embarrassed at having been caught in the middle of a private conversation which Sofia, nevertheless, would have understood was all about her.

She put a small cup of steaming black coffee down in front of me. The picture on the cup was yellowed and faded, showing an image of Naples in front of a smouldering Mount Vesuvius.

I smiled. 'I've never been to Naples. People tell me I should. Would I like it?'

The question seemed to make her even more flustered. There was something about her that made me think she was perpetually on the edge of tears. 'Oh. It's so long since I was there. I was with—' Her words trailed off.

'Elio?' said Federica.

'Yes.' Her voice was little more than a whisper.

We sat in awkward silence for a moment, and then her hands flew to her face. 'Oh, I'm sorry. I forgot the sugar. Would you like sugar?'

'That would be nice.' Fede glared at me as Sofia left the room again. She returned with a sugar bowl, with a faded Venezia logo.

'Big football fan?' I said.

'That – that wasn't mine either.'

'Oh.'

The silence – ever more strained, ever more palpable – continued. Federica, evidently, was not going to say anything that might reduce the level of tension in the room.

Try as I might, I couldn't stop myself from attempting to fill the space with something suitably banal and inoffensive. I looked at the ragged arm of the sofa and smiled at Sofia. 'My cat does this as well.'

She shook her head. 'He's – well, he's not around any more.'

'Oh. I'm sorry.' I sipped at my coffee, too vigorously this time, and felt it scalding the back of my throat.

Federica turned on one of her most dazzling smiles. 'So, Sofia. It's been lovely to be invited round for coffee. What would you like to say to me?'

I could see Sofia's shoulders shaking with the tension.

'It's about Elio. About your father.'

Fede nodded, but said nothing. The smile on her face was a terrible one.

'Someone's kept telephoning me in the past couple of days. Ever since Michele died. A journalist, she said she was.'

'Sara Scarpa?' I said.

'That was the name. She said she wanted to talk about Michele, and about Federica's father. And about—' Silence, again.

'And about *what*, Sofia?' said Fede, measuring out the words slowly.

She nodded, and put her hands to her face, rubbing at her eyes. 'Okay. That Elio and Michele had done favours for the mob. The Mala del Brenta, possibly others. That Giuseppe Lupo himself was a friend.'

Fede was no longer smiling. 'Okay. I understand.' Her voice shook, just a little. 'Is there more?'

Sofia nodded. 'There is. There are stories they'd set up a safe house on Pellestrina for *mafiosi*, and that they knew what became of the proceeds of a jewellery heist in 2003. But Lupo was such a great friend of them both that he refused to implicate them even when he was arrested.'

Fede closed her eyes, and nodded to herself. 'I see. So the suggestion is that my father not only colluded with mafia but actually received stolen goods from them. Is that right?'

'Yes,' she whispered.

Fede continued. 'This is nonsense, of course.'

'Of course,' Sofia nodded, frantically.

'Are you saying "of course" because that's what you think

I want to hear? Or is it what you really believe?'

'I . . . I. . .' Sofia fell silent.

'Fede,' I said, 'that guy who met me on the bus the other day. He said the same thing. About the safe house. And Lupo was arrested after trying to fence two diamonds that were linked with a heist in—'

Fede interrupted me by squeezing my hand so hard it hurt. 'Shut up, Nathan.'

Sofia opened her mouth to speak but Fede leapt to her feet and leaned towards her. 'And you shut up as well, until you decide to tell me the truth. Because I don't believe a word of this crap.'

The other woman shifted in her seat, just ever so slightly. Fede balled her fist, her knuckles whitening. 'What do you want from me, Sofia. Money? Is that it?'

'No, I swear.'

'You make up some shitty story about my father dealing with gangsters, and you think I'll give you money. Or you'll go to the press. Is that it?' she repeated.

'Federica, please listen.'

'I'm done listening.' She stepped towards her, and Sofia cringed backwards.

I laid my arm on hers. 'Fede, don't. Please.'

She spun around, her hand open, and for a moment I was afraid she was going to hit me. There was silence for a moment, as we stared at each other. *If this happens, then everything will be broken*. Then she turned and ran from the room.

I stood there for a moment, trying to make sense of what had just happened, and then I turned to Sofia who was sobbing hysterically.

'I'm sorry,' I said, 'I've got to go. But we'll need to talk about this again.' I fumbled in my pocket for a business card and placed it on the table next to her. She was still crying and I wondered if I should stay with her, make her a coffee, give her a hug. I shook my head. No. Too many misunderstandings already for one day. 'I'm sorry,' I repeated, and left her there crying.

By the time I'd got downstairs there was no sign of Federica to be seen. A bus was receding into the distance. I couldn't make out the number but guessed it might be the service heading for the ferry at Alberoni and on to Pellestrina.

I walked to the stop and checked the timetable. Thirty minutes until the next bus. Shit. I took out my mobile and rang her. It rang and rang and rang until it cut off. I called again, but this time the answerphone cut in immediately. She'd switched her phone off. I heard the bleep after the recorded message and realised that I had nothing to say. Or, rather, that I had a thousand things to say but nothing that would fit into thirty seconds.

Should I call someone? For that matter, would she call anyone after she'd calmed down? Marta? I shook my head. She'd be afraid of upsetting her. Valentina? No. They'd become good friends, but not that good. *Zio* Giacomo? Maybe. I had to admit he'd probably have something suitably wise to say on the subject.

There was plenty of time to kill before the next bus. I'd have a coffee at the bar on the corner and try to get my head together in the meantime.

A car horn parped, making me jump. There was the hum of an electric window winding down, and the driver leaned out.

'Mr Sutherland. Sorry, did I startle you?'

'You did, rather.' I looked closer and did a double-take. It was Busetto, not in his immaculate black *carabiniero* uniform, but rather in shorts and T-shirt.

'You're dressing down today,' I said.

He smiled. 'It's my day off.'

'Oh right. Nice. What brings you to Malamocco?'

'The same thing as you, perhaps? Can I offer you a lift back to Pellestrina?'

I hesitated for a moment. It would be easier, and quicker to accept his offer. On the other hand, enforced conversation for the next thirty minutes or so might be awkward. He made my decision for me, by leaning over and unlocking the passenger side door.

The car smelled of stale cigarettes and air freshener, but was at least cool in a way that the bus would not have been.

Busetto smiled again. 'You're not exactly dressed for the heat, Mr Sutherland.'

'I've been to church. I thought I needed to look smart.'

'You look hot. Here, I'll turn the air con up a bit.' A wave of blissfully chilled air passed over my face. 'This is only a Lancia, but it has its creature comforts.' He paused. 'One can't afford a Ferrari on a *carabiniero* salary, sadly.'

'I don't imagine many people can.'

He shrugged. 'Hmm.' He gestured at the radio. 'Music?'

'That's nice of you.'

'What would you like?'

'I don't suppose you've got any Hawkwind?' He looked confused. 'Don't worry. Whatever you like.'

'Okay.' He pressed play. 'Ariana Grande. It's my daughter's

favourite. I'm starting to quite enjoy it.'

'Ariana Grande and TS Eliot. You're a bit of a renaissance man, *maresciallo*.'

He chuckled. 'Well, it's important. I need to be able to talk to my daughter about something.' He paused. 'So, Mr Sutherland, I take it you were at the service for *signor* Ballarin?'

'We were. It seemed appropriate.'

'It's very good of you to break off from your honeymoon in order to go to the memorial for a man you hardly knew.'

'He was my father-in-law's business partner. There's almost a family link there.'

'Family. Of course.' Why did he have to react to everything I said as if it was suspicious?

'I don't suppose you know when the funeral will be?' I said.

He shook his head. 'Difficult to say. Ballarin died in suspicious circumstances. That means we can't release the body just yet.' He turned to me for a moment and smiled. 'Why, are you planning on going to that as well?'

I shrugged. 'Who knows? It depends what else we have on.'

'I understand. Busy social diaries and all that.' He fell silent, and we sat there without speaking as he guided the car down the long, straight roads to Alberoni and the ferry terminal at Faro Rochetta.

We arrived just as the *traghetto* was pulling away from the dock. He checked his watch. 'Oh, that's annoying. It seems to have left early. Still. That gives us a little more time to chat.' He turned the engine off, and reached into his jacket pocket. 'Cigarette?'

'I've given up, thanks.'

'Well done. I keep telling myself I will when I retire.' He opened the car door, and popped his seat belt. 'Come on, I won't inflict this on you in here. Let's just stretch our legs a bit.'

I got out of the car, into the heat and humidity of the twilight, as Busetto smoked away in silence. He chained one from the stub of the first, and then grimaced. 'Second one's never as good, is it?'

I didn't reply.

'No offence meant, Mr Sutherland, but, for a translator, you seem to know some very interesting people.'

'I'm not sure I do.'

He shook his head. 'You're too modest. Albino Lupo seemed very interested in making your acquaintance. Or at least that of your wife.'

I sighed. '*Maresciallo*, you do seem to have been keeping a very close eye on us?'

'Not at all. But is there any reason why I shouldn't?'

'Spying on people on their honeymoon isn't a very cool thing to do, *maresciallo*.'

'That's not a nice word to use, Mr Sutherland. I just wondered how you came to know Giuseppe Lupo's son, that's all.'

'If you must know, he tried to run me over the other day.'

'My goodness. He seemed to be having quite a conversation with your wife.'

'A very one-sided one. Federica doesn't know him from Adam.'

'I see. It just seemed a little strange to me, that's all. Just a little misunderstanding on my part, evidently.'

The ferry, mercifully, had completed its round trip and

was pulling up to the jetty once more. I got back in the car.

'I'm sorry. Are you in a hurry?'

'A bit of one, yes. I'd kind of like to get back home. It's just Federica – well, she was a bit upset.'

'Of course. That's understandable. I'll get you back as soon as possible. Any plans for the rest of your honeymoon?'

'Nothing specific,' I lied. 'We'll just see what turns up.'

'Lovely.'

He turned the engine on, and we joined the queue of traffic waiting to board the ferry. Ariana Grande blared out from the stereo again.

'Can I ask you something?' he said.

'Sure.'

'Those photographs on your kitchen table. Just remind me again. Where did you find them?'

'They were in a box in the attic.'

'In the attic?'

'Yes. I was looking for stuff for the beach – umbrellas, deckchairs that sort of thing.'

'That sort of thing,' he repeated. 'And you found a box of photographs. Was there anything else in there?'

I paused, perhaps just a little too long. There was, I thought, no need to tell him about the USB stick. 'No,' I said.

Busetto said nothing, and just nodded. We sat in silence for the rest of the journey, listening to Ariana.

He dropped me off just outside the house. 'Thanks for the lift,' I said.

'It's not a problem.'

I tried to open the door, and banged myself against it as it refused to shift.

'I'm sorry, it's childproofed.' He pressed a button on the dashboard, and the door clicked open.

'Good night, Mr Sutherland.'

'Good night, *maresciallo*.'

I slammed the door shut, and made my way to the front door. I heard the sound of the window winding down behind me.

'Oh, and Mr Sutherland?'

I turned around. He was smiling at me.

'You really are a terrible liar.'

Then he wound the window up, gunned the engine, and was gone.

The house was in semi-darkness and I padded upstairs as quietly as I could to avoid disturbing Fede. I could hear her snoring, gently, within the bedroom and I smiled. I turned the doorknob, as quietly as possible.

It was locked.

I nodded to myself. Then I padded back downstairs and into the living room. I shuffled a few cushions around on the sofa. There were no blankets, of course, but in the early summer warmth that wouldn't matter.

Gramsci yowled and prowled around my feet and I hushed him as best I could, throwing a few balls for him to catch until he got bored. There was still some wine in the fridge. And some Campari. I could make myself a spritz Nathan, but that didn't seem like the best idea in the world. Prosecco then. Not that there was anything to celebrate. I could, I supposed, fix myself something to eat, but my heart wasn't really in it. There was, at least, a certain novelty to that.

I put my glass down next to me on the coffee table, lay down on the sofa and closed my eyes. Something needed to be done. I didn't quite know what.

I heard the scrabbling of claws, and then there was a little *miaow* and the sound of something landing on the back of the sofa. I opened my eyes. Gramsci was there, looking down at me.

'You're in disgrace as well are you, puss?'

He looked down at me, and miaowed again.

'I know. Bit difficult, isn't it? I don't suppose you know what to do?' I reached up at him to scratch him behind the ears. He purred for a moment, and then nipped half-heartedly at my fingers.

'No. I don't really know either.' I reached out my hand, and took a sip of my prosecco. It had been in the fridge too long and tasted flat and sour. 'I really don't know at all.'

I put the glass back down on the table, and adjusted the cushion behind my head.

'But we'll think of something, won't we, eh? We'll think of something.'

In the Wolf's Den

'We always wanted children. It seemed we never would. But then our little miracle came along. On the twenty-eighth of September 1978. The same day that Luciani died.'

'I'm sorry?'

'Albino Luciani. Pope John Paul I.' His voice is sharp, as if displeased by my lack of knowledge of – or interest in – the religious affairs of forty years ago.

'I'm sorry. Yes, of course, carry on.'

'Now you might think I went out to the tabacchi *and bought the finest cigar in the shop and celebrated with champagne and oysters. No. The baby was sick, very sick. The doctors said he might not survive the night. And so I went to the nearest church – I can't even remember which one it was – and I sat there and prayed from dusk to dawn. And I promised—' His voice breaks off.*

'You promised?'

He shakes his head. 'Nothing. One does not bargain with God. But any rate, He heard my prayer. And the boy lived.' He smiles. 'Of course, we had to call him Albino. It seemed like a sign.'

I am never quite sure what to make of the Old Wolf's piety.

Does he genuinely believe that the God with whom one does not bargain is the same God who might give advice on possible names for one's son? I think better of asking this question.

'You've mentioned God a number of times. You go to Mass, I understand?'

Lupo nods. 'Of course I do. I was brought up to go to church. Sometimes I miss a Sunday. I try not to.'

'Would you describe yourself as a good Christian man?'

'I don't think about that. God knows. God will judge me. Who am I to say if I'm a good man or not?'

I weigh my next question carefully. Lupo is a courteous host. He is also, even in jail, the kind of host that one does not wish to upset.

'Bergoglio has decreed that members of the mafia should be considered excommunicate.'

He says nothing. I wait for him to respond. I have been a journalist a long time but he – Wolf-like – is better at waiting than I am. 'Pope Francis has said that members of the mafia should not receive Communion at Mass.'

He smiles. Just a little. 'I do know who Bergoglio is. And what excommunication is. But thank you for reminding me.'

'Do you agree with what he said?'

'The Pope can say whatever he likes. I'm not a priest. I don't have an opinion.'

'A priest visits you every week, I understand?'

'That's correct. It is permitted, of course.'

'And you take Communion? The priest gives you the bread?'

'I do. He does.'

'Therefore your priest does not agree with the doctrine set out by the Holy See?'

'I don't know. You'd have to ask him that.'

'Do you think it's appropriate for you to receive Communion?'

'I have no problem with it. Why would I? All of us are sinners, after all.' He looks at me and grins. 'Even you, signor Brezzi.'

'There are degrees of sin, though.'

'I'm sure there are. But it's not for us to judge.'

The Old Wolf, I imagine, has been asked this before and his answers are practised ones. I change tack, just a little.

'You give – have given – a great deal of money to the church of Madonna della Marina in Malamocco,' I say.

He tries and fails to look embarrassed. 'I've done what I can. I'm not sure I've done anything special.'

'You paid for the re-gilding of a seventeenth-century monstrance, window repairs and,' here I have to look at my notes, 'major repairs to an interior wall. This is quite special, surely?'

'It's kind of you to say so.'

'I'm not being kind at all. I just wondered why you felt compelled to make so many large donations to a church which is not your own?'

He nods, as if to himself, and then shifts his chair closer to mine. He leans forward, placing his hands on my knees. I can smell the tobacco on his breath. 'Brezzi,' he says, 'now listen to me, Brezzi, and listen well.'

He is perhaps just ten years older than me, yet for a moment I feel like that young cub reporter on Il Gazzettino, seeing his first dead body on Via Piave. I am unable to stop myself from flinching. I look into his grey, unblinking eyes but cannot hold his gaze.

'Do you want me to say that I gave so much money to the church because I was afraid for my poor soul? Is that what you want me to say?'

For the first time in our conversations I am afraid. This is a man, I remember, who could do me harm if he decided he did not wish me well.

He grips my knees, just a little bit harder, and leans forward. He is smiling now. 'Is that what you want me to say?' he repeats.

I have been a reporter for nearly forty years. In my time, I have interviewed murderers, rapists, the lowest of the low. People who disgusted me. Yet I have never met anyone before who I believed could have me killed if he so wished. I dig deep, find the courage, and dredge up the words. 'Yes. That is what I want you to say. Were you afraid for your soul?'

'Good. Good.' He moves the chair back, the legs scraping against the floor. He sighs. 'And the answer is – perhaps.'

'I see.' I scribble in my notepad, and notice his gaze following my hand. Watching it shake. My breathing has returned to normal, and I decide to risk a follow-up. 'Why Malamocco? It was never your church. Why not your one in Mestre?'

He shrugs. 'It was Vicari's church. It meant a lot to him.'

'That's why you ask for Don Francesco to come and visit you once a week? In memory of Vicari?'

'Perhaps,' he says.

'Or is it that the priest from you own church refuses to give you Communion?'

There is silence in the room. The Old Wolf continues to stare at me and, for a moment, looks older than his years.

'I think I'd like to stop there for now,' he says.

Chapter 32

I woke up to the sound of the Moka bubbling away, and the smell of fresh coffee. Something was prodding insistently at my shoulder.

'Not now, Grams,' I muttered and rolled over in the hope of going back to sleep.

'Hmm. Being compared with an unfriendly cat is not the best compliment a girl can receive first thing in the morning.'

'Fede?' I opened one eye. She gave a half-smile, but looked tired and drawn.

'I've made you a coffee.'

'Thanks.' I sat up, and wished I hadn't. 'Ouch.'

'Are you okay?'

'A bit stiff. Bear in mind that sofa was probably old when your grandad was young. It's not really meant for sleeping on.'

'Sorry.' She looked down at her feet. 'Will the coffee help?'

'Coffee helps with everything. Even deep muscular pain.' I drank a little and, if the aches and pains did not immediately ease, the world immediately seemed just a little more manageable.

'That's better. Thanks.' We sat there and stared at each other in silence. I broke first. 'So. How are you?'

'Not so good, to be honest. How about you?'

'Not good.' I shook my head. 'Do we need to talk?'

'Yes. I think we do. But not here. Finish your coffee and let's go out.'

'Okay. I could do with a shower first.'

'That doesn't matter. When we get back.'

'Fede, I've slept in my clothes on an antique sofa. Parts of my body no longer seem to be responding to instructions from my brain. Please. I need a long hot shower and a shave.'

She tried to look disapproving, failed, and then gave a weak smile. 'Okay. But not too long. I'll make you another coffee as an incentive to get a move on.'

We sat on the *murazzi* and looked out over the Adriatic. There was nothing to be heard except for the occasional cry of a seabird, or the rumble of a passing car from the road behind us.

'So. Last night,' said Fede.

'Last night. Yeah.'

'Sorry.'

'Me too.'

She shook her head. 'Wasn't your fault.'

'I know. But it seemed like the sort of thing I should say. I'm sure I've done something I need to apologise for.' She leaned her head against my shoulder. 'You know, I assumed being locked out of the bedroom was something to be worked up to after years of marriage. I have to say I didn't really expect it on honeymoon.'

'Sorry,' she said again.

'It's all right. Given time I'll get used to the sofa.'

We both laughed, and sat there listening to the sea.

'You never talk about your father, do you?' she said.

I sighed. 'No.'

'Is he still alive?'

'I don't know.'

'You must have some good memories of him?'

I nodded. 'There are some. But when I close my eyes and think back, most things that come to mind are shouting. Tears. Doors slamming. You know why I went to Aberystwyth University?'

'Because it had an excellent modern languages department. Or at least that's what you told me.'

'That was one reason. The other was that it was one hell of a long way away. And one day I realised I didn't have to go home any more if I didn't want to. I kept in touch with Mum, of course. She left not long after I did. I felt bad about that. It must have been lonely for her. Then she died and, well, that was the last time I saw Dad. At her funeral. I haven't been back since. And as I said, I don't even know if he's still alive. I think, in my heart of hearts, that he probably isn't. But I don't need to know.' I sighed. 'I suppose there were good days. There must have been. I think Christmas was usually okay. But that just made January seem worse. The cold, the rain. School. Dad in a foul mood.' I shook my head. 'Bloody hell.'

Fede said nothing, but just sat there and stroked my arm. I turned to look at her. 'It was different for you, of course, wasn't it?'

She nodded.

'That's what I'm trying to understand. I'm not used to people coming from close families. Hell, I'm not used to people coming from *nice* families.'

'This is it. This is the thing, the damnable thing about it. I know my father wasn't the person I wanted him to be. Not the person I thought he was. But they were good days, growing up. And now I'm starting to wonder how much of all that was a lie?'

I shrugged. 'Does it matter? The memories are still good ones.'

She shook her head. 'You don't understand.'

'I don't. But, as I said, I'm trying to.'

'I know. Thank you.'

We sat there in silence again, and I felt happy again for the first time in days. As long as we were here, just the two of us, everything seemed simple and uncomplicated. Yet there was a question that I needed to ask. I knew it would break the moment, but it had to be said.

'What if it's true?'

I was prepared for her to snap; perhaps even to scream at me or to storm off again. But she just stiffened, ever so slightly.

'I don't know,' she said.

'We need to find out, though, don't we? I don't think we can just wish it away.'

'No.'

'So what do we have? One journalist, possibly two, asking questions of ourselves and your mother. And now they're speaking to,' I bit down on the words, 'the other woman' and settled for, 'Sofia.'

'If they are journalists.'

'Exactly. I'm not so sure. So, following Ballarin's death, "people", shall we say, are asking questions of those of us who had more than a simple professional relationship with him. About links with the mob, about Giuseppe Lupo, and about a string of jewellery robberies in the Veneto fifteen years ago. Why?'

'Because they think we know something about it. Thinking *papà* might have confided in us. Or in Sofia. So we need to know more. The question is, how do we do that?'

'I gave it a bit of thought last night on the sofa. First of all, we need to speak to people who might have known Lupo.'

'That would mean speaking to actual *mafiosi*, and I don't think either of us want to go there. How would we even go about it? You can't look at "m for mob" in the *Pagine Gialle*.'

'I've got an idea. We – I – could try to speak to someone in Santa Maria Maggiore.'

'Cellmates?'

'Not necessarily. Think about it, he'd have been a very big fish in a very small pond. Everyone would have known who he was. He might, just might, have spoken to someone.'

'Even if he had, how are you going to get in there?'

'Ah-ha!' I waved my forefinger in the air. 'I've thought of that. I can go through diplomatic channels.'

'You what?'

'I'm the Honorary Consul, remember? The British guy in Santa Maria Maggiore I told you about? Someone tried to steal his phone at a *vaporetto* stop late one night. He beat him up, pretty badly. Hospitalised him.'

'So, what, you can just request an audience with him?'

'Hmm. I'm not sure one "requests an audience" with prisoners. It's supposed to be that they ask to see you. But I'm supposed to see him before they send him home.'

'Okay. I suppose it's worth a go.' She sounded dubious.

'The other thing is,' I took a deep breath. 'I think we need to talk to Sofia again.'

'You do?' Her voice was guarded.

'I have to. Come on, she's the only other one we know who's been approached. She's obviously in a state about it. And it does sound as if she knows something.' Fede said nothing. 'We need to speak to her, properly, even if what she says isn't what you want to hear.'

Fede nodded, and her voice shook as she spoke. 'Okay. But you'll have to do it. I just don't want to be in the same room as that woman. I just can't.'

'You don't have to. I'll do it. I, er, gave her my card, you know. Just in case.'

'I understand,' said Fede in a voice that suggested she very much did not understand.

There was something else I needed to say. I weighed up the possible consequences in my mind, and decided that sooner or later I'd need to say it anyway and that, whilst this might not have been the ideal occasion, I was struggling to think of a better one.

'You know, I was thinking last night . . . as I said, I had quite a lot of time to think . . . about your father and—'

'—that woman.'

'Sofia, yes. I was thinking that, well, it does take two to tango.'

Oh Christ. That could have come out better.

Fede didn't seem to react, beyond a flat 'Meaning?'

'Meaning it wasn't just her fault, was it?' I took a deep breath. 'Elio was the married one, after all.'

'I know. But it does make it easier for me.'

'Yep. I know.'

She patted my shoulder. 'Come on then. It sounds like you've got phone calls to make.'

'I have. But first,' I rubbed my hands together, 'I'm going to buy fish and have a think about what to cook tonight.'

'You'll have to do that later. I've got plans for this morning.'

'You have?'

'Sure. What, did you think I just came home last night, had a big cry and then locked myself in the bedroom?'

'Well. Yes.'

She shook her head. 'Don't start being a disappointing husband. No, I called Margherita. I thought it might be good to talk. And besides, there's somewhere I need to go.'

Chapter 33

The bus journey was less than ten minutes but, even at this time of the year, it would have been an uncomfortable walk in the heat. It pulled up outside a car park, where a few old Fiats and Vespas were parked next to a row of green wheelie bins in front of a crumbling red-brick wall.

'Flowers,' said Fede. 'We should have brought flowers.'

She took my arm and led me through a rusty metal gate, and I realised where we were. Beyond the entrance lay a small octagonal chapel in terracotta brick, surrounded by gravestones and funerary monuments.

I nodded. 'Oh, I see.'

She gripped my arm. 'Sorry. I should have told you. I haven't been here in years. But I thought it would be a good time to pay my respects to *nonno*.' She tested the gate, and it creaked open. 'He's through here, just down the side of the chapel.'

Many of the graves were well looked after, with fresh flowers in vases. Others were crumbling and long-neglected, their inscriptions now only semi-legible.

'Here we are.' She stopped, and crouched down, brushing the dust away from the stone that was inscribed with the name *Ravagnan*.

'Hello, *nonno*,' she murmured. 'I'm sorry. It's been a very long time. I've brought someone to meet you. I think you'd have liked him.'

I knelt down next to her and took my handkerchief from my pocket, to further clear the encrusted dirt. She patted my hand, and we knelt there in silence for a few moments.

She drew my hand to the niche above that of Giulio's. *Stefania Boscolo. Beloved wife of Giulio Ravagnan.* Again, I cleared the dirt from the inscription.

She got to her feet. 'Thank you.'

I hugged her. 'We'll come back. And we'll bring flowers next time.'

She nodded. 'Yes, we should.'

'Is your father here?'

She shook her head. 'No. He's in the cemetery in Malamocco. *Nonno* and *nonna* always considered themselves *Pellestrinotti*. Father not so much. He'd become a sophisticated city boy, after all.'

I heard footsteps on the gravel behind us.

'Federica?'

'Margherita? Lovely to see you.'

Margherita Ballarin smiled at us. Federica brushed the dirt from her hands, and they exchanged an awkward air kiss. 'Thank you for coming out.'

'It's no problem.'

A small lizard scurried across the gravel and over Margherita's sandalled foot, before scuttling away into the shade. She wiped a thin layer of sweat from her forehead. 'It's starting to get hot, isn't it? Properly hot.'

'I don't imagine it's much better in Rome,' said Fede.

'It's worse. Everyone who can gets out of town. Either the beach or the mountains.' She wiped her forehead again.

'I'm told the weather's due to break soon. It feels stormy.'

'It does.' Margherita laughed. 'Listen to us. I thought it was only the English who were obsessed with the weather.' She turned to me. 'No offence. But I don't imagine you wanted me to come out here just to talk about the prospect of rain in the next couple of days?'

'No,' said Fede. 'And I know you have things to do, and I'm grateful to you for coming over here. So I wondered if we might talk about Michele?'

She shrugged. 'I wonder what there is to talk about. We weren't close, as you probably know. And we hadn't seen each other since 2010.'

'I don't understand. I remember you from when Michele and I,' Fede looked at me, 'had a thing.' I smiled and nodded as if to indicate that I was perfectly happy with Federica having had a thing. Which, of course, I was. 'You seemed to get on well then.'

'We did. The trouble started when father died. I inherited his money, and Michele got the apartment. That made sense. I was living in Rome, after all.'

'I see. That seems reasonable.'

She gave a dry laugh. 'You would have thought so, wouldn't you?'

'Michele didn't agree?'

'You might say that. We exchanged some harsh words over it.'

'I'm sorry.'

She shrugged. 'He said it was unfair, that I had always

been Father's favourite, and why should I get all the money when he could have used it to expand his business. We had a blazing row over it. We didn't speak for years after that. Family, eh?'

'And then one year, I decided to come back. 2010 it would have been. Just to see some friends. It was early summer. And I decided it would be good to see Michele again. To make things right between us. More than that, I was worried about him. I'd heard stories. From friends.'

'What kind of stories?' said Fede.

'At first, it was just stuff like "Oh, Michele must be ever so successful these days, he seems to have so much money." And then it was "How on earth does Michele have so much money?".'

I thought back to the church website. 'I've seen a photograph of Michele at Madonna della Marina with two men – Giuseppe Lupo and Sandro Vicari.'

She nodded. 'Two *mafiosi*. Yes.'

Fede took a deep breath. 'So. Did you say anything about it?'

'I did.'

'That must have been an awkward conversation.'

'To say the least. I came straight out with it and asked him exactly how he was coming into so much money.'

'So what did he say?'

'He said he was working hard and building up an important new client base. And I asked him if that client base included gangsters.'

'What did he say to that?'

'That he didn't know what I meant. I told him that I'd

heard he'd been seen on a yacht on Lake Como, in the company of Lupo and Vicari. I asked him if these were the sort of men who were forming part of his new client base.

'At first he denied it. He said, yes, he'd been in Como and, coincidentally, he'd happened to meet the two of them. They'd asked him to come for drinks on Lupo's yacht. Well, as you can imagine,' she laughed, emptily, 'it would have been rude to refuse, wouldn't it?

'I told him that I didn't believe him. He said he didn't give a damn whether I did or not. He was making a success of his life at last, he said, and obviously I couldn't stand the thought of not being the "special one" any more.

'These people are *mafiosi*, I told him. He got angrier, and angrier. They were just businessmen, he said.

'I wasn't sure whether to laugh or cry. Do you know how many times I've heard that in Rome? They're "just businessmen". It's as if repeating the lie enough times will make it the truth. Who knows, perhaps he even believed it himself?

'I told him that you cannot deal with these people, not even once or you will never be free of them. And then I told him that I loved him, and I would help him if I could. But he had to be honest with me.

'I think he hesitated, just for a moment. Then he shook his head, and swore. Told me to get the hell out of his house and to come back when I felt like apologising. When I had some respect for what he'd managed to achieve. When I wasn't so damn jealous.'

She sighed. 'That was the last time we saw each other. The last words we exchanged were angry ones. Nearly a decade ago.'

'I'm sorry,' said Fede.

Margherita shrugged. 'There's nothing to be done now.'

'Just one thing,' I said. 'Why did you want to meet us out here? We could have come over to Malamocco.'

'No.' She shook her head vigorously. 'I don't want to spend more time there than I have to.'

'What's happened?'

'I went out early yesterday evening, just for a walk around the town. To see the places where Michele and I grew up. And then I thought I thought I'd stop for an *aperitivo*, watch the sun going down and decide where to go for dinner.

'And Albino Lupo, it seemed, had just the same idea. He'd seen me sitting alone and wanted to apologise. He was sorry, he said, if he'd upset me earlier. But it would be nice if we could meet up some time and talk about Michele, given that he'd been such a good friend of his father's. He even invited me out to dinner.' She shuddered. 'God, I feel dirty just talking about that man.'

'So what did you do?'

'What did I do? I declined of course. He said that was a great shame, but he hoped we'd run into each other in the next couple of days. He was, he told me, staying very close by.'

'Bloody hell,' I said.

'So a graveyard at the far end of Pellestrina seemed like a suitably remote spot to meet and talk.'

Fede put a hand on her shoulder. 'Thank you, Margherita.'

'It's fine. I hope it's helped.'

'It might have. Are you going to be here for long?'

'At least a few more days. I need to make sure everything's been sorted out with Michele's apartment. There are a number of papers I'll need to dig out, and he was never very good at keeping that sort of thing in order.'

'Okay. Well I hope we can meet again. We'll do something different next time. You must come round for dinner. Nathan's an excellent cook.'

Margherita smiled. 'An English cook. Well, that does sound like an offer I can't refuse.' She kissed first Federica, and then me. 'I'll look forward to it. Let's keep in touch.'

Chapter 34

Prisons, by their nature, are not designed to look beautiful, but, from the outside at least, Santa Maria Maggiore was quite a handsome red-brick building. Certainly, it was hard to imagine one more beautifully situated. Built during the 1920s on the ruins of the convent from which it took its name, it stood amongst the canals and green fields of one of the quieter areas of Santa Croce.

The interior, I knew, was a different matter. Bleached of any colour beyond the filthy grey of discoloured, crumbling concrete it felt as bleak and soulless as any Victorian prison in the UK. The overcrowding that had led to frequent riots in the past had at least been reduced, but the place still stank of desperation.

Santa Maria Maggiore. Where Giuseppe Lupo, once a mafia boss, had ended his days alongside some of the poorest and most wretched members of society.

Jack Stubbs was approaching the end of his sentence and would be released within two months. At which point, two officers from the penitentiary police would accompany him to Marco Polo Airport, put him on a plane to the UK, and the Italian state would wash its hands of him.

The governor had been surprised by my telephone call. Not all consuls were quite so diligent when it came to the rights of their incarcerated citizens, he'd said. I told him that I was an unusually diligent consul; at which point he'd laughed and agreed it would be useful for me to speak to Stubbs and tell him exactly what was going to happen. I asked him if there was anything I should bring, and was told that cigarettes and sweets always went down well.

I hadn't been there in some time. British tourists occasionally got themselves into trouble, but it usually resulted in nothing more serious than a night sleeping it off in a police cell and being shouted at by angry cops the following morning. Prison sentences were rare. Nobody on the security gate could remember me, and they took their time in letting me through. As ever, they seemed baffled by the idea that there was a British Honorary Consul in Venice, and more so by the fact that I would want to visit someone. They scanned me and dusted me down to check for contraband. I'd bought a few packets of cigarettes from my previous tobacconist's, who seemed pleased to see me but also disappointed when I told him I was still quitting. He seemed only half convinced when I told him I was buying them for a man in prison and gave me a wink when I left, as if to suggest I might be tempted to sneak a crafty one. The thought had also occurred to me.

A guard took me through into the interview room.

'Okay. I'll be with you the whole time, but there'll be no trouble with this one. He's a smart guy, kept himself out of trouble. Do you have anything for him?'

I took out the clear plastic bag containing my presents. I'd bought a few packets of sweets and a newspaper as well as the cigarettes. In a thoughtful touch I'd remembered to buy him a lighter as well. The guard checked that the seals were still intact. Presumably the smuggling of something stronger than tobacco had been a problem in the past.

The door opened, and Jack Stubbs came in. I vaguely recognised him from his photograph in the newspapers, although he appeared to have lost a lot of weight. He was dressed in a black T-shirt and jeans, and his face was haggard with a thin layer of stubble.

We shook hands, briefly.

'Mr Stubbs?'

'Hi.'

'I'm Nathan Sutherland, the British Honorary Consul. I just need to check, has it been explained to you why I'm here?'

'Yeah. Briefly. You're going to tell me what happens when I get out, right?'

'That's pretty much it. Now, you know of course that they'll put you straight on a flight to Britain. And, I have to tell you, that unfortunately it will be very difficult for you to return to Italy in the future.'

He laughed. 'Come back to this shithole? I don't think that's going to be a problem, mate.'

'I understand.' I took out the plastic bag of gifts and slid it across the table to him. He saw the cigarettes and shook his head.

'I don't smoke.'

'You don't?' I couldn't keep the surprise out of my voice.

'No. What, do you think everyone smokes in here?'

'Yes. I thought you used them as, what's the word, *currency*?'

He shook his head. 'You watch far too many films, man.'

'I'm sorry. I've got you some sweets as well. And a newspaper.'

He shrugged.

'The paper has last night's football results, if that's of interest?'

He sighed. 'Cigarettes, and a tabloid with the football results. Is that really what you think everyone's like in here?'

'I'm sorry. I don't know you, but I really am trying to help.'

'Sure.' He took the paper from me and flicked through it to the celebrity pages and a photograph of a minor reality show star, wearing a broad smile and little else. He grinned. 'Well, I suppose she'll brighten up the cell a bit, eh?'

I smiled back, as best I could. Then I ran through the protocols of what would happen to him on release day. He nodded away throughout, but seemed less than interested.

'To be honest, mate – I mean, it's nice for you to come out and all that – but all I want to do is keep my nose clean for the next month and get home. And never bloody come back here.'

'I never asked you why you came.'

'Stag night.'

'A stag night. In Venice?'

'Yeah,' he laughed, hollowly. 'We got that one wrong, didn't we?'

'It wasn't yours, I hope.'

'Nah. Friend of a friend. Seemed like it would be a laugh. Again, I got that one wrong.'

'I mean, what is there to do on a stag night in Venice?' I asked, wondering if I really wanted to know.

'Number One Pub Crawl.'

'I'm sorry?'

'Number One Pub Crawl. You go down the Grand Canal on the number one *vaporetto* line, get off at every stop and have a drink in the nearest bar.'

'That's a *thing*? That's an actual *thing*?'

He shrugged. 'Seems it is.'

I suddenly felt very, very old. I shook my head. 'So do you have a place to stay when you get home?'

'Back to Mum and Dad's I guess. I lost my job, of course.'

I made what I hoped was a sympathetic little noise.

'Girlfriend hasn't written in a while so my hopes aren't high there. But at least I'll have a place to stay.'

'I'm sorry.'

'If he hadn't tried to steal my bloody phone none of this shit would have happened.'

I nodded. I'd seen the police reports. Jack Stubbs hadn't just punched him, he'd hospitalised him.

'I know. But it could have been a lot worse. The other party was seriously hurt.' I took a deep breath. 'People can get locked away for a lot longer than this. In some ways you've been lucky.'

'Lucky? Oh, I'm the luckiest man on earth, Mr Sutherland. Christ. What a lucky, lucky man I am.'

'I know that's not what you want to hear.'

He looked at me, and shook his head in contempt. 'What are you, my social worker now? I had a bloody priest come around straight after they banged me up. Asking if he could help. What do I need a priest for, I ask you?'

'Ah. That'll be Father Michael. He feels quite strongly about pastoral care.'

'He can stick his bloody pastoral care where the light of the Good Lord don't shine. So. You've come and read me my rights, is there any reason why you're still here?'

I drummed my fingers on the table. 'There might be.'

He grunted, and shrugged, in a way that suggested I could at least ask even if I should not expect an answer.

'I'd like to talk to you about Giuseppe Lupo.'

A grin slowly spread across his face. The guard stiffened and shot me a look.

'One moment please, Jack.' I turned to speak to the guard and switched to Italian. 'I need to speak to him about this.'

'I don't understand. That's not why you're here.'

'I know.' I'd come prepared for this and had worked out an excuse that, to me at least, sounded on the edge of plausibility. 'He's going to be back in the UK in a month or two. The press will know he was in jail with a gang boss. They'll want to speak to him, know about conditions in Italian prisons, that sort of thing.'

'I still don't understand. Why is that important?'

'Look, you know what press coverage is like of the system here. Do you really want there to be bad headlines in the UK as well? "My Italian Prison Hell", that sort of thing.'

He shrugged. 'Don't see that it'll make much difference to me. Might even be good. Might make some of the silly bastards think twice before coming over here and causing trouble.'

'Maybe. I don't think it'll put your boss in a good mood, though.'

'Hmmph. Maybe so. Okay, make it quick, though.'

'Thanks.' I turned back to Jack. 'So. Giuseppe Lupo.'

Jack grinned, and waved a finger at myself and the guard. 'I understood most of that, you know?'

'You did?'

'Sure. I've learned a bit of Italian in here. Not much else to do with my time.' He shook his head. 'Your accent's not that great, you know?'

'Oh, thanks for that.'

'I even taught some of the others a bit of English. Gave me a bit of an edge.' He nodded at the guard. 'Not him, though. He's not a natural student, if you know what I mean.' The guard stiffened but said nothing. 'So. What do you want to know?'

'First of all, did you know him well? Do you know who he was?'

'I think everyone did. Everyone else in here, well, probably shouldn't be in here. Just petty crooks or unlucky bastards like me. North Africans, East Europeans. Half the poor sods don't know Italian, the other half don't know English. It's tough for them. But we all knew that Mr Lupo was, what would you call him, a mafia don?'

'Close enough. Did you ever speak to him?'

'Sure I did. He liked to practise his English.'

'What did you talk about?'

'Just stuff. Family, friends. The weather.'

'Just that?'

'Just that. What, you think he talked to me about life as a master criminal?'

'I was kind of hoping so. Listen, did he ever talk to you about a man called Michele Ballarin?'

'Nope. Never heard of him.'

'Okay. What about Elio Ravagnan?'

He shook his head. 'Don't recognise the name. Listen, he just wanted to make small talk. Do you know what he looked like?'

'I've seen the photographs.'

'So you know what he was like then. He was just a little old man looking forward to getting out.'

'Did he mention his son?'

Stubbs frowned. 'Had a weird name, didn't he? What was it again?'

'Albino.'

'Yeah, that was it. He got quite upset whenever he talked about him.'

'Really?'

'Yes. Family seems to be important to people in this country, doesn't it? Anyway, old Mr Lupo talked about him a bit. Apparently he was born on the day the Pope died. Not this one, or the one before. I'm trying to think now. Not the German guy. Before him. There was the Polish guy who was there forever, what was his name?'

'Wojtyla.'

'No, that's not him. John Paul the Second, that was it.' I smiled to myself. 'Anyway, not him either. The one before. I don't remember him, maybe you do?'

'John Paul the First.'

'That's the bloke. Anyway, Albino was born on the day he died, so Gramps gave him the same name. Quite a religious bloke he was. Used to see a priest every week.'

'Ah. Do you remember the name?'

'No idea, mate. Came from the Lido, I think. Always turned up late, complained about the boats every time.'

'Little guy? With thick glasses?'

'Yeah, that sounds like him.'

'Okay. That's useful. Thanks.'

'Anything else?'

'Maybe. Did he have any friends? If that's the right word.'

'It's the nick. You don't have friends. You have people who might want to beat you up or nick your stuff – or both – and then you have those who don't. That's all.'

'Okay. Okay, I'm sorry, I'm not a criminal. I don't know how this works. Who did he speak to?'

He shrugged. 'Everyone. Except maybe the Africans. He didn't like them.'

'Yes, but anyone in particular?'

'I suppose the guy he shared a cell with. A guy called Enrico Zanetti.'

'What do you know about him?'

'Just another petty crim. No one special. Not a boss or anything.'

I scribbled away in my notepad. 'Okay. That could be useful. Thanks.'

'Any reason you're asking me all this?'

'I'm trying to defuse a delicate domestic situation.'

'Blimey.' He smiled. 'You've asked a lot in exchange for a pin-up from a newspaper, Mr Sutherland.'

'I know.'

'I'll take the cigarettes, though. And the sweets. Some of the guys here will like them. So, do you really think the papers will want to speak to me?'

'It's possible. The trouble is, you've only been here for a few months. You're not exactly a *cause célèbre*. But they might do.'

'Do you think I'll get some money? What should I hold out for?'

'Whatever they give you, I guess.'

'Good. Might be a bit difficult to find work now. With this on my record.'

'What did you do before?'

'Computer Programmer.' I must have looked surprised. 'That surprises you, eh?'

I was going to deny it, but then nodded. 'Just a bit.'

'What did you think? Football hooligan?'

'The two aren't exclusive. To be honest, I hadn't really thought about it. Look, just a word of advice. If the press do talk to you, try and be subtle.'

'Subtle?'

'Yes. They're going to want to make your experience sound like *Midnight Express*. Now you can do that if you want, but don't go naming names. Don't go talking about Venetian mafia and Giuseppe Lupo.'

'Why not?'

'Because they're the Venetian mafia and he was Giuseppe Lupo. Because it's not a clever thing to do. You understand?'

He nodded. 'I understand.'

The guard looked at his watch. 'Are you nearly finished?'

'I think so.' I got to my feet. 'Okay, thanks, Jack. I hope everything goes as well as it can.'

We shook hands. He patted the newspaper. 'Thanks for this.'

I nodded at the guard. 'I think I'm ready to go now,' I said.

In the Wolf's Den

'Tell me more about Albino,' I say.

He hesitates. 'He was like all boys,' he finally says.

'What do you mean by that?'

'Prone to getting into trouble. I think all of us go through that phase.'

I laugh. 'I think we all do.'

The Old Wolf half closes his eyes. 'But there were other things, of course. When he became a bit older and realised who his father was. He came back home from school one day – I think he would have been about ten or eleven – in tears. Someone had said to him "ask your papà what it feels like to kill someone".'

'What did you do?'

'I told him it was nonsense. And I asked him for the name of the boy who had said this. It didn't happen again.

'But that didn't solve the problem. Now he knew that if anyone bullied him at school, I could make their life a living hell. He became more and more difficult to rein in as he grew older. You know I told you that he was never to come back from school with a bad grade?'

'I remember.'

'I meant that. If he ever did, it was the worse for him.'

I pick my words cautiously. 'What exactly do you mean by that?'

He blocks the question. 'I mean it was the worse for him.'

I decide to push it no further.

'But his grades improved. And I congratulated myself on being a good father. Tough but fair. Then one day,' he sighs, 'one day I heard he'd threatened the headmaster of his school. And I realised just why his grades were improving.'

'What did you do?'

'I put my hand across his face. And he punched me back, and sent me staggering across the room. He told me he wouldn't take it from me any more. He disappeared for three days. Maddalena, of course, was frantic. She blamed me. Probably correctly. He returned, stinking of cigarettes and cheap booze. He went up to his room. And we never, ever spoke about it again. And at that point I realised I hadn't been beating the devil out of him. I'd beaten the devil into him.

'Then, in his late teens, things began to go wrong. For all of us. The good days of easy money were coming to an end. Angel Face was arrested. He turned pentito *and named names in order to avoid a life sentence. I don't think he was ever one for "honour amongst thieves".'*

'You were one of the names, I understand?'

'We were. Both Vicari and me. But Sandro had been well prepared, as ever. There was nothing they could pin on us. But it needed the right people to be paid. We lost much of what we'd built up over the years.' He sighs. 'And that didn't help, of course, with Albino. He said I was weak, that what sort of man was I if I couldn't provide for my family? Provoking me. I think he wanted me to hit him so he could have the satisfaction of hitting me back.

'A number of colleagues didn't wait to be arrested. Some of them went to the South, others fled abroad. Croatia was a good place at that time. Maniero had been friends with people close to the president. Francesco Tonicello went to England.' He chuckles. 'They say he spent ten years there selling newspapers. He's in jail now, as you know.'

'And those of us who stayed went underground for a while. Other gangs formed; continuity gangs. They wanted the Old Wolf to hunt with them, of course. So I did. And, for a while, the good days returned. Money came in, as it used to. Even Albino started talking to me again. We paid the usual money to informers in the police, and after a while we started to feel we could relax again.

'Then one day in early 2006 I took a telephone call from one of my informers. Something was coming, he told me. Something big. Something called Ghost Dog.'

Chapter 35

The walk across town left me feeling uncomfortably hot and sweaty by the time I reached Campo San Giacomo dell'Orio, and the sixty steps to Dario's apartment did not help matters at all. The Costa–Visintin family, it seemed fair to assume, were in better shape than me.

'Nat, how are you doing?' He went to hug me and then decided against it. 'Man, you look hot.'

'I am hot. I've been at a hot prison all morning. Air conditioning doesn't seem to be high on their list of priorities.'

'I used to know a guy who worked there, you know? He said the one good thing about the summer is that it gets too hot to riot.'

'I can imagine. And then I made my way over here. Walking through a hot city surrounded by people seemed better than standing on a hot *vaporetto* surrounded by even more people.'

'You should have taken your jacket off.'

'Yeah. That would have been an idea.'

'Would a beer be good?'

'It would be very good.' He fetched two bottles from the fridge and cracked them open. I closed my eyes, and pressed the bottle to my forehead.

'Better?'

'Much. You know, Dario, I'll never understand how you manage those stairs, every day, in this sort of weather.'

He shrugged. 'You get used to it. Most of the time we're carrying shopping as well.'

'Couldn't we have met at the Brazilians? Or a bar in the *campo*? We could have had lunch.'

He shook his head, and looked serious. 'No. Franco got back to me with some information. And it's stuff I don't really want to talk about in public.'

'Okay, I understand.' I looked around. 'Where's Vally?'

'Out with Emily. I don't want them to hear this either.'

I shook my head. 'God. Is it that serious?'

He nodded. 'I think it might be.'

'God,' I repeated.

He held up the envelope I'd given him with the photographs and the USB stick.

'Let's get started.'

He laid out the six photographs on the table.

'Okay. Franco's managed to identify all of these guys.' He pointed to the top left photograph, a man in dark glasses getting out of a car. 'This is Giorgio Pozzi. From Vicenza. Suspected of drug trafficking, and running arms to Croatia in the 1990s.'

He moved on to the next image. 'Luigi Crovi. Drugs, again. Extortion. Prostitution. Served a short sentence for domestic violence in the mid-'90s.

'This one here is Silvano Gabrielli. Kidnapping, extortion, robbery. Achille Fontana – suspected of the murder of two members of the *San Donà di Piave* cartel. Gino Pattarello – bank robbery. Roberto Rizzi – kidnapping and extortion.'

He sighed. 'All of these guys were senior members of the Mala del Brenta, Nat.'

I shook my head. 'Oh Christ, Dario, this is bad. And it explains a lot.'

'Okay. Tell me more.'

'There's a cop on Pellestrina. *Maresciallo* Busetto. He called round the other day. These photos were out on the kitchen table. I thought he seemed interested in them. Then yesterday he saw Giuseppe Lupo's son talking to us at Ballarin's memorial service. Everything we do seems to link us with these bastards. No wonder he's interested in us.' I rubbed my eyes and took a deep breath. 'Okay. So my next question is – what are these photographs doing in a box in my father-in-law's attic?'

Dario held up the USB stick. 'That's what this is all about, Nat. It's about something called *Ghost Dog*. It all starts back in 1994 with a guy called Felice Maniero. Angel Face, they called him.'

'Okay, I've heard of this guy. Go on.'

'By 1994 Mr Angel Face was pretty much in charge of every form of organised crime in the Veneto. It took about four hundred cops to bring him down. But they did it. He was arrested in Turin and he turned *pentito* to avoid life imprisonment. He named names. Lots of them. There were over four hundred arrests. Mobsters, businessmen, police. Judges, even.'

'Right. And that was *Ghost Dog*?'

'No. That was over ten years later. Thing is with

organisations like this, they always grow back. All the old guys,' he indicated the photographs, 'they just ended up running smaller gangs. Within ten years everything was back where it was before. And that's where *Ghost Dog* comes in. In 2006.'

'Another crackdown?'

'Exactly. The cops had two informants. Let me check a moment.' He clicked away at his computer. 'Franco sent me some further info. Here we are. Stefano Galletto and Giuseppe Pastore. Nobody knows where they are. Either in prison or somewhere else, living different lives under different names.'

'Galletto and Pastore. No one else?'

He shook his head. 'No one else. At least not that Franco knows.'

'Not Giuseppe Lupo? Or Sandro Vicari?'

'No. Again, Franco didn't mention them.'

'But these guys – the guys in the photographs – what happened to them after *Ghost Dog*?'

Dario sighed. 'This is the thing, Nat. They were all on the most wanted list. You'd have expected them all to have been arrested during the crackdown. But none of them were. They just disappeared. Nobody knows where they are now. Britain, Argentina, who knows?'

He plugged in the USB stick. 'Franco's done his best with this. It's an export of an email account. The trouble is, it's encrypted. All he knows is that it refers to something called the *Ghost Dog* account. But the email address,' he sighed, 'that was easier to track down. It was a Hotmail account registered to Michele Ballarin.'

'Shit. Oh shit.'

'I'm sorry, Nat.'

'Dario, I spoke to Ballarin's sister this morning. Together with this, it looks as if Ballarin was complicit in helping known *mafiosi* to flee the country. And if he was,' I paused, 'maybe we need to accept that Elio was as well.'

Chapter 36

We sat in silence for a while. Then Dario patted me on the back.

'Would another beer be good?'

'Bloody hell, it would.' I rubbed my forehead. 'But I'm not going to. I think I'm going to need a clear head.'

'How about some music?'

'Yeah. Yeah, that might help.'

He slid a disc into the stereo and, after a gentle, reflective opening, David Gilmour's power chords thundered out of the speakers.

I raised an eyebrow. '*The Wall?*'

'Yep!'

'Oh good. That should cheer me up.'

I closed my eyes and listened to 'In the Flesh?' and wished that I'd taken Dario up on his offer of a beer.

'Right, how long have we got before Vally and Emily get back?'

Dario checked his watch. 'Perhaps an hour?'

'And I guess you'd like me to be gone by then?'

'Nat, it's not that. It's just that if Vally finds out I've been investigating stuff like this – mafia business – well, it's not going to be good. For either of us.'

'You're right. And I'm sorry. It wasn't fair to drag you into this. Okay, one hour then. I promise I'll be gone by the time they get back. I just need to use your computer, okay?'

'Sure.'

Time finally ran out for Giuseppe Lupo on a baking hot August Saturday. Lupo is now seventy years old, but the greybeard seen in handcuffs outside the carabinieri station on Via Lungomare Adriatico, Chioggia might have been ten years older. Crime may have paid for the elderly member of the Mala del Brenta, but the passing of time has left its scars. Certainly the confused-looking old man arrested on August 28th bore little physical resemblance to the dapper figure of popular legend.

There is still some confusion about Lupo's movements over the past six months, following the attempt on his life earlier this year. Stories are circulating that his most recent place of residence had been at a hotel in Chioggia; whilst other rumours place him on Pellestrina or even in Malamocco.

Lupo is known to have a long, sentimental attachment to the church of Madonna della Marina, having contributed considerable sums to its restoration. A local bar owner, who did not wish to be named, said it was common knowledge that Lupo had attended Mass there on several occasions earlier this year, a claim firmly denied by parish priest Don Francesco.

Gianni Brezzi, *La Repubblica (Veneto edition)*

'Brezzi.' I turned to Dario. 'I've come across this guy before. Have you heard of him?'

He shook his head. 'Not a Venetian name.'

'Good. That should make him easier to find. Can you check the phone book?'

'Sure.'

'Great. In the meantime, I'll check out Lupo's cellmate.'

Enrico Zanetti had not generated anything like the number of column inches that Giuseppe Lupo had. He'd spent three years in Santa Maria Maggiore, sent down for distribution of cocaine. He appeared to have strong links with what remained of Clan Giostrai. And that was interesting. Stubbs had suggested the two men got on well, and yet, from what I'd been able to learn, the Mala del Brenta and Clan Giostrai had been at daggers drawn for years. Prison, I supposed, could make strange bedfellows, especially if one had no choice, but there was something odd about it.

I searched further. Zanetti was a Mestrino by birth but had moved to the Lido a few years ago. Most of his criminal activity seemed to have sprung out of his work with a local travelling fair which had been used as a base for dealing and distribution of drugs. He'd been arrested after beating up a local youth following an argument over a girl. The young man had knocked on his door late at night, to be met by Zanetti swinging a baseball bat. The resulting incident had given the cops the opportunity to investigate further, leading to the discovery of several kilos of cocaine hidden in olive oil canisters, and a number of firearms in Zanetti's garage.

What a lovely man, I thought, as I searched for further stories. There was little more to be found, except a photograph from the *Gazzettino* on the day of his sentencing. I expanded it and looked closer. Then I folded my hands behind my head, leaned back and smiled. Things were, finally, starting to make a bit of sense.

'Nat, this Brezzi guy lives on the Lido. Not far from where Federica used to live.' Dario leaned over my shoulder to look at the screen. 'You look happy.'

'I think I am. I know this guy. I'm sure I do.' I expanded the photograph, just to be sure. But there was no doubt about it. He might have been wearing a suit instead of a T-shirt and shorts but Zanetti, in handcuffs between two police officers, was undoubtedly the irritating little man who'd wanted to be my best friend on the bus the other day.

There was more. Another photograph showed a woman leaving the courtroom, her face not quite concealed behind enormous dark glasses. I expanded it, looking at it this way and that and then closed my eyes thinking back to a few days previously. I opened them again, and took an even closer look. It was definitely her.

'Zanetti's wife, Dario.' I checked her name. 'Giulia Tagliapietra. The woman who's been acting as our cleaner ever since we arrived on Pellestrina.'

'So, what do we do now?'

I smiled 'We do nothing, Dario. Or rather you do.'

'I can't do that, Nat.'

'Yes, you can. Have a nice quiet evening with your lovely wife and lovely girl. You've done more than enough already.'

'What about you?'

I checked my watch again. Early evening now, and too late to consider paying a call on Brezzi.

'I'm going home to cook fish, Dario. And then I'll have a bit of a think . . .'

Chapter 37

I winkled out the last scrap of flesh from the prawn shell, popped it in my mouth, and then pushed my chair back, patting my stomach.

'Happy?' said Fede.

'Happier. Things seem easier after dinner. Actually, things seem easier whilst preparing dinner. You feel in control of things. Butterfly prawns, griddle zucchini. Everything just seems right.'

'That's nice. It was very good.'

'Thanks.' I frowned. 'But I do wonder about the zucchini. That griddle pan isn't quite as good as my own.'

She pushed her chair back from the table and gave me a playful cuff on the back of the head. 'I think we've had the *Masterchef* conversation before. Now, shall I wash up or would that offend your creative sensibilities?'

'No, no. That's fine. Stick the shells in the fridge though. I'll make a stock with them. I might make risotto tomorrow.'

'Lovely.' She took our plates through to the kitchen. 'So, our cleaner is a gangster's wife then?'

'I believe the correct phrase is "a gangster's moll". But yes.'

'So, what's our next step?'

'Tomorrow? I need to have a talk with a guy called Gianni Brezzi. He's a journalist. Lives near your old place up by Santa Maria Elisabetta.'

'Okay. Do you want me to come along?'

'I was wondering if you could meet with Margherita again. She doesn't know me at all, so there's no need for me to be there.'

'Sure. But is there anything else for her to tell us?'

'I don't know. But I'd just like to know if she's heard from Lupo again. And if she knows what he wants.'

'Okay. It's worth a go.' She returned from the kitchen and flopped herself down in her grandad's old armchair. 'Look at this,' she said, rubbing at a mark on the leather. 'I remember him doing this. He fell asleep with his pipe in his hand one night. *Nonna* gave him hell over it the next morning.' She yawned and stretched, setting off Gramsci who repeated her gesture. 'Look at him,' she said. 'Two plates full of seafood and not the slightest bit of interest.'

'I know. I cooked him a prawn especially but he didn't touch it. I think I might have overcooked it.'

'Overcooked it? He's a cat. He's a cat who eats dried food. How can you have overcooked it?' She shook her head, and chuckled. 'Oh this is nice. Just talking about silly, normal things. About ungrateful cats and Grandad's old armchair. Nothing about mafia and mobsters.' She sighed. 'What are we going to do, *caro*?'

I closed my eyes, and shook my head.

And then it came to me. My eyes snapped open and I jumped to my feet.

'I know exactly what we're going to do.'

'You do?'

'Yes. We're going to go to *da Celeste* and have a *sgroppino*.'

'Are you mad?'

'Not at all. It's a brilliant idea. If we stay here, we'll just end up getting depressed. Possibility of drinking too much. Leading to a row. Leading to another night on the sofa for one of us and – I should remind you – it's your turn next time. But if we go out, we'll have a lovely walk under the stars, sit outside looking over the lagoon, enjoy dessert and everything will be as it's supposed to be on honeymoon.' She showed no signs of moving. 'Come on, let's get going.'

She got to her feet. 'Nathan, there's no way a restaurant is going to let us in just to order the cheapest dessert on the menu.'

'Yes, they will. We've spent plenty of money there over the past weeks. They know we're on honeymoon. And, if need be, I am prepared to spend silly money on this as well.'

'You really are mad.'

'I am. But I am also one hundred per cent right. Come on!'

I never made *sgroppino* at home. Not that it was difficult to make. All you needed was to whip together lemon sorbet with a shot of vodka and a dash of prosecco, and pour the results into a chilled glass. There really wasn't much that could go wrong and, even if it did, it was still pretty good.

No, the problem was simply that *sgroppino* was not made for drinking in your living room in front of the television. It needed the other essential ingredients of the company of friends and the open air. Was it a cocktail, or did it actually qualify as a dessert? I didn't care. All I knew was that it was the taste of being on holiday.

So we sat there and drank under the eyes of restaurant staff who, despite occasionally throwing a glance at their watches, nevertheless looked as if they thought this was all quite sweet and if this was what the honeymooners wanted to do, well, they would just keep the restaurant open for us a little bit longer.

Eventually, the owner of the *gelateria* across the street turned off the lights and pulled the shutters down, and the crowd of teens outside – flirting, smoking, some even eating ice cream – decided it was time to be on their way. The head waiter remained a respectful distance from our table but I could tell the moment was approaching when the need to go home and go to bed would outweigh his reluctance to say anything.

'We really should go,' I said.

Fede sighed. 'I suppose we should. It's been lovely though.'

'Yeah. It has. Haven't I been brilliant?'

'Okay. I have to admit you have been modestly brilliant this time.'

I took a banknote out, and tucked it under the empty *sgroppino* glass.

'Are you overtipping through fear?'

'Maybe. But I don't care. They've earned it.'

The head waiter smiled as he bade us good night, and then smiled even more upon spotting the tip.

We made our way back along the *lungomare*. There were still a few pedestrians around, and a couple of kids on bicycles but Pellestrina, it seemed, was going to bed. Far, far in the distance we could see the twinkling lights of the refineries at Porto Marghera. I had never, ever thought of Marghera twinkling before, and I chuckled.

'What's so funny?' said Fede.

'I'm just thinking how lovely a chemical plant looks. And more than that,' I spread my arms wide, 'all this. Isn't it just so bloody wonderful?'

'I told you it was nice.'

'It's more than just nice. It's so lovely. So quiet. You can walk properly without tripping over tourists. The buses and the boats aren't choked with people.'

Fede linked her arm in mine. 'My goodness. Listen to you. You'll be wanting to move here next.'

I paused for a moment. 'Would that be so bad? I mean, really?'

'Ah, imagine the winter. When the wind and rain come in off the Adriatic. The sheer hassle of getting anywhere. And you'd get bored. Eventually even you'd get fed up with *da Celeste*. And they're closed in winter.'

'It's a risk I'm prepared to take.'

'Listen to you,' she repeated, and kissed me. Then she sighed. 'But I suppose we'd better go home. There's a lot of stuff to do tomorrow.'

I nodded. 'You're right, of course. But I'm still thinking about it.'

Judging by the yowling that was coming from inside the house, Gramsci had not taken well to being left on his own. Fede sighed. 'There's another problem for you. Imagine how our neighbours would feel, having to live next to him for three hundred and sixty-five days a year.' She was about to push open the garden gate, when she suddenly stopped and I banged into the back of her.

'Sorry.'

She put a finger to my lips, shushing me.

'What's going on?' I whispered.

'Did you switch the lights off?'

I hesitated. 'Of course I did. Well, at least, I think I did.'

'Look.'

One of the shutters did not close quite perfectly, and we could see a blade of light shining through the gap, occasionally broken by a shadow. As if someone were walking around inside.

'Gramsci?' I said.

Fede gave me a withering look. 'He wouldn't have switched the lights on, would he?' She took her keys out of her bag. 'Come on.'

'Are you serious?'

'Only one person has a set of keys apart from us. I think we can manage this.'

'Only one person that we know of.'

'I don't care. This is my house – our house – now, and I'm sick of this.'

Before I could even think of stopping her, she had pushed the gate open, walked up the short garden path, and opened the front door.

'Good evening, Giulia,' she said.

Chapter 38

Giulia looked startled for a moment, and then gathered herself. '*Signora?*'

'Hello, Giulia. We weren't expecting you.'

She was standing next to the bookshelf. In her left hand, she was holding the postcard that Elio had sent to Federica, the image of the *Virgin in the company of twelve saints.* There was a nasty scratch on her right hand. Gramsci sat on the back of the sofa, looking exceptionally pleased with himself.

'Sorry,' I said. 'He's not very friendly.' I pointed at her hand. 'You want to put something on that.'

'What are you doing here, Giulia?' said Fede.

'I'm sorry, *signora.* I think I left something here when I was cleaning. I knocked at the door but no one answered so I let myself in.'

'You left something here?'

'*Sissignora.*'

'I understand. Can you tell us what it was? Perhaps we've seen it.'

'Thank you, *signora.* I've already found it.' She patted her bag. 'My ID card. It was here on the shelf.'

'Oh that. Well, that's important. Good thing you found it. I wonder what it was doing there.'

Giulia gave a half-laugh, and shrugged. 'I must have put it down while cleaning.'

'You must have done.' Fede nodded at the postcard. 'You like that?'

'It's very pretty, *signora*.'

'Pretty. Yes. I think so too.'

'You're sure it was an ID card?' I said. 'Not your journalist's card?'

She laughed again, nervously this time. 'I don't understand, *signore*.'

I sighed. 'Oh, cut the crap, Giulia. It's late and I want to go to bed. You've been sneaking around here trying to find something. Looking under the floorboards, rearranging books. Ringing up Federica's mother, pretending to be from the press. Trying to find something out. But what?'

She put her hands to her face. She might actually have been crying, but we already knew her to be a good actress.

'Did your husband put you up to this Giulia? Enrico Zanetti?'

She dropped her hands from her face.

'He's not a good man, Giulia. I think you know that as well. Come on. Just tell us. What are you looking for? Just what is it that you think we know?'

'I can't tell you. I'm sorry. I just can't.'

Federica stretched out her hand. 'Okay. Let's try something a bit easier. Why don't we start with you giving our keys back? And the postcard.'

Giulia looked unsure for a moment, then nodded and

reached into her bag and took out a bunch of keys.

Fede stretched her hand out further. 'Thank you.'

Giulia pulled her hand back at the last moment, and dropped the keys to the floor. Fede took her eyes off her for just one moment but it was enough. Giulia punched her in the face and bolted through the door.

I dropped to my knees next to Fede, who had blood streaming from her nose.

'Are you okay?'

'Just get after her.'

'You're sure you're okay?'

'I've got bloody heels on. You get after her.'

Giulia had a start on me but I could see her shadow receding in the distance, in the alley leading to the main road. There was the blare of a car horn, and a screech of tyres, but then she was across and climbing up the stone steps that led to the top of the *murazzi*.

Running after a lone woman late at night was, I thought, something that was ripe for misunderstanding but, fortunately, there was no one else around. This section of the *murazzi* was angled, and the irregular marble slabs were illuminated only by the moonlight, making it difficult to run. She was heading for a gap in the tree-line, towards the beach.

'Giulia,' I shouted after her. 'Don't run. I only want to talk.'

She stopped for a moment, and turned around. I couldn't see the expression on her face, so I held up my hands. 'We can talk about this, Giulia.'

She shook her head, turned, and ran again.

I made to run after her but had taken only a few steps

when I tripped on one of the irregular marble blocks. I put my hands out to break my fall, and then rolled, over and over, down the slope of the *murazzi* until, for the second time in a week, my fall was broken by a bush.

I lay there for a few seconds, my head spinning, and then got unsteadily to my feet. A few cuts and bruises but nothing seemed to be broken.

Giulia, of course, was long gone.

Chapter 39

I poured out a cup of coffee for myself, and a mug of Earl Grey for Federica.

'So,' I said, 'I take it we're not expecting the house to be cleaned today?'

Fede smiled. 'Perhaps not. How are you feeling?'

'Not too bad really. How about you?'

She rubbed the bridge of her nose. 'A bit sore. Nothing serious. How visible is it?'

'You can hardly see it.'

'Hardly?'

'I mean just a little bit.' I frowned. 'This isn't like you, Fede, to worry about something like this?'

'Not me, you idiot, *mamma*. I thought if I had time I might go and see her tomorrow. But if she notices that something's even slightly wrong it'll set her off again. And so "hardly visible" isn't something I can risk.'

'Heh. Right then, I'd better be off. I'll see you later. I'll make us that risotto I mentioned.'

'Lovely.' She touched my cheek. 'You've got a few scratches yourself.'

'I know. I've scrubbed up as best I can. Do I look respectable?'

'Respectable enough.' She smiled. 'Don't worry. They're hardly visible.'

I got to my feet, and kissed the top of her head. 'See you later.' Then something on the mantelpiece caught my eye. 'Hang on, what are these?'

'Those? The keys she threw at us last night, remember?'

I picked them up. The key fob was a little red, white and green stick figure with a football for a head. '*Ciao*' from Italia '90.

'Is something wrong?'

'No. It's just that I was thinking about '*Ciao*' only the other day. I wonder why?'

'There's another thing,' said Fede. 'Those aren't just our keys. There's another one on there.'

'Hmm. Interesting.' I dropped them into my pocket. 'I'll take these with me. Just in case.'

'Mr Sutherland?'

'*Signor* Brezzi. Thanks for agreeing to meet me.'

'No problem.' He smiled. 'I'm just grateful that people still read my words. You don't always expect that as a journalist. Come in.'

He led me upstairs to his apartment. Bright, modern and looking out across the lagoon as far as the *centro storico*.

I nodded in approval. 'Lovely view.'

'Thank you. It belonged to my wife.' He laughed. 'She was always more successful than me, you know?'

'My partner – no, I'm sorry, my wife – used to live around here. Although her flat faced in the opposite direction. Perhaps you know her. Federica Ravagnan?'

He shook his head. 'I don't know the name. Perhaps I'd recognise her. Coffee? Or would you prefer tea? I know the English are supposed to like a cup of tea at any time of the day.'

'Well, I'm an unusual Englishman. I'd prefer coffee.'

'Sure. Come through, we can chat while I'm making it.'

He filled a small Moka for me, and then put a kettle – an electric kettle, no less – on to boil. Then he took a box of Earl Grey teabags from a cupboard, and dropped one into a mug with the logo of Venezia FC on the side.

'Tea? Earl Grey, no less. The same as my wife,' I said.

'Well, I'm an unusual Italian. I worked in London in the early '90s and got into the habit.'

'As a journalist?'

'It was after the 1990 World Cup. All of a sudden the Brits were crazy for Italian football. I had a nice little job there for a couple of years.'

'Italia '90? Wait a minute.' I reached into my pocket and pulled out the keyring, 'is this yours?'

He took the bunch from me and examined them. 'No. They're not mine.' He passed them back. 'But that's a nice little souvenir. *Ciao* was everywhere that year. Anyway, I earned some money from writing about Italian football when I was in England. Enough to buy myself a bit of time when I came back home. Time enough to write about what really interested me.' He poured out my coffee, and then stirred his teabag around, prior to removing it and dropping it in the bin. 'Which, I suspect, is what you want to talk to me about.'

'Giuseppe Lupo. And the mafia.'

'Okay.' He topped up his tea with a little milk. 'Which mafia?'

'Erm. All of them, I guess.'

He grinned. 'Okay. Let's sit down. This might take some time.'

Brezzi sipped at his tea, and a wry smile broke across his face. 'How long have you been in Italy, Mr Sutherland?'

'Over ten years now.'

'Ever spent much time in the South?'

I shook my head. 'Hardly any. To be honest, I don't think I've ever been south of Rome.'

'Well, you should. It's a big country, Italy. Or rather it's a series of small countries all pushed together. So you've never been to Sicily? Or Naples?'

'I'm afraid not.'

'Okay.' He set his mug down. 'I'm going to ask you a question. I don't want you to think too much about the answer. But be honest. What's the first thing that comes to mind when you think about Naples?'

'Pizza.'

He sighed. 'Be honest.'

'I was being honest.'

'Come on now, you're not a tourist. Try harder.'

I paused. 'Football. Diego Maradona. Good food. Bad drivers.'

He shook his head. 'No. You're trying to be polite. I asked you to be honest.'

I took a deep breath. 'Okay then. Extreme social problems. Corrupt governance. *Gomorrah*. And, I suppose, mafia.'

He snapped his fingers. 'That's it. You got there eventually. You English are too polite. If I asked an Italian friend

– someone from the North, anyway – they would have said mafia – or at least '*Ndrangheta* – long before you did.'

'I'm sorry. It's not something I feel comfortable talking about. If I even mention it I worry people will think I'm making a judgement on their country.'

'And that's where you're being very English again. Here, in the civilised North, we feel free to make judgements about the South all the time. A peasant people, still in thrall to their superstitions and their Church. Taking all the money that we generate in the North and spending it – on what? What do we get in return? What do they make, what do they sell? Where is their Benetton, their Parmalat, their FIAT? Nowhere. All they export,' he smiled, 'is crime.'

He sipped at his tea again. 'And this, of course, is a non-sense. Peddled by those who have an interest in promoting the idea of a rich, cultured and civilised North that, in truth, never existed. Separate from the South, they tell us, and all our problems will be solved. If only we were free of *Roma ladrona* – thieving Rome.' He smiled. 'The trouble is, of course, where does it stop? Next step is independence for the Veneto, then for Venezia-Mestre, then for Venice itself and it ends with you declaring independence from the man who lives next door.

'For years we convinced ourselves that the mafia was their problem. Not an issue for us in the civilised North. But we had organised crime as well. We just pretended we didn't. It was, as you English would say, "the elephant in the room".' He smiled. 'Have I got that right?'

I nodded.

'They were here, but we told ourselves they were not organ-ised criminals, they were just criminals. Until, eventually, people just got sick of pretending. It took a lot of very, very brave people to bring them down.'

'It doesn't exist any more then?'

He turned his hand this way and that in order to indicate how unsure he was. 'It exists, yes. I don't know if one can every truly believe that these things can be killed. Let's just say they are less active than they used to be.'

'Did you ever meet Giuseppe Lupo?'

'I did. On many occasions, at Santa Maria Maggiore. The authorities were very accommodating, and he was keen to talk.'

'Why so?'

'I thought a series of conversations with him might form the basis for a book. One day I hope to get around to finishing it. And Lupo saw it as his chance to put his side of the story.'

'What sort of man was he?'

'Oh, he could be delightful. Moderately racist of course, which was regrettable. But good company as long as one kept him on side. You've seen the photograph of him? Shortly after his arrest.'

I nodded.

Brezzi chuckled. 'I interviewed him soon after that. Do you know, he was so, so angry. I genuinely felt I was in the presence of a dangerous man, of someone who could – would – have me killed. And what had made him so angry? The photograph. He said it made him look like an old man. Here, wait a moment.'

He left the room, and was gone for several minutes. I checked the time. Not too bad. I'd still be back late afternoon.

Plenty of time to cook that risotto, or to head out somewhere if not.

Brezzi returned with a magazine in his hand. 'Take a look at this. This was taken just six months after his arrest.'

I recognised the title as the glossy magazine that went out with *Repubblica*'s Friday edition. Then I smiled as I recognised the photograph. Lupo's face, lined with age but his eyes bright and clear, stared out from the cover. I turned to the article. Lupo was sitting on the bunk bed in his prison cell, slightly bent over with his chin resting on his right hand and a cigarette dangling from his fingers. He was wearing a dark suit and looked indisputably cool.

I laughed. 'How did he get away with that?'

'With what?'

'Wearing his own clothes. Smoking in his cell.'

'Oh, that.' Brezzi grinned. 'He was so angry over the photograph of his arrest that he only agreed to do the interview if we made him look good. And the amount of shit we got over it – glamorising crime, that sort of thing.' He shook his head.

'Do you think he . . . ever killed anyone?'

'Personally, no. He was far too smart for that. Do I believe he had people killed? Well, that's another matter. It wouldn't surprise me if he had.'

'Yet he seemed to be a devout Catholic.'

'Oh that's not unusual. Not at all. I think perhaps these people can compartmentalise themselves. Lupo the gangster on one side. Lupo the loving husband, father and churchgoer on the other.'

'He contributed to the restoration of Madonna della Marina in Malamocco.'

'That's right. Throwing money at the Church in the hope that will undo or put right what they've done elsewhere. I'm not a religious man but I assume God's too smart for that.'

'Did he talk about his son?'

Brezzi sighed. 'Oh yes.'

'And?'

'And what he had to say about him I could scarcely believe. I don't know if I'll ever be able to publish it. One moment.'

He left the room for a few seconds, and returned clutching a sheaf of notes. He flicked through it, and extracted the last few sheets.

'Here. This is from my last interview with him.'

In the Wolf's Den

'Ghost Dog *was coming, but Vicari and I had been preparing for something like this for years. What would happen if there was another crackdown? We both thought we were too old to start again. And besides, I was starting to think about retirement. I'd promised Maddalena that I would try and get out.*

'*And, of course, that is not so easy. When one has spent one's whole life as a businessman, it's not so easy to stop being one. It's not so easy to stop making money. Nevertheless, I promised her. Vicari made sure our affairs were in order, and we paid money where it needed to be paid.*

'Ghost Dog *broke our organisation, as you know. Hundreds of* carabinieri *had worked on it for years. I don't know how many informers there were — we know about the main two, about Galletto and Pastore, but there must have been others.*

'*Twenty million euros were confiscated. A further sixty members were arrested. Some of them were bosses from the big cities, friends of mine. This time, we knew, there would be no going back. Nobody trusted anyone any more. But* Ghost Dog *had passed through us, and left Vicari, and me, and our families untouched.*'

Silence hangs thick in the air between us, as solid as the fumes of cigarette smoke.

'There were stories about you.'

He stares at me. He takes out yet another cigarette. I am starting to find it uncomfortable, yet I do not say anything.

'What do you mean by that?' he says.

'There were stories . . .' I repeat, and my voice trails off. Lupo is not about to let me off the hook however, and stares at me with those grey eyes. 'Stories about your loyalty,' I say.

'And those stories were shit.' He almost spits the words out. 'I had been loyal all my life, you understand? I kept to the code. Omertà, call it what you will. I was always loyal. Always.

'But yes, there were stories. That perhaps the Old Wolf had been running with others. That he'd been speaking to the wrong people. Or just that he'd spent too long in church with Vicari listening to the prattlings of priests.

'None of this was true, you understand? None of it. Yet, whenever I met with friends over dinner there would always be something in the atmosphere, something unsaid. An awkwardness. I knew that everyone was too polite to ask the old man directly, but I could tell what everybody was thinking. Why had Ghost Dog left the Old Wolf untouched? For the first time in my life I no longer felt in control of events, but at their mercy.' He clenches his fist, and then, slowly, opens it again. 'Everything I had worked for was trickling through my grasp, like grains of sand.

'Then, one morning, I received a letter in the post. There was nothing in the envelope except for a photograph. It was me, at dinner with Galletto and Pastore. The informers. I remembered the occasion. There had been perhaps twenty of us in the room. The photograph had been cropped, of course, to make it look as if there were just the three of us there. And immediately I thought, who else has seen this? And for the first time in my life – I mean this – I felt afraid.'

'What did you do?'

'I told Maddalena that enough was enough. To start packing. We had money in the bank, we would take the next flight out of Italy. I suggested Argentina. Maddalena said no. Too many Italians. London. Tonicello had hidden out there for years, after all. Nowhere more anonymous than a city of that size. I said yes. We called Albino and told him what we were doing.'

'What did he say?'

'He begged me, pleaded with me not to do it. I should fight my corner he said, like I always had. He would feel dishonoured if I ran away. Papà, don't bring shame on me. If you go now, they will believe all the stories. That sort of thing.'

'But you didn't agree?'

'If it had just been me, perhaps. But there was Maddalena as well. In the end I told him we would think it over for twenty-four hours. I had no intention of doing that, of course, but it gave me time. Plenty of time to arrange flights and somewhere to stay in London. I telephoned Vicari and told him what we were doing. He said he would do the same. And so the next morning we left our house, ready to begin our new life abroad. I remember that morning. The smell of wet grass, and feeling the low winter sun on my face. I thought about how much I would miss Italy. And at the same time I felt excited again, for the first time in years. I felt young once more.

'The next thing I remember, of course, was waking in the hospital in Mestre. I had been badly hurt, they told me, but I would live. It was two days until they told me that I was a widower.'

Silence hangs in the air again. I can think of nothing to say beyond, 'I'm sorry', but he waves my words away.

'Somebody had believed it. All those lies that I was complicit in *Ghost Dog*. Somebody had believed it and put a bomb under our car.'

'You must have had suspicions,' I say. 'As to who was responsible.'

'Oh yes. I had my suspicions at first. I did my best to push them out of my head. But one name kept coming back.'

'And it was?'

He looks surprised. 'Why, Albino, of course.'

'You can't be serious,' I say.

He shrugs. 'Why would I joke about this?'

There is silence once more, and it is a long time before the Old Wolf speaks again.

'I was weeks in hospital, but they took good care of me. I received letters, anonymously. Saying it would have been better for me to have died with my whore of a wife. Telling me exactly what they were going to do to me as soon as I left hospital.

'And so one evening, I discharged myself and went to a Bancomat, which refused to give me money. Impossible, of course. I was a wealthy man. But there I was. Giuseppe Lupo, one of the most respected figures in the Mala del Brenta, standing on a rainswept street in Mestre with not even the price of a cup of coffee in his pocket. All those years had passed, and I had come full circle.

'I took out a fifty-cent piece and thought about dialling Vicari. And then I paused. We had made arrangements together for our future. Our retirement plan, we called it. He would profit from me being out of the way. But Vicari? A man I had trusted with my life?

'I decided I had no choice but to trust him. I dialled his

number and his wife answered the phone. Or, should I say, his widow. He had been killed in a shooting in Padua two weeks previously. Nobody had told me, of course. The official reason was that it was a robbery gone wrong. I didn't believe that for a moment.

'And so I stood there in that phone box in Mestre and put the phone down and cried. There was a kid outside the box, and he saw this old man with tears streaming down his cheeks, and he tapped on the glass. Mister, he said, are you okay? And I smiled and I nodded back at him. But it wasn't okay. Not at all.'

He shakes his head, takes a deep breath. 'I decided not to trust my own son who had, after all, been conspicuous in his absence from my bedside. But there was one man who I thought might be able to help me.'

He is not going to suggest a name to me, so I throw one out to him in the hope that he'll catch it. 'Michele Ballarin?' I say.

He raises his eyebrows, ever so slightly, but says nothing.

'Elio Ravagnan?'

He shakes his head. 'I know the names of course. And I know what you're suggesting. Or, rather, what you're trying to get me to say.'

I smile back at him. 'You really are very loyal, aren't you?'

'There's nothing more for me to say on this, Brezzi. Nothing at all. Ballarin was a friend of mine. That's all.'

'Nevertheless, there were rumours that you'd stayed in his business partner's property on Pellestrina whilst you were hiding out.'

'Rumours. Nothing more. I was arrested in Chioggia, as you know.'

'Trying to fence stolen diamonds, I understand.'

'No.' He shakes his head. 'I had a couple of diamonds from a necklace that I had bought for Maddalena, this is true. Since the "accident", I had taken to keeping them on me for security. Quite simply I needed the money.'

'The diamonds were identified as being part of sets stolen from a jeweller's in Padua in 2003, during a robbery in which the shop owner was shot dead.'

'They were mistaken.'

I persist. 'The X-ray signatures identified them.'

'That's not foolproof, as you know.'

'It was enough for the jury to convict you.'

He nods. Then he gets to his feet, stretches and yawns. 'It was. Ironic, really. If I hadn't had to flee the Mala del Brenta, I would never have been convicted of a grubby little jewellery robbery. And so here I am. At my age. Spending the rest of my days with the Moroccans, the Albanians and the Romanians. Do you know, Brezzi, half the people in here don't even speak Italian?'

'I take it you no longer have any contact with your previous associates in the Mala del Brenta.'

'None at all. That is a chapter in my life which I consider to be closed.'

'And your son?'

He shakes his head. 'That, also, is a closed chapter.'

'You must be lonely.'

He nods. 'I am.'

'What will you do when you get out?'

'I don't know. I imagine I will leave Italy. There are any number of people here who do not wish me well.'

I pause. 'You have access to money, then?'

The Old Wolf grins at me.

'*Your retirement plan? Those other missing diamonds?*'

He says nothing, but just shakes his head and smiles. There is warmth and genuine humour in his eyes now. The Old Wolf is still capable of teaching us a few tricks.

'*I don't suppose you're going to tell me where they are?*' *I say.*

'*Well now. That would be quite a scoop for you, wouldn't it?*'

'*It would.*'

He laughs. '*But I'm sorry. I'm not going to do that.*'

We smile and shake hands. We say goodbye for what proves to be the last time.

Chapter 40

I shook my head. 'It can't be.'

'It seems unbelievable to you?'

'If what Lupo is saying is true, his own son betrayed him. More than that, he was responsible for the death of his mother. I can't believe that.'

'It seems unbelievable, yes. But we're very good at self-deception. Giuseppe Lupo tells himself so often that he's a just a businessman that he starts to believe it himself.'

I nodded. 'A young Englishman in Santa Maria Maggiore tells himself that he was just trying to stop someone stealing his mobile phone. Because the alternative is admitting to himself that a young man spent weeks in hospital with a bleed on his brain.'

'Exactly. It's the same thing. And Albino Lupo convinces himself that he was just following the code of the Mala. He cries for his mother, of course, but the responsibility – he tells himself – isn't directly his.'

'Lupo was in a cell with a guy called Enrico Zanetti. He'd been a member of Clan Giostrai, or at least with what remained of them. And yet I've been told that the two of them were good friends.'

Brezzi shrugged. 'What do you know about this guy?'

'Unsuccessful career criminal. Probably violent. Never made very much of himself. Uneducated.'

'Young guy?'

'Middle-aged. Perhaps in his mid-forties.'

'In good shape?'

'Definitely. Not averse to violence either.'

'So Lupo gets a tough guy as security. Remember, he doesn't have the protection of the Mala any more. Zanetti gets the prestige of hanging around with a proper boss. Prison makes strange bedfellows of people. Who knows, perhaps he thought Lupo would throw a few favours his way when he got out?'

'Including the diamonds?'

Brezzi sucked his teeth. 'Hmm. That would be a big reach. Lupo couldn't tell him directly, of course. Otherwise there'd be nothing stopping Zanetti taking them all for himself when he was released. Lupo was no longer in the Mala del Brenta. He had no one to look after his affairs on the outside.'

'Apart, perhaps, from Michele Ballarin.'

'Perhaps so. He came up in conversation a number of times. He was Lupo's lawyer, as you know. But it was difficult to get him to talk about him. There seemed to be a great loyalty there.'

He opened the file again, and leafed through the contents. 'Here we are.' He jabbed a finger at a photograph of a group of people standing on the deck of a yacht. 'You recognise anyone?'

Most of the faces were unfamiliar to me, but I recognised Lupo, Ballarin and Vicari as standing out from the crowd. I nodded. 'Who are the others?'

'Not people you'd like to meet.'

'Margherita – Ballarin's sister – told me about this. It was true then. But could it have been, I don't know, something unimportant? Trivial, even?'

He shook his head. 'I don't imagine you got invited to stay on Giuseppe Lupo's yacht for doing something trivial. I imagine that level of access would have involved big favours.'

I leaned forward and ran my hands through my hair. 'Oh hell.'

'Not what you wanted to hear?'

I shook my head. 'No. Not at all. But it was perhaps what I was expecting.' I got to my feet, and checked my watch. 'I've taken a lot of your time. All afternoon. But thank you. It's been very helpful.'

'Not at all.' He reached out to shake my hand. 'Mr Sutherland, what are you going to do with this information?'

'I don't know. Hopefully try and prove that my father-in-law wasn't a gangster.'

He gave a thin smile. 'I understand. Just be careful how you go about it. Giuseppe Lupo may be cold in his grave but many of his old associates are still very much alive. As I said, just be careful.'

'I will be. And thanks again.'

I made my way downstairs, and out into the warmth of the early evening, already wondering what I was going to say to Federica.

Chapter 41

'Fede?'

'Nathan, are you finished with Brezzi? We need to talk.'

'Sure. I mean, I'm in the street now. I'll be home soon. Is it important?'

'I think it is. I've been trying to get hold of Margherita all day, and I can't. She's not answering her phone. I called her hotel. She's not there.'

'Could she have gone back to Rome already?'

'She's supposed to be here until the day after tomorrow. But I called her office just in case. They haven't heard from her either.'

'It might just be that she's travelling and she's got her phone off. Let's try again when I get home.'

'Okay.' Fede didn't sound convinced. 'Don't be long.'

'I won't be. Love you.'

'Love you too.'

I was waiting for the bus when the red Ferrari pulled up. A face grinned up at me from the driver's seat. The same man who'd sat next to me on the long, long journey to Pellestrina a few days past. A man who I now knew to be Enrico Zanetti.

'Hello, Mr Sutherland.'

'Signor Zanetti, I believe?'

'How are you today then?'

'I'm well.'

'What brings you to this part of town?'

The last thing I wanted to do was to drag Brezzi into this. 'Just dropping by my wife's old flat,' I said.

'That's nice. I understand you've been to prison as well.'

'And, as I understand it, so have you.'

He grinned. 'That's so funny. Can I give you a lift?'

It would have seemed churlish to refuse.

I sat down heavily, the seats being nearer the ground than any car I'd been in before. It had been years since I'd last had a car. A second-hand Vauxhall something, furnished with crumpled cigarette and crisp packets and yellowing newspapers on the rear parcel shelf.

This was not like that. It smelled of new car and vulgarity. Leather, chrome and polished metal; all immaculate. There were no crumpled cigarette packets. Indeed, I imagined the owner would have you killed if you so much as suggested lighting up.

'I've never been in a Ferrari before, you know,' I said as my chauffeur stomped on the accelerator and the car leapt forward.

It was only a few kilometres from the Lido to Malamocco. Strangely enough, given the speed that we were travelling at, the journey actually seemed to take longer than it should have. Given the use of a muscle car for the evening, my companion seemed intent on thrashing the hell out of it, whether for his own satisfaction, or just to intimidate me.

'I think it's a forty zone here, you know,' I suggested at one point. 'I think there might be a camera here,' at another. Then I winced as I saw the Curve of Death approaching somewhat faster than it should. 'Might be worth slowing down a bit here, perhaps.' Then I clamped my eyes shut, and tried to block out the sound of the engine roaring and the tyres screeching.

I opened my eyes, just a fraction, and saw that we were on the wrong side of the road. A car was speeding towards us, lights flashing and horn blaring. I clamped them shut again as the Ferrari swerved first right then left. The driver shouted something, presumably profane, but the words were carried away by the engine noise.

I pressed my head back against the rest, and gripped the seat with both hands, grateful that it was at least holding me fast. Then the sound of the engine diminished to a low, bassy rumble and I became aware that we were slowing down.

The driver dug me in the ribs, hard enough to get an 'Ow' out of me.

'We're here.'

I opened my eyes. 'This doesn't look like home,' I said.

'Maybe later. *Maybe* later. If you do as you're told.'

'Can I get out?' I said.

He nodded and I struggled out from the snug embrace of the seat and hauled myself to my feet, doing my best to keep my legs from shaking. I looked around and could see that we were in wooded gardens, surrounded by what might once have been agricultural buildings. A restaurant lay at the end of an immaculate gravel drive. An *agriturismo*, I supposed you'd call it. The air was warm, and the first mosquitoes of the season were flying around, but the smell from the restaurant was enticing. That, I thought, was a good sign. If Albino had wanted me dead, I assumed he'd have had me driven into the very deepest, darkest part of a forest somewhere on the mainland and forced me to dig a shallow grave. A restaurant seemed less intimidating.

I turned to my companion. 'You're going to get yourself killed driving like that, you know.'

He shook his head. 'Not me. I'm a good driver.'

'Nobody's that good.'

He grunted, and swore at me. Under his breath but loud enough for me to hear. For a moment, I wondered if I should mention that I knew about Giulia. Was it possible that she hadn't told him of the events of last night? Given what I knew of Zanetti, she might have decided it was safer not to. I decided to keep quiet.

'Come on. You're expected.' He stood to my side and pushed me forward, up the gravel path and into the restaurant.

The interior was wood-panelled and cosy, and packed with diners. Agricultural implements hung from the ceiling, together with enormous hams. 1990s Italo-pop played in the background at a non-distressing volume.

It did not feel like the sort of place where you would be likely to be murdered. Neither did the diners look like *mafiosi*. The nearest table consisted of a family group, grandparents, mum and dad, and a little girl with her hair in bunches and a helium balloon with the number 8 on it, reaching up with a spoon to scrape the last remnants of ice cream from a bowl that was almost as big as she was. Then I remembered Vanni's words on Giuseppe Lupo. 'Looks like everyone's favourite grandpa, doesn't he?'

Okay then. They didn't look like *obvious mafiosi*.

A bald-headed man with a bushy moustache and a waiter's apron came over to us.

'*Signori*?'

My companion nodded at him. '*Signor* Lupo is expecting us.'

'Of course, sir.' He bowed his head and clicked his heels. 'Come with me, please.'

He led us through into another dining room, similarly packed with diners of all shapes, ages and sizes; and through a back corridor lined with wine racks until we reached a wooden door. He took out a handkerchief and dabbed at his forehead before knocking.

'*Avanti.*'

He opened the door and stepped through, then moved to one side in order to make space for me. 'Your guest, *signor* Lupo,' he said.

Lupo beamed, and got to his feet. 'Dear Mr Sutherland, do come in,' he said. Then he looked at his watch and frowned. 'I do apologise. I was going to have some prosecco ready. You are a little earlier than I was expecting.'

'Well,' I said, 'you have a very efficient chauffeur.'

He chuckled, and stroked his beard. 'Enrico gets just a little overenthusiastic when I let him use the car.' He turned to him. 'Enrico, just wait outside please. But come in, come in, Mr Sutherland.' He kissed me on both cheeks. I could feel his muscles beneath his jacket. Albino Lupo kept himself in good shape.

'Sit down. Please.'

The waiter re-entered carrying a silver tray with a bottle

of prosecco and two glasses. I noticed the marque. Not something I had seen in Conad and therefore something, I assumed, that was out of my price range. Albino Lupo's philosophy of life did seem to equate the most expensive with automatically being the best. I was starting to find it all slightly irritating. Then I recalled where I was and who I was talking to and remembered to be scared.

The waiter took a surprising amount of time to wrestle the cork from the bottle, as if his nerves were interfering with his hands. Finally, it slid out with a satisfying hiss and he wiped his hand in relief across his forehead. He poured us two glasses.

'Would you like to see the menu, *signori*?'

Lupo smiled at him. 'Just give us ten minutes, perhaps?'

The waiter nodded and backed out of the room.

Lupo raised his glass. 'Your good health, Mr Sutherland.'

I could certainly drink to that, I thought. 'And yours.' We clinked glasses.

'Thank you for joining me here.'

'Well, thank you for the invitation. It's not often that I'm picked up in a Ferrari.'

'It was short notice. I do apologise.'

'No problem. I should really let my wife know I'm going to be a little bit late getting home, though.' I spread my hands. 'Just married. You know how it is.'

'I'm sorry. That was my fault again.' He paused, just for a moment. 'I'll invite your wife as well.' Another pause. 'Next time.'

'Well, that would be kind.'

He took a drink of prosecco and exhaled in satisfaction.

'Mmm. The best. They keep a wonderful cellar here, don't you think?'

I swirled the liquid in my glass, raised it to my nose and sniffed it gently. I took a small sip and rolled it around my mouth. A horde of tiny golden angels danced on my tongue. 'Excellent.'

'I'm glad. You have a good palate, Mr Sutherland.'

'It's more that I'm used to buying prosecco in one-and-a-half-litre plastic bottles and getting change from five euros. But thank you for the compliment.'

He chuckled. 'Okay. I think perhaps we should talk business.'

I said nothing.

'So. Mr Nathan Sutherland. Translator by profession. Also the British Honorary Consul in Venice. Resident in the Street of the Assassins.'

'You seem to know a lot about me.'

'You have something of a large footprint, Mr Sutherland. Recently married,' he paused, 'to Elio Ravagnan's daughter.'

'Yes. Believe it or not this is supposed to be my honeymoon. To be honest it's not working out quite as I'd hoped.'

'I'm sorry.' He chuckled again. 'I do seem to be apologising a lot, don't I? But I really am.' He paused. 'I could make it up to you, of course.'

I inclined my head. 'Go on.'

'Pellestrina is very nice, I'm sure. But wouldn't you prefer to take your wife somewhere special? The Caribbean? The Maldives? The Seychelles, perhaps?'

'Sounds lovely. I'll need a cat-sitter, though.'

'I'm sure that wouldn't be a problem.'

'I think it might.'

He smiled. Just a little too broadly. 'And now I think you're making fun of me.'

'I assure you I'm not. I'm absolutely serious.'

'You'd find someone. Perhaps your friend, *signor* Costa.'

Dario. He really had done his homework. For the first time I felt unsure as to what to say, and shifted in my seat. I raised my glass, but my prosecco seemed to have vanished.

Lupo looked pained. 'I'm so sorry.' He reached across the table to refill my glass. 'So. I've told you what I know about you. Or at least the most important things. Why don't you tell me about myself?'

'Well now. Would you like me to be honest or tactful?'

'Honest, of course.'

I nodded and took a deep breath. 'Your name is Albino Lupo. Your father was Giuseppe Lupo, a senior member of the branch of the Venetian mafia known as the Mala del Brenta. He recently died after serving a long sentence in Santa Maria Maggiore for his involvement in a jewel robbery and homicide back in 2003.'

Lupo nodded and tapped the side of his glass.

'Very honest.'

'You asked me to be.'

'Would you like to be even more honest?'

To hell with it. I had the feeling he wanted to hear the truth anyway. I drained my glass and set it down.

'I believe you're a gangster. I believe you're also part of whatever remains of the Mala del Brenta. I know that for some reason you have an interest in my wife and myself. I believe that you – or your little helper outside – tried to run me down on the Curve of Death outside Malamocco the other day. And I also believe that – despite having access to more money than I could possibly dream of – the concepts of restraint and good taste are basically foreign to you.'

He nodded again, slowly this time. Then he laughed, gently, and reached across the table to shake me by the shoulder.

'That's funny. I like that. So. What do you expect to happen now?'

'Well, either you shoot me in the head or we discuss this like gentlemen.'

He threw up his hands. 'Mr Sutherland. I am not a barbarian. I would never shoot you in the head.'

'Oh good.'

He smiled. 'I have friends who would do that for me.'

'Oh.'

'But you were very rude about me.'

'You did say you wanted me to be honest. And come on,' I got to my feet, and spread my arms wide, 'this is all a bit of a cliché isn't it? Being "collected" by your friend in the expensive sports car. The restaurant with the private room. The obsequious waiter and the expensive prosecco. What next? Is there going to be a menu with oysters and truffles?'

Lupo coughed and looked a little embarrassed. 'Actually yes. That's exactly what there's going to be.'

'Oh good. Although my wife is going to be very jealous. But, really, this is all just a bit too much classic gangster chic. Isn't it?'

I was staring to enjoy myself now. Perhaps just a little too much. I reminded myself that I was, after all, in the company of a man who had been complicit in the death of his own mother.

The obsequious waiter entered the room again and Lupo nodded at him. 'I think we can see the menus now.'

Oysters. Lobster. Crab. And, of course, pasta with black truffles. I was sure they'd all be exquisite. The wine list was price on application but I was sure that would not be a problem. And yet I really wanted to be with Federica, sitting outside a restaurant on Pellestrina and drinking *vino sfuso*.

As if on cue I felt my phone buzzing in my pocket. Lupo raised an eyebrow. 'Perhaps you ought to take that?'

'It's probably not important.'

He shook his head. 'I think you should check it.' He smiled, and his smile was wider and broader than it had ever been. 'Please.'

I took it out and checked the number. 'It's my wife.'

'Oh well. You must answer it.'

I didn't move.

Suddenly, the smile switched off. 'Answer it. And tell her you are well and will shortly be home.'

I nodded. 'Okay.' I clicked on Receive. '*Ciao, cara.*'

'Nathan. I've been waiting for you. I was getting worried.'

'I'm fine. Really. I met an old friend on my way back and time seems to have got away from us. I'm sorry, we just stopped for a beer.'

She paused before replying. 'Only one?'

'Well, one or two. You know how these things work.'

'Not Dario then?'

'No. An old translating colleague.'

'Oh. That's nice. Will you be home soon?'

'I hope so.'

'Where are you now?'

'Still on the Lido.'

'You have colleagues on the Lido?'

'She's not from here. She's from Venice. She's meeting some friends.'

'She?'

'Anna. I think you might have met her?'

'I don't think so. Okay. Should I go for pizza or, God help me, should I attempt cooking something?'

'No. I don't think I'll be that long. We could go along the road to *da Celeste* when I get back.'

'It's their closing day, remember?'

'Bugger. Sorry.'

'It's okay. Have a nice time with your friend. I'll see you when you get back.'

'I'll pick up some pizza on the way, or cook us that risotto.'

'That'll be nice.'

I heard the unmistakable sound of Gramsci scrabbling away at the furniture. Fede swore under her breath. 'Okay. It sounds like I need to go and entertain your cat. See you later, *caro*. Don't be too late.'

'I won't. I promise. Love you.'

'Love you too.'

I hung up, and tucked my phone away. 'Everything okay?' I said.

He was smiling again. 'Very good. It's an important lesson to learn. How to lie to your wife.'

I yawned. 'Okay. Why don't we get down to cases. It's getting late. I have to go home, apologise to my wife and play with my unfriendly cat. And given that it doesn't even look as if I'm going to get fed, I'll need to pick up something on the way. And trust me, you won't like me when I'm hungry. What exactly do you want?'

'I'd have thought that was obvious.'

'It isn't.' I pushed back my chair, and folded my arms. 'Enlighten me.'

'I want the diamonds that my father was keeping safe all those years.'

'The ones he stole? The ones from a robbery where an innocent man was killed? Why do you think I could possibly know where they are?'

'You don't. But your wife does.'

'That's absurd.'

'No it isn't, Mr Sutherland. Elio Ravagnan and Michele Ballarin used the property on Pellestrina as a safe house for a number of members of the Mala del Brenta – and also my father – from 2006 onwards. Your wife recently received a legacy from her late father, on her wedding day.'

'That was the house. Trust me, she didn't get so much as a sniff of a diamond.' I paused. 'Ballarin could have told you that.'

'He did. He was very insistent about that. But unfortunately I chose not to believe him. After all, Michele Ballarin would have had his own interests in finding them. So, the property now belongs to your wife. If anyone knows where the diamonds are, she will.'

I laughed. 'I'm sorry, but this makes no sense. My wife is an art restorer. She has a small apartment on the Lido. We live in my even smaller apartment on the Street of the Assassins.

A night out for us is the opera once a year – and not even in the posh seats – the odd meal out on special occasions, or a Negroni downstairs at the Magical Brazilians.'

'The what?'

'It's what I call them. Trust me, if she had access to stolen diamonds don't you think we might be living a slightly more *dolce vita*?'

'Perhaps your wife is not being honest with you. Perhaps she's as good at lying to you as you seem to be to her.'

'And perhaps you've spent too much time with crooks, Albino. Normal people don't have that sort of relationship.'

He laughed. 'Don't they? I'm sorry, I was forgetting you're still in what you call "the honeymoon period", Mr Sutherland.' He topped up my glass with the rest of the bottle.

'Aren't you going to join me?'

'No. I have much to do. I'd prefer to keep a clear head.'

'Sensible. Wouldn't do to be driving a car like that after one too many.'

'Quite so.'

'Anyway, I seem to be missing something. Giuseppe Lupo was your father. If anyone would know where the diamonds are then you should.'

'My father and I had a *difficult* relationship in his later years. We didn't speak much.'

'I understand. He attempted to leave the Mala del Brenta. It's a miracle he lived for as long as he did.'

'Ballarin did a good job at his trial. He made sure he was in Santa Maria Maggiore. There haven't been members of the Mala del Brenta there for years. Only cheap crooks, the East Europeans, the Africans. No one important. The population of this city declines every year. That even applies to the prisons.'

'There must be others who would have known.'

'Vicari is dead. Killed in a police shoot-out in Padua years ago. His wife died of cancer in 2015. The two bums who carried out the robbery are also dead. One killed in a street fight. The other one choking on his own vomit in a sordid little flat on Giudecca after overdosing.'

'You could have tried making it up with your father. I'm sure he'd have appreciated a visit or two.'

Lupo sighed. 'Some things are more important than family. My father did something unforgivable. He wanted to dishonour us. But Ballarin and Ravagnan looked after him. They had, you might say, history in this. They helped members of the Mala del Brenta escape after *Ghost Dog*. They gave them a place to stay, gave them documentation, even arranged weapons. And then my old father goes crawling to them for help. For protection. Not from the police but from his own people. And even after his arrest he stayed loyal to them in a way he never was to the Mala. No, Mr Sutherland, if anyone knew where the diamonds were, Ballarin and Ravagnan would have.'

'They might have done. They're not going to tell you now. Killing Ballarin wasn't such a smart move, was it?'

'I didn't kill Michele Ballarin.'

'Someone did. One of your people. The fake journalist perhaps? Or your driver.'

He shook his head in irritation. 'Idiots. All of them.'

'I'm surprised you used them. I didn't realise the Mala del Brenta even spoke to whatever remains of Clan Giostrai.'

He looked surprised for the first time in our conversation. 'Ah. You didn't know I knew that, did you?' He said nothing so I continued. 'Why would you be reduced to using bums from the fairground scene? Unless, of course, you had to.' I smiled. 'You're no longer in the Mala del Brenta are you? This isn't about them. You're working for yourself. What happened? Did they,' I reached for the appropriate word, '*excommunicate* you? Do you have to pay them for protection? Money running out? Cars like yours don't pay for themselves, do they? If nothing else, the way your idiot driver is thrashing it you're going to need a new set of tyres pretty soon.'

Lupo nodded, and drummed his fingers on the table. 'You've been working hard, I see. Which surprises me given, as you say, you know nothing about this.'

'My mother-in-law is upset. Which means my wife is upset. What did you expect me to do?'

'Britain.' He shook his head. 'What a country. Do you all let yourselves be pushed around by women? No wonder you lost the empire.'

'Better that than having an unhappy wife.'

He sighed. 'We're wasting time here. I'm hungry too. I need to eat and then I need to think. So I think it's time for you to go.' I made to get to my feet, but he waved a hand. 'So, when you get home tonight, what are you going to do?'

'Hmm. Pizza first. Perhaps a *spritz Nathan*.'

'A what?'

'It's my own invention. Oh, and then I'll have to throw balls for my cat before he starts destroying things.'

'You let yourself be pushed around by your wife. And you

let yourself be bullied by your cat. What sort of man are you, Mr Sutherland?'

'One who likes a quiet life.'

'So it seems. Well, let me tell you what you're going to do. You're going to get your wife to tell you everything – *everything* – about the relationship between Elio Ravagnan and my father—'

I cut him off. 'And, as I keep saying, there is nothing to be said about—'

'Shut up, you pathetic little streak of piss.' He leaned across the table and swept the bottle and the glasses to the floor. Then he slapped me across the face. Just hard enough to let me know he could have done worse. 'You listen to me now, and you listen good. And if you make one more shitty little joke, one more wisecrack, I'll take the remains of that bottle to your face.' He sat down, breathing heavily. 'As I was saying, you go home tonight and you get your wife to tell you everything she knows about her father, about Ballarin, about my father. Where they met, when they met, the diamonds, everything. And then you come back and you tell me all about it.' I said nothing, and then he reached over the table and grabbed me under the chin, squeezing hard. 'You understand?'

I did my best to nod.

'You get your wife to tell you everything. You beat it out of her if necessary. Because if you don't,' he glanced down at the broken bottle, 'then I will.' He released his grip and sat back down. 'Are we clear now? Are we *absolutely* clear?'

I nodded. 'We are.'

'Good.' He got to his feet and walked around the room,

kicking the broken glass into a corner. He stood behind me, and squeezed my shoulders. 'Enrico will drive you to the ferry terminal now.'

'If it's all the same to you I'd prefer to get the bus.'

He grabbed my hair and yanked my head back, crouching down beside me and hissing in my ear. 'You do exactly what the hell I say, do you understand?'

'I understand.'

He released his grip, and sat back down. 'You can go now. I'll see you soon.'

I got to my feet and walked to the door.

'Enjoy your honeymoon, Mr Sutherland.'

Chapter 42

'So,' said Federica over coffee the next morning. 'What are we going to do?'

'Well, my original plan was to sleep on it.'

'Hmm. Yes, a good plan in some ways. Did it work?'

'Not really. I kind of failed at the sleeping bit.'

She yawned, and I was struck by how pale and drawn she looked. I assumed I looked much the same, with the added attraction of a layer of stubble. I made her a cup of tea, and coffee for myself, spooning in multiple sugars in the hope of taking away the feeling of sand running through my veins.

'Are you worried?' I said.

'Me? No. Are you?'

'Hell, no.' I drained my coffee in one, wincing at the heat. 'Christ, we're both rubbish at lying, aren't we?'

Fede nodded, and forced a weak smile on to her face.

'So it's like this,' I continued. 'Lupo thinks you know where the diamonds are, and you don't.' I paused. 'Actually, I'm assuming you don't?'

Fede shot me a filthy look.

'Okay, okay. Just checking. It would have been easier, that's all. So the problem is that you don't know where they are and we have to find out as soon as possible.'

'So it seems.'

'Which is not going to be easy. We could go to Busetto. Throw ourselves on his mercy. Tell him everything.'

'Which is not much. Anyway, what's he going to do? Give us police protection for the rest of our lives?'

'So, then, we have to find them.'

She yawned. 'Great. Any ideas?'

'Think of everyone who could have been involved with this. Anyone who might have known something, anything about the diamonds. Ballarin, of course.'

'Who's now dead.'

'Margherita.'

'Who's disappeared.'

'I wondered about Brezzi, but I genuinely think he's told us everything he knows. Who else?'

'The priest. Don Francesco. He visited Lupo in prison. It sounds as if they were close.'

'Good. That's a start. Do you think he'll speak to us?'

'I think you're going to have to be properly diplomatic. I don't think priests are very keen on divulging personal information about their parishioners.'

'I can be diplomatic. I'm great at talking to men of the cloth. Just ask Father Michael. Anyone else?'

Fede was silent for a moment. 'There is one other, of course.'

'Who?'

'Sofia. She worked for Ballarin for years. And we know she'd been contacted by Giulia when she was pretending to be a journalist. It seems reasonable that Albino might think she knows something.'

'Okay. This is plenty to work with.' I got to my feet and yawned. 'Christ, I'm tired. And I'm aching. And I'm on bloody honeymoon and now I have to go and talk to a priest about the mafia.'

She gave me a hug. 'I know. Come on then. See you later, unfriendly cat.'

Gramsci miaowed, and turned his back on us.

The smell of coffee and brioche wafted out of Renzo's café. I gave Federica a pleading little look, but she shook her head. 'No time now. We'll grab a *tramezzino* or something after the priest.'

'I can't believe we're having to fight crime on an empty stomach,' I grumbled. We made our way through the *calle* to the main road. There, leaning against the stairs that led up to the *murazzi*, with his phone in one hand and a cigarette dangling from the other, was Zanetti.

'Enrico,' I said. 'Have you been there all night? You must be shattered. You should have knocked on the door, we'd have made you a coffee.'

He said nothing.

'Or a cup of tea. A biscuit, even.' I turned to Fede. 'We do have biscuits, don't we?'

She nodded. 'We do.'

I turned back to Zanetti. 'There you go. You could have had a biscuit as well. Something to keep you going.'

Zanetti looked at me and shook his head. 'What is this?'

'You tell me. Is this your job now?'

He attempted to smile and failed. Then he spat on the pavement, dropped his cigarette and ground it under his heel.

'What do you mean?'

'Oh, it just seems a bit of a comedown, that's all. This is what Clan Giostrai's been reduced to? Chauffeuring and standing around waiting for something to happen, until the boss says they can go home?'

He tensed, and dropped his phone into his pocket. I looked left and then right. The road was clear.

'Must be difficult, I imagine? Not like the old days. Money, booze, drugs. Now you drive a car you can't afford for your greatest rival, and your wife is pretending to be a journalist one day and a cleaner the next. Which, now I think of it, is a really weird job description.'

Fede shot me a glance, wondering where this was going. Zanetti tensed some more, his fingers twitching.

'Ah. You didn't know that I knew that, did you?'

Zanetti's phone buzzed and his hand automatically went to his pocket before he could stop himself. He continued staring at me, blinking furiously now. His phone continued to ring.

'Hadn't you better get that?' I said. 'You don't want to piss off your employer.' Then I paused, just for a moment, and then chuckled. 'Well, I say employer. I mean owner.'

He finally snapped. 'Bastard.' He swung a fist at me but he'd been telegraphing the blow for minutes and I stepped to one side to dodge it. I punched him in the face and he staggered back, dropping to his knees.

'Nathan!' Fede grabbed my arm, just as I was about to punch him again. 'This is stupid. Stop it.'

Zanetti got to his feet and spat blood upon the ground. 'You should listen to your wife, mister.'

Fede nodded. 'He should. There's no need for this, Nathan.'

Zanetti forced a grin on to his face. 'Yes, *Nathan*,' he drew the word out, mocking her accent, 'do as the nice *signora* says.' He wiped blood from his nose and spat once more. 'At least I don't take orders from a woman.'

Federica smiled at him, and I tried to stop myself from wincing. 'As I said, there was no need for that.' She turned, as if to walk away, checking left and right. The street was still empty. 'But I think there's a need for this.'

She spun round, and kicked Zanetti in the balls with all her strength.

He opened his mouth to scream, but the breath would not come and he dropped to the ground gasping.

'Nothing more to say, signor Zanetti?' She put her hand to her ear. 'No? I can't hear you? And now, I think that's our bus coming.'

'You know,' I said, 'that might just cause us both a bit of trouble.'

'You started it.'

'Sorry.'

'Don't be. I think it needed to be done. Come on.' She flagged the bus down, and the doors hissed open. The driver looked out of the window, open-mouthed, at the prone figure of Zanetti.

Federica smiled. 'I think he'll be getting the next one,' she said.

The driver looked at her, then down at Zanetti, then back at Federica. He saw the expression on her face, nodded, and put the bus into gear.

***

Don Francesco was sitting outside the café opposite his church, sipping at a cappuccino and delicately dabbing away the foam moustache it left.

'*Padre*. Good morning.'

He looked up at us both. 'Good morning. Mr Sutherland, isn't it?'

'That's right.'

Don Francesco turned to Fede. 'And—?'

'Federica Ravagnan. Do you mind if we join you, *padre*?'

He looked at his watch. 'Well, I am in something of a—'

Federica beamed at him. 'We won't be long, *padre*. I promise.' She'd started the day in a not-going-to-take-any-nonsense frame of mind.

'Elio's daughter?'

'That's right. I also worked on the restoration of your painting.'

'Ah.' His hand shook a little as his sipped at his coffee, as if in anticipation of a difficult conversation. 'A lovely thing it is, as well.'

'Thank you.' She paused for a moment. 'It's a shame it's not hung in the right place.'

'Oh that. We had to move it, I'm afraid. There was – there was a problem with damp on the original wall.'

'I thought it was due to the light,' I said.

Fede patted my hand. 'No, darling, remember what I said. There's hardly any natural light where it is now. The *padre* wouldn't have moved it because of that.'

'Is that right? Silly me, I remember talking about this with Don Francesco a few days ago.' I turned to the little priest who, once again, had decided his glasses were in need of a good polish. 'I could have sworn you told me it was due to the light. I must have completely misremembered.'

Don Francesco gave a nervous little laugh.

Fede smiled, and gave me a little kiss on the cheek. 'Honestly, darling, your memory.' She turned to Don Francesco. 'You see what I have to put up with?'

'I'm sorry. My head's all over the place at the moment. Of course, the wall where it's hanging now is the one that was repaired.' I paused, and smiled. 'With the money from Giuseppe Lupo and Sandro Vicari.'

Don Francesco's cup clattered in his saucer. 'I don't understand.'

'I think you do, *padre*. Lupo and Vicari paid for the restoration of the roof of your church and a crumbling interior wall. Oh, and a monstrance, just so they could feel good about themselves.'

He dabbed at his forehead. 'Mr Sutherland, the church needs money these days. Gifts from anyone are always welcome.'

Fede looked at me, knowing what was coming next.

'Even *mafiosi*?' I said.

'That's a nonsense,' he stammered. 'And an outrageous thing to say. Quite outrageous.'

'*Padre*, you took Communion to Giuseppe Lupo in prison. What did you think he was doing there?'

'Everyone is entitled to receive the Sacrament, Mr Sutherland.'

'*Padre*, I don't know if you genuinely believe this or if you're deluding yourself because the alternative is uncomfortable. Pope Francis decreed that members of the mafia are to be considered excommunicate. You took Lupo Communion because his own priest refused, didn't you?'

He jabbed a finger into my chest. 'Shut up.'

'You're deluding yourself because the alternative is admitting that your church took money from gangsters.'

'Shut up. Shut up.'

'How much money did they give you, *padre*? Thirty pieces of silver?'

Don Francesco slapped me across the face with surprising strength. I sat there and rubbed my cheek as he glowered at me, red-faced and sweating.

'You know nothing about me, nothing about my situation.' He jabbed his finger towards the church. 'Every year, fewer and fewer people walk through those doors. Every year that building crumbles away a little more. What do you think I do, get on my knees every day and pray for a miracle? Sometimes I've had to make compromises. And you're a lucky, lucky man if you've never had to.'

I held my hands up. 'Okay. Just tell me one thing. Did he confess to you? Towards the end of his life?'

'He did. Of course he did. And if you expect me to share that with you,' he shook his head, 'you are even more deluded than I thought.' He got to his feet, threw some coins down on the table, and stalked off.

Federica sipped at her tea.

'Well then, *tesoro*. How do you think that went?'

'I think we touched a nerve.'

'It seems we did.'

'Uh-huh. A shame really. It was going so well up until the "thirty pieces of silver" bit.'

She sighed. 'Come on then. Sofia next.' She got to her feet. 'I still remember a few things from my Church days, you know? I always liked that line about *covering a multitude of sins.*'

Chapter 43

'You go in,' said Fede.

'You're not coming?'

She shook her head. 'No. It didn't exactly go well last time, did it? You go. It'll be better with just you.'

'You sure? Do you trust me after the way it went with the priest?'

'You'll be better than I will. I can't face it. I'm sorry.'

'That's okay.'

'I'll go and have a coffee.' She jerked a thumb over her shoulder in the direction of a bar. 'I remember that place. It's harmless enough. I'll see you there. If you're good, I'll even buy you a lychee spritz.'

'A *what*?'

'A lychee spritz. They have quite an extensive spritz menu.'

'Too extensive, I'd have said. Somebody actually woke up one morning and decided that what the world needed was a lychee spritz?'

'It seems they did.'

'And this is something you think I need to try?'

'Oh yes.' She frowned. 'Perhaps only once, though.'

'Okay, well you're completely selling me on the idea. I'll

be as quick as I can.' I gave her a kiss, and then pressed Sofia's doorbell. It took a long time before anyone answered.

'Who is it?'

'Sofia. It's Nathan. Can we talk?'

There was silence over the intercom, and I think she swore under her breath, but then the door buzzed and clicked open.

'You're on your own,' she said.

I nodded.

'Good. I didn't feel like another row.'

I noticed a glass of something bright red on the table. Campari? It was still not quite noon. Nevertheless, I felt I was probably the person least equipped to be judgemental on that.

'What do you want?'

'There's something you might be able to help me with. About Michele. About Elio. And about *Ghost Dog*.'

She shook her head. 'I don't know what you mean.'

'You're lying. And very badly at that.'

'I'd like you to leave, please.'

'I'm going nowhere. Not until you tell me what you know about the *Ghost Dog* account.'

'Would you like me to start screaming?'

'Do that. You do that. And then maybe somebody will call the cops and we can all go to the police together. So go ahead. Scream.'

She took a deep breath, and for a moment I thought I'd got this horribly wrong. Then she sighed, slumped into a chair, and drained her glass.

'Can I get you another?'

She nodded.

'What is it? For that matter, where is it?'

'Campari. Next to the fridge.'

Neat Campari. Not even in the fridge but next to it. Ouch. I went through to the kitchen, poured her out a glass that verged on being a bit too generous, and took it back to her. Her hand shook as she reached for it, and she half drained it.

'You're frightened. Okay, I understand that.'

She said nothing, but finished her drink and slammed it back down on the table. I sighed and went to refill it. I poured out a measure and turned to go back into the living room. Then I changed my mind and knocked it back in one, before refilling it for Sofia.

'Okay, let me put this together, piece by piece. I know only one person who could scare someone into drinking warm Campari in the middle of the day, and that's Albino Lupo, right?'

She gave the barest hint of a nod.

'He's been round here?' Again, she nodded. 'He wanted you to tell him everything you knew about Ballarin's relationship with his father. Everything about *Ghost Dog*. And anything – absolutely anything – you knew about what became of the diamonds that were never recovered following the robbery in Padua in 2003. That's right, isn't it?'

'That's right,' she whispered.

'Now, what would a man like that want with people like you or me? What's our connection with him? You used to work for a friend of his father's. So did my ex-father-in-law.' I paused. 'I still don't know if that's right. Never mind.

'In 2006 the *Ghost Dog* operation is launched against the Venetian mafia after two members of the organisation turn *pentito*. There are over sixty arrests. It effectively breaks the power of the Mala del Brenta. But also in 2006, Michele Ballarin allows a suspected *mafioso* to use Ravagnan's place on Pellestrina as a safe house. Just for a couple of days. Just until he could get out of the country.

'And this goes on for the next four years. At least six *mafiosi* in total. Until one day, there's a new guest. Giuseppe Lupo. This isn't just some middle-ranking member that Ravagnan can turn his eyes away from. This is a *boss*. Ravagnan knows that if this ever comes to light, he will end up going to prison for a very long time. Maybe he feels ashamed, dirty after what he's done. But I think it's more than that. I think he knows that if this ever comes to light, his daughter won't love him any more. And I think that breaks his heart, and he decides that enough is enough. Am I getting close here?'

Sofia nodded.

'He tells Michele he can't go on like this. More than that, he says he's going to go to the police. And then, that night, his car runs off the road at the Curve of Death.'

Sofia said nothing.

'I'm right, aren't I?'

She nodded. 'Yes.'

I sighed. 'Okay. Do you want to tell me more?'

'It was almost as you said. Elio and I, in 2006, well, we weren't together any more. That made things awkward in the office.'

'I can imagine.'

'He wanted me to find a job elsewhere. But why should I leave? I'd worked there all my life, back when Antonio was the senior partner. That's when things started to go wrong. When the old man died. I think Michele missed having him around for guidance. Sometimes he needed people to stop him doing things.

'He came into work a few weeks after his father died, in a foul mood, shouting and swearing. I gave him five minutes, maybe ten, to calm down. When I couldn't hear anything more from his office, I took his newspaper in with a cup of coffee. He was sitting behind his desk, with his head in his hands. He was crying. I thought it was because of his father, of course. I didn't know whether to give him a hug or not – you know how men can be funny like that? They don't want to be seen crying.'

I nodded. 'Go on.'

'Then he raised his head, and his eyes were red. I put his coffee and newspaper down, and asked him if he was all right. If there was anything I could do.

'He looked at me, and took a deep breath. And then he screamed, and swept his arm across the table. I remember the coffee going everywhere. Then he called me a stupid bitch and told me to get out.

'I heard him crying again after that. I sat down. Elio came over and suggested we go out for a cigarette together. He told me that Michele had heard the details of his father's will. Margherita got the money. Michele got the house. It would have made sense for Antonio to do that. After all, Margherita was living in Rome. He would have thought he was doing the right thing.

'I didn't understand why Michele was so angry, so upset. I'd never seen him like that before. Elio said he thought Michele had been spending a lot of money recently. Nice new suits, a new car. He was taking more holidays than he used to. Spending money he didn't have on the assumption he was going to inherit from his father.'

I shook my head. 'Blimey, that's a bit of an assumption. The only thing I'm going to inherit is a string of irate creditors.'

She ignored me, and carried on. 'The next day I came in to find a big bunch of flowers from him on my desk. He never apologised to me directly though. I think he was embarrassed and we never spoke about it again.

'Work went on as usual for a couple of months. The atmosphere was dreadful, though. It was difficult enough for Elio and me to be in the same office, and now Michele was constantly stressed. He'd come in late and then work late as if he thought that would compensate.

'Then one day, he asked Elio to spare him a few minutes in his office. They were together for maybe thirty minutes. I remember they both had clients that morning and I had to cancel them. It was embarrassing, I'd almost never had to do that before. Elio came out, shaking his head. He didn't speak to me. He just went into his office and came out with his hat and coat. He said he was going home and that I should cancel his appointments for the rest of the day. I asked him if he was all right, but he just shook his head and said he had something urgent to attend to.'

'Okay. I can have a guess at what that was. Head down to Pellestrina. Make the place look nice. Take up a floorboard and hide a gun underneath it. Extra protection for whoever was going to be staying there.'

'They started keeping a different book for a special group of clients. There was a separate account for them. I wasn't allowed to access it. I'm not sure if I was even supposed to know it existed. But I heard them talking about it, from time to time. They called it the *Ghost Dog* account.'

'I don't understand,' I said. 'Why would you even record that stuff? Surely that could have been compromising?'

'I think it was insurance. For both of them. It was evidence against the other in the event of someone deciding to break the deal.'

I shook my head. This, I thought, was going to break Federica's heart. 'You're saying that Elio was fine with this? With dealing with the mob?'

'I don't think he was ever happy with it. But he needed the money. And having done it once, the second time was easier. The third time, easier still. But Michele pushed him too far. One afternoon, I heard them having a row. Elio was saying he wouldn't do it. That he was out. I didn't know what that meant at the time. Michele must have been worried I'd overhear, so he stepped out of his office and told me I could go home for the day. Of course I did. I didn't want to be there.

'I was the first one in work, as usual, the following morning. Michele came in later as normal. He looked different. So much older. He told me there'd been an accident. Elio had crashed his car just outside Malamocco.

'I don't know if I believed it or not. Elio drove that way home every night. He knew how dangerous that bend was. Michele said he must have been drinking. He told me, again, that I could take the rest of the day off.

'A few days later I took a phone call from a local garage. They wanted to speak to Michele, but he was in a meeting. They asked me to pass on a message. His repair would take a bit longer than expected as they'd had to order a complete new front wing from Turin.'

I took a deep breath. 'You mean Michele ran him off the road?'

'I don't know.' She lowered her head and whispered. 'I don't know if he meant to or not. Maybe he was just angry, maybe it was an accident.' Her voice was barely audible now. 'But I think he did, yes.'

'And you didn't think of going to the police with this?'

'There was no proof of anything at all. And besides, I was scared of Michele. And—' She paused.

'And?'

'And when I told him about the message from the garage, he offered me money. Good money, never to speak about it again.'

I shook my head.

'A few months later I heard about Giuseppe Lupo being arrested in Chioggia. I wondered if he'd been part of the *Ghost Dog* account. There was no proof, of course. A few months later I left the job. Michele had become unbearable. He kept looking at me, as if suspecting that I knew something. He couldn't be quite sure that I didn't. But, of course, all I had was a reference to something called the *Ghost Dog* account and a phone call from a garage.'

'So you said nothing to anyone?'

'No.'

I shook my head again. 'I don't think I'll ever understand this. Elio left his family for you. You must have loved him once. And yet you said nothing. Absolutely nothing.'

She drained her glass and set it down with a crash, her

hand shaking. 'Don't you judge me. Don't you dare judge me.'

'I'm not judging you. But I don't understand you.' I got to my feet. 'I'll see myself out.'

She was already refilling her glass as I slammed the door behind me.

I made my way downstairs. What had Elio intended to do when he left the office for the last time? Had he meant to go straight to the police? Or was he prepared to give Michele one last chance? We'd never know. All we knew was that a USB stick and an envelope full of photographs – the only evidence against Michele Ballarin – had stayed hidden in a box of news clippings and family photos in an attic on Pellestrina.

As good a hiding place as anywhere. So good, in fact, that it had stayed hidden for the best part of ten years.

I walked across the road to the bar, where a lychee spritz awaited me, but could see no sign of Federica.

Chapter 44

She'll be here somewhere, I told myself.

She'll definitely be here somewhere.

I pushed my way through the customers to check the tables at the back.

She wasn't there. Okay, it was crowded. She must have gone elsewhere.

I made my way outside. The only other bar in the area was directly across the road and closed up. She must have gone a bit further afield.

But where?

I went back inside. Two women were standing at the bar. One of them was holding a bored-looking child by the hand, who was rhythmically kicking against the metal rail that ran along the base. I opened my mouth to speak, but the *barista* waved me aside and turned to them instead. He smiled at them. 'I think you were next, *signore*?'

'I think we were.' One of them turned and smiled at me. 'We'll be very quick.'

'I'm sorry, but this is important.'

She switched the smile off. 'We'll be very quick. As I said.' Then she tutted and looked down. 'Mario, what are you doing?'

The small boy had become bored with kicking the metal foot-rest and had moved on to the bar itself. The rhythmic thudding was starting to echo through my head. My mouth felt dry, and in desperate need of a glass of water.

'*Mamma*,' he said, in between kicks. 'Can I have an ice cream?'

His mother sighed. 'Do you have to have one now, Mario?' He nodded.

Thud. Thud. Thud.

'Mario, do stop that.'

Thud. Thud. Thud. I gripped the edge of the bar, my hands sweaty and slippery.

'Oh Mario, which one do you want?' There was an air of desperation to her voice.

The child frowned, as if surprised by the ease of his victory, and stopped kicking. He stared down at his shoes. 'Don't know,' he muttered.

Another sigh. 'Let's take a look then, shall we?'

She took him by the hand and led him to the refrigerator. I seized my chance, and moved into her space, leaning over the bar and waving my telephone at the barman.

Her companion tutted, and tried to elbow me out of the way. 'We're still being served.'

'No you're not.'

'We are!'

'You're not. Look, they're choosing an ice cream. They could be there for hours.'

'We're still—'

I cut her off. 'No you're not. The moment's passed. Sorry.' My hair felt damp, and I swept it back out of my eyes. I waved my phone at the barman again. 'Look, I'm trying to find my wife. I think she was in here maybe ten, twenty minutes ago.' I clicked the button to display the screen saver. 'Do you recognise her?'

'Her? Oh, her I recognise. Yes, she was in here about half an hour ago.'

'Where did she go? Did you see?'

He shrugged. 'She went outside, looked like she was taking a phone call. It was a bit noisy in here, you know?'

He inclined his head ever so slightly in the direction of the refrigerator. Little Mario, evidently, had not found quite the flavour he was after and was becoming disturbingly purple in the face. I suspected I didn't have much time.

'Okay, and then? She didn't come back in?'

'No.' He frowned, as if remembering something. 'Hey, that means she never paid.' He glared at me.

I rummaged in my pocket. 'Okay, I've got this, don't worry. What did she have?'

'Just a spritz. Four euros.'

I slipped a fiver across the bar. 'Keep the change. What happened next? Did you see where she went?'

He looked embarrassed. 'Mister, are you sure you want to know?'

'I'm sure. Come on.'

'A guy pulled up in a car. Nice red sports car. If you see one of those, you don't forget it.' He paused.

'And then?'

'He just leaned out and said something to her. I don't know what it was. And then she got in and he drove off.'

I gripped the edge of the bar, and screwed my eyes closed,

breathing deeply. I swore under my breath, but evidently not under enough as the woman next to me tutted and muttered the word *maleducato*.

'Is everything okay, mister?' said the barman.

I turned and ran from the bar without answering, narrowly avoiding tripping over Mario, now purple-faced and howling with an evidently unsatisfactory ice cream in his hand.

I dialled Fede's number again, and then again. There was no answer. I hadn't really expected there to be one. I ran the length of the street, and then back again but there was no sign of the red Ferrari.

Lupo didn't need me, of course. He only needed Federica. I closed my eyes, and leaned back against a shop window. *Beat it out of her if necessary – if you don't, I will.*

I forced myself to count to ten, breathing deeply. It would be easy, so easy, just to tip over the edge into blind panic. But that wouldn't help Fede.

I'd try ringing her once more. I started walking again, heedless as to where I was going, and pulled my phone out of my pocket.

There was a screech of brakes, and I heard a woman scream. Then someone threw their arms around me and hurled me to the ground.

'Mister, are you all right?'

I nodded. 'I think so.' I looked up to see a young man looking down at me, an expression of concern on his face.

'You nearly walked out into the traffic. I only just grabbed you in time.'

I got to my feet, wincing. 'Thank you. I'm sorry, I just wasn't thinking.'

'You're sure you're okay?' I nodded. 'You've dropped your stuff everywhere. Here, let me give you a hand.'

He was right. My phone had gone in one direction, my wallet in another; and the change in my pocket had scattered across the road.

'Is this yours, mister?' He held out Giulia's set of keys with the *Ciao* keyring.

'It is, yes. Look, I'm very grateful to you. I think you saved my life there.'

He smiled. 'No problem. I guess that's my good deed for the day. *Ciao,* mister.' He gave me a wave, and turned and walked away.

'*Ciao,*' I murmured and looked at the keyring. Why had that been going through my head?

Then it came to me.

Ballarin's desk.

Ballarin's leather-topped desk in his wood-panelled office. With the incongruous little plastic figure of *'Ciao'*.

I held the keys up, my hands shaking. Margherita had mentioned Ballarin's house. She'd said she needed to go round there, just to make sure that everything was in place. Following which, nobody had heard from her.

I took out my phone, sighing with relief when I saw it was still working, and brought up the telephone directory. How many Ballarins were there in Venice? Over two hundred. But only one Michele on the Lido. The address was on Via Sandro Gallo, perhaps a kilometre away. No time to wait for a bus, no time to hope for a passing taxi. I'd have to run . . .

***

I stopped, gasping for breath and sticky with sweat, outside Ballarin's house.

I looked up and down the street, but there was no sign of Lupo's Ferrari. The street was a mixture of shops and residential properties with a steady stream of traffic and pedestrians. When I'd caught my breath, I went up the steps to the front door, put the key in the lock, and turned it.

The door opened.

I lifted the keyring to my lips and gave it a kiss. *Oh bella 'Ciao'!*

I opened my mouth to call for Fede, and then shut it again. Stupid idea. I made my way down the corridor. The walls had once been lined with paintings, which now lay smashed and torn on the floor. I knelt down to look at them. Oil paintings of Venice, their colours now dulled with age. Not the sort of thing I'd have associated with Michele Ballarin. Presumably it was his father's taste.

I took the first door at the end of the corridor. The living room. Again, paintings had been torn from the walls, and the canvases ripped from the frames. Furniture had been overturned, and books pulled from the shelves.

'Fede?' I whispered. 'Fede?' There was no answer, and I breathed deeply, trying to quash the rising tide of panic that was swelling in me. She had to be in here somewhere. She just had to be.

I went back into the corridor, and noticed a thin blade of light from under the door at the far end. I pulled it open as quietly as I could. Concrete steps led downwards, illuminated by a bare bulb hanging from the ceiling.

I made my way downstairs into a garage that seemed far

too shabby for the spotless red Ferrari parked in the middle of it. The rear wall was lined with shelves, all stacked with tools, and a DIY bench had been pushed up against it.

Something wrapped in black plastic was lying on top of the bench.

Something that could have been human-shaped.

God, no.

I forced myself to move closer, and started to pull the sheeting up, just a little.

Oh Christ . . .

Human feet. I almost dropped to my knees, and then I noticed the shoes. Not Federica's.

Oh Christ, thank you . . .

I pulled the sheeting away. Margherita lay cold on the bench, her throat heavily marked. Strangled.

I looked around for something more dignified to cover her with, but could see nothing. I settled for pulling the sheeting over her again, to cover her sightless eyes.

'I'm sorry,' I said.

I looked around the garage once more. She had to be here or . . . I shook my head. Keep it together, Nathan.

I decided to risk it. 'Fede,' I called. And then louder, 'Fede!'

I heard a thumping noise from the Testarossa. A noise, a rhythmic banging coming from under the bonnet. Of course. Luggage space in the Ferrari was in the front. The driver side door was unlocked and I fumbled around under the steering wheel looking for the release mechanism, pushing and pulling at anything and everything I came across until I heard it clunk open.

Federica, trussed and gagged, had been crammed inside

the impossibly small space. I sighed with relief.

'Okay. I've got you. Just give me a minute, I'll get you out of here and then we'll call the cops, okay?'

She nodded, but then her eyes widened and she shook her head frantically.

'It's okay, it's okay. I've got you.'

She continued to shake her head and was struggling to say something. I leaned in further, in order to try and remove the gag.

The lid of the bonnet slammed down on my head and I dropped to my knees, my head spinning. Then it cracked down once more, and everything went black.

Chapter 45

I opened my eyes, and wished I hadn't. I was still in the underground garage, only now the lights were on and were uncomfortably bright. There was a bitter, metallic taste in my mouth and my head ached like a bastard. For a moment, I thought I was going to vomit. I closed my eyes again and took a few deep breaths until the feeling passed and I felt I could risk half opening them.

Better. Not good, but definitely better. I tried to move and realised I couldn't. My hands were tied behind my back and, as I looked down, I could see that my ankles were tied to the legs of the chair.

I felt a hand touching my fingers, wrapping themselves around them and squeezing.

'Fede?'

'You're awake then?'

'Are you all right?'

'That's what I was going to ask you.'

'I'm fine. I think. A bastard of a headache, but I'll be okay. How about you?'

'I'm okay. He punched me in the face, of course. Just because he could.'

'Lupo?'

'No. The other one. Zanetti. He said he was getting his own back for this morning. Said he'd do worse if it was up to him, but orders were orders.'

'Bastard. I'll kill him.'

Fede forced out a dry little laugh. 'That's very gallant of you, *tesoro*, but I don't think either of us are going to be doing any killing any time soon.'

'Why the hell did you get in the car?'

'He'd got my phone number from somewhere. Maybe from *mamma* when his wife was still pretending to be a journalist, I don't know. Anyway, I went outside to take the call and he pulled up. Then he leaned over and told me that if I didn't come with him, all he had to do was make one phone call and he'd have you killed as soon as you left Sofia's flat.'

'And you believed him?'

'It didn't seem like it was a bluff that I could call. He was quite convincing. I didn't think it was something one could really say "Oh, it'll probably be all right" about. Believe it or not, I'm not ready for widowhood just yet.'

'Aw. That's nice of you. What the hell were you doing under the bonnet?'

'Not a lot.'

'You know what I mean.'

'He thought it would be funny. God, you can imagine how hot it was in there. No light. Not being able to move. I started to panic about not being able to breathe and then I heard you calling.'

'Son of a bitch.' I managed to give her fingers a squeeze. As far as I could tell, she was similarly tied up, with her back to me. 'Can you reach the ropes around my wrist?'

'It's not a rope. It's a cable tie. Sorry.'

'Shit.'

'So now what do we do?' Her voice was calm, but I knew that she, like me, was on the edge of panic. I wrestled with the cable tie, but only succeeded in chafing my wrists. I strained my ankles against the legs of the chair, to no avail. Then I started trying to rock myself from side to side.

'What are you trying to do?'

'I'm wondering if I can topple the chair over.'

'Oh. Why?'

'Maybe it'll break. Or just enough to get my legs free.'

'Or maybe it'll be like now. Except you'll be on the floor.'

'Look, I'm trying, okay? I don't know what the hell else to do.' I yanked my wrists once more, and felt the ties dig in, deeper this time. 'Ow.' I swore under my breath.

'Nathan. Calm down. This isn't helping. Whatever's going to happen will be easier if you're calm.'

I nodded, clamped my eyes shut and counted to ten, breathing deeply. For the first time since I was a child, I wished that I could pray and mean it.

Pray.

I thought of Albino Lupo, the man named after the late Pope John Paul – the smiling Pope, the September Pope – kneeling in the front pew of Madonna della Marina, the rosary twisting in his hand as he muttered his prayers and breathed in the dust of centuries.

Praying.

I thought of the photograph on the church website.

Michele Ballarin, laughing and joking with Sandro Vicari and Giuseppe Lupo. Don Francesco, happy to accept his money and not to ask too many awkward questions about where it came from.

What do you think I do, get on my knees every day and pray for a miracle?

My eyes snapped open. 'My God.'

'What's wrong?'

'Nothing. Nothing's wrong.' I began to laugh. 'I think I've solved it.'

Chapter 46

'You what?' said Fede.

'The diamonds. I think I've solved it.' I could hear foot-steps coming down the stairs, and a key rattling in the door. 'Fede, you're going to have to trust me on this, okay?' She gave my fingers a squeeze.

The door opened, and Zanetti stood there, gun in hand.

'Good evening, Enrico.'

Zanetti grinned. 'Mr and Mrs Sutherland,' he drawled, trying his best at an impression of what he imagined a posh English accent might sound like.

I twisted around as best I could, and looked over to where Margherita's body lay on the bench. 'You didn't have to do that,' I said.

Zanetti turned his head to one side, and then the other as if trying to decide. 'No. No, I kind of think I did.' He grinned.

'She was a good woman, Zanetti. She wouldn't have caused you any trouble.'

'Yeah, but she was a good woman making a lot of noise.' He shook his head. 'I don't like that. So,' he shrugged, 'you know?' He grinned again. I wasn't sure if this was all an act, like the amiable idiot routine he'd given me on the bus.

'Will your wife be joining us this evening?'

'I don't think so. We had a bit of a talk after she got back from your house the other night. Things got a bit heated, you know?'

I shook my head. 'Jesus.'

Zanetti continued to grin, nodding his head all the while. Then he walked over to me and punched me in the face. Fede gripped my fingers ever more tightly.

'You know, Mr Sutherland, when we met this morning I was prepared to be nice to you. But you decided to make fun of me instead.'

'Yeah.' I spat blood on to the ground. 'That was a mistake.'

'You're right about that,' he said, and punched me again.

I was prepared for the blow, but, tied to the chair, there was no way to ride it. I felt my head spinning, and I spat out blood once again.

'Stop it. Please for the love of God, stop it.'

Zanetti turned to Federica, and grabbed her by the chin, balling his fist. 'Sure. You want me to start on you instead?'

'Zanetti. Enrico. You don't have to do this. You want me to talk, I'll talk. But you don't have to beat the crap out of us first.'

'Oh, I know I don't need to. But I'm having so much fun.' He shifted his grip to Federica's throat and drew his fist back.

'I see you've started without me.' I shook my head to try and clear it, and looked up to see Lupo stood in the doorway.

I tried to conceal my sigh of relief. Zanetti, I was sure, would have been happy to beat us to a bloody pulp before we could say a word. But there was at least a chance of reasoning with Lupo, dangerous as he was.

Lupo looked us up and down. He cupped my face in his hands; then shook his head, took a handkerchief from his pocket, and wiped the blood from his fingers. Then he turned to Federica, and tutted when he saw her blackened eye.

He looked back at Zanetti. 'You were only supposed to bring them here, not beat them unconscious.'

Zanetti shrugged. 'I just wanted to make sure they weren't going to be any trouble.'

Lupo reached down and tugged at the cable ties securing our wrists. 'I don't think that's very likely, do you?' He looked up at Zanetti. 'Everything went well then?'

'No problems, Albino.' Then he hesitated. 'There's just one thing.'

Lupo's eyes narrowed. 'Oh yes?'

'There's someone else in the house. I don't know who it is. But there's a third person there. His name's Gramsci.'

'Gramsci.' Lupo tried not to sigh, and looked back at me. 'Tell me about Gramsci, Sutherland.'

'He's a cat.'

'Ah.' Lupo nodded. 'He's a cat.' He turned to Zanetti. 'He's a cat, you imbecile!'

'I didn't know!'

I looked at Lupo and rolled my eyes, shrugging my shoulders. 'Staff, eh?'

Zanetti snarled, and I braced myself for another punch in the face, but Lupo waved his hand and shook his head ever so slightly.

'He's no good to me unconscious, Zanetti.'

'Very sensible,' I said, and nodded at Zanetti. 'You should listen to him.'

Lupo came and stood over me, putting his hands on his hips. 'You can stop joking, if you like?'

'Sorry. It's a defence mechanism. I always use it in near-death situations. Kind of hard to break the habit.' Keeping him talking, I thought, would buy us a bit of time. 'I've seen the state of Ballarin's house. There's nothing left to tear apart. He never knew anything about the diamonds. Are you convinced of that yet?'

Lupo shook his head. 'I was certain he knew. But, I admit, I got that one wrong. I don't think he did.'

'No.' The voice was Zanetti's. 'He gave him a safe house. He gave him a weapon. And Lupo never, ever implicated him. Of course he knew where they were.'

'Perhaps he did,' I said. 'He's certainly not going to tell you now. So what did you do? Invite him to meet you in Pellestrina? Giuseppe Lupo's son wanting to make contact, and hopefully carrying on the family business? Ballarin would have been fine with that. Then Zanetti here battered him until he couldn't talk any more and threw him in the lagoon. And now poor Margherita. Did she just walk in at the wrong time? Two murders in a week. In Venice. This isn't going to go unnoticed by the police, Albino. All your hench-man's managed to do is attract their attention.'

Zanetti burst out again. 'She was Ballarin's sister, Albino. She might have known.'

'Two dead for no reason, Albino. And a trail that's not difficult to follow. Hell, I managed it.'

'Albino, listen,' said Zanetti.

'Shut up, you idiot.'

'But Albino . . .'

'I said shut up. You idiot. You cheap, chiselling little crook. Why did I ever get involved with someone from a crappy little fairground gang?'

He turned through a full circle, and spread his arms wide. 'Now look where we are, Mr Sutherland. Signor Ballarin seems to have liked his DIY.' He paused. 'Zanetti does as well. And despite his incompetence I might just give him one final treat. So I'm going to ask you one final time. Very politely. Where are my father's diamonds?'

He stared at me and I stared back at him. Then he nodded to himself, reached into his jacket, and pulled out a gun. He turned to look at Federica, and smiled. She couldn't stop herself from flinching.

I nodded at Lupo. 'Okay,' I said. 'I'll tell you.'

Chapter 47

Lupo's eyes widened. 'You know?'

'Yes. I had some time to think whilst I was being tied to a chair and beaten. It's straightforward enough really.'

Lupo chuckled, and turned to Zanetti. 'See, Enrico, as easy as that. Nobody has to get hurt. Nobody has to get killed.' He looked back at me. 'So . . . ?'

'It's not as easy as that, I'm afraid.'

Lupo sighed and levelled the gun at me.

'Not much of a threat, Albino, as I'm the only one who knows where they are.'

He nodded. 'Okay.' He turned around to face Federica.

'That's not much of a threat either, because if you hurt her there's no way on God's clean earth I'll tell you.'

He turned back to me. 'I don't have to kill you. I could just start with your kneecaps, and then move on to more interesting places.'

I nodded, trying to keep my voice calm. 'You could. Or – and here's a radical idea – you could let us go?'

'What?'

'Easiest for everyone. You let Federica go. You let me go. I'll take you to the diamonds. Then you get the hell out of the country to wherever you want and none of us have to hear anything about this ever again.'

'Albino, he's lying,' said Zanetti.

'Is he?'

'You know he is. He doesn't know where they are. He's just saying this to save his own life.'

'I wonder. I wonder.' Lupo put his head to one side, weighing the gun in his hands.

'You should listen to me, Albino,' I said, 'Zanetti's not got a great track record so far, has he?'

Lupo nodded.

'Oh for Christ's sake, Albino. You're not going to listen to this idiot are you?'

'You know, I think perhaps I am.'

'You'll get us both arrested.'

'It wasn't me who killed Ballarin and threw him into the sea.' He pointed at Margherita's body. 'It wasn't me who put a dead body in his garage.' He ran a hand through his hair. 'Christ's sake, there used to be a time when I had professionals for this sort of thing. Now look at me. Working with someone who used to scam money out of schoolchildren on the roundabouts.'

Zanetti opened his mouth but Albino shook his head. 'Shut up, Zanetti. Just shut up, please.' He looked back at the two of us, and nodded. 'Okay. Cut them free.'

Zanetti tried to stare him down but couldn't hold his gaze. He took a knife from his pocket, crouched next to us, and cut the ties securing Federica. Then he moved on to me, freeing my wrists and then my ankles. He moved the knife to just underneath my chin. 'Stand up. But slowly.'

I got to my feet, rubbing my chafed wrists and feeling the life slowly returning to them.

'We'll need a car,' I said. 'And there's only two seats in the Ferrari.'

'Zanetti, where's yours?'

'It's parked on the street, Albino.'

'Okay, we'll take that.' He turned to me. 'You drive. The woman next to you. We'll be in the back. If you do anything stupid I'll shoot her. Understood?'

'I understand.'

'So take it easy. Try very, very hard not to go over any bumps. Where are we going?'

'Malamocco,' I said. 'I'll tell you more when we get there.'

Lupo nodded at me. 'Okay. Let's go.'

Chapter 48

I parked the car outside the church, and cut the engine. Lupo and Zanetti got out of the back seat, keeping their guns trained on Federica the whole time. 'Okay. Get out. And close the door. Quietly.'

I clunked it shut and took the opportunity to look around. It was dark now and the streets were deserted. We must have spent a long time in Michele Ballarin's garage.

We walked up the short path to the church door. Wooden, iron-barred and very, very shut. Even in Malamocco, churches remained locked at night. I cursed under my breath, and turned around.

'It's locked,' I said, somewhat redundantly.

Lupo shrugged. 'Okay. So we get the priest out. I know where he lives. You walk ahead of me. Just a few feet, eh?'

Don Francesco's house was at the back of the church, and set back from the road. I rang the bell once, twice and then leaned on it. Lupo swore, reached past me, and hammered on the door.

'I was trying to avoid making a noise,' I said.

'Shut up.'

A light came on from inside the house, and a silhouette

appeared behind the frosted glass of the door. Lupo lowered his revolver so that it could not easily be seen, jamming it into the small of Federica's back.

Don Francesco opened the door. He looked angry, at first, upon seeing my face, but his expression changed to one of confusion upon seeing Lupo.

'Good evening, *padre*.'

'Albino? What are you doing? What's going on?'

'I need you to open up the church for me, *padre*.'

'I don't understand? For prayer? What have you done, Albino?'

'Please hurry, *padre*. We don't have long. Open the church. Please.'

'I'm in my pyjamas. I'll just go and get changed.' He waved his hand at Fede and me. 'What are these people doing here?'

'They're just here to help me. And it's a warm evening. Don't worry about getting changed.'

Don Francesco shook his head. 'I'll only be five minutes.' He was about to turn around when Lupo, tired of waiting, raised his revolver and pointed it at him.

'I'm sorry, *padre*. But I don't have five minutes.'

Don Francesco's eyes widened in terror. He nodded. 'I'll get the keys.'

'Don't be too long, *padre*. I wouldn't like to think you were making a telephone call.'

'They're just here.' He opened up a wooden box on a chest of drawers in the hall, and took out a heavy bunch of keys.

'Come on. Let's go.' He waved the gun. 'You first, *padre*.'

'Albino,' I said, 'I'm not saying you haven't thought this through or anything, but it does strike me that walking through the streets of Malamocco with a priest in pyjamas is liable to attract attention.'

Don Francesco shook his head. 'There's a rear door. We can access it via my garden.'

Zanetti smiled, and patted me on my shoulder. 'Not so smart are you, Mr Sutherland? Not so smart after all.'

Don Francesco led us through the garden, the moonlight through the medlar trees casting jagged, expressionist shadows on the ground, to a wicket gate in the wall which scraped across the gravel path as he pulled it open.

'We're doing very well, *padre*. On we go.'

He led us to the side door, shielded from the view of any late-night pedestrians by the high wall, and took out his keys.

Albino looked at Don Francesco. 'Please, *padre*. Don't take too long.'

The little priest looked terrified, his hands shaking as the ancient keys rattled in the lock. The great wooden door creaked and groaned as he pushed it open.

'First you then, *padre*. Then you, Mr Sutherland. And then I'll follow with the *bella signora*.' I turned back, and saw his revolver jammed right up against the back of Fede's head.

I held my hands up. 'There's no need for this, you know? I told you I'd show you where the diamonds are. I still will. But put your gun down. Please? In case anybody gets too excited.'

Albino looked at me and shook his head. Then he pulled the gun back and cocked the trigger. Fede shuddered, in spite of herself.

'Please,' I said.

'*Please . . . please . . .*' he whined, in a mock-English accent. 'You pathetic little shit. If someone threatened my woman I'd have them killed. And all you can do is beg. *Please . . .*' he wheedled again.

'Albino, if I called her "my woman" she'd kick my sorry arse all the way to England and back again. Come on. If you shoot, someone will hear, someone will come. Just put the gun down. Then you can take what you came for, everyone will be happy and no one has to get hurt. Or at least no one else has to get hurt. Is that so bad?'

He stared at me and his hand trembled for an instant. Then he nodded and lowered the gun. 'We're wasting time.'

'We certainly are. *Padre,* take us through to the sacristy, please.'

He led us through by the dim beam of the light on my mobile phone, briefly genuflecting and crossing himself as we passed in front of the altar and muttering under his breath. He unlocked the sacristy door, and stepped through.

'*Padre,* we need some lights on.'

He nodded and flicked a switch. There was a brief hum of electricity, and then the lamps set into the walls flickered into life.

Albino released his grip on Fede and stepped into the room, covering us all with the gun.

He nodded at me. 'Sutherland?'

'Come on, Albino,' I said. 'Don't you know?'

Zanetti looked around the sacristy, turning through a full circle. Then he stopped and stared at the painting of the *Virgin in the company of twelve saints* and began to laugh.

I smiled at Albino. 'Look,' I said. 'Zanetti's worked it out.'

Zanetti reached into his jacket, and took out the post-card from Elio. 'Albino, Giulia took this from their house the other night. Ravagnan had it sent to his daughter. It's the same painting!'

I nodded at him. 'The first restoration job that Federica ever worked on. And a painting that used to be on the opposite wall.'

'And moved to the wall that was restored by Lupo and Vicari.' Zanetti let the postcard drop to the floor and ran to the painting, running his hands over the canvas and then tugging at the frame. Federica winced.

He turned to Don Francesco. 'We need to get this off the wall. Get a spade, a pickaxe. Anything like that.'

'This is a church! Why would we have a pickaxe?'

'I don't care. Get anything as long as we can lever that thing off the wall.' He turned to Albino, and tapped his forehead with his index finger. 'See! Good old Enrico's not so dumb after all, is he?'

Lupo looked at Zanetti, and then at me. He sighed. 'Go on then, Enrico. Tell me more.'

'Ravagnan's daughter, Albino! That's why he sent her the postcard.' He jabbed his finger at the wall. 'That's where they are.'

Lupo nodded. 'And so when we remove the painting, we break open the wall and find a hidden chamber with the diamonds?'

'That's it.' Zanetti turned back to Don Francesco. 'Anything you have – a spade, a pick. A tyre iron.'

Albino rubbed the bridge of his nose, and waved his hand to shush him.

'No,' he said.

'We're wasting time, Albino. I don't know how long it's going to take us, but the sooner we start, the sooner—'

'Shut up, please, Enrico.'

'But—'

Albino walked over to him, and placed an arm around his shoulder. 'Shut up, please. Just for a moment. You see, Enrico, Mr Sutherland is counting on us hammering away at a brick wall for hours in order to buy some time.' He turned to look at me. 'Isn't that right?'

I shrugged, and smiled apologetically.

'I don't understand,' said Zanetti.

Albino patted his shoulder. 'No. No, you don't, do you? But do try to think. Just a little. Vicari and my father had these diamonds put aside as a sort of insurance policy. Something they could get hold of in minutes. Imagine, now: Vicari lives in Malamocco. So close to his beloved church. Imagine, then, that one day he hears from his informers that the police are preparing to act. Perhaps his bank account is frozen already. He phones my father and tells him they have to move, right now. They just need the diamonds. But above all, they need to move quickly.'

'I still don't—'

Albino screwed his eyes up as if in pain. 'Mr Sutherland. Would you like to tell him?'

I coughed, gently. 'What Albino is trying to say, Enrico, is that in a situation where even the matter of a few minutes could mean the difference between life and death, having to hammer a hole in a brick wall in the middle of a church would be likely to slow you down a bit.'

Enrico's face fell.

'Sometimes, Enrico, a postcard is just a postcard.'

'I don't understand. Why move the painting then?'

'Just a distraction. That's all.'

Albino shook his head, and turned away from Zanetti in disgust. 'I'm getting tired, Sutherland and I want to be away from here.' He raised the gun again.

'Come on, Albino. You're a smart guy. You can work this out. Somewhere in here.'

He turned around to look at the display cases. Vestments, chalices, pyxes and ciboriums. Ornate candlesticks, finely embroidered purificators and corporals, and faded, rotting altar cloths from centuries gone by. And there, in the middle of them, its gold glowing against its dull and worm-ridden case, was the monstrance. A fragment of the Crown of Thorns, set in a perfect crystal reliquary.

Albino looked at it, and then at me. And a smile slowly broke out across his face.

I nodded. 'Of course it is. Where else would it be? This was nothing to do with the saving of souls. This was Vicari, the master jeweller, the master forger. Hiding something in plain sight and setting up a decoy with all the nonsense with the painting.'

Federica smiled. 'Of course. *Covering a multitude of sins.*'

'Diamonds drilled into the frame. And covered with a thick layer of gold paint.'

Albino ran his fingers down the front of the display case. Then he took his revolver, smashed through the glass and reached through to pull the monstrance out. Even in the dim light I could see that he'd scratched himself and the back of his hand was bleeding, but he appeared not to notice.

He laid the gun down. Fede and I exchanged glances, but he caught sight of us and shook his head. 'Zanetti, keep them covered.' He reached into his pocket, and took out his car keys. Then he ran his thumb over the curve of the outside edge of the monstrance, back and forth, back and forth until he found something – a tiny little raised edge – under the pad of his thumb. He took the keys between thumb and forefinger and began to scratch away, slowly at first, then more vigorously until I could see flecks of gold clinging to his hand. Then a moment, just a moment, of metal catching against something else. He stopped scrubbing at the frame and picked away at the gold with his fingernails until they were bloody. Slowly, ever so slowly. I tried to move closer, just a step, in order to see more clearly, but Zanetti waved his gun at me.

Albino bowed his head for a moment, and smiled. He held the monstrance above his head, as if raising the Communion chalice; then brought it to his lips, and kissed it.

Zanetti ran his free hand through his hair, and laughed. 'We've done it. I don't believe it, Albino, but we've done it.'

'Yes, Zanetti. We have. Haven't we?' Lupo's voice was empty of any emotion, his expression blank.

Zanetti continued to laugh. 'Christ almighty, we did it. We're rich.'

Lupo shook his head, and his expression changed. He smiled at him. 'We?'

Zanetti stopped laughing. 'What do you mean?'

'Oh, Enrico,' I said, 'what do you think he means?'

'Albino, I don't understand.'

'Enrico, Enrico. This was never a partnership. Albino only needed you because he knew you'd been Giuseppe's cellmate. There was a chance, no matter how slim, that he might have told you something. When he found out you knew nothing at all, it was still worth keeping you on to do the dirty work for him.'

'Albino, tell him that's not true. I know I made mistakes, but I worked hard for you. I did everything you asked me to. Everything.'

'I know you did, Enrico. I know you did.' Lupo continued to smile at him. 'But I've thought about this and I don't think there's anything else I really need you to do.'

'Fuck you, you prick. I've done all the shit work for you, so you could keep your hands clean.'

'You did. But the trouble is, you really didn't do it very well.'

'Fuck you, Lupo.' Zanetti levelled his revolver at him, his hand shaking with rage.

Albino shook his head – 'Bored with this now' – and shot him through the chest.

Zanetti fell to the ground, as the four of us stood there, listening to the echoes die away.

'Albino, for the love of God, what have you done?' Don Francesco stammered out.

Lupo put a finger to his lips to shush him, and then turned to me. 'Thank you, Mr Sutherland. I'm grateful. Really. But the bargain only held up until now.' He raised his gun again. 'I am sorry. Perhaps my father would have done otherwise. But that was his weakness.'

He aimed the gun at Federica but before I could move, Don Francesco had stepped between them. 'You won't do it,' he said.

'You think so?'

'I know so. Because I am going to walk out of here now

and call the police. I knew your father, Albino. He was a good Christian man. He would never kill a woman. And he would certainly never kill a priest.' He turned his back on us and walked towards the sacristy door.

'Don Francesco. If you don't stop, I will shoot you.'

The little priest, to his credit, did not even break his stride. Albino swore, and pushed Federica to one side, the better to aim. Before Don Francesco had even laid a hand upon the door, Albino had shot him in the back, the noise deafening in the tiny space.

Albino stood motionless, as if overwhelmed by what he had done, his gun hand trembling. It was only a moment, but it was enough. I threw myself at him, sending him tumbling backwards into the display case. His hand tightened upon the gun, and I grabbed his wrist with both my hands, not daring to trust my strength with just the one. I forced his hand upwards, as he loosed a shot into the air. Then I pushed it back, through the broken glass of the case. He screamed as the jagged edges dug into his flesh, and dropped the gun.

He no longer had the weapon, but Albino had one great advantage over me. Quite simply, he was very, very good at casual violence. He brought his head down on my nose, whilst at the same time kneeing me in the stomach. I staggered back, gasping for air, giving him time and space to punch me in the face, sending me reeling back across the room.

I could see Federica kneeling by the door, next to Don Francesco. Why the hell hadn't she got out while she could? Then I noticed the priest's body shudder. He was still alive.

Try as I might to gather myself, my head was still spinning and I was in no condition to stop Albino from punching me again and knocking me to the floor. He made as if to kick me in the face, and I feebly attempted to throw up my arms to protect myself. Then he stopped, and grinned down at me. No. Better to have me conscious. He stepped back, bent down and picked up the gun. He turned to Federica.

'This is the last thing you'll ever see, you bastard.'

He didn't even get the chance to raise the weapon. Two bullets slammed into his chest, sending him spinning backwards. He dropped to his knees, before a third shot knocked him flat. I could see his head, turned to one side, his eyes searching for the monstrance which lay on the ground close by. His fingers reached out for it, just brushing the casing.

'*Papà*,' he said.

Zanetti had raised himself to his knees, his revolver trembling in his hand. The other clutched his chest, and I could see the blood pouring through his fingers. He inched closer and closer to Lupo, who tried to raise his own hands in a desperate attempt to protect himself, still struggling even in the last moments of his life. Then Zanetti fired directly into his chest. Once. Twice. And again and again until the magazine was empty and the revolver clicked.

Zanetti knelt over him, silhouetted in the dim light, and wreathed in smoke from the revolver. Then he dropped it to the floor with a clatter. He reached for the monstrance and slowly, ever so slowly, pulled it towards him.

'Mine,' he managed to croak out. 'Mine.' And then he collapsed on to Lupo's chest.

I looked across the room to Federica, still kneeling next to Don Francesco. The sound of gunfire was roaring in my ears but I could still hear the sirens outside.

Chapter 49

Busetto held the monstrance up to the light. The crystal refracted a small rainbow on to the far wall that shimmered and wobbled as the *maresciallo* shifted it from hand to hand.

'Lovely, isn't it?' he said.

'Too lovely. Federica gave me the idea. That thick coating of gold around the outside. It looked so vulgar compared to the rest of the piece. Now at first I thought it was just the work of a mafia thug with no taste. But then I read in Brezzi's notes about the rest of Vicari's work and it confused me. The master craftsman, the master forger. Why had he done such a crude job on this? As if he was throwing money at it, just for the sake of it.

'And then I got it. He wasn't showing off. He wasn't being vulgar. The thick gold layer was to conceal the diamonds that he'd drilled into the casing.'

Busetto continued to turn the monstrance over and over in his hands. 'Brilliant in some ways,' he said. 'A small, local church has a beloved relic repaired. It comes back looking bright and shiny and new. That's enough for them. Who'd think of asking any questions? Who'd even think of complaining that it looked just a little bit too bright?'

'Exactly. It could have sat there for years until such a time as Lupo or Vicari wanted it back. Think of it. Just another relic hiding amongst hundreds of other relics. No need for extra security. Nobody really believes there's a fragment of the Crown of Thorns in there. So, easy to retrieve when required.' I reached out my hand. 'May I?'

Busetto nodded. 'Of course.'

I picked it up, feeling its weight in my hand. Then I swivelled my chair around and held it up to the light streaming in through the window. I narrowed my eyes against the glare, the better to see the thin filament inside. Had it genuinely been placed upon the head of Christ?

'So what are you going to do now, Mr Sutherland?'

I shrugged. 'I don't know. It's not my decision. It's Federica's house and she's not really decided yet. There are still a lot of memories locked up there.'

'Do you think you'll come back to Pellestrina?'

'I hope so. Lovely as it is it's not given us quite the honeymoon we deserved. I think it owes us a proper holiday. Yes, I think we'll be back.'

Busetto smiled. 'Well, if you do come, give me a call. We should have a beer together.'

'Thank you. That's kind. I thought for a long time that you thought I was a crook.'

'I did. I thought both of you were.'

'Okay. That's less kind.' We both laughed. 'I might still take you up on that beer, though. How's Don Francesco?'

'He was badly hurt but he'll be fine. It might be some time until his flock sees him back in the pulpit, though.'

'I must go and see him. I owe him my thanks. We both

do. I admit I got him wrong. For all his talk of having to make compromises, he was braver than I thought. Perhaps even braver than he thought. And what about Giulia?'

Busetto sighed. 'I don't know what she'll do now. But it's bound to be better than life with that pig Zanetti.'

'I imagine so. I feel sorry for her to be honest. Will she be charged with anything?'

He shrugged. 'I doubt it. What would the charge be? Cleaning someone's house without their permission?'

The light shining through the window was now casting a long, attenuated shadow of the thorn – if that's what it was – on to Busetto's desk.

I smiled at him. 'So. What do you think?'

'About what?'

'About this. Is there genuinely a fragment of the Crown of Thorns in there?'

'Who knows? But if it gives comfort to people then where's the harm?' He smiled at me. 'It might surprise you, Mr Sutherland but I still go to Mass every Sunday.' He reached out his hands, and gently took the monstrance from me, placing it between us. 'So tell me, what do you think it is?'

'Oh, I'd have thought that was obvious,' I said.

He shook his head. 'Enlighten me.'

I reached out my hand, and traced my fingers around the layer of thick, gold paint.

'The stuff that dreams are made of,' I said.

Chapter 50

Federica linked her arm in mine. 'You're sure then, *caro*?'

I nodded. 'I'm sure.'

'I'm sorry. I think perhaps you still liked the idea of living here.'

'Oh I did. I still do in some ways. There's something so incredibly romantic about it. But—' I paused.

'But?'

'But then Dario phones and wants to go for a beer, and it's ninety minutes away. Or the boys on Giudecca want to play cards. And the Honorary Consul thing would be finished. I mean, how many tourists have even heard of Pellestrina, let alone know how to get there in an emergency.' I shook my head. 'No. It's a lovely idea. But it'd never work.'

'We could have rented it out.'

'We could. But it wouldn't seem right. Not to me. Somehow people are still living on this tiny spit of land. Four thousand of them. There's an airport within twenty kilometres and yet kids here need to take two boats just to get to school. There's something brilliant about that.' I shook my head. 'Let's just sell the place and be done with it. And then maybe we'll read one day that the population is four thousand and one. Or four thousand and two. Or maybe more. That'd be enough for me.'

She squeezed my arm. 'Proud of you, *caro*.'

'Oh, I don't know why. But I'm proud of you, of course.' I looked at her. 'So are *you* sure about this?'

She said nothing, and we stood and stared at the newly erected For Sale sign in silence for a couple of minutes, just listening to the sound of the seabirds circling and feeling the sun upon our faces. Soon it would be time for lunch. One final, splendid lunch with crabs and mussels and squid and too much prosecco. And then the long journey home with a grumpy cat. Gramsci was playing in the garden, scrabbling away at the grass in search of the Unluckiest Lizard on Pellestrina.

Fede broke the silence. 'I'm sure,' she said.

'But your father—' I began.

She shushed me. 'It's not his house any more. Nor mine, nor *nonno*'s, nor *mamma*'s. It doesn't belong to any of us now. It's time for somebody else to move in. Time for them to write their own stories here.'

'He wanted you to have it, though.'

'He wanted lots of things. But above all he wanted me to be happy. And I am. And so his work is done.'

'I wonder if we'll ever come back?'

'I hope so. Maybe once a year, just to remember. But maybe not to stay.' A mewl came from the long grass. 'And certainly not with him.' She paused. 'Maybe *papà* wasn't much of a husband, you know?' Her voice broke, just a little. 'But from what we've found out, he was a better man than I gave him credit for. He tried to do the right thing in the end.'

We stood there in silence, as I let her cry. Then I wiped her tears away, and pulled her to me. 'Hey now. Are we okay?'

She nodded.

'Time to go then?'

'Time to go.' She took a deep breath, then looked at me and smiled. 'Except, of course, it's not.' She broke free of my embrace and ran towards the house. She fumbled with the keys, rattling them in the lock, and disappeared inside. She was back almost immediately, clutching something to her chest. I saw her throw the keys over her shoulder, and heard the chink as they landed on the path outside the door.

She checked her watch, and then kissed me on the cheek. 'We've just about got time for lunch.' She nodded at Gramsci. 'It'll be good for you to steel yourself before you try to get him home.' She linked her arm in mine, and we walked off towards *da Celeste*. Her eyes were red, but she was smiling as she looked down at the book in her hands.

It was, of course, *Pinocchio*.

Glossary

agriturismo	typically a small farm converted for use as a restaurant or holiday accommodation
avanti	come in (in the context used here)
avvocato	lawyer
bacino	the San Marco basin, typically used to refer to that area in front of Piazza San Marco, where the Grand Canal and Giudecca Canal merge
beh (or *be'*)	audible equivalent of a shrug
boh	dunno
bricola (pl. *bricole*)	two or more pieces of wood, linked together and fixed into the base of the lagoon in order to indicate the navigable path through the water
carabinieri	a branch of law enforcement in Italy. They differ from the state police in being a military organisation not a civil one, but their responsibilities are broadly similar
centro storico	historic centre. In Venice this is typically used to refer to the main area of the city and not the outlying islands

chi è?	literally 'who is it?', a common question when answering the door phone
da portar via	to take away
Dio mio!	my God!
dolce vita	the sweet life, the good life
forza	take courage! Come on!
gelateria	ice cream shop
Il Gazzettino	a daily newspaper of Venice and the Veneto
Gomorrah	an exposé of organised crime in Italy, by Roberto Saviano
liceo	high school
lungomare	seafront
maleducato	rude
murazzi	the system of seawalls, in Istrian stone, that protect Pellestrina from the Adriatic sea
neonati	literally 'new born', the name given to tiny baby fish, typically sardines or anchovies
nonno/nonna	Grandpa/Grandma
'Notti Magiche'	'Magic Nights', the official anthem of the 1990 Italian World Cup
omertà	the mafia code of silence
Pagine Gialle	the Yellow Pages
pentito	one who has broken the code of *omertà*
piano nobile	the principal floor of a *palazzo*, typically the second storey in Venice
questura	police station
La Repubblica	Italian newspaper of the centre-left

Risorgimento	the reunification of Italy, led by such great figures as Garibaldi and, in Venice, Daniele Manin
salve!	hi!
straniero	foreigner
tabaccheria	cigarette shop
tesoro/caro/cara/vecio	terms of endearment
traghetto	ferry
tramezzino	the traditional Italian-style sandwich; triangles of white bread with the filling typically heaped up in the middle
tranquillo	don't worry, keep calm
vaporetto	the style of boat used in the public transport system in Venice
zio	uncle

Historical Notes

Until the mid-1980s organised crime in the Veneto was the province of a small number of disparate criminal gangs such as Clan Giostrai, the Veneziani, the Mestrini and the San Donà di Piave cartel.

This began to change due to the influence of the Sicilian mafia. Throughout the late 1960s and the 1970s, policy had been to separate high-ranking members of the mafia from their colleagues, by incarcerating them far away from their usual place of activity. The effect was the opposite of the one intended, as local gangsters began to seek them out and learn from them; most prominent among them Felice 'Angel Face' Maniero. By 1990, the Mala del Brenta had effectively absorbed all the other major criminal gangs in the Veneto into itself, under the control of Maniero.

In 1994, faced with life imprisonment, Maniero turned *pentito*, leading to the arrest of over 400 members of the organisation, together with a number of judges, policemen and businessmen. Many of his allies and henchmen fled abroad, including Francesco Tonicello. A master forger, and responsible for fencing artworks, antiques and stolen jewellery throughout Italy, he was arrested in London in 2005 whilst selling stolen newspapers from a kiosk. Maniero himself was released from prison in 2010, only to be sentenced to four more years in 2020, this time for domestic abuse.

Reorganising as the Nuova Mala del Brenta, many members continued their criminal activity, often working with disaffected youth gangs in the major cities of the Veneto.

The organisation, however, was dealt a further significant blow by the *Ghost Dog* operation of 2006. The testimony of two *pentiti*, Stefano Galletto and Giuseppe Pastore, led to sixty arrests, including many of the local gang leaders in the bigger cities.

Much of the credit for this is due to Francesco Saverio Pavone, the 'Iron Magistrate'. A man of great courage and integrity, his death from the Covid-19 virus on Monday 16th March 2020 was widely mourned.

Acknowledgements

As ever, most of the locations in the book exist and are as described, the great exception being the imaginary church of Madonna della Marina.

I am, as always, greatly indebted to my wife Caroline who gave me a copy of Rita Vianello's *Pescatori di Pellestrina* as a Christmas present, which proved to be invaluable in researching the history of the island and its fishing traditions. Equally valuable was an extended visit to the island, cycling the back roads, walking the *murazzi* and eating quite a lot of fish.

I've taught a number of young people from Pellestrina over the years – too many to mention, but I must thank them for their recommendation of *Ristorante da Celeste* as a place to eat. It's always a pleasure to go there.

My continuing gratitude to all those of you who take the time to write. It's greatly appreciated.

I finish, as ever, with my thanks to my agent John Beaton; to Krystyna, Rebecca, Jess, Andy and everyone at Constable; and, of course, to Caroline.

Philip Gwynne Jones, Venezia 2020
www.philipgwynnejones.com